PRAISE FOR BARRY EISLER

"Eisler combines the insouciance of Ian Fleming, the realistic detail of Tom Clancy, the ennui of Graham Greene, and the prose power of John le Carré."

—*News-Press*

"Furious and creative . . . Rain's combination of quirks and proficiency is the stuff great characters are made of."

—*Entertainment Weekly*

"No one is writing a better thriller series today than Barry Eisler. He has quickly jumped into my top ten best American mystery/thriller writers, along with Michael Connelly, Lee Child, Walter Mosley, and Harlan Coben . . . Rating: A."

—*Deadly Pleasures*

"Written with a delightfully soft touch and a powerful blend of excitement, exotica, and what (ever since John le Carré) readers have known to call tradecraft."

—*The Economist*

"Barry Eisler serves up steamy foreign locales, stunning action, and enough high-tech weaponry to make for an A-plus read."

—*New York Daily News*

LIVIA LONE

ALSO BY BARRY EISLER

A Clean Kill in Tokyo (previously published as *Rain Fall*)
A Lonely Resurrection (previously published as *Hard Rain*)
Winner Take All (previously published as *Rain Storm*)
Redemption Games (previously published as *Killing Rain*)
Extremis (previously published as *The Last Assassin*)
The Killer Ascendant (previously published as *Requiem for an Assassin*)
Fault Line
Inside Out
The Detachment
Graveyard of Memories
The God's Eye View

SHORT WORKS

"The Lost Coast"
"Paris Is a Bitch"
"The Khmer Kill"
"London Twist"

ESSAYS

"The Ass Is a Poor Receptacle for the Head: Why Democrats
Suck at Communication,
and How They Could Improve"
"Be the Monkey: A Conversation about the New World of
Publishing" (with J. A. Konrath)

LIVIA LONE

BARRY EISLER

THOMAS & MERCER

Published by Thomas & Mercer, Seattle

www.apub.com

Amazon, the Amazon logo, and Thomas & Mercer are trademarks of Amazon.com, Inc., or its affiliates.

ISBN-13: 9781503939660 (hardcover)
ISBN-10: 1503939669 (hardcover)

ISBN-13: 9781503939653 (paperback)
ISBN-10: 1503939650 (paperback)

Cover design by Rex Bonomelli

Printed in the United States of America

First edition

For the sheepdogs

1—NOW

Billy Barnett dug the Asian chick sitting next to him. She was slim and petite, but with a nice little rack shown off by a form-fitting, long-sleeve yoga shirt. He'd asked if she was coming from a late workout when he'd first sidled up next to her at the bar at Ray's, dipping his head close so she could hear him over the music from the jukebox, and she'd told him yeah, a workout that had earned her a drink, and he'd laughed and asked if he could buy her one, and she'd said sure, a white wine wouldn't be so bad. He'd been surprised by that—her hair was dyed peroxide blonde and she was wearing a lot of purple eye shadow behind a pair of over-sized, horn-rimmed eyeglasses, and a chick with a look that wild would ordinarily be the type for tequila shots, say, or maybe a vodka martini with a twist if she was trying to play it more upscale. But hey, whatever.

So he'd asked her name, which turned out to be Sue, as though that mattered, and he'd ordered her the wine she wanted, with a Bulleit back for himself, and they'd bullshitted about how she'd just moved to Marysville because her ex-husband was here and they had joint custody of their kid, and now she had to get a job and deal with interviews and how was she going to find anything half as good as what she'd left in

LA, personal assistant to some movie producer Billy had never heard of. But fuck, he didn't care about her story. What mattered was that she'd come to Ray's all made up even after a workout, street clothes still in a big backpack so she could show off that sweet body in her yoga outfit, and wearing flip-flops like she couldn't wait to get barefoot and jump straight into the sack. All meaning she was looking for a little action, right? Practically begging for it.

Ray's closed at two—less than an hour away. Billy knew he shouldn't think about that, shouldn't imagine it. He was in Ray's four, maybe five nights a week, his neighborhood place since being released from the Monroe Twin Rivers Unit the previous month. Hell, Ray, who was tending bar tonight and was himself an ex-con, knew Billy, even called him by his nickname, Barn. If this Asian chick kicked up a fuss, Ray's would be the first place the cops would come looking. And they'd finger Billy just from the description: *Big, solid-looking guy; long, dark hair; accent straight out of Beaumont; spends his time at Ray's? Gotta be my man Barn. Let's pick him up, bring him in for questioning. Send his ass back to Monroe and we never should have let him go in the first place.*

But shit, the bourbon was giving everything that vibe, that great, invulnerable *up* feeling like he could do anything he wanted, take anything he wanted, *get away* with anything he wanted. He lifted his glass and drained it, closing his eyes for a moment to savor the sweet smell in his sinuses, the sting in his throat, the mushrooming impact inside his head, and he heard the crack of balls on the pool table, and felt the steady stomping beat of Bruce Springsteen's "Spirit in the Night," and he opened his eyes and looked at the Asian chick, and she was smiling at him, and he wanted to, he so fucking wanted to.

And besides, Asian chicks put up with a lot of shit, didn't they, rather than have to deal with public humiliation? It was why there were so many molesters on Japanese trains, it was too crowded for the girls to move away and they'd silently endure almost anything rather than draw attention to themselves. That's what he'd heard, anyway, he'd never been to Asia but he'd always wanted to go.

Well, maybe you can take a little trip there tonight.

And even if she did go to the cops, there were a half dozen people in here, including Ray himself, who would attest that she'd shown up in that tight yoga outfit and the garish makeup, and eased out of her sweatshirt like a striptease, and flirted with Billy for hours, laughing at his jokes, touching his arm, letting him buy her drinks. How would she explain all that?

Of course, the real problem was more Hammerhead than the law. Not that the guys had any moral qualms about some slut getting what was coming to her, but a member drawing heat due to repeated sexual assault charges wasn't particularly good for business, and Billy was already semi in the shit for just that reason. His orders were to keep a low profile following his release—stay clear of the gang, stay out of trouble, head back to Seattle when the weekly meetings with the state-appointed therapist were done and he was no longer being watched so closely.

But shit, the way he liked to play it, who would ever even know? He almost never needed to threaten, and only twice had he had to resort to the hunting knife he kept in a leather sheath attached to his belt. No, he knew how to do it right. Get the chick alone, start to get rough with her, and then, when she tried to stop him, accuse her of leading him on. His size and sudden anger always scared them, threw them off balance, chilled them right out. Yeah, this hot little Asian chick would give it up. Even persuade herself it was her decision, or at least her fault. And she'd know no one would believe her if she tried to claim otherwise.

He gestured to her nearly empty glass. "Like another?"

She shook her head. "Three's my limit. Especially after a workout." She smiled shyly, as though confessing something shameful. "I'm such a lightweight. I think I've already had too much. But you go ahead, if you want."

He did want. He did indeed.

He nodded to Ray, then pointed at his empty glass. Ray picked up the Bulleit bottle and strolled over. "You guys good?" he said as he refilled the glass to three fingers. One of the benefits of being a regular—Ray didn't stint on the refills.

"No more for me," the Asian chick said.

Ray nodded. "Last call in fifteen. Just so you know."

Billy watched Ray stroll away, then raised his glass to the Asian chick and said, "Here's to life's little pleasures." He tossed the whole thing back, tilting his chin up to ease the whiskey's passage. He set the glass back on the bar and closed his eyes, just savoring the moment. Damn, he loved good bourbon. One of the things he'd missed in the joint. One of many.

When he opened his eyes, the Asian chick stretched her arms back, and oh, man, that little rack wasn't so little after all, was it? "Well," she said, reaching down to the foot of the barstool and retrieving her backpack, "I should get going—that interview in the morning."

Billy looked her up and down, not caring what she made of it. Damn, she really was a hot little slut. It wasn't just the bourbon. He'd wanted her the moment he'd caught her eye as she walked in. And she was drunk now, and they were going to walk out together, and if she was carrying a backpack, especially a big one like that, it probably meant she'd arrived on foot—otherwise, she would have left her gear in the car. It was all working out so perfectly, it was almost too good to be true.

"Yeah, getting late for me, too." He stood and dropped a couple of twenties on the bar, then slipped her sweatshirt off the back of her barstool. "Here, let me get that for you."

"You don't have to—"

"No problem," he said with a smile. "No problem at all."

Billy led the way, holding the door for her, letting his gaze slide down past the backpack she had slung over a shoulder, admiring her ass as she squeezed by. He waved a goodnight to Ray, who nodded in return, his face impassive, probably knowing what Billy was up to, but also knowing it was none of his business.

A moment later, they were out on the sidewalk, the door swinging shut behind them with a slowly dying squeak, the music from the jukebox suddenly muted. The warmth of the spring evening had died away, and the late-night air was cool and slightly moist. A half moon hung low in the sky, its edges softened by mist. On one side of the bar was a pawnshop, its interior dark behind barred windows. Opposite, what was once a parking lot, now fenced off and colonized by weeds. Other than the sound of distant eighteen-wheelers on the interstate and a few crickets, the area was silent. Billy nodded, liking the whole lonely vibe, just the two of them at last.

"Where are you parked?" he asked.

The Asian chick glanced at her sweatshirt, as though she wanted it back but was afraid to ask. Billy liked that.

"I'm not. I walked from my workout."

Just like he'd thought. Perfect.

"You're walking home, then?"

"That's the plan, but—"

"I'll walk you. Neighborhood's not safe this time of night."

"Look, you really don't have to—"

"Hey, I insist," he said, some edge in his tone, letting her know he'd be insulted if she refused his offer. "You just point the way."

The Asian chick hesitated for a moment, clearly unsure of how to handle this. "It's just a dump on the other side of the park. I've barely moved in, the place is a mess . . ."

"Well, hell," Billy said with a good-natured laugh he knew would put her at ease. "I wasn't expecting you to invite me in. I'll just see you to the door and say goodnight."

Nothing to argue with in any of that, was there? And sure enough, after a moment, the Asian chick nodded and said, "All right, then. Thank you. The park *is* going to be kind of dark at this hour."

Yes, it is, pretty little thing. Yes, it is.

They headed down the sidewalk, passing not a soul, just closed storefronts and empty lots. The Asian chick was asking him questions, making small talk out of skittishness. Billy responded, but automatically, barely even hearing his own words, the bourbon buzzing in his brain. All he could think about was how dark the park would be. How deserted.

And then there it was, just ahead, so still, so perfect. There was a sudden hush as they crossed inside; even the crunch of their footfalls on pavement vanished, replaced by the soft, stealthy squish of grass. There were no lights anywhere, just weak moonlight and shadows under the trees. The Asian chick wasn't talking anymore. Billy watched her out of the corner of his eye. A warm hit of adrenaline snaked out through his torso at the realization of where they were, how helpless she was now, how he could do anything he wanted.

"It's getting chilly," the Asian chick said, maybe just to hear the sound of her own voice.

They were almost halfway across. Dead center. Even the interstate trucks were barely audible now. There was a small copse of trees ahead. That would be the place. Billy could feel himself stiffening at the thought.

"Oh, I don't know. Feels all right to me."

"I guess you're warmer-blooded than I am. Could I have my sweatshirt now?"

"Sure you can. No problem." But he kept walking. The trees were just thirty feet away now.

"My sweatshirt," the Asian chick said. "I'm cold."

Billy didn't answer. Twenty feet to the trees now. Ten.

"Hey," the Asian chick said. "Did you hear me?"

He stopped and turned to her. Nothing but shadows here, and the trees would soak up sound. If she made any.

"Oh, I'm sorry," he said, smiling. "Lost in thought."

She stopped and looked at him. "I said I'm cold."

God, she looked so fucking tasty in the faint light. So vulnerable. His heart was thudding hard. He could feel it in his chest, his throat.

He took a step toward her. "Well, shit, honey, I can take care of that. Warm you right up."

She flinched and shook her head. "What? No. I just want my sweatshirt."

"Sure, we'll spread it out right here on the grass. It'll be fine."

He tossed the sweatshirt on the ground next to her. He was going to follow her down when she knelt to retrieve it, but she didn't. She just stood there, looking at him. Well, that was all right. Lot of ways to skin a cat.

"Come on, now," he said, moving closer to her. "I'll make you feel good. You'll see."

She stepped back. "Look," she said, with a little quaver. "I just want to go home. Okay?"

God, he liked the fear in her voice. Loved it.

"I told you I'd get you home, didn't I? You doubting me now?"

"What? No. I just—"

"Don't you give me a hard time. I was nice to you tonight. Bought you all those drinks, didn't I?"

"Yes, it was nice of you, but—"

"Then don't you think you should be nice back?"

"That's not the point. I mean, it's just, I don't want—"

He stepped in suddenly and seized her by the shoulders. He squeezed hard, letting her feel how strong he was, how in control. How much damage he could do if she gave him a reason.

"Stop," he said, giving her a single brisk shake. "Just stop now. Stop your talking and listen to me."

He could feel the tension in her body. The growing panic. Fuck, he was so hard.

"I've been nice to you," he said, keeping his grip tight. "All night. And all I want is for you to be nice back now. Are you telling me you won't? Is that it?"

"Come on, stop," she said, her voice high now, like a child's. "You're hurting me. Stop."

It was such a turn-on, the way she was talking. He relaxed his grip and eased the backpack off her shoulder, letting it drop to the ground. It was heavier than he'd expected. Must have had some weights inside, something like that.

He caressed her neck for a moment, then let his hands drift to her elbows, his thumbs brushing the edges of her breasts along the way. He squeezed her arms to her sides and brought her closer. "Come on now. Just a kiss. Is that so much to ask, after I've been so nice to you?"

"Don't," she said, again in that high voice. "I don't want this."

"Like hell you don't," he said, and it was so perfect, the way she was afraid, the way she was resisting him, it was everything he always loved, everything he'd hoped it would be, and he was going to do her now, right here in the park, on the cool grass, make her take everything he had to give her, and she'd never tell anyone and she'd never forget it, either. God, he didn't know what he'd done to deserve her walking into Ray's tonight. It really was too good to be true.

He snaked a hand behind her neck and started to pull her in to make her kiss him, but she pressed her palms against his chest and pushed him away. It surprised him—she was stronger than she looked. The workouts, he supposed. Seemed they were paying off. Up to a point.

He grabbed her shoulders again and twisted suddenly and hard, bringing her to the grass on her back, coming down on top of her, straddling her hips.

"No," she said, panting. "No, I don't want this. Stop."

She tried to shove him away, but Billy took hold of her throat—not hard enough to choke her, but hard enough to let her know he easily could. With his free hand he started working his belt buckle. "Don't you be a little bitch now," he said. "You better just be nice."

But the pressure on her throat didn't settle her the way he'd expected. She didn't even try to pull loose. Instead, she put her hands on his left knee and pushed it wider, then somehow twisted and slid her right knee through the opening under his legs, all the way to her chin. He noticed her foot was bare—the flip-flop must have come off when he'd taken her down—and then he felt the foot on his hip and somehow she kicked his leg back. He almost collapsed on top of her but threw his arms forward and caught himself just in time, thinking, *Goddamn little bitch, gonna make you pay for that.*

He started to push himself up, but she was shoving his right knee now, and she twisted, and her left knee was coming through, the same way the right one had, the foot bare again, and suddenly both her legs were wrapped around his lower back, and he was confused because this was what he wanted, to get between her legs, but it wasn't like that, she felt too in control, and he realized, holy shit, it was a jiu-jitsu move he'd seen guys practicing in the yard, "pulling guard" they called it, he knew the trick but it was so out of context here. Well, an Asian chick, he supposed he shouldn't be surprised she might know some jiu-jitsu or whatever. It didn't scare him. Just made him angry that she thought she could fight him off with a few martial arts moves.

So he planted his left foot firmly on the ground and reared up, at the same time pulling his left arm back and cocking it into a fist, a fist he was going to smash down into her face and never mind leaving marks on her, he was past that now and she deserved the lesson. But she reacted so quickly, it was almost like she'd been expecting the move. She jerked his right arm across his body and shot her right leg into the air, past his left ear, crashing the crease of her knee down on the back of his neck. Billy saw stars and felt an adrenalized surge of rage. He tried to say, *Bitch*, but the word wouldn't come, because now she had wrapped her free leg around the foot of the leg that had come down on his neck, and she was scissoring his throat or figure-fouring it or something. The pain was ungodly, Billy couldn't breathe, he felt his tongue protruding, being squeezed forward by the pressure, and he tried to jerk his arm free so he could access his knife, but the bitch was holding his wrist so tightly it was like she knew the knife was there, and he couldn't get loose, and there was a crazy ringing in his ears and he tried to reach around his back with his left hand to get to the knife, *the knife*, but the bitch took hold of his sleeve and stopped him, and he panicked and tried to stand but the bitch twisted and broke his balance and he collapsed on his side, eyes bulging, legs churning, lungs screaming, his brain feeling like it was going to explode out of his head, and he scratched at her leg but the material on the damn yoga pants was slippery and his fingernails grazed right over it, and the moonlight and shadows on the grass began to disintegrate into gray, and the ringing was receding now, too, fading into a quiet, dying buzz, and he felt his bladder let go, and his vision darkened, and the world shrank to a pinprick, and his last thought before everything went black was *Too good to be true.*

2—NOW

Livia knew less than five minutes might be inadequate, so she kept the strangle in place, breathing steadily to slow her heart rate, craning her neck from side to side to ensure they were still alone. But she wasn't unduly concerned. At this hour, what park wouldn't be deserted? Deserted was why Billy had wanted to come here. And what was sauce for the goose was sauce for the gander.

While she waited, she ran her fingertips over her hands and face—the only parts of her that weren't covered in thick Lycra. She didn't think he'd managed to even once touch her skin, but it was best to be sure. She detected no scratches, meaning no DNA left behind under his nails. The wig was still in place, too, and beneath it, a hair net. So no telltale hairs anywhere, either.

She knew from his file—the same file that had told her where she could find him—that Billy wasn't exactly the most popular member of Hammerhead. He was a dependable soldier, true, but his penchant for rape was creating liabilities the gang didn't welcome. Another arrest, and he'd be looking at a fall long enough so that maybe he'd be willing to testify about some of the higher-ups. Said higher-ups might have decided to make that kind of thing impossible. That would be her own theory, anyway, and she was a damn fine cop.

And beyond Hammerhead, Billy had gambling debts, drug debts, and enemies from prison, too, so the list of suspects for Marysville PD to run down would be long. But how hard would they really try? White supremacist rapist ex-cons who wound up quietly dead tended not to command a maximum of investigative attention. They'd check out Ray's, of course, and they'd hear about an Asian girl with platinum hair, or maybe a wig. But so what? Even if by some chance the detective assigned to the case was motivated enough to try to collect physical evidence, the only thing Livia had touched in the bar was the stem of her wineglass, which she'd discreetly wiped with a napkin before leaving. She'd taken the glass with her to the restroom after her last sip and cleaned it with hydrogen peroxide wipes, on the admittedly remote chance that anyone might try to recover DNA from the mystery woman's saliva. If Billy had asked why she was taking her wineglass to the restroom, she would have smiled and told him she'd heard too many stories about date rape drugs to leave her glass unattended in a bar. But he hadn't seemed to notice or care. And there was a security camera over the entrance to the place, but she'd been careful to keep her face down when passing it. Anyway, beyond the wig, there was all the makeup, the nonprescription eyeglasses, and the fact that she looked and was playing it a decade younger than her actual thirty years. No, the platinum-haired Asian girl would be a dead end. The working theory would be that whoever she was, she had functioned as a decoy, a honey trap, sent to Billy's favorite bar by an enemy to lure him into the park, where a waiting accomplice had approached from behind and strangled him.

When she was sure there was no longer even the remotest chance of revival, she relaxed the strangle and eased out from under the body. She stood and glanced around, ready to grab her gear and take off if necessary, but the park remained still and silent. She looked down at his face for a moment, pale in the faint moonlight, the eyes staring sightlessly past her, the mouth agape in a pantomime of astonishment. She felt strong. Satisfied. Triumphant. *Alive.*

But it was too soon for feelings. She still had to focus.

She pulled the hydrogen peroxide wipes from the backpack and quickly went over his fingertips, making sure plenty of the liquid got under his nails. Just a precaution and probably unnecessary, but she was adrenalized from the encounter and it was possible he'd scratched her without her feeling it, even now. Then she stepped back into her flip-flops, picked up the backpack and her sweatshirt, and walked briskly across the park to a maintenance shack in the northwest corner. She circled it to confirm she was alone—no teenagers hooking up, none of Marysville's homeless using the spot for the night—then paused on the side farthest from the street to look and listen. Nothing.

She set down the backpack, unzipped it, and removed a heavy-duty plastic contractor bag. She stepped out of the flip-flops, then stripped off the yoga pants and shirt like a surgeon peeling back a pair of post-op latex gloves—outside over the inside, to minimize any contamination. The sports bra came off last. She tossed it onto the rest of the clothes, then paused for a moment, suddenly aware of a slight breeze, the cool air delicious all over her body.

Not now. Later.

She knelt and loaded everything into the contractor bag, the wig and glasses included, pressing out the excess air and tying it off when she was done. From the backpack she pulled underwear; riding leathers, gloves, boots, and a full-face helmet; and a belly bag concealing her duty weapon, a Glock 26. She donned all of it, then zipped the contractor bag into the backpack, slipped her arms through the straps, and continued out of the park along a residential street. In the distance, a dog barked once, then was silent. Other than that, still nothing.

At the intersection of a four-lane road, she hung back in the shadows until two night-owl cars had passed her position and it was quiet again. Then she lowered the helmet visor and crossed the road into the parking lot of the motel where she'd parked the bike. It wasn't her registered ride—she loved that Ducati Streetfighter more than anything she'd ever owned, but it was too unusual, and therefore too memorable, a machine for what she had done tonight. No, for nights like this one, she used something she had built herself from parts, most of it a Kawasaki Ninja 650. The Ninja was one of the most popular bikes around, so not something anyone would much notice. And because she kept it separate from her residence, it couldn't be connected to her regardless.

There it was, parked in back where she'd left it. She undid the disc lock, the steering lock, and the cable lock she'd run through the rear wheel and around a signpost. She stuffed the cable lock in the backpack and pulled out a florescent vest, which she slipped over the leather jacket. Nothing stealthy about her appearance now—just a good, honest citizen and responsible rider. The kind that made cops feel comfortable. The kind they tended to ignore.

She drifted out the other side of the motel parking lot, keeping it in first, the engine growling softly. In three minutes, she was heading south on Interstate 5, the wind whipping past her, the throttle open, the bike thrumming between her thighs. She resisted the urge to tuck in and gun it, not wanting to take any unnecessary chances. Even if highway patrol might be willing to offer a little professional courtesy to a fellow cop, a traffic stop would place her in the vicinity at around the time Billy had shuffled off his mortal coil. And while she knew she could outrun and outride anyone who tried to pull her over, a high-speed chase would entail its own set of risks.

Considerations like these were always involved when she hunted down a repeat-offending, misdemeanor-pleading rapist scumbag. This time, though, there was even more at stake. Yes, this time, the rapist scumbag's death was going to be the occasion for a big funeral, a send-off white supremacist–style, attended by the entire Hammerhead gang. And what Livia learned from that funeral would give her what she needed to go after the real prize: a senior Hammerhead named Timothy "Weed" Tyler, who was about to finish a sixteen-year prison stretch at Victorville.

The last time Livia had seen Tyler, he had been one of her captors. And he was the only person alive who might be able to tell her what had happened to her sister, Nason. Nason, her little bird, who had been missing since they had both been trafficked from Thailand as children.

3—THEN

It was the end of the rice harvest when the men came to the village and took Livia and her sister Nason. Livia was thirteen. Nason was eleven. Their parents had sold them.

It had been morning, the time the children ordinarily would have been feeding the chickens, except that this year there were no more chickens in the village, or pigs for that matter, or even dogs. The last three harvests had been poor, and everyone was hungry. Livia caught worms, frogs, spiders, even scorpions, but it was hardly enough, and the emptiness in her belly gnawed at her constantly, sometimes merely an itch, more often an angry, throbbing ache.

Their father had told them to play outside, which he sometimes did when he was irritable, so they went out to the dirt in front of the small thatched hut and pretended to be different animals—fish swimming in the river, birds flying across the sky, tigers creeping stealthily through the jungle. It was one of their favorite games, and in fact Nason's birdsong imitations were so uncanny that Livia's pet name for her was "little bird." They laughed delightedly whenever Nason got real birds to answer, and the game distracted them both from thoughts of the food they didn't have.

They were Lahu, one of the hill tribes living in Thailand's mountainous forests along the Burmese and Laotian border. But borders, like the outside world generally, were largely an abstraction for Livia. There was a single radio in her village, used mostly for music. The only television was a tiny vintage model that, when the weather was right, displayed snowy images picked up from a Burmese station somewhere to the north. She had heard of something called the Internet, but had little idea of what it could be.

Livia spoke some Thai from the provincial school she sometimes attended, and wanted to learn more. But her parents didn't see why anyone would need a language other than Lahu. Besides, in better years, there were too many chores to allow for frivolities like school: rice to be planted and then harvested; well water to be fetched; game to be hunted. By the time she was six, Livia was already expert with the *a-taw*—the Lahu machete used for everything from clearing a trail to felling trees to butchering a chicken; the *law-gaw*, the sickle used for threshing rice; and the *heh hga geu dtu ve*, a wicker cage in which a small chick was placed in the forest to attract jungle fowl, which could then be shot with a *ka*—a crossbow of ancient but effective design.

Though Nason was only two years younger than Livia, she was small for her age and not very strong. Livia worried about her. She had seen what happened to the smallest piglets in the litters born to the village sows. Denied access to their mothers' teats by their greedy brothers and sisters, the little ones quickly weakened, and it was never long before the villagers butchered them for their scant meat. Livia hated it. She would push away the stronger siblings so the little ones could get a turn at a teat—she would even feed them herself—but it was never enough. She knew Nason needed someone to help her, too. But their parents were too busy to give the girls much attention, and their brother

Zanu, fifteen, handsome, and already the topic of marriage gossip in the village, couldn't be bothered. Livia would have to protect Nason herself.

One night, lying on the pallet she shared with Nason, separated from the rest of the hut by a curtain, she heard her parents talking in low voices about the government in Bangkok, how it was trying to stop the hill tribes from farming by their traditional method of cutting and burning. Something about the environment. Her mother was frightened. How would they eat? Her father said they would have to find the girls jobs. Livia didn't think that sounded so terrible, but for some reason her mother strongly protested, even daring to raise her voice. But Livia's father silenced her by asking if she would rather see her children starve.

Nason stirred. Livia handed her the small wooden protection Buddha she had carved herself, and which they both liked to keep by the pallet. Sometimes holding the Buddha helped Nason sleep. Then Livia stroked her hair to soothe her, but Nason's eyelids fluttered open. She moaned and rubbed her stomach.

"Here, little bird," Livia whispered, reaching into a small shoulder bag. "I saved this for you."

It was a durian fruit, Nason's favorite. Livia had found it deep in the forest, fallen and overlooked by others foraging for food. She had badly wanted to eat it herself, but knew Nason might wake up hungry.

"No, Labee," Nason said, calling Livia by her Lahu name. "It's yours. You need it, too."

"I don't. I had some already. I'm full."

She knew Nason didn't believe her. But was there anything more persuasive than hunger?

Nason looked longingly at the fruit. "We'll share it, then."

Livia nodded and took a small bite. And made sure Nason ate the rest, encouraging her to go slowly so it would last.

When the durian was gone, she snuggled closer to Nason and put her arms around her. And somehow, despite the hunger, despite her parents' frightening words, when she heard Nason softly snoring again, she slept, too.

The men came not long after.

Livia and Nason were out playing, as their father had directed them. Livia was laughing at the way Nason was shimmying her body like a fish when they heard an unfamiliar sound—a car engine. Livia looked up and saw a rusting white van bouncing toward them along the rutted dirt road, a plume of dust behind it. She and Nason stopped their game and stood, watching.

The van slowed and crept closer, stopping just in front of them. Three men got out. Livia immediately disliked them—they looked crafty, like slinking dogs hoping to steal a morsel. One of them, taller than the other two and with prominent cheekbones that made him look like a skull with eyes, was holding a photograph—the photograph that belonged to her mother, Livia realized in confusion. One of the villagers who had a camera had taken the photo a year earlier, then had it developed for their mother in nearby Chiang Rai. The photo was of Livia with her arms around Nason in front of their hut, both in their finest clothes—brightly colored embroidered dresses, the traditional garb of their people. Her mother treasured that photo and kept it in the cooking area in a jar to protect it from dampness. How did these men get it? And what were they doing with it?

The skull man looked at the photo, then at Livia and Nason, then at the photo again. He nodded to the other two men, then began walking toward the hut. One of the two, who had a dirty, patchy beard, followed him. The other, whose shaved head was overlarge and unnaturally square, stepped forward and grabbed Nason by the wrist. Nason whimpered and tried to jerk free, but the man simply turned and began pulling her toward the van. Too startled to think, Livia grabbed Nason's other wrist and pulled in the opposite direction, at the same time calling out to her parents, her voice high and frightened. For a moment, the man dragged both of them along, but then Livia planted her feet and strained harder, and managed to stop the man from any further progress. But the bearded man must have come up behind Livia, because he threw an arm around her waist and hoisted her into the air, breaking her grip. Enveloped by the stink of vinegary sweat, Livia scratched the man's arm from elbow to shoulder. He cried out in anger and she tried to scratch him again, but he wrapped his arms around her and began carrying her toward the van. She panicked and tried to break loose but couldn't. Then she saw that the other man had picked up Nason, too. She stopped struggling—she would never let anyone take Nason without going with her—but she screamed for her parents.

She twisted in the man's arms and craned her neck, and saw them. They had come to the door of the hut, but they were just standing there, watching, doing nothing. Zanu came and looked, too, but their father pushed him back inside. And then her mother turned away, sobbing, and her father simply motioned to the men with a backward flick of his fingers. Livia was beyond terror now . . . why weren't her parents doing anything? She couldn't understand. It didn't make any sense.

The men shoved her and Nason into the van. The interior was filled with children—eight of them, including Livia and Nason, some of them crying and babbling in the various languages of the hill tribes, others mute and trembling, their arms wrapped around their knees. The air was damp and fetid with the smell of sweat and urine and feces. There was a fourth man inside, too, and he pulled Nason and Livia in and rolled the sliding door closed behind them. The other two men got in front—one in the driver's seat, the other in the middle. Livia fought her way to the window on the other side. She wiped a clear swath through the moisture and grime and saw the skull man give her mother the photo, then count out a stack of baht into her father's hand. She shook her head in shock and incomprehension.

The skull man got in the van and they drove away. Livia watched through the streaked glass as her mother went inside, still sobbing.

Her father remained, his eyes straight ahead, not on the van, one hand clutching the baht, the other rubbing his thigh as though trying to wipe something from his palm. The van went around a bend in the road, past the village's rickety wooden shrine, the kind every village had to ward off evil spirits . . . and suddenly the hut, her parents, the village . . . all of it was gone.

She heard Nason behind her, crying, "Labee, Labee!"

Livia maneuvered around several other crying children and threw her arms around her sister.

"It's okay," she said, fighting her own tears and panic. "It's okay, Nason. I'm here. I'm here. I'm here."

The van stopped at two other villages and picked up five more children. Then they drove through the forest for a long time, gradually heading down the mountain. Livia had no idea where they were going. The men spoke Thai and sounded like they were from the city, but that was all she could tell. Amid the stink and the sobbing and the bouncing from the ruts in the road, she held Nason and whispered to her that she was here, that she loved her, that they would be okay.

"But where are we going, Labee?"

"I don't know."

"Why aren't Mama and Papa coming, too?"

"I don't know that, either." She thought back to the conversation she'd overheard, the one where her parents had argued about the girls getting jobs—could this be what they had been talking about? But then why would the men have paid her parents if the jobs hadn't even started?

Not really believing it but needing something to tell Nason, she said, "I think maybe Mama and Papa got us jobs. To make money, so we can buy food."

She hoped that the notion of having something to eat would help, but her words only made Nason cry harder. "But why wouldn't they tell us?"

Livia had no answer to that. She remembered how opposed her mother had been to the idea of jobs, and she felt a chill steal into her belly.

"I don't know, little bird," she said. "I don't know."

At midday, they stopped in a clearing and the men pulled the children out of the van. Livia stood in the tall grass and held Nason's hand, blinking in the glare of the scorching sun, her skin sticky with sweat. She tried not to be afraid, but she didn't like that they had stopped. The van was horrible, but she had quickly become accustomed to it. She wasn't afraid of the van anymore. She was afraid of what would happen next.

The four men stood around the children as they unloaded them from the van, obviously intent on preventing any escape. But one boy must have been planning for this moment, because as soon as his feet touched the grass, he took off running. One of the men grabbed the boy by the shoulder, but the boy squirmed free and raced away.

The boy had gotten not thirty feet when a man popped up from the grass like a tiger and clubbed him across the face with a forearm. The boy flew through the air and landed on his back. The man hauled him up, slung him over a shoulder like a sack of rice, carried him back, and dropped him on the ground in front of the children. And then, with no expression and no sound, the man pulled off his belt and began to whip him. The boy writhed and shrieked, but the man continued, his expression almost bored.

Some of the children turned away. Others were crying. One threw up. Livia, without thinking, shouted in Lahu, "Stop it! Stop!" And then, remembering her Thai lessons, shouted it in Thai.

None of the men even looked at her, least of all the one whipping the boy. She watched, horrified, holding Nason's sobbing face to her chest so she wouldn't see, then glanced at the other children to see if anyone else would at least protest. One of them, a Yao boy, she thought, looked older than the others. Certainly he was bigger, almost as big as the men, though not as big as the skull-faced one. But he did nothing.

It went on for a long time. And then, as suddenly and dispassionately as he'd started, the man stopped. He looked at the other children, as though mildly curious about which one he would whip next, and Livia thought his eyes were as flat and cold as a snake's.

If they had been deeper in the forest, Livia could have found one of the herbs her people used for cuts and pain. But in this grass, there was nothing. She wanted to go to the boy and try to comfort him, but Nason was holding her too tightly, still shaking and crying. So Livia stood still and whispered to Nason that it was all right, she was here, she wouldn't let her go, they would be all right.

One of the men unzipped his pants and urinated into the grass, not bothering even to turn his back to them. Livia realized she needed to go, too. She didn't want to ask permission—it felt like a bad idea, and besides, it wasn't as though they would allow her any privacy. She imagined waiting, and realized she couldn't. So she squatted, lowered her pants as little as possible, and peed. She kept her arms in front, covering herself as best she could, and stared fixedly at the grass, her face burning with shame.

When she was done, she hurriedly pulled up her pants and stood. She glanced at the men. None of them said anything. But she didn't like the way they were watching her.

Some of the other children, realizing it was okay, followed suit. But most of them, it seemed, didn't need to go. They had already lost control of their bladders—and some, of their bowels—in the van, or while the man had been whipping the boy.

The other men relieved themselves, too. Then they smoked cigarettes while the children squatted on the ground, most of them softly moaning and crying, the only other sounds the buzz of insects in the trees and the call of birds in the distance. Then the tall man looked at his watch and nodded to the others. They gestured to the van and kicked the children to make them move. Livia got up quickly, Nason clutching her arm. She wanted to go before the other children so she could be next to the window. If she could see outside, she might learn something, something that could help them. Despite the kicks, some of the children remained frozen in place, crying helplessly. The man who had whipped the running boy pulled off his belt and drew back his arm, and the stragglers hurried forward, too.

Back in the van, Livia found herself next to the boy who had been whipped. She touched his arm and whispered in Lahu, "Are you okay?"

It was a stupid question, she knew. Of course he wasn't okay. None of them was okay. But she had to do something.

The boy looked at her, his eyes red. His lips were swollen and bloody, probably from when the man had clubbed him to the ground.

"Are you okay?" Livia tried again, this time in Thai.

The boy said something Livia couldn't understand—Hmong, she thought, but it was slurred because of his lips and she wasn't sure.

"Thai," she said. "Do you speak Thai?"

The boy looked left and right as though searching for something, then said in Thai, "Where? Where we go?"

Livia shook her head helplessly.

They were quiet for a moment, then she pointed to herself. "Labee," she said. "I am Labee."

The boy nodded and pointed to himself. "Kai." Then he added, "Where we go, Labee?"

She shook her head again. She wanted to tell him he was brave, but couldn't remember the word.

4—THEN

They drove for hours past sprawling fields and terraced paddies, by streams sparkling in the harsh sunlight, through small towns with wires strung on poles along the road. Livia leaned against the metal side of the van. The bumps made it uncomfortable, but this way Nason could use her as a cushion. At some point, she woke and realized she'd been dozing. The bumping was gone. She looked out the window and saw the road was paved. She had only seen one paved road before—the narrow, winding one connecting her village with those of the other hill tribes—and she was amazed to see how long and straight this one was, going on and on for what must have been kilometers.

They stopped twice more. At one of the stops, the men handed out rice crackers, which the children devoured, and then bottles of water. No one tried to run. Livia told herself she would have if she hadn't needed to take care of Nason, but she wasn't really sure.

As night fell, they reached the edge of a giant city. Livia had never seen so much concrete, so many cars, such massive buildings. Even from inside the van, she could hear the noise of the place, feel its swirling energy. She was pretty sure this was Bangkok, which she of course understood was the capital of the country, but which until that moment had existed in her mind mostly as a kind of dreamland described in schoolbooks, not a real place she might ever actually see. A part of her was fascinated, amazed, by the sheer density of it all. But more than that, she was just frightened. She thought this must be where the men were taking them—where else would there be to go, after a city so enormous? What would happen to them here, in a place with so many people, of whom she and Nason knew none? A city this big could swallow them whole, and no one would ever even know.

And then, in the distance, against the violet and indigo of a darkening sky, she glimpsed a line of giant monsters lit from below and looming over a vast body of water. Everywhere there were enormous boats and rectangular metal boxes bigger than the van, bigger than two vans. Then she saw a sign in Thai: *Laem Chabang Port*. Was this the ocean, then? And were those monsters actually . . . machines, of some sort? Yes, they were. She saw some of them holding the metal boxes aloft with strings, moving them to and from the boats. The sides of the boxes were marked with huge white letters in languages Livia didn't know. And then a wave of terror stole through her: were these men taking them to another country? She had barely gotten over her fright at being swallowed up in Bangkok. She couldn't even comprehend what might lie beyond it.

Nason must have sensed her fear because she squeezed her arm and whispered, "What is it, Labee?"

Livia put an arm around and her and pulled her close. "Nothing, little bird. Nothing."

They drove on, finally stopping alongside a wall of the giant metal boxes, stacked seven high and lined up as far as Livia could see. A single box lay in front of the others, displaced from the wall. One of the men got out. He opened a door on the box, looked around, then nodded to the other men. One by one, they began taking the children off the van and pushing them into the box. Livia was terrified—what was in there?

What would happen to them? How would anyone ever find them in one box out of thousands? But there was nothing she could do. She had to be brave for Nason.

Livia and Nason were last. Nason was crying again, clinging to Livia. As two of the men pushed them toward the box, Livia, desperate, said in Thai, "Where? Where we go?"

Both of the men laughed. One of them looked at Livia in a way that made her want to cover herself. They shoved Livia and Nason inside, then stood blocking the doorway.

Livia looked around. There was nothing bad inside the box, at least. Actually, there was nothing at all. Just a few plastic buckets. But the emptiness was itself somehow terrifying.

Two of the men came inside and handed out more rice crackers and water. All of it was gone in seconds, and the men handed out more. While the children ate, one of the men gestured to his crotch, then to his backside, then to the buckets, grunting with each gesture. Livia understood. The buckets were toilets. They were going to be in this box for a long time. She fought back panic.

The men backed out and closed the door behind them. A quiet wail went up at the sound of bolts scraping into place. Nason stood trembling and clutching Livia, who held her and tried to keep her bearings in the dark. But after a moment, she noticed it wasn't fully dark. There were holes cut along the top of all the walls. For air, she realized. But the holes were letting in a little light, too.

She made her way carefully to the door, Nason trembling by her side, and tried to open it, but of course it was useless. She tried to think, to figure out something to do.

"Who speaks Thai?" she called out in Thai. There was nothing but the sound of sniffling and quiet sobs in response, so she called out again, "If you speak Thai, answer!"

She heard someone say, "I speak Thai." The Hmong boy, she thought, recognizing the slight slur from his swollen lips. Kai.

27

Someone jostled her. Livia resisted the urge to shove the careless child away.

"Listen!" she said. "We have to be careful, how we move. Or we hurt each other. You understand?"

"I understand," Kai said.

"You are Hmong?" Livia asked.

"Yes, Hmong."

"Then say my words in Hmong. And ask in Hmong who speaks Akha, Lisu, Karen, or Yao. You understand?"

Soon they were communicating simple messages translated from one language to another and to yet another. There wasn't much to say—*Walk carefully so you don't step on people who are lying down; the buckets are for toilet; calm, we have to stay calm.* There seemed barely any point to it, but it helped to feel there was something to do.

No one knew who the men were or where they were taking the children. One sobbing child reported that she had heard about men like these, that they took children to eat them. Livia could feel panic steal through the space as the message was translated and repeated. She said in Thai, "That's silly. If they want to eat us, they feed us more—make fat." That seemed to calm the panic a little. She hoped it was true.

After that, it grew quiet again. Livia wondered if there were other people on the boat, people other than the men. Maybe people who could help them. She picked up one of the buckets and told the children she was going to bang it against the door. Maybe someone would hear and help them.

"No!" the Yao boy said. "Stupid idea. Don't make men angry."

"No," Kai said. "Good idea. We try. Try something."

"Make men angry bad!" the Yao boy said.

The other children murmured support for whichever side they favored. Livia decided to just do it. She wished she had a heavy stick or a metal bar—it would have made a louder sound.

She slammed the bucket against the door once, then a second time with more confidence, then a third time even harder. The Yao boy yelled at her to stop, but it felt good to do something, anything, rather than just waiting.

Immediately after the third bang, she heard the sound of the bolts scraping. She stepped back. The door opened, silhouetting the figure of a man outside. She couldn't see his face, but she thought it was one of the three who had taken her and Nason. He said in Thai, "If you make noise again, we whip you. All of you."

The door closed and the bolts scraped back into place. There was no more noise after that, other than the sounds of quiet crying. The Yao boy said, "I tell you! You stupid girl! Get us all whipped!"

At some point, Livia lay down with Nason on the cool metal floor and managed some sleep—a fitful sleep in which she dreamed she and Nason were being chased in the forest by monsters, horrible monsters with the bodies of men and the faces of tigers. Nason screamed and Livia heard one of the man-tiger monsters roar as it pounced—

She jerked awake and glanced around wildly, frightened and disoriented. Nason was clutching her and wailing and everything was moving, swaying. Some of the children had fallen down; others were still on their feet, their arms spread for balance, their eyes wide with terror.

"Why box moving?" Kai cried out in Thai. "Why?"

"Box alive!" someone else called out. "Going to eat us!"

The words were repeated in other languages, and in seconds the box was filled with a terrified cacophony of unintelligible cries.

"It's not alive!" Livia shouted. She could feel the box swaying as it moved. "They move it, with a machine and a string. I saw. I saw before."

Some of the children repeated her words in other languages, but it was useless—the rest were too frightened to listen or understand.

The box continued to sway slowly from side to side. Livia looked through the holes and saw they were moving up, and then sideways, and then down again, down, down, and then there was a loud thud and suddenly everything was still again. No, not still—there was a vibration under them. There was a sharp smell in the air, like burning plastic. Livia thought the machine had moved them from land onto a boat, that the vibration was a motor, like the one on a motorcycle or in the van. And the smell . . . some kind of gasoline? She thought about trying to tell the other children, but she didn't know whether it would calm them or frighten them more. So instead she just held Nason and whispered, "It's okay, little bird, it's okay. I'm here. I won't let you go."

After that, it was quiet for a long time. Even the children who had been crying the most grew silent—asleep, maybe, or else too exhausted even to weep. There was a strange sense of movement, a mild rolling, almost, but Livia got so used to it, and to the vibration, that she had to think about the sensations to realize they were there.

Livia lost track of time in the dark—dozing but never really sleeping; waking but never really feeling awake. If they were on a boat, were they moving? And if they were moving, where were they going?

It was so hard to not be afraid, but she couldn't stop her thoughts. Had the men forgotten the children were in here? Or had something happened to the men, and now no one would be able to find them? She thought about banging with the bucket again, but what if all it achieved was getting everyone whipped with belts? Or worse, what if no one came at all? She decided to wait, to keep the possibility open just in case. But she was so hungry, and thirsty, and the crackers and water were all gone. And it was getting cold. She pulled Nason closer and tried to warm her with her own shivering body.

At some point, she realized she could see a little—the box was filling with a dull, gray light. She looked through the airholes and realized she was seeing the sky. It was morning. There was a new smell amid the stink of the buckets and the children's fear—something salty, a kind of tang in the air Livia couldn't place. She watched the sky get lighter. There were clouds, and the clouds were moving. But was the wind pushing the clouds, or were they on a boat, a boat that was moving past the clouds? She was afraid of the answers to her questions, but it was horrible not to know.

Some of the other children noticed it was getting lighter, too. They discussed as best they could what it meant, whether they were moving, where they were going. Who these men were who had taken them. And whether they were coming back. There were no answers, and after a while, they all grew silent again.

Time passed, and then she heard the sound of bolts scraping on the door. She'd been praying the men hadn't forgotten them, but at the sound of the bolts, she was suddenly afraid again. Who was coming? And what would they do?

The door opened, silhouetting three men outside. Livia squinted and saw it was the same three who had taken her and Nason from the village—Skull Face and Dirty Beard and Square Head. She glanced beyond them to try to get her bearings. Yes, a boat, they were on a boat, an enormous boat—the string machine must have swung the box, as she'd suspected. But aside from that, she could see nothing, just a vast expanse of sky. She didn't know what had happened to the fourth man, the one with the belt. She didn't care. She just hoped they were going to get something to eat.

Skull Face remained standing in the doorway. One of the other two came in and replaced the used buckets with empty ones. The third handed out bottles of water and little metal cans with pictures of food on them. Livia realized there was food in the cans, but didn't see how to get to it. She looked for an opening, a top, but couldn't find anything. Other children were similarly perplexed. The man who had handed out the cans laughed. He took Livia's can and fingered a ring at the top of it, then pulled back the ring and the metal top peeled off. Instantly Livia smelled something so savory and delicious it made her salivate. She held out her hand greedily and the man, laughing again, gave the can back to her. She almost upended it into her mouth, but then remembered herself and exchanged it for Nason's closed can.

Nason needed no prompting—she dug into whatever was in the can and began devouring it.

Skull Face was watching her, seemingly intrigued that she had given her open can to Nason. But Livia didn't care about that. The smell was making her head swim. She pulled the ring back just as the man had done, and the top of the can peeled off like a magic trick. She dug in and winced—the edge of the can was sharp, like a knife. But she was too hungry to care about a cut. She brought the can up, tilted her head back, and poured the contents into her mouth. She thought she had never tasted anything so delicious—balls of meat, some kind of noodles, and a tasty, tangy sauce. She actually moaned with relief and realized the other children were making a similar sound.

The men watched and waited while the children ate. It took a while because the children were wiping and licking every last drop of sauce out of the cans. A few of them cut their fingers on the edges, as Livia had done, or even their tongues, but none seemed to care very much beyond a momentary wince. Livia showed Nason to be careful, then handed over her can when she had finished eating from it so Nason could lick it clean, keeping the top for herself.

One of the men walked around with one of the buckets, indicating to the children that they were to throw their empty cans in it. Livia finished licking the top and was ready to throw it in the bucket when she realized—the edge of the top was so sharp, it could be useful as a weapon. She glanced at the men, saw that no one was watching, and quickly slid the top into the back pocket of her pants.

Just in case.

5—NOW

In a little under an hour and a half, she was in Seattle's Georgetown neighborhood, once a thriving center of manufacturing, now an unlikely amalgam of small industry, hipster eateries, and container shipping yards wedged between Interstate 5 to the east and the Duwamish Waterway to the west.

She rode in along the overpass above the Union Pacific rail yard, cut across to Airport Way, and drifted into the gravel parking lot of the office trailer park at Corson Avenue, where she killed the engine and dismounted. Tentative yellowish light seeped over from the sodium-vapor streetlamps nearby, but beyond that, the area was pooled in shadows. She raised the helmet visor and tasted a morning moisture in the air, heard the whoosh of the earliest commuter vehicles on the freeway overpass above and behind her. Beneath the overpass, at the bases of the giant support columns, were a few cardboard shelters, their inhabitants silent, doubtless sleeping.

She unlocked her trailer, which she rented under a fictitious name and paid for in cash, rolled in the bike, and removed the magnetically attached stolen license plate. Then she pulled off the backpack, shoved the plate and the florescent vest into it, re-shouldered the pack, secured the trailer, and headed south along the sidewalk.

Thirty yards down, she paused to remove the helmet. She shook out her hair and glanced back. Nothing stirred. She put the helmet in the pack and moved off again.

Five minutes later, she reached her building, a three-story brick colossus dominating the western half of her fantastically misnamed dead-end street—South Garden. Built a hundred years earlier as a can and bottle manufacturer, it was now shared by an auto-wrecking operation, a metal recycling plant, and a machine shop run by the guy who owned the building. The guy had been there for decades, and had suffered enough break-ins that a few years earlier he had been thrilled to rent the third-floor storage space over his operation as a loft to the investigating SPD officer. The space—three thousand square feet cluttered with unused machine tools, featuring a kitchenette so spare it might embarrass a college student and a bathroom not much bigger than what you could find on an airplane—wasn't well suited to human habitation, but it was perfect for Livia. She liked being on the border of the polluted Duwamish, with its crumbling brick warehouses, their windows shattered, corrugated eaves rusting like dried blood, smokestacks inert and anachronistic. And the area's solitude, particularly late at night, was unmatched. Best of all was the access to tools she could use for motorcycle maintenance and repairs. The property developers were working with city hall to turn the warehouses into condos and upscale offices with views of the Duwamish, and one day, she knew, she would be sad to see her ghostly, brooding neighbors blazing with light and life. Well, nothing lasted forever. She knew that better than most.

There were multiple CCTV cameras installed around the building, trained on the doors, garage bays, and ground-floor windows, all of which were also alarmed. Ordinarily, the security wasn't a problem, but after killing someone like Barnett, she didn't want to be recorded entering at an odd hour. Late-night coming and going could be explained, of course, if it ever came to that, but it was always safer to have nothing to explain to begin with.

She set down the backpack and removed a mountaineering grappling hook—four steel prongs she had coated with spray rubber and attached to a length of knotted climbing rope. She re-shouldered the pack, took hold of the rope, and swung the grappling hook up onto the fire-escape landing. The hooks caught with a quiet thud, and she was up the rope, arm over arm, in under five seconds. She paused on the first landing to reel in the rope, scooted noiselessly up the remaining sets of stairs, raised the window, and slipped into her apartment.

The lights were off, but there were so many windows exposed to the city's ambient glow that the space was never really dark. Everything was exactly as she'd left it: mattress on the floor in the corner. Desk and chair alongside it. Dresser and wardrobe opposite. Next to the window and fire escape, a small shrine. Several judo and jiu-jitsu gis hanging from pegs on the wall. A cinderblock-and-plank bookshelf containing a row of volumes, among them Alice Vachss's *Sex Crimes*, and *The Essential Abolitionist*, John Vanek's comprehensive guide to human trafficking. Everything else belonged to the shop—drill presses, grinders, lathes, and the other tools of the trade, most of it older, put in storage here on the third floor as the shop acquired newer, more efficient equipment.

She checked the mobile phone she'd left on the rug alongside the mattress to corroborate that she'd been in all night. Not that it would come to that, but she'd put away enough rapists based on cell phone metadata to know not to take the chance. No messages. Good, everything was good. Just a few small matters to take care of, and she could relax.

She opened a window on the southwest side of the loft and turned on the industrial fan facing out from it. The electric motor and loud rush of the blades brought the still space to life, and a cool breeze immediately drifted past her as air was drawn in from the fire-escape window and sucked out by the fan. She grabbed a steel bucket and placed it under a shredder, moving quickly and easily, the layout and the machinery all comfortable to her, familiar. The press of a button, and the shredder started up with a loud whine, its twin shafts spinning toward each other, the teeth of each sliding smoothly into the grooves of its counterpart. She tossed in the stolen plate. There was a brief metal shriek, and then the plate was gone, reduced to confetti-sized scraps deposited at the bottom of the bucket.

She shut off the shredder and carried the bucket over to an oxy-acetylene torch next to the fan. She attached a rosebud tip, pulled on a pair of welder's goggles, fired up the torch, and melted the license plate scraps, keeping the torch moving to make sure she didn't go through the bottom of the pail. The contractor bag with the wig and other potentially contaminated materials went in next. She scoured everything down with the 6,000-degree flame. Billows of black smoke rose from the pail like an evil spirit, but the fan sucked it all away and expelled it, and in seconds, the contents of the pail had been reduced to an undifferentiated, glowing lump.

She killed the torch, removed the goggles, closed her eyes, and let out a long breath. Out of danger now. And nearly done.

Keeping the lights out, she stripped off everything—the gloves, the boots, the leathers, even her underwear. The riding gear got hung near the door. The underwear she threw into a small washing machine in the kitchen, along with some other laundry, running it on a hot cycle. She grabbed a yogurt drink from the refrigerator, keeping one eye closed to preserve her night vision against the interior light, chugged it, and chased it with a big glass of water. Then she took the hottest shower she could stand, washing her hair, scrubbing her body with an exfoliating cloth, standing in the billowing steam to let the heat boil the last of the night's tension out of her. She wasn't worried about the open windows. The Glock, always close at hand, was on the toilet tank next to her.

When she was done drying off, she went back to the shredder. The contents of the bucket had cooled, and she threw the entire thing in, bucket and all, collecting the newly made confetti in a new contractor bag. She'd get rid of the bag in some dumpster tomorrow, but even if it were found here tonight, it could no longer incriminate anyone in anything.

The first light was beginning to show in the eastern sky. She turned off the fan and closed and locked the two windows. Just one last thing to do.

She knelt on a mat in front of the shrine—a small wooden Buddha, an incense brazier, and a photograph of her and Nason, all that remained to her of when they were girls in the forest. She set the Glock on the mat next to her, lit the candle and the incense, and placed her palms together at her forehead in the traditional *Sampeah*, closing her eyes and dipping her head forward as she did so.

"I love you, little bird," she whispered in Lahu. "I will never forget. I will never stop looking. And one day I will find you."

She paused, and added in English, "I'll learn something at the funeral. Something I can use against Weed Tyler. I'm so close, little bird. I've waited so long. And I know you have, too. I know."

She maintained the pose until the incense had burned low. Then she slipped into bed and lay on her back. She would use an eyeshade soon against the morning sun, but for now it was still dark enough. She breathed slowly in and out, the sheets cool against her skin, a slight tingle in her extremities.

She closed her eyes and in her mind replayed everything about the evening. Studying Barnett's file. Reconnaissance of the neighborhood. Buying the wig, the glasses, the yoga outfit, all for cash from stores outside the city. The ride into Marysville that night. Stripping off the leathers and putting on the makeup in a fast-food restroom. Walking into the bar, nervous as the whole thing went live. Catching his eye. The flush of excitement as he sauntered over.

Her heart began to beat harder, and she parted her lips to draw more air. She flexed her legs and brought her knees up a few inches from the mattress, the sheets sliding smoothly under her toes and the balls of her feet.

The smell of his bourbon as he got increasingly drunk, whatever self-control he had fading, his judgment occluded. The way he looked at her. Knowing what he was thinking, planning.

She shifted her weight to one shoulder, then the other. Her knees widened and one of her hands drifted down between her legs.

The way he had grabbed her shoulders and shaken her. How he had tried to pull her in and make her kiss him.

"No," she breathed aloud, her fingers pressing, rubbing, moving. "No. I don't want this."

How he'd ignored her pleas and thrown her down on the grass. His weight as he straddled her.

Her fingers were moving faster now, harder, her breathing loud in her ears. She could feel the pressure building inside her. "No," she said again. "No."

His hand on her throat. The sound of his belt buckle.

She sat up and twisted around, her knees spread wide, her free hand gripping the bedsheet, her arm taking her weight. She rocked her hips against her fingers and moaned.

Squeezing his neck, feeling it being crushed in the figure-four of her legs.

The pressure was unbearable now. She gripped the sheet harder and spread her knees wider.

The way he'd scratched at her leg, his efforts frantic at first, then increasingly feeble. Knowing she'd stopped him. Denied him every option. Taken complete control—

And then the pressure exploded, and she cried out, the pleasure obliterating Barnett, obliterating the memories, obliterating everything.

Eventually, it began to slacken. She shuddered once as her consciousness reconstructed itself, then turned onto her back. She lay there, her heart slowing, her breathing coming back to normal, her muscles relaxing as sleep overtook her.

The sun was still below the horizon, but the loft was filling with soft gray light. She reached sluggishly for the eyeshade, not even aware of the tears streaking her face.

6—THEN

At one point during the day, the men came with blankets. They threw them on the floor and left, the bolts scraping into place after they closed the door behind them.

Livia grabbed one blanket for Nason and herself, and the other children immediately followed suit. But there was no need to hurry—there were enough for everyone. In fact, there was exactly one extra, which the Yao boy took for himself so that he had two. Livia gestured to his extra blanket, then to herself, indicating he should give it to her because she and Nason had only the one. But the boy shook his head and clutched both blankets close to his body.

Livia took a step closer and gestured to the extra blanket again. "You give," she said in Thai.

The Yao boy shook his head again and took a step back.

Livia handed the blanket to Nason and advanced on the boy. "You give," she said. "One each. Not two. One."

The Yao boy backed up until he hit one of the metal walls and could go no farther. He clutched the blankets tightly and bared his teeth at Livia.

She didn't care that he was older and bigger. It wasn't fair that he had taken two blankets. And it wouldn't be good for anyone if the stronger children figured out they could take what they wanted from the weaker ones. She advanced, stopping just a few feet away from him. She looked directly into his eyes and stuck out her hand, the gesture not a request but a demand.

Despite his size, the Yao boy looked uncertain. But he wouldn't surrender the blanket. Livia prepared to grab it, thinking she would punch him in the face or kick him in the place it hurt boys most if he tried to pull it away.

But just before she went for the blanket, Kai came up alongside her and stood facing the Yao boy, his shoulder almost touching Livia's. He was smaller than the Yao boy—smaller even than Livia—but his voice was firm as he pointed to the Yao boy and said in Thai, "You give. Give blanket."

The Yao boy bared his teeth at Kai as he had at Livia. But when neither of them backed away, he grunted as though in disgust, tossed one of the blankets at Livia, and slunk away to one of the corners of the box.

Livia nodded to Kai, then took the blanket to Nason. If they snuggled closely, one blanket would be enough to keep them warm, and the other they could use as a pallet. She realized this would be a good idea for the other children, too, and explained it carefully in Thai, waiting patiently while the message was translated from one language to another. Like most of her ideas, she didn't know if it would help much, but it gave them something to do and seemed to make the others feel a little better.

That night, while she snuggled close to Nason in the dark, Livia folded the top of the can nearly in half to make one edge stick out and to make it easier to hold without cutting herself. She gripped it tightly between her thumb and fingers and touched the edge with her free hand. It wasn't as sharp as an *a-taw*, but it would slice deeply if she slashed with it. She slid it into her back pocket, and slept better feeling the small, hard shape beneath her.

Several days passed. Once in the morning and then again at night, the men handed out food in cans and bottles of water, and replaced the stinky buckets with fresh ones. At night, they carried flashlights, which they would shine at the top of the box and then watch by the reflected light while the children ate. Livia didn't like their expressions. They looked like hungry cats eyeing trapped mice. Like they wanted something from the children, but for some reason weren't taking it. Yet.

On their fourth night on the boat, when the men came with the food and water, they smelled of alcohol. Their faces were red in the glow of their flashlights, and they licked their lips while the children ate from the cans. It was enough to make Livia remember what one of the children had said—that she had heard about men like these, men who ate children. It seemed too horrible to be true, but Livia knew from the feverish look in their eyes, the way they rubbed their mouths with the back of their hands, that they were going to do something bad. But what?

When the children were done and had thrown the empty cans into the dirty buckets, Square Head, who was standing next to Livia and Nason, glanced at Skull Face and raised his eyebrows as though asking a question. Skull Face nodded—and Square Head seized Nason by the wrist. Nason cried out and tried to pull away.

"You come," Square Head said in Thai.

Livia grabbed Nason by the other wrist, just as she had in front of their hut, a time that seemed impossibly far away now. She felt like she was having a nightmare. Why were the men trying to take Nason? She thought about the folded can top in her back pocket. But how could she use it against three men?

"Why you take her?" she cried out in Thai. "Why?"

Square Head was still pulling, but only hard enough to keep Livia from pulling Nason back. He looked at Skull Face as though waiting for him to decide.

Skull Face laughed and shone his flashlight in Livia's face. She raised one hand against the blinding light, hanging on to Nason's wrist with the other.

"For fun," he said. "We take her for fun."

For a moment, Livia didn't understand. Fun? They wanted Nason for a game? It didn't make sense—

And then she was overwhelmed with a horrified understanding. "No!" she cried out. "No, please, no."

Skull Face laughed again. "No? Why?"

Livia struggled to hold back tears. "She too young for fun. Please."

Livia felt Skull Face looking at her, and she had the horrible sense that he knew her, knew her better than she knew herself. She tried to think of what to do, and then Skull Face shone the flashlight on Nason and said to Square Head, "Enough. Take her."

Square Head started pulling again. Livia grabbed Nason's wrist with both hands and tried to pull back, but the man was too strong. Nason looked at Livia and screamed, "Labee! Labee!"

Livia was being dragged along behind Nason. She couldn't stop them. But she couldn't let them do this to Nason. She couldn't. Without thinking, she looked at Skull Face and screamed, "Take me! Not her, take me!"

Skull Face, already red from the alcohol, flushed more deeply. His nostrils flaring slightly as he breathed, he said to Square Head, "Wait."

Square Head stopped pulling, but didn't release Nason's wrist.

Skull Face shone his flashlight at Livia. "You want us to take you?"

Livia shook her head, squinting. "She too young. Please."

"Then you? You want us to take you?"

Livia couldn't answer.

Skull Face shrugged and nodded at Nason. "Okay," he said to Square Head. "Take her."

"No!" Livia shouted. "No, you take me. I want you take me."

Skull Face looked at her. His sunken eyes were black.

"What if we like her better?"

"No, she no better. Please. You take me."

"Why?"

"She too young."

"You mean . . . you'll be more fun?"

Livia was so relieved that Skull Face seemed to be listening, she was barely aware of her own terror. "Yes. I more fun. Please. Please take me."

Skull Face nodded to Square Head, who released Nason. Nason stumbled into Livia and clung to her, crying. Livia looked at Skull Face. He shone his flashlight on the ceiling and gestured to the door, smiling.

"It's all right, little bird," Livia whispered. "It's all right. I have to go with them, but not for long. I'll be back very soon."

Nason clung harder. "Why, Labee?"

"It's too much to explain. Just a little while, and I'll be back."

Nason shook her head and cried helplessly. "I want to go home."

Livia thought of their parents, and almost said, *We don't have a home.* But that would be needlessly cruel. So instead she whispered, "So do I, little bird. So do I."

"Why can't we?"

"I'll try to find a way. But for now, I need you to be brave and wait for me to come back. Will you do that?"

"But I'm not brave, Labee. I'm not."

"No, that isn't true, little bird. You are brave. You just don't know it yet. But you are."

Livia tried to pry herself away, but Nason clung to her.

Livia's heart was pounding. She didn't know these men. She had no reason to trust them, and every reason not to. They weren't even Lahu. And even if they had been, look at what her own parents had done.

What if you do what they want, and they break their promise? Their promise not to hurt Nason?

She didn't know. She couldn't even fully acknowledge the possibility. She just had to try. She couldn't live with herself if she didn't.

Kai came and put his arm around Nason. Livia disengaged and nodded to Kai. He nodded back. She couldn't tell what he was thinking. Nason continued to cry, but at least there was someone with her, someone who cared enough to try to comfort her.

Livia straightened, clenched her jaw to keep her lips from quivering, and walked through the door to whatever was outside the box.

The first thing she noticed was the wind—cold and strong and clean. It made her realize how rank the air inside the box had become. The sky was dark, but there must have been lights on the boat somewhere because she could see well enough. She looked around, trying to learn something that might be useful, anything. They were standing in a long, narrow space, with a high metal wall to one side and more of the boxes stacked opposite. On either end of the long space, she could see nothing but darkness. On the other side of the wall was a tall post, like a tree with lights up and down it. Maybe if she could get to it and shimmy to the top, she could see more? But she couldn't see how she would reach it, even if she could outrun the men. And besides, what would happen to Nason if she tried?

She couldn't be sure, but a boat this big, and the port, and the foreign letters she had seen . . . they had to be on the ocean. The thought was as terrifying as it was bewildering.

She watched while the men closed the door and secured the bolts. It was a simple mechanism, but she saw no way it could be opened from inside.

The men motioned that she should come with them, and she obeyed. They wanted her to cooperate, and she had to give them what they wanted. Or they would take it from Nason instead.

They walked toward what she thought from the direction of the wind was the side of the ship, the boxes to their right, the wall to their left. A short way down, there was a gap among the row of boxes, as though one stack had been removed, or left out. The men motioned.

Her heart pounding, her throat constricted, Livia walked into the gap, the men close behind her.

She stopped in the center and turned. The light was dim and the space felt like a cage. There were stacks of boxes to three sides. The floor was covered in some kind of fake grass—she could just make out the color green in the faint light, but the feel under her bare feet was scratchy. She wondered absently why someone would want to make fake grass. What kind of world was this?

One of the men came toward her. Square Head. His face was silhouetted and she couldn't see his expression. For some reason, she felt glad of that. She didn't want to see their faces.

The sound of the wind was deadened inside the space, and Livia could hear the man breathing heavily, see it in the rise and fall of his chest. He said in Thai, "Get on your knees."

Livia didn't understand. She had been terrified the men were going to do to her the thing that made babies. The thing she and all the Lahu children saw dogs doing, and sometimes heard their parents doing. But then why would he want her on her knees?

She knelt and started to cry. She hoped the men couldn't see it.

Square Head pulled open his pants. Livia shook her head, not understanding.

Square Head pointed to her mouth, then to himself, then to her mouth again.

A wave of nausea coursed through her. No. He couldn't want her to . . . what, kiss him? There? It was disgusting, why would anyone want that?

She thought of her parents, of her father gripping the handful of baht, and cried harder.

Square Head stepped closer. He smelled like curry, a spice Livia had always liked but which was suddenly repulsive.

"Mouth," he said in Thai. "Mouth."

She closed her eyes and held her breath and tried to do what he wanted. But it was all so sickening that she gagged again and again until finally she jerked her head away and threw up. He waited a moment and then made her continue, holding her hair and thrusting himself in and out of her mouth while she squeezed her eyes shut and tried desperately to conjure something good, a happy memory, some secret imagining these men couldn't know or reach. But nothing came. So she gagged and sobbed and thought of Nason, of how much worse it would be if this were happening to her little bird instead of to herself. She clung to that thought and endured one second to the next, not knowing when it would end or how.

Finally, the man moaned as though he was hurt and something squirted out of him, something hot and slick and slimy. Livia gagged and tried to pull away, but he held her hair tightly and kept moving. When he finally let her go, she leaned over and threw up again.

It was the same with Dirty Beard, and then with Skull Face. When they were all done, Livia collapsed to her side, retching, her stomach convulsing but with nothing left to throw up.

The men lit cigarettes and watched her. After a few minutes, her roiling stomach subsided. She spat until there was nothing left to spit and sat up.

Skull Face smiled at her. "You fun," he said. "So fun. You stay fun, and we won't do this with your sister, okay?"

Livia was too exhausted to respond. But amid the horror and revulsion, she felt a tiny sliver of hope. She had protected Nason. She could do it again, if she had to. To protect her sister, she would do anything.

She didn't know that, in the end, it wouldn't be enough.

7—NOW

Livia woke after only an hour, before the alarm went off. She had been too excited to sleep deeply—from killing Barnett, of course, but even more because of everything that was going to happen next.

She rolled out of bed, opened a window, and inhaled the air of a spring morning far too glorious for the Jeep. She rode the Ducati to headquarters, tossing the contractor bag near a homeless encampment under the interstate along the way.

She was at her desk well before roll call—her usual practice, and it was important not to do anything out of the ordinary immediately after a kill. No news about Barnett, but it was still early. Probably Marysville PD hadn't even had time to positively identify the body. She wouldn't be surprised if Hammerhead learned of his demise before word reached Seattle PD. It didn't matter. People would be talking about it soon enough either way.

In lieu of anything on Barnett, she worked her usual caseload. In the last week, she'd arrested a peeper in Ballard and a man exposing himself in Olympic Hills, so things were momentarily light. But she also had a sex worker victim, raped by a john out by Sea-Tac. The prosecuting attorney wasn't going to like this one—not a good victim, meaning not sufficiently sympathetic to a jury, as though only nuns and candy stripers could be raped—and Livia knew she needed an unusually strong case if she was going to persuade the prosecutor to go to trial. She'd already identified a suspect, and was now looking for ways to connect him with similar attacks. There had to have been others—it was just too unlikely this was the first time the guy had decided to attack a sex worker. If Livia could find his other victims and persuade them to come forward, it would go a long way toward getting the prosecutor off his politically calculating ass and putting a serial rapist behind bars.

Sometimes, she almost wanted the prosecutor to say no, or to plea the charges down. It was a reason, an excuse, to do it her way instead. But she knew she had to be careful of that temptation. There was a balance. She respected the system, but she wouldn't be a slave to it. Her real allegiance was to her victims, and if the system didn't get them justice, she would get them justice another way.

She'd been at it for close to forty minutes when her lieutenant came in—short, brown hair neat, expression wide awake despite the early hour. Donna Strangeland. A Brooklyn transplant with an accent to match, and a damn good cop. It was odd—some of the women on the force dealt with discrimination by identifying with the men, competing with their sister cops, putting them down, trying to step over them like crabs in a bucket. But a few dealt with it through mutual support and solidarity. Donna was in the latter camp. Beyond which, Livia had never seen a better interrogator. The woman could project incredible levels of compassion and understanding even to the most vile criminals. Murderers. Child rapists. Sadists. She made her suspects feel she understood them, and that if they would only explain to her, be honest with her, open up to her, she could forgive them. Something about her made them crave understanding, the possibility of forgiveness, to the point where Livia had seen her get people to sign confessions stained with their own tears. She was like some kind of surrogate mother, persuading her suspects to trade honesty for the chimera of her love.

She had explained to Livia it wasn't exactly an act. When she walked into that interrogation room, she set aside all her horror, her disgust, her rage. She always looked for something that would enable her to feel sympathy, and then focused on that thing, not allowing herself to feel anything else. Until after she'd gotten a signed statement, of course. But first she made her suspects want that confession almost as badly as she did.

"Guess I shouldn't really be surprised to see you," Donna said, pausing on her way to her office and sipping the department's strong-smelling coffee from a Styrofoam cup. "Though I did think you might throttle it back a little after the last two."

She was talking about Ballard and Olympic Hills—both closed cases now. "Yeah," Livia said, lacing her fingers and stretching her arms over her head to crack the knuckles. "I was going to. But something turned those guys into what they are. So I thought I'd poke around a little. See if there was a teacher, a coach, whatever, picked up for moles-tation. Cross-reference. Maybe I can spot the next one before it happens. Plus there's my Sea-Tac victim. Prosecutor's not going to like her."

None of it was a lie. Not really. It was just a matter of emphasis.

Donna nodded. If it had been anyone else, she might not have bought it. But she knew Livia's habits. Her obsessions. "All right," she said. "See you at roll call."

"You bet. Unless you have something for me now."

"I always give you the child stuff, Livia. No one else wants it, anyway."

Almost no one who had kids, or even nieces and nephews, could handle the child cases. It was too much to bear. But everyone knew that for Livia, it was a crusade.

"Just asking."

Donna nodded. "By the way. Word from the chief. There's a guy coming in. Homeland Security. Something about a joint anti-trafficking task force. They're looking for the right personnel, and it sounded up your alley. You interested?"

"Maybe. Any other intel?"

"That's it. You know the feds. All very hush-hush. But if it's DHS, it's safe to say there's an overseas component. And maybe some kind of terror angle, I don't know." She paused, then added, "I don't know if it's about kids. Certainly could be."

Overseas . . . right now, she didn't want anything that would distract from the Hammerhead funeral. Or from Weed Tyler, whose release was imminent, who was the only possible key to what had happened to Nason. Livia nodded and said, "Can I think about it?"

Donna took a sip of coffee. "I don't even know when the guy's coming in. We'll learn more then."

"Great. Thanks."

Roll call was the usual—an hour of updates on what had happened the night before; discussion of changing policy and procedures governing the use of force; information-sharing on open cases. Just before dismissing everyone, Donna glanced at her tablet. "Oh, look at this," she said. "Seems one Billy Barnett has met his maker."

Some of the assembled detectives raised their eyebrows. Others glanced around, looking for clarification. Outside Sex Crimes and the Gang Unit, Barnett was hardly a household name.

"Hammerhead soldier," Donna said. "And twice-convicted sex offender. Got himself strangled in a park up in Marysville. Just released from Monroe, too. Terrible loss for humanity."

"Marysville PD like anyone for it?" That was Suzanne Moore, another good cop who, like Donna, had early on taken Livia under her wing.

"Yeah, about a hundred different people. Barnett wasn't exactly Mr. Popularity. One theory is he tried to rape the wrong girl. But more likely, Hammerhead itself did the hit. Barnett's last trip to Monroe caused them a lot of headaches. Good chance they decided they didn't want any more of his bullshit."

Suzanne laughed. "Always good when the garbage takes out the garbage."

There was a generalized murmur of assent to that. Then Donna said, "There's a third possibility, and it's one we need to be aware of. Another gang might have been behind this. If so, there are apt to be reprisals. So work your CIs. If there's going to be trouble, we want to spot it in advance. Speaking of which, Barnett was a Texas native, but G thinks Hammerhead is going to bury him locally, at Crown Hill. If so, all of Hammerhead's going to be there. Now, the G guys will be all over the periphery—high profile, as a deterrent in case Deuce 8 or the East Union Street Hustlers or whoever decides to show up looking for trouble. But we'll want to look sharp, too. A Hammerhead white power funeral is like a full moon on a hot, humid night. It just gets people riled."

Livia raised her hand. "If there's going to be a funeral, Lieu, I wouldn't mind swinging by. Check out a Gossamer, get a little intel about who's who. We know Barnett didn't always rape by himself, and most of his vics were afraid to come forward once they learned they were dealing with a gang. I want to know who he was close to. With Barnett dead, if there's another Hammerhead rape, chances are it'll be one of his good buddies."

The Gossamer was a handheld cell phone tracker that could place a mobile phone to within less than a yard of its actual location. SPD had a half dozen of them, all purchased with a grant from the Department of Homeland Security. The public knew about the location-tracking function, of course, but what wasn't as widely understood was the technology's versatility. The devices could track dozens of phones simultaneously, and could be programmed to key on the proximity of any two cell phones, or five, or ten. The G-unit used them to head off gang battles, setting their Gossamers to sound an alert if phones known to be carried by members of rival gangs were converging in a way that suggested a street fight was imminent. Narcotics used them to map the movements and associations of known traffickers, and to eavesdrop on their conversations. And High Risk Victims used them to uncover networks of pimps, their suppliers, and their customers.

Because of the DHS grant, inventory was monitored closely. But Livia had thought of a way around that. She'd only been waiting for the right moment to act, and if Barnett's funeral was going down in a day or two, the moment was now.

Donna nodded. "Makes sense. I'll send the paperwork to the Tool Shed." She took a moment to look around at the assembled detectives, then said, "All right, everyone. Let's go get 'em."

Livia's expression remained perfectly neutral—a routine request, a routine permission granted. But inside, she felt the familiar stirring. The heat. The power. The *dragon*.

Go get 'em, she thought. *Oh yes, I will.*

8—THEN

Every night after, it was the same. The second time was nearly as bad as the first. But by the third time, Livia at least knew what to expect—what the men wanted, and more or less when and how it would be over. The men must have loved curry, because they always stank from it. And when they smelled like alcohol, too, they were rougher with her, like they were trying to hurt her, and they laughed when she gagged or threw up. But she was able to endure it because she knew doing so was protecting Nason.

After that, time didn't pass so much as it blurred. She sat in the box with the other children, and knew it was day from the light coming through the airholes, and knew it was night when the light faded and they needed the blankets to stay warm. The only breaks in the monotony happened each morning and evening, when the men brought food and water and changed the buckets. After each evening feeding, Livia would go outside the box with the men and numbly do the disgusting thing, then come back and hold Nason, allowing herself to cry noiselessly only after Nason had fallen asleep.

By now, she knew there were no "jobs." As hard as she searched for a way to explain it away or alter it, she couldn't deny the essential truth. She and Nason . . . their parents had simply sold them, the way they would sell a chicken or pig.

One night, the alcohol smell was especially strong. Livia's stomach sank at the realization that outside the box it was going to be even worse than usual. But there was nothing she could do. She would have to endure it for Nason.

When she had finished her food, she stepped toward the door to go out with the men. But Skull Face smiled and said, "No. You stay."

Livia watched him, uneasy. It would be a relief to not have to do the disgusting thing. But she sensed something dangerous in Skull Face's smile, some trick.

"Why?" she said, hating that she had to ask, but needing to know.

"You no fun anymore. We want new fun."

Livia felt heat spread from her stomach to her limbs. Was he talking about one of the other children? Surely he couldn't mean—

Skull Face pointed to Nason. "Take her."

"No!" Livia screamed, in her panic reverting to Lahu. "No, no, no!"

The other two men moved forward. Livia shoved Nason to the back of the box, as far from the door as possible, then turned to face the men, blocking Nason with her body. "No!" she screamed again, in Thai this time. "You say, you promise!"

Skull Face laughed. Livia turned so her arm would be hidden, then slipped the can top from her back pocket. She would slice the first man who tried to get past her to Nason.

Skull Face was laughing harder. He took a bottle from inside the jacket he was wearing and began to unscrew the top. The alcohol, Livia realized.

And then a vivid image flashed inside her mind: the way they killed snakes in the village. Not by cutting off the tail.

By cutting off the head.

Skull Face raised the bottle to his mouth and tilted his chin up to drink. Livia took an enormous breath and raced forward, screaming with all her heart and lungs, the piercing wail of it exploding within the confines of the box like a thunderstorm. The men flinched. The children covered their ears.

Skull Face saw her coming and tried to move away. But before he could reach the door, Livia leaped, her free hand grabbing at his jacket, the other hand swinging the can top down and around like a tiger claw, slashing it across his eye. Skull Face shrieked and staggered back. Livia crashed into him and they both fell to the ground. Livia tried to slash his face again, but his hands were up and she succeeded only in cutting his arms. She darted her head in, got her teeth around the meat under one of his thumbs, and bit as hard as she could, bit the way she'd imagined doing every time they had made her do the disgusting thing, and Skull Face howled and jerked his hand free and she slashed at him again, trying to get past his arms to his face and especially his eyes. There was blood in her mouth and on her face and she felt a savage excitement at the smell and taste of it, the awareness that she was hurting Skull Face, maybe killing him.

And then she was being pulled backward, and she twisted and slashed with the can top and cut one of the other men across the cheek. He yelled and she tried to slash him again, but the other man grabbed her arm and pulled it behind her back. She felt a jolt of pain in her shoulder, and the bloody can top was pulled from her fingers. The man threw an arm around her stomach, jerked her high into the air, and slammed her down onto the metal floor. Livia saw stars and the breath was knocked out of her.

After that, everything was confusion—Skull Face rolling back and forth on the floor, wailing, his hands covering his face; the other men trying to help him; the children retreating to the walls of the box, screaming and crying. Livia tried to yell at them to run, *run!* But she couldn't breathe. She watched, agonized, as the other men pulled Skull

Face to his feet and dragged him through the door. The children could have easily rushed past them, but none of them tried, not even Kai. They all just sat and cried, their backs to the walls, their arms around their knees.

Then the door slammed closed and the box went dark. Livia heard the bolts scraping into place, the clank of the lock closing. And then there was nothing but the sound of the children's tears and the sharp smell of the men's blood.

Amid the other children's sobs, she heard Nason crying, "Labee, where are you? Labee?"

She managed to draw a breath and sit up. Her shoulder hurt from the way the man had jerked her arm. She swallowed to wet her throat and said, "I'm here, little bird."

"Where?"

"Follow my voice. I'm sitting in the middle of the box."

She kept talking, and it was almost like one of their games. A moment later, Nason stumbled into her, then collapsed into her arms, crying. Livia stroked her hair and whispered to her that it would be all right, it would be all right.

"Why you did that?" she heard someone call out in Thai. "Why?"

It was the Yao boy, the coward. Livia considered not answering, but then said, "Why you no run?"

"Run? Run where?"

In fact, it wasn't an unreasonable question. Livia didn't really know what was out there. A boat, yes, but beyond that she barely had any idea. Were there other people? The boat was so big, there must have been. But where were the people? And would they help?

"You want stay here?" she said. "Like chicken in trap?"

"Yes!" the Yao boy said. "In here food. Water. What if now men don't come? What if men mad now? No bring food! No water!"

A low, collective moan of terror filled the box. But Livia didn't feel frightened. She felt rage—rage at the Yao boy's cowardice, and even more that he didn't care what she was being forced to do to keep the men happy while he cowered in the box, warm and safe and well fed. If the men hadn't taken the can top from her, she would have found the Yao boy and slashed him with it. Well, she didn't need the top. She could hurt him with her nails, and her teeth.

But no. She had to take care of Nason—that was what mattered. So she said, "You could run. But you no run. What happens, you did, not me."

She wanted to believe that. But she didn't. She knew she'd wounded a tiger. And that the tiger was going to come back.

9—THEN

Sometime later, Livia was awakened by the sound of the bolts scraping back. She sat up instantly, her heart pounding. Nason, obviously still on edge, sat up with her, gripping Livia's arm.

The door opened and the men strode in. This time, they didn't point their flashlights at the top of the box. They swept them back and forth, shining them straight into the children's terrified faces. Livia held up a hand to shield her eyes as the lights flashed on her and Nason. She squinted to try to see, and saw a pair of legs approaching. She scrambled to position herself in front of Nason, but something must have happened because suddenly she was on her back, her head throbbing, her ears ringing, and Nason was screaming from all the way at the front of the box, and Livia tried to stand but a wave of dizziness and nausea coursed through her and she fell. "Nason!" she cried out. "Nason!"

And then the door closed, and the bolts scraped into place, and Nason was gone. Livia drew in a long, hitching breath and shrieked into the darkness.

10—NOW

The next day, Livia got confirmation from the G-unit: Billy Barnett would be laid to rest at Crown Hill Cemetery at eleven o'clock the following morning. The G guys would be out in force to deter rival gangbangers from causing trouble, and to take them down if deterrence failed.

Livia went to inventory—a.k.a. the Tool Shed, a.k.a. the Bat Cave. Gossamer usage was monitored closely, in accordance with an SPD contract with the manufacturer, and a detective requesting one of the units needed permission from a lieutenant or higher, and had to fill out nearly as much paperwork as for a sniper rifle.

The Tool Shed was run by a civilian SPD employee named Alvin, a ginger-haired computer geek who looked twenty years younger than his actual forty-five. Alvin ran his operation like an OCD military quartermaster, demanding every i dotted, every t crossed. And God help you if you were an hour late returning something you had checked out from him.

But he also had a crush on Livia, blushing under his spray of freckles when she came by to sign out some equipment. And even more when she came by just to say hello. She was pretty sure he would cut her a little slack if she were to return one of his toys in, say, less than factory condition.

She took the elevator to the basement, walked down the fluorescent-lit corridor, and saw Alvin standing behind the checkout window like a postal clerk or pharmacist. She'd never once been down here and failed to see him at the ready. Sometimes she wondered if he ever went to the bathroom. But she'd decided this was something best left a mystery.

She waved. "Hey, Alvin."

He waved back. "Livia. That's funny—I just received a permission slip from Lieutenant Strangeland for a Gossamer."

She smiled. "Well, what a coincidence."

He laughed awkwardly. "Right. Of course. Well, I've got one right here for you. Charged up and ready to go. You have the form filled out?"

"No, I thought I'd fill it out here. If I'm not taking too much of your time."

"What? No, of course not. Here you go."

He produced one of the Gossamer forms—how long will the unit be out, what is its intended use, who authorized, et cetera. While she filled it out, she guided him through some small talk, mostly about how things looked for the Mariners this season, how exciting it would be to have Browner back with the Seahawks, that kind of thing. Alvin was a sports fan, and though Livia wasn't, she wouldn't have been worth much as a detective if she didn't know how to shoot the shit about politics, sports, the weather, and a variety of other such topics. When she was done with the form, she slid it across the counter to him.

He examined it carefully, frowning after a moment as she'd expected. "Uh, three days . . . you're really supposed to file an extension if it's going to be longer than forty-eight hours."

"I know. It's this Hammerhead funeral. It's tomorrow, but I want to make sure I have time to follow up on what I learn there."

He rubbed the back of his neck. "I get it, I just . . . look, would you mind if we make it forty-eight, and if you need it longer, I'll fill out the extension myself."

She smiled. "You're sweet."

He blushed. "No, I mean, I just know you're busy."

"Well, so are you."

"Not like you. That Montlake case? I just read an article about the survivor in the *Stranger*. Did you see it?"

Livia nodded. Of course she'd seen it, a follow-up on the brave woman who had survived the sadist who had broken into the Montlake home she shared with her lesbian partner, torturing, raping, and repeatedly stabbing them both before in extremis the partner fought back and saved the other victim's life. The rapist had used the women's love for each other, their mutual devotion, to control them while he tortured and raped them. That case had hit close to home, and when she tracked the rapist down, it had been hard for Livia not to kill him. But at least the system had worked, and he'd been sent to prison forever.

"She said you were her rock," Alvin said. "From the first interview all the way through sentencing and even after that. You really help people, you know?"

For a moment, she forgot she was manipulating him, and was genuinely moved. "Thanks, Alvin."

"No, thank you. So, anyway, okay with forty-eight, and then a de facto automatic extension? Just between you and me."

She wondered for a moment who was manipulating whom. Then she held out her hand in mock formality and said, "Deal."

Alvin smiled and they shook.

Maybe he'd manipulated her a little—he'd have to have some skills to manage all the competing requests he received, and the egos behind them. But it didn't matter. She'd gotten Alvin to agree to bend the rules. And she knew that once you'd gotten someone to say yes to one thing, it was easier to get him to say yes to the next. Like, say, going easy on the paperwork if a Gossamer were to suffer some sort of mishap. Because she needed one of the units for a little longer than forty-eight hours. She needed it for when Weed Tyler was released from Victorville.

And maybe even beyond that.

11—THEN

Eventually, the dizziness and nausea slackened and Livia was able to sit up. Her head still throbbed, and a spot over her ear was tender when she touched it. She realized the men had hit her with something harder than a hand, though the flashlights had been so blinding she hadn't even seen it happen. She sat and waited, feeling miserable and powerless and alone. All she could do was hope, and try not to imagine what they were doing to Nason.

At some point, she realized she could see—morning had come, and light was beginning to creep through the airholes. "Nason," she whispered helplessly, clutching herself by the shoulders. "Nason."

The inside of the box grew lighter, and she heard the sound of the bolts. She stood and rushed to the door. If the men didn't have Nason, she would get past them and find her, somewhere on the boat, somehow.

The door opened. It was the three men, Nason just ahead of them. Livia was so overcome with relief at the sight of her sister that her knees wobbled and tears ran from her eyes. The men pushed Nason inside, and she stumbled into Livia's arms. Livia gripped her tightly, stroking her hair. "Little bird," she whispered, her throat so tight she could barely speak. "Little bird, are you all right? Are you all right?"

For an instant, just having her in her arms, Livia was sure Nason was okay. But then she realized something was wrong. Nason wasn't answering. And she wasn't hugging Livia, clinging to her the way she did when she was frightened. She didn't have her arms around Livia at all. One hand hung limply at her side. The other was in front of her, raised to her mouth. Livia took a half step back and was shocked to see that Nason was sucking her thumb—something her sister hadn't done since she was very small. Livia looked in her eyes and whispered, "Nason, Nason, are you all right?"

Nason was looking at her, but more she was looking . . . through her.

Livia took her by the shoulders and shook her once, then again. "Nason!" she said. "Nason!"

It was as though Nason couldn't hear her. Or see her. As though she didn't even know Livia was there.

Livia glanced down and saw blood on Nason's pants, between her legs. She tried to tell herself it must be something else, something that had spilled. But she knew it was blood. She could smell it.

She stared at the men, for the first time seeing the bandages around the faces of Skull Face and Square Head and on their arms. They were all holding long sticks, and some distant part of her registered that probably this is what they'd hit her with. Skull Face looked at Livia and started to raise his stick, but Dirty Beard shook his head and gripped Skull Face's arm. Skull Face shook off the man's hand and smiled at Livia, the smile distorted by pain or the tight bandage or both.

Everything Livia had ever felt was replaced by an eruption of pure, black hate. A bloody mist filled her vision, and she charged screaming at Skull Face, her teeth bared, her fingers raked back like claws. But this time he was ready for her. His stick flashed forward and caught Livia in the stomach. The breath was driven out of her and she collapsed to the ground, her midsection an exploding ball of pain.

Skull Face squatted close to her. "Your sister was fun," he said. "Maybe later, we'll come back for more fun with her."

Kai rushed over. Skull Face stood and raised his stick, but lowered it when Kai stopped and knelt next to Livia, his hand on her shoulder. Livia scrabbled her feet to propel her body toward Skull Face, because nothing mattered except getting at him, scratching him, clawing him, biting him, killing him. But her stomach was so clenched she couldn't breathe. She stared up at Skull Face, kicking and grimacing. He was still smiling. Dots began to dance in Livia's vision, and the box filled with gray. The gray became everything, and then even that was gone.

12—THEN

Livia was lying on her back in the forest and it was raining. Drops fell from the tree branches onto her cheeks and her eyelids. She heard someone calling her name from far away, but she didn't answer. She felt safe in the forest and didn't want anyone to be able to find her there.

And then her eyes fluttered open, and the forest was gone, and the raindrops were from a water bottle, and the person saying her name was Kai, who was sitting next to her and sprinkling water on her face. Her arms and legs twitched, and she moaned and sat up, panting for a moment while a wave of dizziness engulfed her and then passed.

"Nason?" she said, suddenly unsure of which was the dream—the forest, or this.

"Here," Kai said. Livia saw that Nason was right next to them, lying on her side on a folded blanket. Her knees were drawn up to her chest and her eyes were open. Her thumb was still in her mouth.

Livia felt her face contort, and tears flowed from her eyes. "Oh, little bird," she said, her voice cracking. "Little bird."

She lay down behind Nason and put one arm around her, stroking her hair the way she did when she was trying to help her sleep. "Little bird, little bird," she whispered between sobs. But Nason gave no sign she even knew Livia was there.

After that, when the men brought food and water, they carried long sticks, as though expecting the children to attack them. When they looked at Nason, their faces seemed worried, which Livia didn't understand. But for whatever reason, they didn't take Livia or Nason outside the box again, or anyone else. They brought food and water and changed the buckets and said not a word.

Days passed, and Nason remained like that, not talking, not responding to being talked to. She would eat when Livia fed her and drink when Livia tipped a bottle to her lips, and use the bucket when Livia led her to it. But other than that, she remained on her side, curled up, her eyes staring at something Livia couldn't see.

Livia tried to tell herself it wasn't her fault. But she knew why Nason had been bleeding. Because the men did to her the thing that made babies. But they hadn't done that to Livia, and maybe the Yao boy had been right . . . maybe they wouldn't have done it to Nason, either, if Livia hadn't made them so angry. Maybe they had hurt Nason worse than they would have if Livia hadn't attacked them. Something had happened to Nason's mind; she could see that. Maybe the men had hurt Nason so much that Nason had found a way to just . . . go away? Yes, maybe that was it. Livia tried to cling to that hope, and to believe that maybe, when Nason did come back, she wouldn't even remember what the men had done to her because in a way she hadn't been there when it had happened. But would she really come back? How? When? And if she didn't, how could it not have been Livia's fault?

More days passed. And as terrible as it had been when the men had been taking Livia outside the box and making her do the disgusting thing, the way they had hurt Nason, and Nason's unresponsiveness, was so much worse.

Every night, Livia slept curled up behind Nason, whispering her name and stroking her hair until she herself was overcome by sleep.

During the days, she never left her side. And when the men came with food and water, Livia made sure to stay as far to the back of the box as possible. When she heard the bolts scraping open, she would stand Nason up and gently ease her against the wall, then position herself in front of her. That way, if the men tried to grab Nason, Livia could see it coming and fight them. She didn't have the can top anymore, and the men had been opening the cans themselves and keeping the tops since Livia had cut them. But she still had her teeth. She could leap at them, and bite their noses and ears and lips.

But the men must have known what she was thinking. One morning, they came in and began handing out food from the back of the box, rather than from the front where they usually positioned themselves. Dirty Beard stood to Livia's left and Square Head to her right while Skull Face stayed in front of the door. She felt something was wrong, that they were trying to trick her, and as she swept her head from one side to the other, trying to watch both men at once, Dirty Beard stepped in and grabbed her hair. She screamed and twisted toward him, terrified they were going to take Nason again. Square Head gripped her shoulders from behind and pulled her to the floor. Panic surged through her and she squirmed to her stomach and tried to bring her knees forward. But one of the men knelt on her back, pinning her to the ground. She grabbed for Nason's ankle, as though she could fuse them together and stop the men from pulling them apart. There was a sting in her neck, and all at once her limbs felt heavy, too heavy to move. The weight on her back seemed to spread all over her body, as though she was under the box instead of inside it.

"Little bird," she whispered, and then she was gone.

13—NOW

Barnett's funeral was everything Livia had hoped for.

It was a perfect spring morning in Crown Hill Cemetery—cherry blossoms blooming, birds singing, a breeze stirring the tree branches. Over a hundred Hammerheads were there to pay their respects to poor Billy, some rolling in on Harleys from as far as Reno and Missoula. There were denim kuttes heavy with Confederate flags and Iron Crosses. Lots of tattooed arms, and a good number of faces and necks, too. Steroid-swollen bodies. Bourbon toasts and Sieg Heil salutes. Livia recognized most of the local leadership, having spent a year with the gang unit before making detective. The G-unit's mandate was to know everything about Seattle-area gangs, and to make sure the gangs knew they knew, as a means of deterring violence. Livia had wanted access to that intel, so that when she was finally able to get to Weed Tyler, she would be ready.

A hundred mourners logically meant an equivalent number of cell phones, but the Gossamer picked up half again as many. Burners. The gangbangers knew better than to carry their personal units alongside the disposables they used for business, but it was a pain to switch off one phone every time you were going to use the other, or to leave one at home when you were out on your hog and didn't know who might be trying to reach you on which. And switching burners frequently was a hassle, as well—so many people to apprise of your new contact information. So in the battle between security and convenience, sooner or later convenience almost always emerged victorious. And it only had to win once for the cops to own you.

Livia kept a discreet distance from the funeral, dressed in a conservative skirt and blouse and wearing dark glasses against the late-morning sun. She even laid flowers in front of a marker, standing with head bowed for a few minutes as though in silent contemplation. Which was more than enough time for the Gossamer nestled in her purse to identify every cell phone in the cemetery. She confirmed the data had been stored in the unit, then headed out, face downcast, just another bereft visitor weighed down by the cemetery's solemnity.

She didn't go straight back to headquarters. Instead, she drove to the loft, the top of the Jeep off to take advantage of the weather. Ordinarily on so fine a day, she would have used the Ducati, but changing in and out of leathers wasn't always feasible, and she'd seen enough horrific motorcycle injuries to refuse to ride without the proper equipment.

A couple of the guys on a smoking break outside waved as she headed in the first-floor entrance. Everyone knew she lived on the third floor. She imagined they must have speculated about her solitary existence, but it didn't matter. They were friendly enough. She waved back and took the stairs three at a time, unlocking and then double-bolting the door behind her.

She laid the Gossamer on her desk, brought over a set of watch-repair tools, and removed the back of the unit. From her gun safe, she retrieved a circuit board she had created from parts purchased from Radio Shack—battery, transistors, memory card, antenna. Visually, her homemade board was a clone of what she had observed on a previous experiment opening up a Gossamer. Of course, hers was nothing but a simulacrum, but it didn't need to function. It just needed to look right.

She brought the homemade board over to the desk and set it down alongside the Gossamer, from which she carefully removed the circuit board. She spent an hour soldering the Gossamer's innards into a shell she had designed to house them. When she was done, she closed up the shell and tested the unit. It worked perfectly. She smiled in satisfaction. She'd always been good with tools.

Next, she placed her homemade board inside the original Gossamer casing, screwed the unit closed, and placed it on the base of a hydraulic press. She turned the press on and waited for a moment, listening to the mechanical whine growing louder and smoother as the machine warmed up. Then she pulled the lever and watched as the steel cylinder descended and crushed the unit flat. The results were extremely satisfactory, but she repeated the process twice more to ensure the absolute maximum devastation, then used a tweezers to pick out and pocket the few pieces with markings that might have identified them as not native to a Gossamer. When she was done, she poured the pulverized remains into a bag and headed back to headquarters, tossing the marked pieces along the way.

Back at the Bat Cave, she made sure to look worried and chagrined. "Alvin," she said. "You're going to kill me."

He raised his eyebrows. "What is it?"

She placed the bag on the counter. "I was cutting across the pedestrian overpass at the Light Link University Street Station. And I dropped the Gossamer."

He blanched. "Oh, no."

"Oh, yes. I ran down as fast as I could. But a train had already come. And . . ."

She lifted the end of the bag, and what looked like nothing other than the crushed remains of a genuine Gossamer came sliding out onto the counter.

For a moment, they were both silent. Alvin put a hand over his mouth and just stared at the mess, his expression crestfallen. Then he sighed. And then he moved his hand—and Livia saw he was smiling.

"I have to tell you," he said. "I've had equipment misplaced before. Lost. But this . . ." He shook his head and started laughing.

Livia maintained her worried expression. Of course, claiming she'd lost the unit would have been easier. But more suspicious, too. A cop who claimed something had been lost might have stolen it. A cop who brought back something flattened to a pancake was at worst guilty of carelessness.

"It's not funny," she said. "What's going to happen?"

He waved a hand. "Don't worry. I'll take a picture and email it to the company. They'll send a replacement. I've got the budget to cover it. No one has to know exactly what happened. Someone dropped a unit and a train ran over it, simple as that. I won't even tell the lieutenant, okay?"

She offered him a small, worried smile. "Really?"

"Really. It's not a big deal. I mean, it's not like you threw it under a train on purpose, right?"

She laughed. "Now, why would anyone ever want to do that?"

14—THEN

Livia was riding an elephant through the jungle. Which was strange, because she had never ridden an elephant before. The sensation was pleasant—a rhythmic swaying as the beast lumbered forward, causing tree branches to brush past her cheeks. But the forest had such a strange smell to it—not the smell of trees and wet and earth she loved. Instead, something sharp and unnatural.

And then she realized with a weary sadness that there was no elephant, and there was no forest—it was another dream, like the last time. But she kept her eyes closed anyway, not wanting to be awake, wanting so badly to stay in the forest, even if it was only a dream.

But she couldn't hold on to it. The sensation of riding an elephant faded, and she could feel that she was lying on her back. The ground under her was hard, and that swaying feeling and the smell she had thought were part of her dream, were something else. There was a vibration beneath her, and a distant, mechanical hum, the kind she'd first heard when the machine had moved the box onto the boat. But this vibration was stronger; the humming, louder. She heard hushed, unfamiliar voices speaking words she couldn't understand. The dream broke into fragments, and everything came rushing back. She sat up and cried out in panic, "Nason?"

A woman was kneeling next to her and jerked back as Livia sat up. She was holding a cloth—had she been using it to stroke Livia's cheek? Was that what had felt like branches in the dream? The woman's skin was tea colored, and black hair flowed from beneath a colorful scarf, but her eyes were different. They weren't round like those of the pasty white people—"trekkers"—who sometimes visited the village, but they weren't long and narrow like those of the hill tribes or Thais, either. Livia had never seen a face quite like it—the cheeks broad, the forehead high, the nose long and narrow. The woman's expression was concerned, even kind.

The woman said something in a soothing tone, but Livia couldn't understand her. Everything here was different. The light was brighter, the air smelled cleaner, the tangy salt smell of the ocean was gone. She saw there were other people around, nine of them including Livia. But none she recognized. Who were these people? Where had the children gone? Where was Nason?

"Nason?" she said to the woman. "Nason!"

The woman shook her head, clearly not understanding. She said more words in her incomprehensible tongue. Livia shook her head in frustration and looked all around. She could see she was in a metal box again, but a different one. They'd moved her while she'd been sleeping. And all the children—Kai, the Yao boy, everyone . . . they were gone.

"Nason!" she shouted. "Nason!"

Most of the people were adults. About half looked Asian—Chinese, maybe. The other half looked like they came from the same strange tribe as the scarf woman. There were two children, both about Livia's age. She thought they might be Indian, but wasn't sure. She had only ever seen pictures in the textbooks at the village school.

Livia got to her feet. She swayed for a moment, feeling weak and thirsty. "Thai?" she said in Thai, looking from one face to another. "You speak Thai?"

They all stared at her, their expressions blank. No one responded.

Livia switched to Lahu, already knowing it would be useless. "Lahu?" she said. "Can any of you speak Lahu?"

The expressions didn't change.

Livia jammed her fists against the sides of her head. What could she do? What could she do?

She noticed everyone was sitting in clusters, talking to the people nearest. So some of them spoke each other's languages. But none spoke Livia's. She had never so badly needed to talk to someone, just to be understood, even if they couldn't answer her questions. But she was completely cut off.

She sank to her knees and covered her face in her hands, sobbing. The scarf woman stroked her hair and spoke more alien words. Her tone was soothing and she was obviously trying to help. But she wasn't helping. No one could help. Nason was gone and Livia had no idea where she was, or how she was, or what had happened. She didn't know where she herself was, or where she was going, or what would happen when she got there.

When she was too exhausted to cry anymore, she slumped against the wall. Maybe she could do what Nason had done—just go away. Just go away until things got better. Or maybe she could die. She knew she would die if she stopped eating. The thought was immediately appealing. Something she could do to make things better, something she could control. She would stop eating and drinking. If this was all a nightmare, eventually she would wake up. If it wasn't, she would die. Either alternative was better than this.

But what if Nason needed her?

She squeezed her eyes shut and groaned through gritted teeth. She had to stay alive. No matter what, she had to do that. Until she found Nason, until she found out what had happened to her.

Yes. She could die after that. She could die whenever she wanted to. They had taken so much from her, but no one could take that.

Several days and nights passed like this. Men came with food and water and buckets like before, but different men—white men, their skin the color of cassava paste. Two of them were bigger than the Thai men, their bodies thicker with muscle. The third was stringier. All of them had shaved heads and tattoos up and down their arms. She didn't like the way they looked at the people in the box. Skull Face and his men had felt like cats who would enjoy hurting the children, tormenting them—as eventually they had. But these men felt worse. When they looked at Livia, she felt they saw nothing but an animal, or not even an animal, just a thing. They could feed her, or clean her, or beat her, or kill her, and none of it would make them feel anything at all, neither enjoyment nor regret.

Whenever the men came, she tried to ask them about Nason. Of course they didn't answer. Probably they didn't even understand. She thought about banging on the side of the box, the way she had before. But Skull Face and his men had been prepared for that, and probably the pasty white men would be, too. Probably trying it again would only get her whipped.

She thought constantly about running. But there was always at least one man guarding the door. She did manage to look outside whenever they were in the box. She was amazed by what she saw—hills to one side; broad, grassy fields to the other. This was a river, wider than any she'd ever seen in the forest. They weren't on the ocean anymore. And this was a different boat—much smaller than the first one.

At least the new men didn't try to take her outside the box. At least there was that.

The box got stiflingly hot during the day, much hotter than the previous one. And it got colder at night. The men had given them each a blanket, but by the time the sun came up and gray light began to creep into the box, Livia was always shivering.

One evening, a little while after they'd been fed, about half the people began to groan and clutch their stomachs. Soon they were vomiting into the buckets. Something must have been wrong with the food. Livia knew herbs that might have helped—but that was the forest, and the forest had never been farther away.

The next morning, three of the sick people were dead—the scarf woman and the two children. Livia had seen dead bodies before—mostly old people from her village. She wasn't afraid. She was disappointed. If she had eaten the bad food, maybe she would be dead now. The thought produced a pang of guilt—what if Nason needed her?—but she couldn't help looking enviously at the three bodies. Their faces seemed so peaceful.

The other ones who had been sick were weak, but otherwise seemed okay. The rest of the people moved the bodies next to a wall and covered them with a blanket.

When the men came with food, they checked under the blankets. They saw the people were dead, but left them there. They fed everyone and changed the buckets as always and then left, ignoring anyone who tried to talk to them. Livia didn't understand. She knew the bodies would start to smell soon. They had to be burnt or buried.

Another day passed. Livia's anxiety about Nason gnawed at her constantly. It was as though someone had cut something away from her—an arm, a leg, a part of her heart—and now whatever was gone had been replaced by a raw, throbbing ache. She tried to make herself go away the way Nason had done, but it didn't work. The most she could manage was a kind of half-awake, half-asleep state. She would curl up on the floor, facing one of the walls, not thinking, not feeling, not connected to anything, just an object passing through time.

That's what she was doing when the shooting began.

15—NOW

The cell phone metadata Livia had harvested at Billy Barnett's funeral was an absolute who's who of Hammerhead—not just the numbers of the phones themselves, but also the numbers the phones were used to call, as well as when and where the calls were placed. She knew it would be a boon to the G-unit, though probably they had come up with reasons to collect their own. But while she was always happy to help the G guys, she was looking for something special—a lever long enough to dislodge Weed Tyler. And after a frustrating few days of analyzing the data, she was pretty sure she had found it.

She hadn't managed to turn up anything interesting about any of the regular cell phones, the ones gangbangers used for their personal lives. So she turned her attention to the burners that were relatively easy to associate with the regular cell phones because their owners were too lazy not to carry around both at the same time. But even that offered nothing she could use.

The final step was the ghost numbers—the ones she couldn't immediately place alongside those of specific personal phones. She knew the ghost phones belonged to Hammerheads because the units had been at the cemetery when Barnett was buried. But figuring out which ghost phone went with which gang member was laborious.

One burner, though, stood out. It had been purchased five years earlier. That in itself was interesting—five years was far longer than even the most operationally lazy gangbanger would hold on to a phone he'd purchased for purposes of anonymity. But the phone was interesting, too, because it was used only in connection with one other number— another burner, naturally. Livia focused on the movements of the two numbers. One of them changed position only late at night, typically between the hours of one and five o'clock. The other rarely budged. A classic booty call pattern, except these booty calls were happening regularly, and went back a long time. Whatever was going on, it was a safe bet the participants were trying to keep it quiet. Which would explain why they each had a burner they used for nothing but each other.

The first phone spent most of its time in a Shoreline apartment rented by Michael "Mech" Masnick. She knew Masnick from her days with the G-unit. He was one of the up-and-comers, a popular guy with a lumberjack's beard and the stature of an NBA forward. Despite his size, he was considered to be one of the saner Hammerheads, though not someone to be fucked with, either. The "Mech" was short for "Mechanic," a nickname Masnick had earned for his facility with motorcycle repairs.

The second phone, the one that rarely moved, was associated with a house in nearby Bothell, owned by a woman named Jenny Jardin.

Who just happened to be Weed Tyler's wife.

16—THEN

Livia scrambled to her feet, confused and frightened. Outside the box she heard shouting, explosions like the fireworks they used in village celebrations. Her first thought was, *Nason?*

But Nason wasn't there. For a moment, without Nason to protect, Livia was paralyzed. There was another series of loud bangs. Something—a rock? A metal stick?—hit the outside of the box and made it ring like a huge bell. Livia backed up against the far wall. If something came through the door, she wanted to be as far from it as possible.

There was more shouting, more loud fireworks. Several moments of ominous silence. And then there was a huge bang just outside the door, and the door was yanked back and the box filled with brilliant sunlight, and then the sunlight was gone, replaced by fog, but the fog stung Livia's eyes and her throat and made her cough and drool and gag. She stumbled for the door, choking and blinded. People smacked into her from both sides, but she kept moving, desperate to get away from the choking, stinging fog.

She tripped on something and fell to her hands and knees, retching. She scrubbed her eyes with the back of a hand, and for a moment her vision cleared. She was amazed to see that she'd made it out of the box. It was sunny, the fog was gone, and the boat wasn't moving—it was stopped, on the side of the river, next to a platform with machines and buildings on it. There were men swarming everywhere, wearing plastic masks and black uniforms. They all had guns—long guns, machine guns or rifles like the ones she had seen on the fuzzy village television. Were they trying to take her?

Even choking and half-blinded, she realized she would never have a better chance to escape. She started crawling in the direction of the platform. Maybe if she stayed low, no one would see her.

But something slammed into her back and drove her to the ground, knocking the breath out of her. She craned her neck and saw one of the men in black clothes, a big man, standing over her with his foot on her back. She struggled and squirmed, but she couldn't move. The man turned his masked face this way and that, occasionally glancing at her as his head swept left and right, the long gun he was carrying pointing wherever he looked.

There was noise everywhere—shooting and shouting and a weird, rippling wailing sound, like an animal shrieking but louder and unnatural.

Finally, the noise stopped. The big man removed his mask, then knelt behind her and pulled her wrists behind her back. She struggled, terrified, but couldn't stop him. Something encircled her wrists—something flexible but also strong—and then tightened.

She tried to squirm free, but it was useless. All of it was useless. Why couldn't she have eaten the bad food? Or just stopped eating, and drinking, too? She would never be able to help Nason, she would never even know what had happened to her. And now these men were going to hurt her, make her do more disgusting things, and how could she stop them? Her parents had sold her, and Nason was gone, and she had no one in the world. Her face twisted in torment and she sucked in a long, sobbing breath, and then another, and then the helplessness and emptiness and despair consumed her and she tilted back her head and wailed.

The man reached down and pulled her up by the shoulders. She didn't even think about running. How could she run, with her wrists tied behind her? Where would she go?

The big man said something to her, but she just kept crying. She was so tired of gibberish, of people talking to her with words she couldn't understand. All she wanted was to know where Nason was. And if Nason was dead, then she wanted to die, too. She didn't care about anything else.

The big man gripped the underside of one of her arms and pulled her along to the dock. Through a blur of tears, she saw more people, and realized from their blue uniforms, like the ones on the Thai officers who had sometimes come to the village because of some problem, that they were police. The realization wasn't heartening. She didn't know these people and didn't trust them. That they wore uniforms could be good or it could be bad. And what difference did it make, anyway?

Some other people from the box were already on the dock. They were sitting cross-legged, and, like her, their wrists were tied behind their backs. Other police were leading more of them to the dock, all with their wrists tied. Livia turned and saw two of the men who had been feeding them on the boat facedown on the ground, not moving, blood pooling around them. The police must have shot them. It didn't make her happy, or sad, or anything at all. When they were alive, she'd needed them for food and water. Now she didn't. So it didn't matter whether they were alive or dead.

The big policeman said something to her again, but the gibberish only made her cry harder. He put a hand on her shoulder and pushed down, and she realized he wanted her to sit. But she didn't want to sit. And she didn't want to listen. So she resisted his pushing, crying uncontrollably. The man pushed more. Livia's legs wobbled, but she wouldn't let him push her down.

And then a blue-uniformed woman with deep brown skin came and shoved the big man back. Livia couldn't understand the woman's words, but she was clearly angry and admonishing the big man. They argued for a moment, and then the woman pointed off to the side. The man glared for a moment, then stalked off in the direction the woman had indicated.

The woman leaned forward so her head was on the same level as Livia's, and looked in Livia's eyes. She said something. Livia had no idea what, but her tone was soft and her eyes were filled with kindness. Livia looked at her skin, fascinated. She was the color of chocolate, darker even than the darkest people among the hill tribes, but her eyes were lighter, her lips and cheeks fuller. Livia had seen such people on the village television, and she realized distantly that she had always assumed television was the only place they existed. She blinked her stinging eyes, trying to adjust. What was real? What was television? Was the village a dream? Where was Nason?

The chocolate woman kept talking—softly, gently, reassuringly. Livia recognized the tone as the way she herself would talk to a sow feeding a litter and nervous about Livia's approach. It made Livia feel better. And then, still talking in her soothing tone, the woman stepped behind Livia, and all at once Livia's hands were free. She pulled her arms around and massaged her wrists. The woman tossed something onto the ground, and Livia saw it was some kind of plastic, and that the woman had cut it with a knife she was holding. The woman folded the knife closed and returned it to a belt filled with tools, including a gun in a special holder.

Another big uniformed man rushed over and started arguing with the chocolate woman, gesturing to Livia and then to the cut plastic binding on the ground. He was obviously unhappy that Livia was untied. But the chocolate woman wouldn't back down. She raised her voice and stood close to the man's face until finally, like the first man, he walked off, snarling some words as he did so like a dog slinking away from a fight.

Livia sat in the hot sun for hours and watched, trying to understand. Dozens of people in different uniforms rushed back and forth, taking notes and photographs; picking up things too small for Livia to see and putting them in plastic bags; talking to each other and into little boxes Livia thought were radios. The chocolate woman stayed close the whole time. She gave Livia a bag of something salty and crunchy to eat and a can with a sweet drink inside it, and she wouldn't let anyone bind Livia's wrists the way they had done to all the other people. Livia wondered whether it was because she was a child. She didn't know, but at least she wasn't tied. Being tied was horrible.

A car pulled up and more people got out—people with Asian faces, not chocolate or pasty white. They squatted and talked to the people from the box, and after a while the police began to remove the wrist bindings. The Asian people tried to talk to Livia, but she couldn't understand any of them. In Thai and Lahu, she said, "Nason, my sister, do you know what happened to my sister?" over and over, but none of them understood her any better than she understood them.

The police took them all to a big, modern building—a hospital, Livia realized from the people in white coats, although she had never been to anything more than the hill tribe clinic near her village. Livia sat in a small room on a table covered in soft white paper, the chocolate woman leaning against the wall opposite. A pasty man in a white coat came in. Livia knew he was a doctor—he had an air of authority about him, and the instrument for listening to hearts was hanging around his neck. He said some words, then tried to touch Livia with the instrument. But the thought of this strange man—any man—touching her was horrifying. She jerked away and bared her teeth. He took a step back, then frowned and came forward again. Livia put her hands on the table, ready to spring past him and run. But the chocolate woman talked to him the way she'd talked to the other men, and after a moment, he walked out.

The chocolate woman gestured to herself and said, "Tanya." Then she gestured to Livia and raised her eyebrows.

Livia understood. The chocolate woman was saying she was called Tanya. And asking what Livia was called.

"Labee," Livia said.

Smiling, Tanya held out her hand and said, "Hi, Labee."

Livia looked at Tanya's hand. Was she supposed to hold out her hand, too? She did, the same way Tanya had.

Tanya laughed. She took Livia's hand in her own and gently moved it up and down. Livia understood—they didn't use the *wai* in the West, the slight bow with the palms pressed together and the fingers up. They shook hands. Tanya was introducing herself. She was being nice. She'd been nice since the moment she had chased away the big policeman and cut the ties off Livia's wrists.

It was good that someone was being nice to her. But while Livia was grateful, she didn't trust it, either. Niceness could disappear at any moment. Maybe Tanya would get bored. Maybe something would make her angry. Or maybe she would sell Livia, the way Livia's parents had.

So no. Livia wouldn't trust Tanya, even though the woman was being nice. She wouldn't trust anyone.

They waited. A woman in a white uniform brought food on a tray. Though Livia was painfully hungry, she wasn't sure she should eat, because eating would keep her alive. But then she thought of Nason. So she devoured everything on the tray—chicken and rice, a sweet drink, and a weird, jiggly, translucent red cube that tasted like berries. Tanya stepped out when Livia was done, and came back a moment later with another tray just like it. Livia finished everything on that one, too.

They waited more. There was a telephone in the room. Like so many other things she was seeing here, Livia knew what a telephone was, but had never used one. From time to time, the phone would ring, and Tanya would pick it up and talk into it, then put it back the way it was. On one of these calls, though, she didn't put it back—she nodded vigorously, and spoke excitedly, then handed the phone to Livia. Livia stared at the phone, uncertain, and Tanya gestured to it, as though expecting Livia to do something. Livia raised the phone to her face and looked at it. She could hear a tiny, tinny voice coming out. A woman's voice, and she was speaking in Thai: "Hello? Hello, are you there?"

The feeling of someone she could understand, who would be able to understand her, was so overwhelming that Livia's throat closed up and tears spilled from her eyes. Tanya stroked her arm, and strangely it looked as though she might cry, too.

Livia raised the phone to her ear the way Tanya had. "Yes," she managed to croak in Thai. "Yes, I here. Please, please, do you know Nason? My sister. Where she is?"

"Hello? Your sister?"

"Yes, yes, my sister, Nason. Where she is? Please."

"I . . . I don't know that, but we're going to try to help you. Are you Thai? The translators thought you might be."

"Yes, I am Lahu."

"You came from Thailand?"

"Yes, yes."

The woman said words Livia couldn't follow.

"Please, please, slower," Livia said. "My Thai no good."

"I'm sorry," the woman said. "I work for the Thai government. In America. In Washington. The capital of America."

Livia was confused. "America . . . what? Why?"

"You're in America. In Llewellyn, Idaho."

America? No. That couldn't be right. But they'd been on the boat for a long time . . . had they crossed the ocean? Livia had never felt so disoriented, so cut off from everything she knew. She might as well have been told she was on the moon.

She desperately wanted to understand the woman's other words. "Lew-el-in?" she said carefully. "I-da-ho?"

"A town in America. And I am with the Thai Embassy in Washington."

It was so frustrating not to know the words. "Em-ba-see?"

There was a pause. "Okay, the first thing is to find a Lahu speaker to talk to you."

"Yes, please that! Please Lahu."

"All right. The police will take care of you there. Until we find a Lahu speaker."

"Wait, wait, my sister, Nason. Where she is?"

"The police can help with that."

"But—"

"The police will help. We'll find you a Lahu speaker. You're going to be okay."

"But—"

Livia heard a click. After a moment, there was a buzzing in the phone. She looked at it, not understanding, put it to her ear once more, then realized the Thai woman was gone. She handed the phone back to Tanya and started to cry again.

Tanya stroked Livia's shoulder and spoke in her soothing voice. She handed Livia a square of delicate white paper, like paper for the toilet. Livia looked at the paper, not understanding. Tanya smiled, took the paper back, then gently touched it to Livia's cheeks. Livia was confused—they used this kind of paper for drying tears, not just for the toilet? It was a small thing, but everything was so overwhelmingly alien here that this drying paper upset her and made her cry harder. But she raised the paper to her cheeks and dabbed at them, because it seemed to be what Tanya wanted.

After that, they just waited. More doctors came and went. Tanya spoke to them. They didn't bother Livia.

Periodically, voices came out of Tanya's radio. The radio was attached by a spiral cord to a little black box clipped to the shoulder of Tanya's uniform. A microphone, Livia understood, like the one on the karaoke box in the village. Tanya would pick up the microphone when the voices came out of the radio and talk into it. One of these conversations lasted longer than the others. Tanya glanced at Livia while she spoke, and it sounded like she was arguing. When the conversation was over, she squatted so she was looking up at Livia, who was still sitting on the table. She spoke some words—a question, from the tone—and Livia could tell she was sad, or uneasy, which made Livia uneasy, too. A moment later, another blue-uniformed woman came in, this one pasty white. Tanya gestured to the pasty woman and said to Livia, "Camille."

Tanya was introducing this new police person. Which meant she was leaving. Livia had been right. She knew not to trust Tanya. Not to trust anyone.

Livia turned her face away and said nothing. She heard the women talking, and then the sound of the door as it opened and closed. When she looked again, Tanya was gone, replaced by Camille.

Someone brought more hot food on a tray—some kind of meat, and vegetables Livia didn't recognize. She devoured it all anyway. Then they brought her a blanket and a pillow. She slept curled up on the table, waking up frightened and disoriented several times during the night, and dreaming she was back in the forest with Nason.

In the morning, Tanya returned with several new people: three pasty men in suits and neckties, and a woman in western clothes but with a Lahu face. The woman looked at Livia and said in Lahu, "Hello, I'm Nanu, though here I'm called Nancy. Are you the one called Labee?"

Even more than when she had spoken on the phone the day before to the Thai woman, Livia was overwhelmed at being able to understand someone, and this time someone who spoke her own language. "Yes!"

she said, nodding vigorously and wiping the tears that had sprung to her eyes. "Yes, I'm Labee. Please, do you know where my sister Nason is?"

"We don't know, Labee, but I want you to tell me everything you can so we can help. Was your sister with you on the boat?"

"Not on this boat. On a different boat. A bigger one. The one that took us from Thailand."

"All right, wait just a moment, I'm going to translate what you said for these people. They're going to try to help. All right?"

Livia nodded vigorously, her jaw clenched shut. Now that she could be understood, it was almost impossible not to talk.

Nanu translated, talking more to the men in suits than to Tanya or the other policewoman. Then she turned back to Livia. "Labee, the small boat you were on, the one that brought you here, came from Portland."

"Portland?"

"Yes, a city on the West Coast of America. Was Nason with you when you were put on the small boat from Portland?"

An image of Nason, mute and vacant and bleeding, flashed across Livia's mind, and she pushed it away. These people were trying to help. To help, they needed information. And the more they learned from Livia, the more she might learn from them.

"I . . . I think so. The men who took us made me go to sleep. When I woke up, I was on the small boat. And"—her voice caught for a moment, and she forced herself to continue—"Nason was gone."

"Do you know how long you were on the big boat?"

"I'm not sure. We were in a box. But I think . . . maybe a week. Is this really America?"

"Yes, it is. A week would have been long enough to reach Portland. Were there other people with you on the big boat?"

America. Livia still couldn't believe it. It was so dizzying, disorienting. She pushed the feeling away and forced herself to focus. "Yes, eleven other children, plus Nason and me. Hmong, Yao . . . all from the hill tribes."

Nanu translated for the men in suits and talked back and forth with them. Then she said to Livia, "Some of these men are with the Immigration and Naturalization Service. That means they're experts on human smuggling."

"Human smuggling?"

"What happened to you and your sister. And the other children. Smugglers take people from poorer countries to richer ones."

"You mean, they steal people?"

"Yes, that's exactly what it means. And sometimes they even steal children."

One of the men said something to Nanu. Nanu nodded and said to Livia, "There's a lot of human smuggling from and through Thailand, and these men are trying to stop it. They want you to tell us about the men who took you so they can find and arrest them."

Livia told them everything she could about Skull Face and Dirty Beard and Square Head. The men asked lots of questions, and Nanu translated back and forth.

At one point, Nanu asked, "Did the men . . . hurt you or your sister, Labee?"

The way she said it, Livia understood how she meant *hurt*. Without thinking, she said, "No. They just kept us in a box, like the one on the small boat. And they whipped a Hmong boy named Kai, when he tried to escape."

Nanu looked at her, and Livia sensed she understood Livia was lying about the men not hurting her and Nason. But Nanu didn't press. Not that it would have mattered. Livia was too ashamed of what the men had done to her, and too guilty about what they had done to Nason. She would never speak of it to anyone. Never.

Tanya said something to Nanu, who translated, "Where can we find your parents, Labee?"

Livia was immediately suspicious. "Why?"

Nanu nodded as though she already understood. "Labee, did your parents, did they . . ."

"My parents are dead."

Nanu translated, and several minutes of animated talking followed. One of the pasty men in particular seemed to dominate the conversation. He was taller and more heavyset than the others, with a stripe of charcoal-colored stubble around his head but otherwise completely bald. His eyes were widely spaced behind wire glasses, and his ears were soft and meaty, the lobes as thick as little thumbs. As Livia looked from him to the other two men and back again, she realized his clothes seemed finer—blue with vertical white stripes, while the other men's suits were solid gray. If the other two were from this Immigration and Naturalization Service, this man was from something different. Did America have a royal family, like Thailand? But no, though the other two seemed to defer to the man, they weren't deferring the way Thais deferred to the king. What, then? Was he just rich?

Gesturing to the bald man, Nanu said, "Labee, this gentleman is Mr. Frederick Lone. He's very concerned about your welfare."

Livia narrowed her eyes, suspicious. "Why?"

"The men from Immigration and Naturalization . . . they think they should send you back to Thailand."

Livia felt a bolt of fear and nausea. "What about Nason?"

"I understand. But these men don't know what else to do with you."

"I won't go back. Not without Nason."

"What I'm trying to tell you is, Mr. Lone shares your concerns. You were the only child on the boat. There were two others, but they died en route, apparently from food poisoning. Mr. Lone understands your predicament and wants to help."

"Help how?"

"Mr. Lone is an important man in this town. He owns several businesses—an ammunition factory, a pulp mill—that employ a lot of people. His brother is a US senator—a powerful man in the American government. Mr. Lone's children are grown, but he and his wife will take you into their home until something more permanent and satisfactory can be arranged."

Livia looked at Mr. Lone, not trusting him, not liking him. But she felt the same way about all these people. Even Tanya.

"Can Mr. Lone find Nason?"

Nanu spoke with Mr. Lone, then said to Livia, "Mr. Lone is very well connected, through his business interests and through his brother. And he promises to try."

If America was like what the hill tribe people said about Thailand, Livia knew a rich man could be more useful than the police. Not that she could trust his words. But what choice did she have? She couldn't go back to her parents. She wouldn't. And if Nason was in America, Livia needed to be in America, too. She would find Nason somehow, help her somehow.

"All right," Livia said. "If he can find Nason."

Nanu spoke again with Mr. Lone, who looked at Livia and nodded as though eager for her to understand.

"Yes," Nanu said. "He says he knows how important Nason is to you."

It was only much later that Livia realized how ominous those words really were.

17—NOW

It was pretty obvious from the cell phone metadata what was going on between Masnick and Weed Tyler's wife, but metadata alone might not be enough to ensure Masnick's compliance. For that, Livia wanted something a little more . . . persuasive.

So late at night, she started riding up to Bothell, where Jardin lived with her teenage daughter in a two-bedroom ranch. She would park the Ninja in the shadows of a construction site near the house, set the Gossamer to spoof a cell phone tower for any calls coming to or from the two cell phones of interest, and then wait, sitting on a cinderblock, thinking of Nason, crickets chirping in the dark around her.

The first two nights, she got nothing. On the third, the Gossamer lit up with an incoming call. Livia listened in with an earpiece, her heart pounding with hope.

"Hey, you can't come tonight." A woman's voice. Presumably Jardin.

"Damn, are you sure? I was just about to head over." This time a man. She had never spoken to Masnick in person and so couldn't be certain, but it had to be him.

"I'm sorry. It's Vela. Her light's still on. She hasn't been sleeping well."

Vela was Jardin's daughter—the one she'd been pregnant with when Tyler had been sent to Victorville. The girl was a high school sophomore now. Livia had been right. The woman on the phone was Jardin.

"It's okay," the man said. "Nobody's fault. I was just . . . I wanted to see you."

"I know. I wanted to see you, too." There was a pause, and she added, "Mike, what are we going to do?"

Bingo. And not Mech. That was a gang moniker. She called him Mike, a more intimate form of address.

There was another pause. Masnick said, "I don't know."

"He gets out in a week. Why do you think Vela's not sleeping?"

"I know."

"I want to tell him."

"Jesus, Jen, we've been over this. That's just not an option."

"Then what is?"

"I'll think of something."

"In a week? We've known this was coming for years."

"I'll think of something. I'm not going to lose you. I love you, Jen."

"I love you, too."

"Listen, I'm going to leave the phone on. If she falls asleep, call me, okay? I just miss you."

"Okay. I should go."

"I'll think of something. I promise."

They clicked off. Livia confirmed the unit had recorded the conversation, then removed the earpiece and sat for a moment, stunned despite what she had already suspected.

I'll think of something, he had said.

Well, maybe he wouldn't have to. In fact, she might just think of something for him.

18—THEN

Livia moved in with the Lones. She disliked them intensely—Mrs. Lone especially. She sensed Mrs. Lone, with her pinched face and expensive-looking necklaces, resented Livia's presence in her house. Or that she just resented Livia.

Livia had never seen such grandeur, except on the village television. The house had two floors—four, if you included the basement and the attic—with common areas downstairs and bedrooms above. The property was enormous, surrounded by sloping grounds and perfectly manicured green grass. It had columns, with the flag for America waving from one of them alongside a massive front porch. Inside was really *inside*—no breeze from without, no humidity, no sounds. Livia couldn't even tell if it was raining except by looking through the windows. Some of the floors were made of smooth stone; others were wood, covered with soft rugs. There were paintings on the walls. There were machines to make the air inside dry and cool—too cool for Livia, who needed extra blankets to be comfortable at night. There was no shared village spigot or privy; instead, the house had five separate rooms for toilet and cleaning. No one took dirty clothes to the river here, or hung them on a rope in the sun—instead, they used cleaning and drying machines. There was a giant refrigerator for keeping food cold, and even for making ice. The ice was the one thing about the house Livia liked. She was fascinated by how cold it was, and hard, and how she could make it melt by swirling it in her mouth. But she learned not to take it if Mrs. Lone was in the kitchen, because Mrs. Lone would watch her as though expecting her to steal something.

But despite the house's size and luxury, Livia didn't like it. It wasn't just that everything about it was so unfamiliar. There was something . . . not real about the place, something uncomfortable. Life in the village had been so communal, with all the people living and working and even sleeping side by side. But the Lones seemed not to spend much time together. Maybe it had been different when their children—four sons, Livia understood—had lived in the house. But the sons were grown now, and gone, and the Lones seemed to live separate lives. Mr. Lone left for work early in the morning, before Mrs. Lone rose. Mrs. Lone dressed in nice clothes and was out for much of the day—for what Livia didn't know, since the Lones had a maid and a gardener and even a cook, so it wasn't as though there were any chores to do. For the most part, Livia ate her dinners alone in the cavernous kitchen. Sometimes when Mr. Lone came home from work he and Mrs. Lone would eat together, but Livia rarely heard them talking. Other times, Mrs. Lone spent evenings at something she called her "bridge club."

On her very first morning in the strange house, Livia was greeted by Nanu, who explained that Mr. Lone had hired her to teach Livia English. Livia had to learn quickly, Nanu told her, because there were only two months left in the summer, and then Livia would have to go to the junior high school in Llewellyn, where as a thirteen-year-old she would be enrolled in eighth grade. Livia was terrified of going to school in this strange place, but recognized she had to do what Mr. Lone told her. If he decided he didn't want to keep her in his house, she didn't know where else she would go.

Besides, learning English wasn't a bad thing. Not being able to communicate, not being able to make anyone understand her, had been a horrible experience, and the feeling of it lingered. Livia didn't want to be dependent on translators, or anyone else. She wouldn't be helpless. She was in America now, and as daunting a prospect as that presented, it was also good. Because being in America, and speaking English, was how she would find Nason.

Mr. Lone had explained through Nanu that "Labee" was a strange name for Americans, and that he and Mrs. Lone wanted instead to call her Livia, an American name—the same way people called Nanu Nancy. Would that be all right?

Livia didn't think Mrs. Lone wanted to call her anything at all, as she never said Livia's name and in fact barely spoke to her, preferring a grudging nod or forced smile on those occasions when simply ignoring Livia wasn't feasible. But regardless, Livia welcomed the change. Labee was her name. But "Livia" felt like someone else, like a shield or disguise, something behind which she could conceal her real self.

So Labee became Livia, and sat with Nanu every day at the polished wooden table in the Lones' dining room, uneasy in the strange, cushioned chair, glancing suspiciously at the giant light hanging above them, a thing with arms like an octopus made of hundreds of little pieces of cut glass, what Nanu called a "chandelier," their voices echoing off the room's cream-colored walls. A maid would bring them lunch at noon. Nanu told Livia they should try to use only English even during their break, but Livia sensed the woman missed her other language, and sometimes she would relent while they ate. She told Livia her mother had been trafficked from Thailand to America, just as Livia had been, and that Nanu had been born here and was therefore automatically a citizen. Her mother was put to work cleaning big American houses like this one, and Nanu had helped, until she managed to get a better job, translating part time for the Thai Embassy in Washington. But Mr. Lone had paid her even more than what she made at the embassy to come to Llewellyn and tutor Livia, for which she was grateful. Mr. Lone was a powerful man, Nanu told her, and Livia was lucky he had taken an interest in her welfare.

After lunch, more women would come to the house, all pasty white Americans, each a teacher from a local school, whom Mr. Lone was paying to spend some of the summer tutoring Livia in math, science, and social studies. As the sun moved westward in the sky and the dining room gradually filled with its golden light, Livia learned about algebraic equations, and the characteristics of unicellular and multicellular life, and the origins of the American Revolution and Civil War. Math was her favorite because she needed so little English to understand it. For the other subjects, Nanu translated. There was a lot to learn and none of it was easy, but the feeling of being able to control something, the possibility of mastering it, was galvanizing for Livia, and she studied diligently even through dinner, even in bed. Eventually, she would become too tired to focus, and feel herself slipping in and out of wakefulness while she practiced her English drills with a tape recorder.

But no matter how tired she was, she never went to sleep without first kneeling in front of the window so she was facing the world outside, and whispering in Lahu as though Nason could actually hear her, "I love you, little bird. I will never forget. I will never stop looking. And one day I will find you."

Every evening, when he returned to the house, Mr. Lone would stop by the dining room, his tie loosened and a drink in hand, and ask about Livia's progress. Livia could tell from the smell that it was an alcohol drink, something she didn't like because Skull Face and the other men had liked alcohol drinks, too. Nanu issued glowing reports, and in a matter of weeks, Livia was able to answer Mr. Lone's questions directly. And every day, she asked him a question of her own: "Please, Mr. Lone, have you learned anything about my sister Nason?"

"I haven't, Livia, but I promise I'm trying. And please, feel free to call me Fred."

When he was gone, Livia asked Nanu to explain the phrase "feel free." It seemed that while on the one hand, Mr. Lone was giving Livia the choice of what to call him, on the other he was also letting her know his own preferences. It also seemed that in America, using the first name implied familiarity, while the last name was generally more respectful but also more distant. Livia decided that as long as she had a choice, she would use Mr. Lone's last name. She hadn't liked him from the beginning. And she sometimes didn't like the way she thought he was looking at her. It reminded her of Skull Face.

Livia welcomed the constant studying. The more she learned, the more in control she would be. And studying was the only thing that could put Nason out of her mind. Studying and sleeping—when she wasn't doing one or the other, anxiety plagued her like an illness.

The only break in the routine came on Sunday mornings, when the Lones took Livia to church. For these occasions, she had a closet full of dresses they had provided, dresses she found ugly and hard to move in. But she did her best not to reveal her discomfort—not just with the clothes, but with the whole experience. She knew about Christianity—half the rich Yao tribe were Christians, having been converted by missionaries—but Lahu beliefs were less distinct, and more flexible. Livia understood there were spirits inhabiting the trees and rocks and rivers, and this made sense because trees and rocks and rivers were real. But an invisible being that was at once everywhere and yet nowhere? That seemed silly to her, and she was amazed people could believe it. When Mr. Lone asked, as he invariably did, whether she had been moved by the service or the sermon, she would tell him, oh yes, it was so beautiful, so profound—a word Nanu had taught her—even though in fact she could only understand snatches. The truth was, she resented that these people seemed to want her to share in their silly beliefs. Why did they even care?

On weekends, the Lones had visitors, sometimes many of them. Everyone wore nice clothes, and an extra maid and cook would hand out drinks and bite-sized food on trays. Mr. Lone would call Livia in and introduce her to people, telling them how smart Livia was, how fast she was learning English and adapting to her new life. Livia could understand only part of these conversations, but she didn't need words to know these people were all afraid of Mr. Lone, or wanted something from him, or both, and that's why they came to his house, not because they liked him or wanted to be real friends.

One of the people Mr. Lone introduced her to was named Garry Emmanuel, the chief of Llewellyn's police department. "Chief Emmanuel knows about Nason," Mr. Lone said. "He's doing everything he can to find her."

Nanu had told Livia that in America it was considered impolite not to look in someone's eyes. For Lahu, it was different—looking in the eyes felt like staring, or aggression. So she looked at Chief Emmanuel. She didn't like what she saw. Hair cut close and the color of metal; jowly cheeks and a white mustache; cold blue eyes and a smile she knew he thought would fool a dumb little girl like the one looking up at him and having trouble meeting his eyes.

"That's right," Chief Emmanuel said. "I'm making sure Llewellyn PD is using all our contacts and resources. We'll find your sister, don't you worry."

Livia didn't like his promise. Because how could he really know? She would have been more reassured if he had just said he would try.

But maybe she was being too suspicious. This place . . . everything was so different from her people and the village. Maybe she just didn't understand. And what choice did she have but to try to be patient, and helpful, and to hope?

So she merely thanked Chief Emmanuel for his kindness and told him how important it was to her to find Nason.

The other visitors would make sorrowful faces and tell Livia she was so "brave" to have suffered her "ordeal," how "blessed" she was that Mr. Lone had decided to raise her in his own house. Livia wanted to take their pity and fling it back in their faces. But she knew the role Mr. Lone wanted her to play, and she needed to please him. So she smiled politely and thanked the visitors for their concern, and told them, oh yes, she certainly was lucky, and the Lones were so generous, and Llewellyn was the most beautiful place she had ever seen.

But Llewellyn wasn't beautiful. It was alien. And there was something . . . rotten about it, something she could sense in the way people watched Mr. Lone and interacted with him, something dark and somehow even shameful. It reminded her of a smell—the one that would come from under the hut when a small animal had tunneled into a hole there and died. Everything would look fine, but until the animal's carcass was found and removed, there would be that smell.

19—THEN

One evening, while Livia was drying off after a shower, the little lock on the bathroom door popped and the door swung open. She jumped back, startled and afraid, covering herself with the towel.

It was Mr. Lone, his tie loosened, his drink in hand. He must have come home while she had been in the shower. That's why she hadn't heard.

She watched him, confused and anxious. Had he learned something about Nason? Had he wanted her to know right away?

He looked her up and down, his breathing slightly elevated, his face red. The alcohol smell was strong.

"Why was the door locked, Livia?"

She didn't know how to respond. "I . . . I lock when I shower."

"You lock *it*. But you shouldn't. We're a family now. We don't keep secrets from each other."

She wanted to argue, to tell him she didn't have any family, except for Nason. And why was he accusing her of secrets? She only wanted privacy while she was in the bathroom. She was the one who should have been accusing him, because it wasn't right that he had unlocked the door like that.

But it was his house. And she didn't know how to express these thoughts. So she only said, "Is it about Nason?"

"Not as such," he said. "Not directly. It's actually about you."

He took a sip of his drink, then waited a moment as though expecting her to respond. When she didn't, he said, "I've had to pull some strings, call in some favors, but it's going to be formal. I meant it when I said we're a family now. Because Mrs. Lone and I are going to adopt you. You'll be Livia Lone, and an American citizen. How does that sound?"

It sounded terrible, actually, as though she was being thrown in some sort of cage she could sense but not clearly see. And why was he telling her this here, now?

"I . . . I don't know."

"Well, it's a lot to think about, certainly. But I feel . . . it's all going to work out. I'm glad you came into our lives, Livia. Four sons, but never a daughter. A family isn't the same without a daughter. It's what I've always wanted. And I think . . . I don't think it's an accident that you came to us. I believe God heard my prayers, and answered them. Do you believe that?"

"I . . . I think so." She didn't, though. She only wanted to say what he wanted to hear so he would go away and she could lock the door again. It wasn't right that she had to stand here talking to him, her hair dripping wet and with nothing but a towel in front of her.

"So I don't want locked doors between us. No secrets. Or . . . maybe there's a better way to put it. I want us to be able to trust each other with our secrets. Not hide them. Do you understand?"

His words, and the way he was looking at her, were making her increasingly anxious. "I think so."

He smiled. "What I'm saying is . . . I want you to trust me."

"All right."

"Do you, Livia? Do you trust me?"

She knew she should say yes, but she couldn't. She tried to think.

"You . . . you been very good to me."

"Have been. I *have* been very good to you."

"Yes. You have been. Nanu tries to teach me that grammar."

"*Is* trying. But do you trust me?"

Why was he asking her these things? While she was standing dripping wet in a towel?

"I . . . I only a little know you. Only know you a little, I mean."

He nodded gravely. "Yes. And I want you to get to know me better. Really know me. And I want to really know you. All right?"

Just go, she thought. *Just go*.

"All right."

He stepped closer and she shrank back. But the wall was behind her, and all she could do was press up against the cold tiles. He put his hand on her shoulder. She wanted to push it away, but she was afraid of what that would mean, what he would do. And she was angry, angry that he had unlocked the door and come in without asking, that he was asking her these questions, that he was looking at her in a bad way. She knew she should look in his eyes, but she was afraid he would see her anger and it would upset him. So she looked down—the Lahu way, not what Nanu had told her was the American.

He caressed her shoulder for a moment, then leaned closer.

"Good," he said. "Very good. We'll come to trust each other. I'm sure of it. And we'll keep each other's secrets. That's so important, Livia."

Livia nodded and tried not to grimace.

"And no more locking the door, all right? That's not what people do when they trust each other."

He squeezed her shoulder and walked out.

She didn't bother with the lock again after he had left—she thought it could only make problems if he caught her, and besides, the lock had proven useless.

She didn't like that he had come into the bathroom like that. But what could she do? It was his house, he had the right to go where he liked.

But. But. But.

The way he had been looking at her. The way he had stepped too close and touched her.

Her mind flashed to the deck of the boat, and Skull Face and the other men, and what they had made her do. She shook her head, trying to make the image go away. Were all men like that? They hadn't been in the village, but . . . maybe that's because in the village, Livia and Nason were part of a family. Or at least, that's how it had always seemed. Until her parents had sold them. But once they were alone, were all men like this? How could she ever be safe?

She opened drawers, not entirely sure of what she was looking for, and paused when she saw a metal hairclip. She picked it up and examined it, considering, then pushed it into the crack under the door, tapping it into place with the bottom of a heavy drinking glass until it would go no further. She turned the knob and pulled hard, but the door wouldn't budge.

She nodded, satisfied. Mr. Lone had told her not to lock the door, and she hadn't. But now it couldn't be opened, either.

20—THEN

The day before school was to start, Livia met with Nanu for the last time. The other tutors had stopped coming the week before, to prepare for their classes. And now it was time for Nanu to return to Washington. Livia was sad she was leaving, and frightened, too. Nanu felt like her last connection to a world that was beginning to seem like a strange and fragmenting dream. There was still so much she didn't understand—not just about the language, but about the people, the place, the customs. As strange and uncomfortable as everything was, she had gotten used to the routine—the dining room, her teachers, studying until she was exhausted at night. Even the church. Tomorrow, everything would change.

At noon, Nanu stood and they began heading toward the front door. There would be no lunch today because there would be no afternoon tutoring. Livia wasn't sure what she would do—she had never had an afternoon to herself. Study, she decided.

"Wait," Livia said, realizing Nanu had forgotten something. "Your books."

Nanu glanced back at the textbooks she had left on the table, then looked at Livia. "They're yours now."

Of course. It made sense. But it also made Nanu's departure more real. And more final.

At the door, Nanu paused and turned. "Are you nervous about tomorrow?" she said.

Livia nodded. She wouldn't have admitted it to anyone else, but she didn't mind telling Nanu.

Nanu smiled. "You'll be fine. You're ready. I can't believe how far you've come in just over two months."

All morning, Livia had been hoping Nanu would offer to stay in touch—give her an address, a phone number, something. But she hadn't. Livia looked at her, afraid to ask.

Nanu raised her eyebrows. "What is it?"

Livia hesitated, then blurted out in Lahu, "Could I write you? Or call you? Just . . . to tell you how I'm doing at school?"

Nanu looked down for a moment, then said in English, "Mr. Lone doesn't think it's good for you to talk in Lahu. You know that."

Livia switched back to English. "But we can talk in English. Or write. It will be good practice for me."

"He doesn't think you should talk to *me*."

"What? Why?"

Nanu sighed. "He thinks you'll make better progress if we're not in touch. That your English will get better faster."

"But it's been getting better with you."

"Yes. But now you're going to be in school every day, using English every day with other students. You'll make American friends. They'll want you to be American, too. Not Lahu."

"But I am Lahu."

Nanu shook her head. "You have to try."

"I don't want to."

"*I* want you to."

Livia switched back to Lahu. "Then call me. Write to me."

Nanu shook her head again and looked around, almost as though concerned someone was listening. She said in English, "No, Livia. It isn't a good idea. It would make trouble for us both."

Livia tried, but couldn't understand. Nanu seemed almost . . . frightened. But of what?

"Trouble why? How?"

Nanu frowned. "It's too much to explain. I have to be careful, all right? I have people who depend on me. I'm sorry, Livia. And I'm so proud of you. But I have to go. And I won't be in touch. I'm sorry."

Nanu turned, and in the instant before she was gone, Livia thought her face looked almost ashamed.

Livia stood in the doorway, her body rigid, her lips pursed. She wasn't frightened anymore. She was angry. She watched Nanu get into her car and pull away from the curb. Nanu didn't even glance back. A few seconds later, she was gone.

At least she didn't try to sell you, Livia thought.

But she wasn't entirely sure that was true.

21—THEN

That evening, Livia took a shower while the Lones were out. She liked having the house to herself. And she felt safer showering when Mr. Lone wasn't home.

She was rinsing the shampoo from her hair when she heard someone try to open the bathroom door. She pulled back the curtain and peeked out, her heart racing.

"Hello?" she called.

"Livia? What did I tell you about locking this door?"

It was Mr. Lone. He must have come back. And Mrs. Lone must still have been out.

Livia's hands started to tremble. She stepped out of the shower and pulled a towel around herself. She glanced down at the hair clip wedged under the door. "It not locked. I no . . . I didn't lock."

She saw the doorknob turn back and forth. Then nothing. She waited. Had he gone away?

The door exploded inward with a giant *boom*, bouncing off the wall and back. Mr. Lone strode in, catching the door as he moved and flinging it out of the way again.

"What did I tell you?" he shouted. "What?"

Livia backed away, terrified. She tried to think of words, but her mind was suddenly frozen. She could smell the alcohol, that awful smell.

"I no . . . I no . . ." she stammered.

He came closer and leaned forward so that his face was just inches from hers. "You what? You disobeyed me, didn't you?"

"No! I . . . I . . ."

His arm shot out and he snatched the towel from her body, yanking it so violently that she was nearly pulled into him. For a second she managed to cling to it, but he tore it from her hands and flung it behind him. Livia shrank back against the wall, trembling, covering herself with her arms.

Mr. Lone stepped in and leaned so close that she could feel his breath on her face. "Are you going to lock the door anymore?"

She looked at the floor, her face burning with shame and fear, her arms in front of her, her body contorted as though trying to fold in on itself.

"No," she managed to whisper through a constricted throat.

"Look at me when I talk to you, Livia." His voice was nearly a growl.

She couldn't.

"Look at me!" he shouted.

She stared up into his eyes, grimacing with helplessness and terror, her breath whistling in and out of her nostrils.

"This kind of disobedience," he said, his voice lower again. "After all I've done for you. Taking you into my home. Making you my daughter. Providing for you. Trying to find your sister. And I have some news for you in that regard, did you know that? Yes, I have some news."

For an instant, Livia forgot everything else—her fear, her shame, her nakedness. "What?" she said. "What news? About Nason? Please, what?"

"Really? Why should I tell you now, when you're so ungrateful?"

"Tell! Please!"

"You want me to be honest with you, is that it Livia? Open? Not to keep secrets?"

"Yes. Please. I want."

"You want *that*."

"Yes. I want that."

"And yet look at you. Locking the door. And then standing here in front of me, trying to cover yourself. What are you hiding from me, Livia?"

"What? No, not . . ."

She couldn't find the words. Everything Nanu had taught her, it was all suddenly gone. She was confused and afraid, and the feeling of what the men on the boat had made her do mushroomed in her mind like an evil spirit, and Mr. Lone knew something about Nason and he wasn't even telling her.

"Not what, Livia? Stand up straight. Lower your arms."

She couldn't. She tried to make her arms move. But she couldn't.

"That's fine. If you want to hide from me, I'll hide what I know about Nason. It's up to you."

He turned as though to leave.

"Wait!" Livia shouted. "Wait."

He turned and looked at her, saying nothing.

Her lips were trembling. Her arms and legs were worse. She dropped her head and did her best to stand up straight. Then she lowered her shaking arms. She gritted her teeth, trying desperately not to cry.

"All right," Mr. Lone said. "That's good, Livia. That's a good girl."

Her vision blurred. She blinked, and saw tears hitting the tiled floor.

"Now, would you like to learn about Nason?"

As desperate as she was to hear, all she could manage was a nod.

"Look at me, Livia. Look at me when I talk to you."

She looked at him. And saw the bulge in his pants, the same as the men on the boat. She had already known it would be there.

He reached out and brushed away her tears. His touch brought a wave of nausea, and made her cry harder. But she didn't flinch.

"Your sister is all right, Livia. I know where she is."

One of Livia's hands flew to her mouth and she sobbed. She clasped her other hand over the first, pressing her palms in hard, trying to stop herself from crying, but another sob erupted, and then another. Her legs wobbled, and she reached for the towel rack to steady herself.

"Yes, Nason is all right, but she is in some danger. We have to be very careful about how we try to help her, do you understand, Livia? Very careful."

Livia shook her head, still sobbing. She didn't understand. She didn't understand any of it. Danger? Nason?

"Don't cover yourself," he said sharply. "I told you."

She hadn't even realized her arms had moved back in front of her. She managed to part them a little.

She breathed in and out and tried to concentrate, to think of the words she needed. "Why she danger? Why—"

"Why *is* she in danger?"

"Yes, why that. And we help. We"—she tried to remember the English grammar for necessity, couldn't—"we help. Help. Help Nason. Please."

"Yes. We're going to try to help. But it's going to take time. And it's very important that the men holding her not know we know."

"Why?"

"I can't tell you that right now."

"Why?"

"I just can't."

"Where she is? Please."

"Where *is* she?"

"Yes, yes, that!"

"I can't tell you yet. You have to trust me. Just as I'm trusting you, by telling you this much. Do you understand? I'm telling you because I trust you, Livia. But if we tell anyone else, even Mrs. Lone, it creates danger for Nason. I'm doing all I can. Now, do you trust me?"

She felt her arms trying to move in front of her. She stopped them.

"Yes. That's right, Livia. That's a good girl. You trust me, don't you?"

She nodded.

"And you respect my position as head of the household, yes?"

Again she nodded.

"Then show me you trust me. Show me you respect me. Show me."

What could she do? She looked down and parted her arms while the tears ran down her cheeks.

He reached behind him and picked up the towel, then stepped close and wrapped it around her. She felt a sob shake loose, and bit down hard to stop the next one.

"Don't do that with the door again," he said.

She shook her head and managed to say, "I won't."

"When I have updates about Nason, I'll want to know I can share them with you. Privately. In this bathroom, in fact, where no one else can hear us. Do you understand?"

She nodded.

"Look at me, Livia."

She did. And for a moment, her fear, her confusion, even her thoughts of Nason . . . it was all gone. She stopped crying, feeling nothing but an overwhelming, burning hate. It felt like a force, like something radiating from her yet also somehow separate. Something that was new inside her and still relatively small, but that one day could become big. Terrifying. Could he sense it? How could he not?

"Tell me you understand. Say it."

She let her vision defocus, so she was looking more through him than at him. That was better. Yes. It was better not to have to see him.

"I understand."

He nodded. "That's a good girl." He leaned forward and kissed the top of her head. "We'll talk again soon. I promise."

She pulled on clothes the instant he was gone. Then stuck her head under the faucet in the bath and washed her hair again, scrubbing the spot his lips had touched.

Nason. Was she really all right? In danger of some kind, yes, but still, all right?

Part of her thought she shouldn't believe Mr. Lone. But how could someone lie about something like that? And besides, she had to believe him. She just had to. She had to believe that Nason was all right. That somehow, soon, they would be together again.

She stood in front of the mirror, pulling a comb through her damp hair. She was amazed Mr. Lone hadn't seen her hate. But she could tell he hadn't.

She couldn't say why, but she realized she needed to hide her hate. Her hate had made her feel strong. And it was better if he didn't know she was strong. Because her hatred . . . could be a kind of warning.

And she didn't want to warn him. She wanted to *surprise* him.

With what, she didn't know yet. But something.

22—THEN

School was horrible. Livia had thought her English was good enough, but it turned out that listening to Nanu and the other tutors in a quiet room where she could see everyone's face was one thing. A noisy room from far away, and without being able to ask questions if she didn't understand something, was another.

Some of the teachers were nice, but she didn't like the children at all. At best, they ignored her. A few treated her as a curiosity, staring at her and asking if it was true they ate bugs where she came from. Livia wanted to tell them that when you're hungry enough, you eat anything, but she knew they were stupid and had never gone to bed with anything other than full bellies and they would never understand. So she didn't bother answering.

Some of the children were mean. They made fun of her accent and her struggles with English. They had heard she was Lahu, and spread rumors that she liked to eat dogs, warning the other children to be on the lookout for their pets when Livia Lahu was around. One group of bullies in particular, ninth graders led by a blond boy named Eric, would sometimes surround her and chant, "La-*hoo*, La-*hoo*," drawing out the second syllable in long, mocking high voices. Other times, one of them would sneak up from behind and knock her books out of her arms, then run away while the others laughed at her helpless fury. And they'd repeatedly ask if she was going to jump out a window onto a fence and kill herself. That taunt she didn't even understand.

She hated them. She hated anyone who took advantage of people who were smaller or weaker. And she hated herself almost as much, for being so small and weak. She told herself the bullies were stupid and soft, that none of them could handle an *a-taw*, or stalk a bird in the forest, or avoid the plants that could make you sick and find the ones that could be used as medicine.

But none of those things mattered here. No one knew Livia was good at anything, and they wouldn't have cared even if they did.

Her only refuge was homework. It was hard when the teachers were talking—there was so much she would miss. But when she was studying, she was in control. When she didn't know a word, she could look it up. If a problem was difficult, she could do it again and again until she had it right. And she was good at memorizing things. It was almost as though studying enabled her to slow down the world, to pick out of the air things that would otherwise fly past, and hold and examine and incorporate them. She needed to study—not just because of how isolated she felt at school, but because of how powerless she was in the Lone house.

A few times, Mr. Lone's brother Ezra, the senator, came from Washington to visit. He was tall and bald like Mr. Lone and had the same wide-set eyes, but whereas Mr. Lone was stocky, Senator Lone was trim and fit-looking. When Mr. Lone introduced them, Senator Lone stooped and shook her hand. "I am so delighted to meet you, young lady," he said. "I've heard your progress has been remarkable. Under any circumstances, but especially following an ordeal like yours."

She had to consciously keep from wrinkling her nose in disgust at the mention of her "ordeal." And he sounded like his brother—another mark against him.

"Thank you, Senator," she said, having been coached by Mr. Lone to call him that. "It's very nice to meet you, too." It wasn't hard to say. She was getting good at lying, at saying the right words so other people couldn't know what she was really thinking.

She glanced over at a man standing behind and slightly to the right of the senator. The man was watching her with an odd expression—both intense and dispassionate, as though she was an exotic bug he had pulled from under a log in the jungle and was now examining with detached fascination. The way he was standing, she sensed he was with the senator, though in what capacity she didn't know. He was short, but heavily muscled, with a neck that looked as thick as a thigh and ears that protruded from beneath a blond crew cut. He was wearing a suit, but didn't seem comfortable in it the way Mr. Lone and the senator seemed in theirs. For some reason, even though he didn't have a uniform or a gun, he reminded her of the Thai soldiers who sometimes passed by the hill tribe villages looking for opium growers.

Senator Lone glanced back. "Oh, I'm sorry. This is my legislative aide, Matthias Redcroft. Matthias is the unsung hero behind all my legislative accomplishments—my right-hand man. Matthias, this is Livia, my new niece."

Matthias smiled and extended his hand. "Hello, Livia."

Although they looked nothing alike, when the man smiled he reminded Livia so much of Skull Face that a wave of nausea coursed through her. She shook his hand and managed to stammer out, "It's nice to meet you." And then she excused herself to go to the bathroom, where she washed her hands with the hottest water she could stand.

Twice a week, when Mrs. Lone was out with her bridge club, Mr. Lone would come into Livia's room. If she was already in the bathroom, it would start there. If she was studying on her bed, she would walk to the bathroom ahead of him. There was something about the bathroom he seemed to like. She would undress as though getting ready to shower, and he would open his pants and watch her while he touched himself. It was important to him that she look at his face the whole time. He would say the same strange things to her—trust was so important, and he would never hurt her, but he was taking care of her and she owed him this much and really it was only a little considering how generous he had been and how he had brought her into his house and under his protection and made her his daughter—while he touched himself faster and faster. And then his face would contort and he would moan, and the slime would come out and spill to the tiled floor. Then he would sag against the sink, panting, while Livia balled up toilet paper, wiped up the slime, and flushed it down the toilet. Then he would close his pants and tell her he was so glad they trusted each other the way they did, that she was obeying him the way she did, the way she should. And that Nason was all right, and he was doing all he could.

She still didn't know whether to believe him about Nason. But she was afraid of what she might do if she thought he was lying. She might just despair—stop eating, stop drinking, stop caring about anything. Or she might take a knife from the kitchen and hide it in the bathroom and stab it into his belly again and again while he was opening up his pants. And then use it on herself.

So she told herself that probably he was telling the truth about Nason, or at least not completely lying. He was rich and powerful, wasn't he? And friends with the chief of police? With a brother who was a senator? So many people seemed afraid of him, or in awe of him. A man like that would have ways of finding someone, if he wanted to.

There was so much she didn't know or understand, but she wasn't stupid. She knew he might be holding back information about Nason to make Livia more cooperative. But her need to believe about Nason was so strong that she could endure what he liked to do in the bathroom. It was disgusting, but not as disgusting as what Skull Face and his men had made her do. It would happen, and then he would leave, and she would get dressed and lie down on her bed and study even harder. The bathroom became just another secret, something to close up and hide in a dark mental box, alongside the hate she kept there.

23—NOW

Masnick was careful about his burner, mostly keeping it powered off and never turning it on alongside his personal cell phone. But once Livia knew the burner was his, all she had to do was start tracking the personal unit. So when the personal unit showed up at the Trader Joe's in Shoreline one morning two days after Livia had listened in on Masnick's conversation with Jardin, Livia made sure to be there, too, picking up some frozen dinners, a container of mixed berries, a box of cereal, and a few bottles of wine.

Masnick was perusing the endless refrigerated shelves of beer with names like Ice Harbor Runaway Red Ale and Reuben's Brews Robust Porter and Snoqualmie Falls Wildcat IPA. She headed toward him, her eyes on the shelves, drifting along until her cart smacked into his with a metal clang. "Oh!" she said. "I'm sorry. I should pay more attention to where I'm going."

He looked at her face, then glanced down to take in the rest of her. She was wearing yoga tights, the outfit calculated to get his attention. She didn't doubt Masnick's feelings for Jardin, but in the end he was a Hammerhead—not a species renowned for worship of monogamy.

"Uh, no," he said, looking into her eyes and smiling. "That's okay."

She smiled back. "This'll teach me to do the grocery shopping before I've had a cup of coffee. I need to figure out where things are around here."

"What, are you new in town?"

"Yeah, up from San Francisco. Still getting my bearings."

"Well, if you like coffee, Seattle's the right place."

"That's what I hear. Though I'll tell you, San Francisco's pretty hard to beat in the coffee department. Got any recommendations?"

He laughed. "I tend to fuel up at a place called Black Rock. You're not going to find as much here in Shoreline as in Seattle, or in San Francisco, I guess, but with Black Rock you won't miss it, either."

She gave him an appreciative nod. "Thanks. I'm Suzy, by the way."

He gave her body another look, then extended a hand. "Good to meet you, Suzy. I'm Mike."

She shook his hand, holding it just a tad longer than decorum alone would dictate. "Well, Mike, do you mind if I take advantage of short acquaintance to ask you another question about the neighborhood?"

He glanced at her shopping cart. She could see him doing the math based on her groceries—a woman living alone. A woman who might enjoy a glass of wine before eating her microwaved dinner, to take the edge off. And maybe another with dinner, to keep the edge off. And maybe another after dinner, to kill the edge entirely.

"Hey, happy to help."

"So, I've got a Westie mix. Ginger's her name. Where's a good place to take her to let her off the leash?"

"Easy. Saltwater Park."

"Yeah?"

"Yeah. It's at Richmond Beach. Right here in Shoreline." He looked her up and down again. "And you look like you're into staying fit, yeah?"

"You guessed it."

"Well, you'd be amazed at the workout you can get going up and down the stairs there." He smiled. "I go a lot around sunset. Probably be there tonight. You should come by. You could introduce me to Ginger."

She smiled back. "I might just do that, Mike."

24—THEN

Over the winter holidays, Livia heard the doorbell ring, and then voices in the foyer. The voices died down, and she thought whoever had come to the door had left. But a little while later, when she emerged from her room to get a snack, she found Mrs. Lone sitting at the kitchen table with a visitor. They were drinking coffee and laughing. Livia thought she had never seen Mrs. Lone so at ease and happy. But as soon as she saw Livia, her face closed up into its customary pinched look.

The visitor smiled when he saw Livia, then pushed back his chair and stood. He looked a little older than Mrs. Lone, with hair the color of sand mixed with ash. He wasn't a big man, but there was something . . . solid about him. The way his feet were planted on the ground, the way his arms hung at his sides, maybe. It was as though he was relaxed, but also ready.

Mrs. Lone didn't get up. Her voice cool, she said, "Livia, this is my brother. Officer Harris."

The man glanced at Mrs. Lone and laughed uncomfortably. "Jeez, Dotty, you make it sound as though she's committed a crime."

Mrs. Lone made a noise that might have been meant as a laugh, but came out more as a grunt.

The man walked over to Livia and held out his hand. "If you want to be friends, you can't call me Officer Harris. You have to call me Rick. Okay?"

Livia had learned a lot about how to shake hands since that first time with Tanya. Reminding herself to look in his eyes, she took Rick's big hand in her smaller one and gave it an awkward squeeze. Rick squeezed back. It was only a slight squeeze, but she was aware of the strength behind it.

Rick smiled and released her hand. "It's nice to meet you, Livia."

This was one of the first things Nanu had taught her, and there had been countless opportunities to practice it at the Lones' parties. So it was easy to respond, "It's nice to meet you, too."

"I've heard a lot about you. Dotty told me you got straight A's last semester."

If Mrs. Lone had told him anything at all about her grades or anything else, Livia thought, it could only have been because he had insisted. She glanced over and saw Mrs. Lone watching them. As always, there was something suspicious in the woman's expression. And this time, somehow, something envious, as well. Livia didn't know why, but she could tell Mrs. Lone didn't want Livia talking to her brother.

But she knew the mention of her grades was intended as a compliment. It would be rude to offer nothing in return. So she nodded and said, "Yes."

"That's amazing. I mean, six months ago, you barely spoke a word of English, is that right?"

"Mr. Lone—and Mrs. Lone—they got me tutors."

"Well, that was good of them. But even so, that's quite an achievement. I think you must be very smart."

"I . . . study a lot."

He laughed. "I studied a lot, too. And I grew up speaking English. But I never got straight A's."

Mrs. Lone had called him "Officer." Livia knew the woman wouldn't like it, but she couldn't resist asking. "Are you . . . a policeman?"

Rick nodded. "Twenty-five years on the job in Portland."

Portland, she thought. *Nason.*

"What kind of policeman?"

Mrs. Lone stood. "Livia, my brother had a long drive from Portland, and he's probably tired. So . . ."

Rick gave his sister a strange glance—half amusement, half annoyance—then looked at Livia again. "You know how you can tell you're getting older? When your little sister starts treating you like an invalid. I'm a homicide detective, Livia. That means—"

"Murder," Livia said.

Rick laughed. "Sorry. I should have known you'd know the word. Anyway, yes, just a humble Portland cop, taking a few days to visit his sister and her family."

Knowing again that Mrs. Lone wouldn't like it, Livia said, "What about you? Your family?"

Rick shrugged. "Being a cop can make it hard to have kids and all that. So no, Dotty and my four nephews are my family." He smiled. "And now you."

She didn't know why, but that shrug was the first thing Rick had done that didn't strike Livia as genuine. And while his answer about not having a family of his own had been smoothly delivered, Livia wondered why he felt he needed to explain. At least when he said she was his family now, it didn't bother her—unlike with Mr. Lone, coming from Rick it didn't sound like a threat or a trap. And he'd left out Mr. Lone when describing who was his family—what did that mean?

She didn't know what to make of it all, and wanted to think about it later. So for the moment, she just said, "Okay."

"I'm going to be here for a few days. If you ever feel like a break from studying, I'd love to hear about how things are going—school, life, whatever."

The whole time they'd been talking, she'd been expecting him to say something about her "ordeal" or her "bravery." She was intrigued, and glad, that he hadn't.

Mrs. Lone's pinched look became even more cramped. Not wanting to upset her or to offend Rick, Livia only nodded.

Rick reached for her hand and shook it again. "All right, then. It's really nice to meet you, Livia. I hope we'll get a chance to chat some more."

25—THEN

During the same holiday Rick was there, the Lones' four sons visited. Mr. Lone briefly introduced them to Livia, and they all reacted to her with varying degrees of curiosity, discomfort, and pity. Ordinarily, Livia preferred to eat alone in her room, using homework as an excuse, but while the sons and Rick were in the house, Mr. Lone insisted on taking everyone out to restaurants. These dinners were painful affairs, during which Livia could feel acutely that everyone wished she wasn't there— everyone but Mr. Lone, who seemed to enjoy showing her off in public, and Rick, who was the only one who talked to her, even though her responses were awkward and uncertain.

One morning, Mrs. Lone came to Livia's room and told her Mr. Lone was taking everyone to brunch. Livia understood this wasn't an invitation, and that Mr. Lone was insisting. But she thought she couldn't stand another meal with these people. So she said, "My stomach hurts. I think I'm going to stay in bed."

Actually, her stomach did hurt. A few months earlier, she had started to bleed, and it was happening now. She knew what the bleeding was—it had to do with making babies, and in the village, the women used rags during the days when it happened. Here, they didn't use rags; there were special pads that absorbed better. Mr. Lone had told her to ask for anything she needed, but she didn't want him to know about the bleeding. Her body was beginning to change, with hair between her legs and bumps on her chest where before there had been only skin and muscle, and his bathroom visits had become more frequent, his staring while he touched himself more intense. So she used some of the spending money he gave her to buy the pads in a store, hiding them under her bed when she didn't need them, and putting the ones she'd used at the bottom of the kitchen garbage when no one was around.

Mrs. Lone stood in the doorway, her pinched face looking like someone was squeezing it from both sides. "Your stomach? Nothing contagious, I hope?"

Livia wondered why the woman was asking—she'd never given any indication before that she was concerned about Livia's health, or anything else about her. Was she really afraid someone might catch something from Livia? Or did she suspect Livia was bleeding, with the question a way to try to confirm?

Not knowing what was the right course, Livia decided on ambiguity. "I'm not sure."

"All right. I'll tell Mr. Lone." She closed the door, her footfalls fading as she walked down the hallway.

Livia understood the "I'll tell Mr. Lone" was Mrs. Lone's way of indicating that if it were up to her, Livia wouldn't even be allowed in the house, let alone receive invitations to brunch. But she was used to Mrs. Lone's little indications, and they bothered her less now than they had at first. The main thing was, she didn't have to suffer through another meal with all of them.

She went back to her books. The echoes of conversation downstairs became more animated, then were cut off by the slam of the front door. She heard car doors opening and closing, engines starting, tires on gravel . . . and then, finally, the house was mercifully quiet.

Five minutes later, she heard one of the guest room doors open. She frowned—someone must have stayed behind. She heard a cough, and thought it sounded like Rick. She heard his footsteps moving down the corridor, then the buzz of coffee being ground in the kitchen.

The whole time Rick was staying with the Lones, Livia had been thinking about Portland and Nason. And trying to weigh the risks of asking for his help. It felt dangerous, and she knew Mr. Lone would be furious if he found out. But in the end, she decided she had to try.

She went to the kitchen. Rick was sitting at the table, sipping coffee from a mug stamped "Llewellyn Lions"—the name of the high school football team—and reading the newspaper. He smiled when he saw her and put down the paper.

"Livia—I thought you went with them to brunch. Sleeping late?"

"Studying."

"You're a hard worker."

She nodded.

"But don't you ever . . ."

She waited for him to go on, but it seemed he had thought better of it. He poured some coffee from a carafe into the mug. "You want some?"

She was surprised. "Coffee? I never had it. *Have* never had it."

"How old are you?"

She was going to say thirteen, but then changed her mind. "Almost fourteen."

"Well, I'd say that's old enough for just a taste. Though you might not want to mention it to my sister." He smiled. "Unless you want to get me in trouble."

Livia couldn't help smiling back. "No, I won't tell her."

"Okay, then." He walked over to the refrigerator and took out a carton of milk, then pulled a box from a cabinet. "Turbinado sugar. That's good. A little molasses tastes great in coffee. I generally drink mine black, but for your first time, milk and sugar's a good idea."

He took another mug from a cabinet, poured some coffee in along with a big serving of milk, added two spoonfuls of sugar, stirred it all together, and gave the mug to Livia. She smelled it suspiciously, then took a little sip—and then a bigger one. It was delicious. She'd never tasted anything like it.

He must have seen her expression, because he smiled and said, "Not bad, huh?"

She nodded, happy to have discovered something so tasty, and liking that it was a secret from Mrs. Lone. "It's really good."

"Well, you can't drink too much of it. You're not grown yet, and caffeine can make you jittery. But a little won't hurt you. Just remember, you didn't get it from me."

"Okay." She took another sip, then said, "What were you going to ask before?"

"When?"

"You said, 'But don't you ever . . .'"

"Oh, that. I don't know. Something about school, I guess. But you know what? I don't even remember much about school. I actually hated it."

She cocked her head, suddenly intrigued at what felt like a confidence. "Why?"

"Ah, it's a long story. I just never felt like I fit in. I was glad when it was over. I'm better at being a cop than I was at being a student."

Livia glanced around. "You . . . didn't want to go to breakfast?"

He took a sip of his coffee. "I begged off. It's great to see everyone, but sometimes I need a little space. You know?"

"Yes."

"And tomorrow's Christmas Eve, so it's going to be the big church thing. Does Fred make you go to church?"

"Yes." She didn't like talking about Mr. Lone.

"Yeah, I figured. Well, I'm not really the churchgoing type. To each his own, I guess."

She looked at him, desperate to ask, but also afraid. She sensed she was crossing lines she couldn't clearly see.

A strange expression settled into his face—compassion, but also something . . . concerned.

"How's everything going, Livia?"

Somehow, she could tell he didn't mean it in the usual polite, surface way. That he was really asking. Really wanted to know. Maybe even really . . . cared?

She bit her lip. She so wanted to ask him.

"What is it?" he said. "Honey, if something's wrong, you can tell me."

No, she thought. *I can't tell anyone. Ever.*

But she could ask him. She had to.

"My sister," she said. "Nason." From no more than saying Nason's name, the tears welled up. She wiped them violently away, furious at herself for crying.

"I heard about your sister, hon," he said. "I'm so sorry."

She nodded. "No one knows where she is. What happened to her. Even if—"

She couldn't finish the sentence. But she didn't need to. He nodded, waiting for her to go on. She could tell that Mr. Lone had told him nothing. But did that mean Mr. Lone *knew* nothing?

She cleared her throat. "All anyone knows, I think, is Portland is where we were separated. Portland is where she disappeared."

He nodded. "PPB knows about it. And I talked to all my contacts so they would understand it's personal, too. You know, my beat is homicide, but there are cops who specialize in child matters, that kind of thing. I made sure they're all looking for your sister."

She was stunned. "You . . . you did that?"

"Jesus, of course I did, Livia."

She started crying again. She couldn't help it. She'd gotten so good at hardening herself against cruelty, she hadn't been prepared for his kindness.

He tore a paper towel from the dispenser and handed it to her. While she wiped her face and sniffled, he reached for her shoulder. She jerked back.

Instantly he raised his hands, palms up. "I'm sorry, honey."

She shook her head. She hadn't sensed he was going to touch her in a bad way. But . . . she didn't like being touched anymore. By men, especially.

She wanted to tell him it wasn't his fault, because what he had done for Nason was so nice, so good. But there was no way to explain. She shook her head and said, "No, no, *I'm* sorry."

The way he was looking at her . . . she had the strangest sense that maybe he knew. Or knew enough. Even without her telling.

"It's okay," he said. "And you don't have one thing to be sorry for, do you understand? Not one."

She nodded and wiped her eyes. "Did the special police you know . . . did anyone . . ."

He shook his head. "No. I'm sorry, there's not a lot to go on, and no one has been able to find anything. But I'm not going to give up. And I won't let anyone else, either."

"What about the men who took us? The Thai men? I described them all to the people from the Immigration and Naturalization Service." She pronounced the unfamiliar words carefully.

"As I understand it, that's a dead end. No one knows who the men are or how to find them. I know the police have your description, and if they catch anyone who looks like that, they'll be questioned very closely."

"Will you tell me if that happens?"

"Of course."

She pursed her lips, frustrated. To be right here, able to ask a Portland police officer, and still not find anything useful . . . it was maddening.

"What about the men on the boat? The boat from Portland. How did the police even know there were smuggled people on it?"

"That's funny, I had the same question. I asked around. Word is, it was an anonymous call to Chief Emmanuel of Llewellyn PD. Seems like a rival gang dropped a dime."

"Dropped a dime?"

"An expression. It refers to the days when public phones only cost a dime. Someone wanting to turn someone in would use a public phone so the call couldn't be traced. So 'drop a dime' came to mean an anonymous tip to the police."

"Why would someone do that?"

"Could be a lot of reasons. A business rival, disrupting someone else's shipment. Payback for something. Maybe something else personal. Hard to say. The caller had specific information about the barge and the timing. Llewellyn PD doesn't have much experience with people smuggling, so they called INS. There must have been a lot of cops and agents on the dock the day they rescued you."

She nodded. "I heard the police killed two of the smugglers. But that they caught one. Maybe he knows something?"

Rick smiled. "You have good cop instincts, you know that? And yes, you heard right, two of them died in a gunfight when the police rescued you. But no, the third guy's not talking. Says his dead brother handled all the logistics—the communications, the contacts with people who hired them. He says he didn't know anything, didn't even know you were all kidnapped."

"He's a liar."

"I know. And I wish there were a way to prove it. The AUSA—that's the Assistant United States Attorney, the federal prosecutor, the person responsible for putting people in prison when they commit federal crimes like kidnapping and people smuggling—the AUSA threatened him with a lot of prison time if he wouldn't talk. But the guy still claimed to know nothing."

"So they'll put him in prison for a long time?"

"Twenty years. Maybe less, with time off for good behavior."

She thought of Nason. "That doesn't sound like so long."

"No, you're right. In a just world, it would be longer."

"And . . . does anyone know who the other people on the boat were? Where they came from? The boat from Thailand had thirteen children. But when I woke up, it was a new boat, and the Thai children were gone and all the other people were new. They spoke languages I didn't know."

"This guy they caught, Timothy Tyler—goes by 'Weed,' by the way—he says he doesn't know where you all came from, or who provided you. And he's stuck to that story. The others were from a lot of different places—China, Guatemala, Sri Lanka—a mix."

"What does that mean?"

"Well, it's hard to say. It could mean a lot of things. But in general, it means Weed's gang or whoever hired them thought they had a willing buyer, or buyers, somewhere as far east of Portland as Llewellyn. And maybe farther east. Modern-day slavery is all over the place. Not just Portland, not just Llewellyn. Everywhere."

"Who was going to buy us?"

"No way to know at this point. Could have been a nail salon, agricultural interests . . . or some sick homeowner, who wanted a maid he didn't have to pay or account for."

"But the children on the boat. Me, and the two who died. They were going to sell us, too?"

"Yeah. People buy children, too, I'm sorry to say. I think you can imagine why."

She didn't have to imagine. She knew. And Rick probably knew she knew, but was too respectful to say so.

"What about the other people on the boat from Portland? What happened to them?"

"Well, they were all adults, and they were all here illegally, so my understanding is they've been repatriated. Sent back to the countries they came from. You were the only kid who survived the trip, so that made you a special case. The truth is, INS didn't know what to do with you. I guess Fred pulled some strings."

"Strings?"

"Sorry, another expression. It means . . . used influence. He knows a lot of people. And then there's his brother, Ezra, the senator. You've probably met him."

Something in his tone made Livia sense he didn't like the brother much more than he liked Mr. Lone. She wanted to ask, but only said, "Yes."

She wanted to tell him that Mr. Lone said he knew where Nason was. But what if telling Rick made things worse for Nason? The last time she had thought she was protecting Nason, she had caused her to be hurt, hurt so badly. What if that happened again? What if Mr. Lone were telling the truth, and had located Nason through his contacts, his senator brother, something like that, and now Livia did something stupid like tell the wrong person, and got Nason hurt again?

She couldn't risk that. She couldn't.

But there was one more possibility. And this was her chance. She had to tell him.

She cleared her throat again and said, "There's one thing I didn't say to the other police who asked me. And I want to tell you. But you have to promise not to tell anyone else. Not Mrs. Lone. Not Mr. Lone. No one."

"Why, honey?"

"You just have to promise."

"Whatever you tell me, I'll try to help. But I won't be much use alone."

Livia considered. It was a good point, and she hadn't thought of it.

"Okay," she said. "You can tell the other police you trust. But I want this . . . just please, I need your help. Please."

"All right. Okay."

"You won't tell?"

"I won't tell."

"Do you know a Thai policeman?"

"You mean, a certain Thai policeman?"

"No, no, I mean, do you know Thai police*men*. Any Thai policemen."

"I don't. But I work with people who would know the Thai police, yes."

All right. It wasn't quite what she'd been hoping for, but it would have to be enough.

She told him how her parents had sold her and Nason. She described Skull Face and Dirty Beard and Square Head, leaving out the parts she couldn't talk about—parts she thought he might sense regardless. Most of all, she described where her parents lived, in enough detail so that the Thai police could go to the village.

"But you can't tell any Thai policemen where I am," she said. "I don't want my parents to know. I never want to see them again. Ever. I don't even want anyone to contact them now, but they're the only ones who know who they sold us to. So maybe they can help find Nason. And"—her eyes filled up and she blinked away the tears—"I love her. Even more than I hate them."

"You don't even want your parents to know—"

"No. They don't deserve to know *anything*. Not even where I am. Not even if I'm alive."

He nodded. "All right."

She thought about how her people hated the Thai police, whose only job seemed to be to stop the hill tribes from cutting land in the forest where they could plant food. Some people tried to pay them bribes. The police took the money, then drove the people off their land anyway.

"And also," she said, "the Thai police will tell you they visited the village, but that my parents didn't know anything. Then you'll pay them, and they won't have"—she groped for the word, got it—"they won't have earned it."

"Livia, no one's going to pay the police—"

"I don't know how it is in America. But in Thailand, the police aren't good. They don't let my people farm the way we need to. If you ask for something, they expect something back. So they'll lie and tell you they did what you asked, so they can make you do something for them in return. You need"—she struggled again, then remembered the word—"proof. Proof they did what you asked. Otherwise they'll lie."

"All right. What kind of proof?"

"My mother has a photograph. Of Nason and me. The Thai policemen should take it. And send it to you. Then I'll know. I'll know they really went to the village. I'll know they really asked my parents. At least I'll know that."

Maybe she should have said, "*We'll* know that." But even though he seemed kind, she knew Rick wasn't an ally. She didn't have allies. And she didn't want them. In the long run, the only person she could depend on was herself.

26—THEN

Livia passed the first day of spring semester in a daze of nausea and shame. The day before, Mr. Lone had come to her room. That much she had been expecting—it had been almost two weeks since the last time, and with Rick and the sons gone, and Mrs. Lone at her bridge club, one of his visits was inevitable. Livia had just wanted for it to be over so she wouldn't have to dread it again, at least for a while.

But it didn't happen the way it usually did. Mr. Lone had screamed that he had found her pads, the ones she used for her period. He accused her of hiding things from him again. And then he shoved her onto the bed, knelt on her back, pulled down her sweatpants and underwear, and pushed his fingers inside her, all the while whispering, "Now we'll see, now we'll see," while Livia cried and struggled.

She hadn't slept at all that night, and no matter how hard she tried, the next morning she couldn't push away the memory, the disgusting invasion of his fingers moving and stabbing inside her, the helplessness of being held down like that. The worst part was that as awful as it had been, she knew it was nothing compared to what Skull Face and the other men had done to Nason, and knowing this only magnified her own pain.

She wandered outside at recess and stood in the shadow of one of the oak trees at the edge of the school grounds. The day was warm, and an impromptu touch football game was underway on the grass on the eastern side of the building. Other children were clustered around the rows of picnic tables alongside the school's brick wall, watching the game, laughing as they squinted against the sun, talking with each other. Livia felt apart from all of it, as though some secret pollution had made its way inside her, a pollution the other children must have sensed even if they couldn't really know.

She noticed a boy come through the doors at the back of the building—the new boy, Sean something, an eighth grader like her who the teacher had introduced in homeroom. Sean's father had been hired for an important job in Mr. Lone's ammunition factory, the teacher had explained, and that's why Sean had transferred to Llewellyn in the middle of the school year. The teacher had invited Sean up to the whiteboard to say a few words about himself. Livia had watched him, small for his age, walk slowly to the front as though agonized by each step, and she realized he was shy, maybe even more shy than she was. He had caramel-colored skin peppered with freckles, almond-shaped eyes, and dark, kinky hair. It looked like one of his parents was black, and the other Asian. Maybe it made him feel awkward, because almost all the other students at the school were pasty white. If so, she understood how he felt.

But when he tried to speak, Livia realized his shyness was something else. Sean stuttered. Only a little at first, but the moment it happened, the other children started laughing, and then the stuttering got worse. The teacher tried to stop them, but succeeded only in converting outright guffaws into suppressed sniggers. Sean managed to stammer out a few more words, then returned to his seat, his eyes downcast, his caramel-colored cheeks inflamed. Livia felt sorry for him, and wanted to yell at the other children to stop, but she knew all that would accomplish would be to make them laugh at her, as well.

He paused now at the corner of the building and looked over at the football game, at the children sitting at the picnic tables. Holding his books in one hand, he placed the other against the brick wall as though seeking reassurance, then stood there for a moment, his head poking past the corner, his body behind it. He didn't notice Livia, and no one else seemed to notice him. Then he turned and started walking back toward the entrance.

The doors opened again, and Eric, the ninth grader who liked to taunt her about her accent, strode out, his two bully friends behind him. Livia instinctively tightened her hold on her books.

"Hey," Eric said loudly. "It's Stutter Boy."

Sean stopped and looked at Eric and the other two, his expression worried.

Eric came closer. He smiled. "Say something, S-S-S-Stutter Boy."

Sean shook his head and took a step back.

Livia felt paralyzed. She wanted to help. She knew she should. And in her life before, before everything that had been done to her and Nason, before she'd been brought to this horrible place, before Mr. Lone had made her feel so poisoned and alone and helpless . . . she would have.

At the same time, she was relieved that Eric and the other two were bullying someone else. And even as she realized it, she was engulfed by a wave of shame.

Help him, she thought. But she felt so weak. So useless. So afraid.

Eric took a step closer. His smile faded. "Say something, Stutter Boy. Or I'll *make* you say something."

Again, Sean's only response was a shake of his head. It was the oddest thing—his face was frightened, but there was something in his posture that seemed . . . prepared, somehow. He had turned his body slightly so that his left side was facing Eric, and with one hand he was holding his books close to his chin, almost like a shield, while his other hand was up and open in a gesture Livia thought was meant to look placating, but that also looked . . . practiced, somehow. Deliberate.

Eric shot out a hand and knocked Sean's books out of his arm. They hit the ground, but Sean didn't look away. He kept his hands up, palms forward, elbows close to his body.

One of Eric's bully friends laughed and said, "I g-g-guess you're going to have to make him, Eric."

Eric grunted a laugh, then reached for Sean. What happened next went so fast that Livia wasn't sure what she had seen.

Sean grabbed Eric's incoming wrist and pulled it hard. At the same instant, he planted a foot on Eric's thigh and launched himself into the air in some kind of somersault. He caught Eric's arm between his legs, and for a moment just hung like that, suspended upside down from Eric's body, supported only by his grip on the wrist and his legs clamped on the arm. Eric was pulled into a crouch by Sean's weight. He staggered once as he tried to keep his balance, then fell to the ground with a surprised yelp. Sean hung on to the arm, his ankles crossed over Eric's chest, his back arched. Eric's friends watched bug eyed, apparently too shocked to intervene.

"You g-going to bother me anymore?" Sean said.

Eric kicked and struggled. Sean arched his back more, and Eric yelped again, louder this time.

"You going to bother me anymore?" Sean said. Livia noticed that this time, he didn't stutter.

Eric thrashed harder. "Let me go, you little fucking—"

Sean arched further. Eric yelled in pain.

Sean lifted his head so he was looking directly at Eric's red, contorted face. "You going to bother me anymore?"

"I'm gonna kill you, you little—"

Again Sean arched. This time, Eric positively shrieked. Livia glanced over to the side of the building and realized some of the other children had heard it. They were looking left and right, but couldn't see around the corner.

"You going to—"

"No! No! I'm not going to bother you anymore. Let me go! Let me go!"

Sean released Eric's arm and scuttled off him, then came quickly to his feet. Livia noticed that he kept his hands in front of his face as he stood, as though in anticipation that the other boys might rush him. He took a long step back and watched them warily.

But if he was worried, he didn't need to be. The other two were too shocked, and maybe too afraid, to do anything but gape at their fallen friend, who was cradling his arm now and actually crying. "Why did you do that?" he said, his voice high. "You broke my arm. You broke it." Then he drew in a long, hitching breath and sobbed, "Oh, God, it hurts, it hurts."

"It's not broken," Sean said. "Just sprained." Then he added, "This time."

After a moment, Eric managed to get to his feet. His friends didn't help him. And when he walked back toward the school, cradling his injured arm and still crying, they didn't even get the door. They just followed him, looking at each other and then at Eric and then at each other again. Before disappearing inside, one of them glanced back at Sean, and the hurt and resentment Livia saw in his eyes was the expression of a child outraged that someone had confiscated a favorite toy.

And then they were gone. Sean picked up his books and sat on one of the benches near the doors. Livia noticed he was shaking a little. He looked up and saw her watching, and she quickly looked away.

The bell rang, and the children who had been playing football and laughing at the picnic tables began to come around the corner and dutifully file inside, none of them even glancing at Sean as they passed him. After a few minutes, the area was deserted. Other than a few birds chirping in the surrounding trees, the schoolyard was suddenly silent.

Livia came out from behind the oak tree and started toward the building, her heart pounding, her books pressed across her chest. Sean watched wordlessly as she approached.

She stopped in front of him. He looked up at her, and she thought he seemed very sad. She didn't know why, but she felt like crying. But hers wasn't a sad feeling. Instead, she felt fierce, awake, electrified, as though for so long she'd been suffocating and suddenly had witnessed a way she could breathe. For the first time since the van had pulled up in the forest and Skull Face had gotten out, she wasn't afraid of anything—only that this boy might say no to what she had to ask him.

"Please," she said, her voice nearly a whisper. "What you did? Will you teach it to me?"

27—THEN

It turned out that what Sean had done was called jiu-jitsu, a way small people could fight bigger ones. It had been invented in Japan and then honed and popularized in Brazil, and Sean's father had learned it from some people named the Gracies after he'd left the Marines and gone to live in Rio. Sean told Livia his father had been making him train since he was little, and that he would ask if his father would train Livia, too. Sean's house was across the street from the school, and they walked over together when classes were done.

"Is your father home now?" Livia asked, thinking of how late Mr. Lone sometimes worked.

"Not yet, but soon," Sean said. "He made a deal with his boss that he would start early every day so he could come home early, too."

"So he would have time to train you?"

Sean nodded quickly but otherwise didn't answer, and Livia wondered if there was more to it than that.

Sean's house was two stories tall, with a porch that wrapped all the way around the front and side. There was a big green lawn, too, and though it was nowhere near as grand as the Lones' mansion, Livia sensed Sean's father must be reasonably important to be able to afford something as nice as this.

"Is your mother home?" she asked as they walked up the front steps.

Sean looked down. "She's n-not with us."

It was the first time Livia had heard him stutter since they'd left school together. She realized her question had made him uncomfortable. Was this why his father came home early every day—because his mother was gone? Without thinking, she said, "My parents aren't with me, either."

Sean glanced at her, then down again, and then back. "Did they . . . l-leave you?"

She didn't want to lie to him, but she wasn't inclined to explain, either. So she simply nodded.

"I'm sorry," he said. His face was sad, the way it had been after the fight.

They took off their sneakers in the foyer—Sean explained it was their custom not to wear shoes in the house—then made peanut-butter-and-jelly sandwiches. The kitchen was clean and functional—not showy like the one in the Lone house, but more comfortable, and somehow more real. Sean poured them each a glass of milk, and they sat at a table overlooking a small, green backyard bracketed by a tool shed and a swing set. While they ate, Livia asked Sean all about jiu-jitsu. What he had done to that bully Eric was wondrous to her, magical, and she felt she had to learn everything she could before it was somehow taken away as suddenly as it had appeared.

Sean seemed to enjoy sharing his knowledge. He told her about what it meant to establish your base, and achieve a dominant position, and take away your opponent's options until the only option left for him was to submit.

"Could you have really broken his arm?" Livia asked, still amazed.

Sean nodded. "But I'm glad he didn't make me."

"Your father would have been mad?"

Sean laughed, and Livia saw a little red creep into his cheeks underneath the freckles. It was the first time she had heard him laugh, and she liked it—there was something shy about it, as though his own laughter had startled him and he wasn't sure he should trust it.

"My father taught me to fight because of bullies. He hates them. If I broke Eric's arm, my father would probably give me a medal."

Livia decided she liked Sean's father. "Then you won't get in trouble for what happened today?"

Sean shook his head, but his expression turned sad again. "No. He'll be proud of me."

Livia didn't understand his ambivalence. "But aren't you proud, too?"

"I . . ." his voice trailed off, and then he continued. "I wish they'd just leave me alone."

"But sometimes they won't leave you alone. Sometimes you have to *make* them."

She hadn't meant to respond so fiercely. But was there anything more true than that?

She heard the front door open. Sean looked up and called out, "Hey, Dad."

A baritone voice came from the foyer. "Hey, tiger. How was your day?"

"It was okay. I have a friend here."

The voice called, "Oh?"

A moment later, a handsome black man strode into the kitchen. He was tall and broad shouldered, the sleeves of his button-down shirt snug around his biceps, with posture as straight as a telephone pole. Livia was surprised, and realized she had been expecting Sean's father to be Asian, since Sean had told her jiu-jitsu originally came from Japan, and for the mother to be black. She was also surprised by the man's size, because Sean was so small.

The man stopped and looked at Livia. His eyebrows went up and his face broke into what looked to her like a surprised smile. "Well, hello there," he said.

"Dad," Sean said, "this is Livia. Can we train her in jiu-jitsu?"

Sean's father laughed. "Could you maybe finish introducing us first?"

Sean reddened. "Um, Livia, this is my dad."

Livia stood, as Nanu had taught her. She wanted to make a good impression so Sean's father would agree to be her teacher. What was Sean's last name again? Ueno . . . Uenoyama, that was it.

"Hi, Mr. Uenoyama. It's nice to meet you."

Sean's father smiled. "Oh, Uenoyama is Sean's mother's name. Mine's Freeman. Malcolm Freeman. But please, don't even think about calling me Mr. Freeman, unless you want to make me feel old. You can just call me Malcolm, okay?"

Livia nodded. "Okay."

"So you want to learn jiu-jitsu, Livia?"

"Yes," Livia blurted out. "Please that." She realized in her eagerness she had lapsed into a strange construction, so she amended. "Yes, please."

"Well, it would be good for Sean to finally have a partner his own size, I'll say that. How often can you train?"

Livia was surprised. She expected Sean would have had dozens of training partners. Hundreds. How could everyone not want to learn jiu-jitsu? She shook her head, not understanding the question. "As often as you can teach me."

Malcolm raised his eyebrows. "Well, Sean and I train every day. And if you train every day, you'll learn fast, that's for sure. But do you have time with all your schoolwork? Is this going to be okay with your parents?"

Livia felt a bolt of panic. She hadn't thought of that. Mr. Lone wouldn't like her being out of the house so much, she knew that. And how would he ever allow her to learn something she could use to fight?

But she had to find a way. She had to.

Malcolm seemed to sense her unease. He said, "You want to talk to them first?"

"They're not my parents," she said, terrified she was making a mistake in telling him. "I'm . . . I stay with Mr. and Mrs. Lone."

"Oh," Malcolm said, with a long, significant nod of his head. "I've heard about you. You're the Lones' adopted daughter, is that right?"

She hated to be called that. It made it sound like Mr. Lone owned her. She nodded.

"Well, I see Mr. Lone every day at work. I imagine I could speak to him on your behalf, if you like."

For some reason, the notion frightened her. "I don't . . . I don't know if he'll listen."

Malcolm smiled, a warm, confident smile, and despite herself, Livia felt reassured. "I wouldn't worry about that," he said. "Mr. Lone is the boss, true, but you'd be surprised how few people have my skills—just the skills he needs in that big ammunition plant of his, as it happens. Why, he had a headhunter looking for someone like me for nearly a year. I think he'll be amenable. On two conditions."

Livia was suddenly afraid again. "Yes?"

"One, you have to promise your grades won't suffer. I have a feeling that will be Mr. Lone's first objection, and I'll need to be able to assure him."

Livia didn't hesitate. "I promise."

"Second, however often it turns out to be, when you're on the mat, you're nowhere else. This is no strip-mall dojo. Sean and I train hard. It's a real commitment. And if we're going to train together, I need you to commit to it, too. There's no shame if that sounds like too much for you. But my time is valuable. So decide now. Don't disappoint me later."

Again, Livia didn't hesitate. "I won't disappoint you. I promise."

Malcolm nodded. "You know what? I have a feeling you won't." He opened the garage door. "Well, are you ready? I guess we can roll around for just the one day before we get Mr. Lone's permission for something longer term."

They went out to the garage. Livia had never seen anything like it. There were no cars inside. Instead, the floor was covered with a cushioned mat. At the periphery were various devices—leather-covered bags hung by chains from the ceiling; a thick wooden pole with sticks like arms and legs branching out from it; pulleys and weights and climbing ropes. Malcolm took a white uniform from a wall peg and handed it to Livia. "This one's clean," he said. "One of Sean's. It should fit you fine."

Livia hefted it. It was soft and surprisingly heavy. "What is it?"

"That's a jiu-jitsu gi. Sometimes we train without one, but a gi's the right way to start. There's a bathroom just inside. Why don't you change in there, Sean and I will get changed out here, and we'll get started. Sound good?"

Livia nodded, then raced off to the bathroom, ecstatic. Just before she closed the door, she heard Malcolm whisper, "Damn, son!" And Sean, his tone exasperated, whisper back, "Dad!"

She wasn't sure what it meant, but for some reason it made her smile.

28—THEN

That first day, Malcolm taught Livia the fundamental jiu-jitsu positions: mount, where you straddle your opponent's chest; guard, where you fight from your back and entangle your opponent with your legs; and hooks-in, where you get your legs around your opponent from behind. Everything about it clicked for her. Jiu-jitsu was like a language her body had always known how to speak—she had only needed to hear it.

She was terrified Mr. Lone wouldn't allow her to train. So when he came to her room the next night and asked what it was about "this jiu-jitsu thing," she was ready. She closed the textbook she was studying and sat up on her bed. Then, with planned nonchalance, she said, "The new kid, Sean, likes it. And I don't have any other friends."

She'd been at the school for over a semester now, and given Mr. Lone's concern with appearances, she knew he'd be worried people might find it strange that his adopted daughter had no friends—even if he himself would prefer it that way.

"Yes, his father told me. But it's about fighting, yes?"

This was the part that really worried her—that Mr. Lone would object to her training with Sean and Malcolm because he wouldn't want her to learn how to fight. But seeing the way he was looking at her now, she realized that despite his question, he didn't take the notion seriously. He towered over her. He would never be able to imagine the nervous little girl before him might find a way to protect herself.

Let alone hurt someone else in the process.

"I guess," she said. "But mostly I just want to have a friend."

There was a long pause. Livia tried not to let her anxiety show on her face. She didn't know what she would do if he said no. She couldn't imagine it.

Finally, he said, "All right. Sean's father was quite persuasive about the health benefits. And he wants his son to have a friend as much as I want you to."

Livia was so awash in joy and relief that his lie about wanting her to have a friend didn't even bother her. He didn't want her to have a friend. He just thought that on balance he would have to accept it. And it was interesting that Malcolm seemed to have talked more about the health aspects than about the fighting. Had he sensed Mr. Lone might not like the latter?

"I'm trusting Malcolm," Mr. Lone said. "Do you see how important trust is?"

Livia nodded. "Yes."

He glanced down the hallway, then back at her. "But there are different kinds of trust. I trust Malcolm as my employee. You might trust him as a teacher. But *our* trust is different. The way we know each other is different. Do I need to remind you that what we share with each other, we don't share with anyone else? Because no one would believe you if you tried to tell them about us. It's too special, no one else would even understand it. Not to mention it would be dangerous for Nason."

Livia no longer knew what to think about Nason. Maybe Mr. Lone knew where she was. Maybe he was lying. Either way, he wasn't going to tell her. So she tried not to think about it, pinning her hopes instead on Rick.

"I know," she said. "I don't tell anyone."

"You *won't* tell anyone."

She hated the way her English deteriorated when she talked to him. But she shook it off and said, "I won't tell."

He nodded. "Then you can do the jiu-jitsu. Right after school, and home no later than five thirty."

She suppressed the triumph she felt. "Yes, no later than five thirty. And Saturday and Sunday mornings, too." Anticipating his objection, she said, "And if my grades go down, I cut back. I *will* cut back"

"If your grades go down, you'll stop. I want to see straight A's, just like last semester."

"All right."

He looked at her suspiciously, as though he sensed a missing part, something she was hiding.

Mrs. Lone called from downstairs, "I'm heading to bridge club. Back in a few hours."

The front door closed. A flush crept into Mr. Lone's face. He glanced at the bathroom, then back to Livia.

She clenched her jaw and stood, then walked to the bathroom, his footsteps close behind her.

While it went on, she tried as always to think of something else, to project herself somewhere else. This time, she focused on how one day, she might use jiu-jitsu the way Sean had.

Of course, Sean had warned Eric. Had given him a chance. She would never do that. She would break the arm right away.

To start with.

29—NOW

For the rest of the day, while she worked at tracking down other potential victims of her Sea-Tac rapist, Livia kept tabs on Masnick's phone via the modified Gossamer. It showed up at Saltwater Park at Richmond Beach that very evening. She'd been right—Masnick might have been in love with Jardin, but that didn't mean he was faithful to her. She confirmed there were no other Hammerhead phones in the vicinity. Good. No backup meant he didn't suspect anything. No friends meant he wasn't planning a gang rape. No, Masnick just wanted to get to know his new neighbor a little better. And maybe get lucky afterward.

She used an alligator-clip sheath to secure the Vaari, her favorite fixed-blade knife, in the side pocket of a pair of cargo pants, slid the Glock into a bellyband holster, pulled on an oversized fleece, and rode out in the Jeep.

There were clouds overhead when she got there, but it was clear in the west, the sky streaked with pink, and as she walked down to the beach, the last of the sun was slipping below the horizon. A dozen or so people strolled at the water's edge, some of them with dogs, and the sounds of conversation and an occasional bark were mostly swallowed up by the vast openness of Puget Sound. She sat on a bench overlooking the scene, concealed the Glock beneath her thigh, and waited.

The pink in the sky was just past its peak and it was growing dark when Masnick came walking along the path to her left. He saw her and waved.

"Hey," he said as he got closer. "I was hoping I might run into you. Mind if I take a load off?"

"Please," she said, gesturing to the space next to her.

Masnick sat, then looked around. "Where's your pooch?"

She looked at him. "The truth is, Mike, there is no pooch."

He frowned. "No pooch? Why'd you tell me there was?"

"I guess that was a bit of what you might call subterfuge. To get you to meet me someplace private. I didn't think you'd want anyone to overhear what we have to discuss."

"What the hell are you talking about?"

"I'm talking about Jenny Jardin. You know, Weed Tyler's wife."

He blanched. "What the fuck is this?"

"Relax, Mike. I'm on your side. Assuming you're on mine."

"I'm not on anybody's side. I want to know what the fuck you want, Suzy or whatever the hell your name is."

"It's Livia. Livia Lone. Seattle PD." She pulled her badge from inside the fleece.

He glared at the badge for a moment, then stood and leaned in, towering over her. "You really think you can shake me down with some bullshit about someone's wife? You think anyone's going to believe your lying ass? I ought to face-fuck you sitting right here. Hell, call my bros, they'd love a taste, too. Put the hammer to you good."

She smiled, eased out the Glock, and pointed it at him. "I guess you could, Mike, but if you tried, I'd shoot you right through your cheating little heart. But hey, it's your blood. And I'm used to the paperwork. So knock yourself out."

He glanced at the Glock, then back to her. "You know what? I've got better things to do than listen to some whackjob bitch cop talking out her ass."

It wasn't a bad bluff. But she knew he was going to fold. She just had to show him who was holding the winning hand.

She pulled out a cheap Dictaphone she'd used to record the conversation. "Why don't you listen to this?" she said. "And then we'll figure out what to do about it."

She hit "Play." And watched as his eyes filled with rage.

30—THEN

Livia trained with Eric and Malcolm two hours a day, seven days a week. She couldn't get enough of jiu-jitsu. She borrowed books on the topic from Malcolm and studied them in her room, closing her eyes and mimicking the techniques depicted in the photographs inside, imagining herself using jiu-jitsu against Skull Face and Dirty Beard and Square Head, breaking their elbows and knees and necks. By the time spring semester was over, she was nearly as good as Sean—especially fighting from the guard, her favorite position, on her back with her legs around the attacker's torso. And she still had her straight A's.

The bullies left Sean and her alone now, though people sometimes teased them because they spent so much time together, saying they were "doing it," and laughing and making gross gestures when they would leave school together to go to Sean's house. As long as she had jiu-jitsu, Livia didn't care.

Rick had come to visit again—and he brought the photograph with him. The Thai police had questioned Livia's parents, who claimed they thought the girls were going to get jobs in Bangkok and denied taking any money for them. Rick promised that her parents didn't know where she was or how to find her, but also told her he could get word to them if she changed her mind. She knew he meant well. She also knew her mind would never change.

Rick had asked her again if everything was all right. The way he looked at her when he asked, the concern in his expression, made her sense he had suspicions about Mr. Lone. But Livia was afraid to tell him. She didn't know what would happen if she did. Maybe it would be bad for Nason. Maybe it would be bad in some other way. And besides, Mr. Lone was probably right—no one would believe her. They would just say she was having nightmares about her "ordeal" and attributing them to Mr. Lone, or something like that. Better to endure what happened in the bathroom, and not take chances.

Lying in bed when her studying was done, she would think about what Rick had told her, about how Weed Tyler's gang or whoever hired his gang had buyers in Llewellyn or farther east. Buyers. That explained the food and the blankets, and why they hadn't harmed the children. They'd whipped the Hmong boy, Kai, when he tried to escape, but they hadn't really harmed him, at least not as a product they planned to sell. And it was the same for her. What they had been making her do on the deck of the ship at night didn't leave visible marks. No one would know how they'd used her on the way to Portland.

But they *had* hurt Nason. Badly. Why? Why would they have harmed their own merchandise?

To punish you, she thought. *Because you attacked them. You cut Skull Face's eye.*

She covered her face and sobbed silently into her hands. *Please not that. Please.*

But what else could it be? Probably the men hadn't intended to harm Nason, only to use her, the way they had used Livia. But they had been drunk, and Livia had enraged them. It was her fault. What had happened to Nason had been her fault.

Most of the time, she could push that thought away. When she couldn't, it made her want to not be alive anymore. To stop eating, the way she'd considered on the boat.

But by the morning, the horror would have receded, and she would find a way to eat breakfast. She'd been a coward about so many things. To stop eating, to make herself die, when Nason might still need her would be beyond cowardice. It would be a crime.

She held on to jiu-jitsu like a drowning person clutching a life raft. She and Sean trained harder in the summer—four hours instead of two, and sometimes longer. Livia would go to his house after lunch, where they practiced together until Malcolm came home, and then they would train with him until it was nearly dark. Sometimes Malcolm asked if she wanted to stay for dinner. She did want to—very much—but she also knew Mr. Lone wouldn't like it. So she told them the Lones liked her to be home for dinner, and Malcolm didn't press.

Sometimes while Livia and Sean did drills, Malcolm punched and kicked the various leather bags, including a smaller one shaped like a teardrop that he punched really fast. Livia told Malcolm she wanted to learn those things, too. He showed her how to generate power, and how to hit with her elbows and knees because they were smaller and harder than hands and feet and could do more damage with less risk of injury. Livia overdid it at first, turning her skin raw and bloody. But the raw spots healed and then covered over with callouses, just as her fingers had from gripping and twisting the heavy cotton gi, and soon she could hit as long and hard as she wanted.

By the end of the summer, Livia could consistently beat Sean in free training. The first time it happened, Sean had been uncharacteristically sullen afterward. But maybe Malcolm had talked to him, because after that he was always gracious when she won. Sean was stronger, but Livia had become more technical—and, as Malcolm had frequently assured them both, sufficiently good technique could overcome strength.

"But if you want to keep getting better," he told them, "you have to start mixing it up with new opponents. I think this fall, you should both go out for the wrestling team. It'll be different than jiu-jitsu, but that's a good thing."

Livia was doubtful. "But . . . are there girls on the team?"

Malcolm shrugged. "Not that I know of. But that doesn't mean they're against the rules, right?"

Livia nodded. The idea made her nervous. Jiu-jitsu was so private. It was just the three of them, in Sean's and Malcolm's garage. If she wrestled, there would be a whole team. Matches. Audiences. People would notice her. And she didn't want to be noticed. It was safer not to be.

"Livia, you'd be a hundred-and-one-pounder," Malcolm went on. "And Sean, you'd be at a hundred-and-eight. You'd have to learn takedowns, different rules, new habits. But I could teach you the basics. I think even as freshmen, you could both make the high school team. Experience in wrestling would make your jiu-jitsu stronger."

That was all Livia needed to hear.

31—THEN

Malcolm was right: even though they were only freshmen, Livia and Sean both made the wrestling team. Sean was good, but Livia was better—undefeated at 101 pounds in the regular season, losing only to a stronger and more experienced senior in the semifinals of the state tournament, and placing third in the state overall. People stopped making fun of her, and somehow even the word "Lahu," which the bullies had originally used to taunt her, became a kind of trademark, with the Llewellyn fans in the bleachers chanting, "La-*hoo*! La-*hoo*!" to cheer Livia on when she took the mat.

Her growing popularity was unsettling. She was still shy. She was still afraid that no matter what she had, it could all be taken away in a sudden, horrible instant. And the secret of what she had been forced to do on the boat on the way to Portland, and what Mr. Lone was still making her do in his own house, made her feel ashamed and apart. She knew no one would understand it. And if anyone ever found out, they would treat her like something diseased and polluted. And the really horrible part was, she knew they would be right. She *was* polluted.

Tainted. And worse, a failure, a fraud, for not having protected Nason, and even more for having incited Skull Face and his men into hurting Nason so badly that her little bird's mind had just . . . flown away. The only way she could live with how loathsome she sometimes felt was to wall it all off and focus on school, jiu-jitsu, and wrestling. But if anyone ever learned the truth, that wall would crumble. And she could never, ever let that happen.

Most boys seemed intimidated by the wrestling—by a girl who regularly beat boys on the mat. But some didn't seem to mind, and began to ask her out on dates. She always told them she was too busy. Sometimes they asked if she was Sean's girlfriend. His stutter had faded away, like something he had outgrown, and nobody made fun of him anymore. She would tell them no, that wasn't it, she and Sean were just friends and training partners. Which was true. Although sometimes she would catch Sean looking at her in a way that made her wonder. The rude ones asked if she was "maybe into chicks." She didn't think she was. She wasn't into anyone. What she knew of sex was painful and humiliating and disgusting. She didn't know why people were so fascinated by it. The only thing she wanted more than for Mr. Lone to stop was to find Nason. She would have been happy to never go near sex for the rest of her life.

She was unbeaten again in the regular season of her sophomore year. There were articles about her in the newspaper, describing her as a "phenomenon." Reporters interviewed her at practice, always making sure to note how wonderful it was that the Lones had taken her in, and asking if she attributed at least some of her success to Mr. Lone's hardworking example. She said as little as possible, afraid of causing a problem if she were to say the wrong thing.

Mr. Lone sometimes came to her matches. She wished he wouldn't. It was disgusting to have him watching her do something she loved so much. And although she had grown increasingly confident that he would never see her as anything but a helpless little girl, she didn't think it was a good idea for him to watch her beating boys, even if they were just teenagers her own size and not tall, full-grown men like him.

In fact, not only did he seem unconcerned about her wrestling prowess, he seemed to take pleasure in it. And why not? People were eager to attribute her success to him. In one of her classes, they had learned the story of the Greek King Midas, who turned everything he touched to gold. Even though the story was about a curse, not a blessing, she thought that was how Mr. Lone liked to be perceived, as someone who turned everything to gold. His businesses; his money; and now, his wrestling phenomenon, straight-A, adopted Lahu girl. It was galling to have him bask in her reflected glory, but she refused to dwell on it, ignoring him as much as possible when she saw him in the stands. She had gotten good at feeling as little as possible when he did the bathroom thing, and it was easy to do so elsewhere, too.

Livia and Sean were the only Llewellyn wrestlers to make it to the states that year—Livia at 108, Sean at 122. Sean placed fourth. Livia finished second, pinned in the third round of the finals, the loss again to a senior. When Livia walked off the mat, furious at herself and near tears not just for losing, but at the horror of having been *pinned*, there was a cluster of reporters waiting to talk to her. She took a deep breath to pull herself together.

When the reporters and well-wishers were gone and the next match was underway, she walked to the corner of the gym, where she started stretching to warm down. She had seen Mr. Lone in the stands, but he rarely came over to talk to her at matches, having learned that she would ignore him. Malcolm had driven her and Sean to the tournament, and she saw them approaching now.

She bent at the waist and touched her toes, taking a moment to collect herself. Seeing Malcolm and Sean was making her feel emotional again.

When she was ready, she straightened. They had stopped a few feet away and were watching her respectfully. They didn't hug her. They knew that, off the mat, she didn't like to be touched.

"You were amazing," Sean said.

She didn't feel amazing. But she couldn't say that without implicitly putting down Sean—after all, he hadn't even made it to the finals. So she just said, "So were you."

"No, you were *really* amazing."

He was so nice, and so earnest, she couldn't help a little smile. "Thanks."

"Congratulations, girl," Malcolm said. "Thought we'd give you a minute with your adoring public before we bothered you."

That made her smile more.

"You need anything?" Sean said.

She realized she was thirsty. "Actually, I'd love a Gatorade."

"I'll get one from the concession stand. Dad, you want anything?"

Malcolm shook his head. "I'm good."

"Okay. Be right back."

Sean walked off. Malcolm watched him for a moment, then turned back to Livia. "How you feeling?" he said.

Livia shrugged. The way he was looking at her . . . she knew if she tried to speak, she would cry.

"You pissed at yourself because you lost?"

She nodded and felt her eyes fill up. "He pinned me," she whispered.

Malcolm squatted so he was looking up at her. "Girl," he said, and she was surprised by the thickness she heard in his voice. "I could not be prouder of you if you were my own daughter."

She tried to blink back the tears, but couldn't. "But I lost."

"No, you won. Every match of the entire season until that one. And that boy was a senior. Two extra years of experience. And a lot more upper-body strength. Now, the boys aren't getting any stronger. But your technique keeps getting better. Next year is your year. And the year after that. No one's going to be able to stop you. And no one's going to pin you again, that's for damn sure."

She wanted to believe him. It made her cry harder.

"I want you to know something," Malcolm said. "I'm only going to say it this one time, and not in front of Sean."

She wiped her eyes with the sleeve of her sweatshirt and looked at him, confused.

"You've been a good friend to my son. Best he's ever had. And it's not my place or my purpose to compare the two of you. I love you both."

Livia had heard him say that to Sean before, but never to her. Even her own parents had never said it to her—it wasn't the Lahu way. Of course, even if they had said it to her, she would know now it was a lie. But when Malcolm said it . . . it was confusing. She believed him, but didn't want to. It made her feel good and upset at the same time. Like his words were pulling hard at something she wanted to let go of, but couldn't.

"The thing is," he went on, "Sean is talented. Very talented. And disciplined, too."

"I know."

He shook his head. "But not like you. You are one in a million. The kind of athlete most coaches wait their whole lives for, and never actually get." He looked down for a moment, then back to her. "Sean will probably compete in college. He hasn't decided yet. If he does, he'll be good. And I'll support him every way I can."

She didn't understand what he was trying to tell her. "I know," she said again.

His gaze was intense, almost fierce. "But you could be better than good, Livia. Your talent could take you as far as you want to go. Anywhere. All the way. I don't know if you know that. But I want you to know it. Maybe you're not hearing it from anyone else, and that would be a shame. Because sometimes we need to hear it from someone else.

So you're hearing it from me, okay? However far you want to go, your talent is your ticket. And if you don't believe that, you're making the worst mistake I can imagine."

She started crying again. She so wanted to believe him. That, despite everything else, there was something special about her, something worthwhile.

"You believe what I'm telling you?" he said.

She nodded uncertainly.

"Have I ever told you anything that turned out to be untrue?"

She shook her head.

"I want to hear you say it."

She cleared her throat and looked at him. "I believe you."

"Good. But there's something more important than that."

She looked at him. "What?"

He pointed at her. "You believe in yourself. No matter what. You understand me? You believe in yourself. And there is nothing that is ever going to stop you."

She wanted to thank him, but her throat had closed up and the words wouldn't come. All she could do was nod. But it seemed that was enough. Malcolm took one of her hands in both of his and squeezed it. She almost drew back out of habit, but didn't. It was okay.

"You're going to be fine, girl. You got people who care about you."

She saw Sean walking over. She eased her hand away and wiped her face.

"Hey," Sean said, and the concern she saw in his eyes threatened to bring on another bout of tears.

Sean handed her the Gatorade. She unscrewed the top, put the bottle to her lips, tilted her head up, closed her eyes, and drank. By the time she had chugged half of it, she was in control of herself again. She took a deep breath and said, "Thanks."

Sean shook his head. "You're going to win the whole thing next year, Livia. State champion for sure."

She managed a smile. "You sound like your dad," she said, and they all laughed.

On the way home, sitting in the back of Malcolm's car, she wondered whether she could really be as good as Malcolm had said. She didn't think he was lying. But at the same time . . . there must be something wrong with her. Something that had made so many bad things happen. To herself, and even more to Nason. She could forget it when she was training, and when she was competing. Sometimes when she was studying. And when she slept, if she wasn't having bad dreams.

But it never really went away. In the end, it was always there. And she knew it always would be.

32—THEN

A cheerleader named Katy was having a party at her house after the state tournament, and had asked Livia and Sean to be there. Sean begged Livia to come with him, and though she didn't really want to go, Livia had never forgotten her shame at not having helped Sean when Eric and his buddies had him surrounded and outnumbered. Sean was her friend—her only friend. If he wanted her at the stupid party, she would go.

But the party was a pleasant surprise. Everyone was nice to Livia, congratulating her, saying they were so proud of her, telling her they were sure she was going to be state champion next year. Even Eric the bully, a junior now, came over and told her he was sorry he had been "such a dick" to her when she'd first come to Llewellyn. She told him not to worry about it, but the truth was, his apology meant nothing to her. In her mind, behavior was the truth, not words.

There was a bowl of punch at the party, and after drinking a cup, Livia felt strange—light, relaxed, happy. Everything seemed so funny and good. She was going to have another cup, but Sean told her to be careful because the punch was "spiked."

"Spiked?" she asked him.

"Someone put vodka in it. You can't really taste it because of the fruit juice, but it's in there." He smiled. "I had some, too."

Livia was confused. Was this how alcohol made you feel? But it was a nice feeling, not at all what she would have expected. She thought alcohol could only make people cruel and violent and disgusting.

"Maybe . . . it's more the person than the alcohol?" she said aloud.

Sean laughed. "What?"

She realized it must have sounded weird and felt her face get hot. "Nothing."

He looked at her more closely. "I think you're a little drunk."

Her face got hotter. "Maybe."

"It's nice. I don't think I've ever seen you laugh as much as you have tonight."

She realized that was true. She didn't laugh much. She had when she was little, before the white van had pulled up, before everything had happened. Before she'd lost Nason. She was suddenly ashamed.

Sean must have sensed the change in her mood, because he said, "I'm sorry. I just meant . . . I don't know. I like when you're happy. Really like it."

"I should go," she said.

"I'm sorry," he said again.

She shook her head. "It's not you. It's nothing."

"Can I walk you home?"

She wasn't sure she wanted company, not even Sean's. But she knew her sudden mood shift had worried him. She didn't want him to think it was his fault.

There was an elementary school in the Lones' neighborhood, about a half mile from the house. Sean sometimes walked her home after they trained in his garage, but Livia didn't like him coming all the way to the house, and this was where he ordinarily turned back. But tonight, for some reason, they wound up sitting on the swings behind the school, just drifting back and forth a few inches, the metal chains squeaking softly, a full moon shining brightly overhead. It wasn't terribly cold for March in Llewellyn, and their hats were in their pockets, their coats unzipped. Livia closed her eyes, liking the slight wind on her cheeks, the smell of the night air, the feeling of being bathed in moonlight.

She sensed Sean was looking at her, but didn't open her eyes. After a moment, she heard him say, "I'm sorry if I . . . if I said the wrong thing before."

It made her sad that he thought it was his fault. But there was no way to explain. So she only said, "I'm sorry I don't laugh more."

"You laugh enough."

She laughed, because that was so untrue.

"See?" he said, and she laughed some more. It felt good to laugh. Then she thought of Nason again, and told herself she shouldn't be laughing.

"Can I tell you something that's always bothered me?" she said. It helped that they were side by side on the swings, that she didn't have to look at him while she talked.

"You can tell me anything."

She sighed. "That first time I saw you. When you put the arm bar on Eric. Remember?"

He laughed. "You think I'd forget that?"

No, of course he wouldn't forget it. It was a dumb thing to say. She almost changed her mind, but not saying anything felt too much like cowardice, and it was cowardice she needed to confess to.

"I should have helped you. I mean, you didn't need my help, but I didn't know that. I was just . . . afraid."

"That's okay. I mean . . . I would have been afraid, too."

"They used to bully me, too. And for a second, when I saw them bullying you . . . I was glad. Because it wasn't me." She glanced at him. "I'm sorry."

For a moment, there was only the creak of the swing chains. Then he said, "Has that really been bothering you this whole time?"

She wanted to look at him again, but couldn't. "I'm sorry."

"It's okay. You don't have to be sorry. You didn't even know me. I mean, you'd help me now, right?"

She looked at him and said fiercely, "Yes."

He smiled. "I mean, not that I'd need it. Even if I only placed fourth today and you came in second."

She laughed. It really was so good to laugh. It made her sad that she couldn't seem to do it more.

They were quiet again. Then Sean said, "Can I ask you something?"

The gentle movement of the swing, back and forth, was pleasant. Calming. She looked at him and nodded.

"Everyone at school thinks your parents died, and that's why the Lones adopted you."

She turned her head and looked at the trees. They were pretty in the moonlight, all silver and black.

"But my dad . . . he was stationed in Southeast Asia, and he said your parents might have sold you. Is that true?"

She'd wondered from time to time how much he knew, how much people speculated. She supposed it didn't matter now. And she didn't want to lie to Sean the way she had to the police.

She kept her eyes on the trees. "Not just me. My sister."

"Where's your sister now?" she heard him say.

"I don't know."

"I'm so sorry, Livia."

She nodded and silently said *Nason*. The name felt odd in her mouth—duller, somehow, disconnected. The alcohol, she supposed.

They were quiet again for a moment. Then Sean said, "My mother . . . she left us when I was seven."

She glanced at him. "That's terrible."

"There was a guy she knew, in Rio. She was already seeing him before we moved back to the States. I guess she missed him more than she wanted to be with my dad. Or with me."

"Rio . . . but I thought she was Japanese. Uenoyama, right?"

"There are a lot of ethnic Japanese in Brazil. She didn't have brothers or sisters, so my dad told her parents we'd use Uenoyama for me, to carry on their family name. I wanted to change it when she left us, but my dad told me not to. He doesn't want me to hate her. Or, I guess, forget her. Or something. I think he still loves her. I mean, he hasn't had any girlfriends or anything."

"You don't . . . she's not even in touch with you?"

"She left us a note. That was it for a long time. Then she tried calling, but I wouldn't talk to her. Now she sends me a card when it's my birthday. I don't open them. I just throw them away."

They were quiet again. Then he said, "It messed me up for a while. I had a lot of anxiety. I lost weight, and then I started stuttering. That's when my dad got really serious about the jiu-jitsu. I mean, come on, half-black, half-Asian, and a stutter? He was worried I'd get the shit beaten out of me every other day. And he was right."

Even though his story was sad, she smiled. "I really like your dad."

"Me, too. And he really likes you. He helped me with the bullies, but . . . I didn't have any friends. Before you, I mean."

"I didn't have any before you."

"But now you're really popular."

"Please."

"You are. Can't you tell? Everyone loves you."

"They don't know me."

"Do I know you?"

She looked at him. His face was so earnest, it made her sad. "I don't think anyone really knows me."

"I want to."

She felt confused. Part of her liked what he was saying. And wanted to hear him say more. Even wanted to respond. But it also made her afraid.

"I should go," she said. She let her heels drag along in the dirt, and the swing came to a stop. She stood and turned to him, looking at the ground, wanting to say goodbye, unsure of why she wasn't.

Sean got off the swing and faced her. He reached out and touched her shoulder. Which was strange, because he never touched her off the mat. No one did. But for some reason, it didn't bother her. *The alcohol*, she thought again.

She realized he was touching her . . . differently. So gently, just her shoulder. She looked at him, then down again, confused. His hand came up, and the back of his fingers brushed her hair, her cheek.

"Livia," he said, and it was almost a whisper. He started to lean closer.

She shook her head. "I . . . I have to go."

She turned and ran toward the Lones' house. She didn't want Sean to see her cry.

33—THEN

She had just changed into sweats and gotten into bed when the door to her bedroom opened. Mr. Lone, of course. She sat up, her heart pounding in anxiety and disgust. What was he doing? He never did the bathroom thing late at night—only when Mrs. Lone was out of the house. Where was she?

He stood in the doorway, wearing a robe over his pajamas, watching her. "You're back late," he said.

"There was a party."

"Ah, a party." He stepped inside the room, closing the door behind him. He looked at her. "Well? Was the party fun?"

"It was okay."

"I didn't know you liked parties."

"I—I don't like them. Sean wanted to go."

"Ah, Sean. Your friend."

She didn't know what to say to that. If he was here for the bathroom, she wanted to just get it over with.

He sniffed. "Is that alcohol I smell?"

"No," she said, without thinking.

"Don't lie to me, Livia," he said, his voice louder.

"I—someone put something in the punch. I didn't know."

"Oh, but you know now?"

"I didn't know until after I drank."

"My God, you're not even sixteen, and you're drinking *alcohol*? In my house?"

"It wasn't in your house—"

"That's hardly the point. The point is, it's illegal, Livia. You committed a crime. And you're my daughter. I'm responsible for you. Does that not mean anything to you?"

She'd been feeling so many things earlier in the day. When Malcolm told her he loved her. When people were congratulating her at the party. When she and Sean had talked in the playground, about things they'd never talked about before. When he had touched her shoulder, and her hair, and her cheek, and started to lean closer.

But it was all being smashed now, broken apart, taken from her.

Mr. Lone walked over. He stopped at the edge of the bed. She could hear his breathing. And see the bulge under his robe.

"I guess you're old enough for almost anything now, Livia. Is that it? Maybe I just haven't appreciated that. That you're old enough."

"Please," she said, and hated herself for it.

His breathing was getting louder. He reached for her hand, and placed it on the bulge.

She tried to satisfy him with just her hand. But it wasn't enough. He made her do the other thing, too, the thing Skull Face and the others had made her do, the thing with her mouth.

She managed not to cry. But all she could think about was that Sean had wanted to kiss her. And she'd run away. Run away to this instead.

34—NOW

When the recording ended, Masnick's face had turned so white that Livia wasn't sure whether he was going to cry, or attack her. To help him make the right choice, she kept the Glock on him and gestured to the bench. "Why don't you sit down, Mike?"

He shook his head. "I got nothing to say to you."

She sighed. "Don't you think we're a little past that? I told you. I'm on your side."

He glanced at the Glock. "You always point a gun at a guy when you're on his side?"

She smiled. "Only when I'm not sure if he's on mine."

He hesitated, then sat, watching her, saying nothing.

She lowered the Glock a fraction. "Look, we both know what's going on. Weed gets out in less than a week. And that's it for you and Jenny. And 'that's it' is the best case. 'That's it' assumes no one ever finds out. Because if anyone were to find out? About a Hammerhead shacking up with a brother's wife, and while the brother was in prison, no less, on a fall he took for the gang? Well, shit, we both know the Hammerhead penalty for betrayal, Mike. You guys use hammers. Starting at the feet, and working your way up. It's not a good way to die."

Livia could hear his breath whistling in and out of his nostrils. He looked so scared, she realized he wasn't going to be able to think clearly. And while sometimes that was a good thing, this time, fear might be counterproductive. Because fear might prevent him from seeing that although she was threatening him, she was also his only hope.

"But here's the good news," she said. "I want to take Weed down."

He blinked. That hadn't been what he was expecting.

"Yeah, that's right," she went on. "I'm not interested in you. I'm not interested in Hammerhead. This is strictly between me and Weed. Give me what I need. And all your problems are solved."

He squinted at her. "You expect me to betray a brother?"

"I expect you to protect yourself. And Jenny. What do you think Weed will do to her?"

He laughed. "Yeah, there's just one little problem with your 'Hey, Mike, I'm your friend, just here to solve all your problems' bullshit."

"What's that?"

"The only cunt who's threatening to make any of this bad shit happen is you."

She nodded as though considering. In fact, she'd been ready for that reaction. She shrugged. And tossed him the Dictaphone.

He flinched—obviously, it was the Glock he'd been focused on. But he caught it smoothly enough.

"It's yours," she said. "I don't have a copy." He'd know not to believe that, but it didn't matter, either.

He looked at the Dictaphone, then back at her. "What's your point?"

"My point is that my little recording isn't the only threat. If I could find out, so could someone else. And regardless, Weed is still coming home to his wife and daughter. And when he does, no matter what else happens, you and Jenny . . . that's over."

"Oh, and you want to help me with that."

"I don't want to help you with anything, any more than you want to help me. You want Weed out of your life. I want something I can use against him. That's all this is about."

He scratched his head and said, "Look, I'd help you if I could. But I don't know anything. Weed's been in prison. I mean, he's practically clean now."

She chuckled. "You trying to tell me Hammerhead doesn't have something sweet and moneymaking all set up for him when he gets out? After he does sixteen years for the gang? Come on."

There was a pause. She was pretty sure she had him. Just one more nudge.

"Mike. I know you told Jenny you'd think of something. But there's nothing else. This is it. This is your chance. Don't blow it."

There was another pause, longer this time. She let the silence do its work.

He looked at her. "I give you something you can use, and that's the end of this? No more recordings, no more threats, no more bullshit?"

"Yes."

"I have your word on that?"

"Yes."

He leaned closer. "Good. Then you have my word, too. And my word is, if you fuck me on this, Livia, then I better be dead at the end of it. Because if I'm not, I'll find you. And if you think being a cop will protect you, you don't know me. And if you think what Hammerhead does for betrayal is bad, I swear, by the time I'm done with you, you'll be begging for just a nice little hammer. Begging. So you better know what the fuck you're getting into if you and I make this little deal of ours."

She looked at him, letting him see she respected the threat, but that she wasn't afraid of it, either.

"Tell me," she said.

35—THEN

Livia's junior year went by in a blur. Neither she nor Sean ever mentioned what they had talked about in the playground that moonlit night, or what had almost happened.

Livia's focus on school, jiu-jitsu, and wrestling was more intense than ever. Even Malcolm grew concerned about her dedication, telling her it was important to throttle back sometimes, to find some balance. She knew he meant well. But he didn't know what she was enduring in the Lone house. He didn't know the only way she could push it all away was to obsess about the things she cared about, the things she could control.

She wondered if Rick knew, though. He visited once during the summer and then again in the fall. Both times, he seemed to go out of his way to find a moment alone with Livia, a moment in which he asked her how she was, how everything was going, was everything okay. The way he looked at her, the tone of his voice, always made her feel like he sensed something, but wasn't sure what. Maybe it was too hard for him to face because it was his brother-in-law, his family. Maybe he couldn't fully accept what was happening to Livia because if he did, he would have had to accept that his sister, Mrs. Lone, knew what was happening, too, and did nothing.

Livia wasn't certain Mrs. Lone knew, of course. But over time, she had decided that for the woman not to see, she must have been willfully closing her eyes. The bridge club meetings were just too convenient. And besides, Mr. Lone had started coming to Livia's room even when Mrs. Lone was home, typically at night, presumably after Mrs. Lone was asleep. But would he really have taken the risk if he hadn't known Mrs. Lone already knew . . . and that she was unwilling to do or say anything about it?

Livia did sometimes consider confiding in Rick. Or in Malcolm, who also periodically asked how things were in the Lone house, how they were treating her, in a way that made her feel he might suspect. But she was afraid to trust anyone, even Rick or Malcolm. She no longer really believed Mr. Lone knew anything about Nason, even though she continued to cling to that hope. But telling Rick . . . who knew what might happen? And if she told Malcolm, wouldn't it put his job at risk? And that was assuming anyone else would even believe her story. Probably they wouldn't. Just as Mrs. Lone averted her eyes because she didn't want to know, so many people were in thrall to Mr. Lone and his brother, who together were responsible for the prosperity of the entire town. They'd all believe the traumatized little Lahu girl was lying or delusional rather than face the truth—that their local deity was a monster.

Besides, next year she would graduate. She would be eighteen, and could go anywhere, do anything. She thought she knew what she wanted, too: to be a cop, like Rick. She would carry a gun. She would find the monsters and put them in prison. Or maybe even shoot them. She would protect people like herself, people like Nason, from people like Skull Face and Mr. Lone. She would move to Portland, where

Nason had disappeared, and keep looking for her there. Be a cop during the day and maybe go to college at night. She hadn't told anyone—she was afraid if she didn't keep her plans secret, Mr. Lone would do something to spoil them—but she was pretty sure this was the right path for her. All she had to do was endure Mr. Lone for one more year, and she would be free.

Senator Lone continued his visits. In a way, he was even creepier than his brother. Partly, it was the widely spaced eyes, staring in slightly different directions. Partly it was his legislative aide, Matthias Redcroft. Whatever Redcroft did for the senator, it wasn't just legislation. The way he was constantly an arm's length away, gazing at the senator worshipfully while at the same time coldly observing his interactions . . . something about him seemed sick to Livia, though she could see nothing wrong with his body. When the senator visited, she did her best to stay away from both of them, but Redcroft especially.

Malcolm had been right about the year being hers—Livia went undefeated in the regular wrestling season, after which she crushed every one of her opponents in postseason competition, winning her first state championship by pinning her opponent in the first round of the finals. When the referee raised her arm in victory, she had never felt so filled with happiness. For just that instant, there was nothing else—no Skull Face, no Mr. Lone, not even Nason.

And then, as she walked off the mat and saw Malcolm and Sean waiting for her, their faces beaming with joy and pride, she felt something well up that she couldn't stop. They both put their arms around her and hugged her while she cried uncontrollably, and somehow it was okay that they were touching her off the mat, it didn't feel wrong or make her flinch at the other, horrible ways she had been touched, and the suddenness, the shock, of how good it felt to be hugged by her best friend and her jiu-jitsu teacher made her cry harder. She hugged them back, clutching them, sobbing, afraid if she let them go something could tear them away from her.

When she finally managed to disengage, she saw that Malcolm's eyes were wet, too, and so were Sean's. She laughed delightedly at the sight of it.

Malcolm shook his head as though in wonder. "Did I tell you, girl?" he said. "Did I tell you this was your year?"

She laughed again and wiped her face. It didn't help, though. She was still crying.

Sean was wearing a huge grin. "Livia, you were amazing! Like a hurricane! I think I'm lucky we're in different weight classes."

She felt a little guilty for getting all the attention. "You were amazing, too."

He shrugged. "Third place."

"Come on, one-twenty-nine is a tougher division. Next year we'll both be first." She glanced at Malcolm and smiled. "Ask your dad, he's never wrong."

Malcolm smiled back. "She's right, tiger. The other top three in your weight class were all seniors. A year of experience is huge. Next year they'll all be at college, and the experienced senior is going to be you."

The three of them drove back to Llewellyn in Malcolm's car. Livia couldn't stop smiling. Winning the state tournament had been the best night of her life. And she was imagining a way it might get even better.

36—THEN

Malcolm dropped her off at the Lones' house. Katy was throwing another party, like the year before. Livia wondered whether Sean would walk her home again after. Whether he might try to kiss her again. She'd been thinking about that a lot lately. She thought she wanted him to. She wanted to know what it was like to kiss someone. And she wanted it to be Sean. The way he'd touched her the year before . . . it had been so gentle, so tentative, it hadn't bothered her. When she looked back on it now, she thought Sean touching her like that had actually been quite lovely. She wanted him to do it again. To look at her, and whisper her name the way he had. To lean in the way he had. *Yes*, she thought, smiling. *Please, that.*

She had just finished showering and dressing, and was combing her wet hair in front of the mirror in her bedroom, when the door opened. She turned and saw Mr. Lone. She hadn't been expecting that—Mrs. Lone was home, and it was too early for one of his night visits.

No, she thought. *Not now. Not tonight.*

"Congratulations," he said, one hand resting on the doorjamb, the other holding a drink. His tie was loosened, his suit jacket open.

He took a sip from the glass. "I would have said so at the tournament, but you seem not to like talking with me at your wrestling functions."

She surprised herself by thinking, *Yeah, no shit.* Ordinarily, she just endured him. Even in her mind, she didn't argue. She didn't talk back.

"Why is that, Livia? Are you ashamed of me?"

She glanced down. "I'm going to a party," she heard herself say. "I want you to leave me alone."

If her thoughts were surprising, the words outright stunned her. Who had just said that?

He stepped into the room and closed the door. "What did you say?"

She felt the fear rising up, trying to assert itself. "Leave me alone."

"I don't even know what that means. Leave you alone? You're in my house."

Her heart began to pound. But not in fear. In anger. Her fear had always been stronger than her anger. But this time felt different. This time, the anger felt like something alive, dangerous, uncoiling inside her. A snake. A *dragon*.

"I saved your life, Livia," he said, his voice rising. "Made you my daughter. And a daughter has obligations to her father. That's the way God made the world. You're lucky I haven't demanded more of you. I could have. Until you're married, your body is my right. Do you understand me?"

Some distant part of her realized this was the way he always went about it. Every time he did something worse to her, he worked himself into a tirade first. Maybe he needed to do that, to justify what he wanted from her. It seemed he was going to do it now.

"I've been patient with you," he went on. "Respectful. I waited, until I thought you were old enough for different experiences. Until I thought you were ready. Well, maybe I've been overly solicitous. Maybe you were ready before I thought. Maybe you're ready now."

She could feel the dragon unfurling its wings, opening its claws. "Leave me alone," she said again, still not looking at him.

He placed his drink on the bureau and came closer, stopping in front of her and leaning down until his face was just a few inches from hers. "You little ingrate. After everything I've done for you? I found your sister for you. Do you ever want to see her again? Do you ever want to see Nason?"

Nason's name in his mouth was suddenly sickening. An atrocity. She looked up at him, her lips drawing back. "You're a liar," she said, her voice nearly a whisper.

His face darkened. "That's enough. Take off your clothes. Get on the bed."

Her breath felt hot now, like smoke coming from a fire burning in her lungs. "No."

For a second, she saw complete shock in his eyes. Then he grabbed her by the shoulders and shook her. "You will obey me!" he shouted.

Without thinking, she dropped back with one foot, forcing him to straighten his arms, and shot her hands up under his elbows, breaking his grip. Then she stepped in and shoved him in the ribs, harder than she had ever shoved anything in her life. He stumbled back and almost fell, but hit the wall and recovered his balance.

"Get out," she said, her voice alien, low and dangerous and hot with rage. The dragon's voice.

"Bitch!" he shouted, and charged her. She couldn't get out of the way in time, and he slammed into her and knocked her back. Her head hit the edge of her desk and there was a huge flash of white light. Then everything went away.

She felt a throbbing in her head, and then the room came swimming back into focus. Her sweater was pushed up and her pants and panties were off. She was on the floor looking up at him, his knee digging into her bare stomach. He ripped loose his belt.

"Selfish little bitch," he said, panting. "Tonight you pay me what I'm due. All of it. Every last bit."

The throbbing in her head stopped. She felt no fear. It was gone, incinerated by molten rage. A red haze crept into her vision. The dragon that had merely been stirring was fully awake now. It had taken control of her. It *was* her.

She shoved his knee off her, twisted, and scooted her hips out to the left. Before he could react, she grabbed his lapels and reversed directions, shooting her right knee past his body, working her foot through, and wrapping her legs around his back. The guard. Her favorite.

For one second, he looked almost happy. And why not? He was between her naked legs. What he'd always wanted. He tried to get his pants open, but she pulled him forward so he couldn't. Then his expression changed to anger as he realized he wasn't in control. She was.

He straightened and tried to shake loose, but couldn't. He straightened more, lifting her, then slammed her down against the floor. She saw stars. His height gave him leverage, and his anger was giving him strength. He slammed her again. This time, it knocked some of the wind out of her. He went to do it a third time.

She jerked open his right lapel with her left hand and slipped the fingers of her right hand inside it, high up, alongside his neck. He slammed her down, and as his head rocked forward with the impact, she reached behind his neck with her left hand and got her thumb inside the left side of his lapel, near the back of the collar. She whipped her left arm around his head, dropped her elbows close to her body, and squeezed, the bones at the outer edge of her forearms crushing the sides of his neck like the tongs of a giant walnut cracker. A cross-collar choke, one of the first moves Malcolm had taught her.

His face reddened and veins stood out under his scalp. He tried to break loose and she squeezed tighter with her legs. He tried to push himself up off the floor, and she uncrossed her ankles and kicked out one of his legs. He managed to get his hands on the floor and push himself up, and she hung on, squeezing harder, crying now, screaming, a lifetime of fear and grief and hatred and rage surging up through her arms and out her mouth. His eyes bulged more and his tongue stuck out and a sound came from his throat—a rattling, gurgling, breaking sound. She screamed louder and squeezed harder, looking into his dying, terrified eyes, imagining herself squeezing so hard her arms would go through his neck and cut his entire head off. Harder. *Harder.* She couldn't have stopped if she'd wanted to. And she didn't want to. Stopping was the last thing she wanted.

All at once, his struggles faded. His eyes rolled up, his tongue flopped loose, and his body went limp on top of her. She hung on, sobbing, squeezing.

She wasn't sure how much time went by. A few seconds. A few minutes. Then the door opened. Livia looked up and saw Mrs. Lone, her mouth hanging open in shock. She must have heard the commotion, and become so concerned she couldn't ignore it. Her face contorted. And then she screamed.

Livia squirmed loose from under Mr. Lone's limp form and got to her feet, panting.

"What have you done?" Mrs. Lone screamed, her eyes wide and horrified. "You little whore, what have you done?"

The red haze was fading now, colors returning to normal. But Livia's breath still felt as hot as smoke.

"You . . . you killed him! You filthy little slut, you whore, you killed him!"

Livia pulled down her sweater and glanced at him. He was lying facedown, his arms at his sides, not moving. Had she killed him? She hadn't meant to. Or had she? She hadn't been thinking. Something had just . . . switched on. Taken control.

"I'm calling the police," Mrs. Lone said. "Right now." She turned to go.

"Yes, call them. I want to tell them how your husband has been abusing me since I was thirteen. And how you knew all about it."

Mrs. Lone stopped and turned back to her. Her eyes narrowed to slits. "You filthy, lying whore," she hissed.

"If you didn't know, why do you keep calling me a whore?"

For a long moment, Mrs. Lone stood frozen. Then she made a hitching, choking sound, as though she was going to vomit, and began to cry.

"You killed him!" she sobbed.

A strange coldness came over Livia. The dragon was suddenly gone, replaced by a feeling of perfect clarity. She picked up her panties and pulled them on, then her pants.

"No one has to know," she said. And it was true. She was amazed at how quickly and clearly she was able to see it, see all of it. Almost as though some part of her had realized tonight might happen, and had been prepared for it. "No one has to know anything."

Mrs. Lone raised her hands to the sides of her head. "What are you talking about? My husband is dead! You killed him!"

"No. We think he had a heart attack. He came to my room to congratulate me for winning the tournament, and then he collapsed."

Mrs. Lone stared at her mutely.

"If you tell anyone I killed him," Livia said, "I'll tell them why. It's that simple."

"No one's going to believe you, you lying piece of refugee trash!"

"I don't know. Why would I have killed my great benefactor? For the rest of your life, they'll always look at you, and wonder whether I was telling the truth. And how it could be that you didn't know."

Mrs. Lone made the vomiting sound again, but otherwise said nothing.

"Call nine-one-one. Tell them you heard me yell. He was lying on the floor when you got to my room. I told you he collapsed. You tried to revive him. CPR. But you were panicked and you didn't know how. You were hitting him, trying to wake him up. That's why he has marks on his neck."

"They'll do an autopsy. They'll know it's a lie."

Livia realized on some level that the woman was listening to her, her objections now only practical ones, as though she wanted to be persuaded and just needed to be presented with a way.

"You know the police. They'll listen to you. They were all tied up with him, I could see that, his friend Chief Emmanuel especially. Chief Emmanuel won't want a scandal any more than you do. I think he knew more about your husband than you'd like. I think a lot of people knew, like you did, and won't want anyone to know they knew. If you tell the police the right story, they won't investigate."

Mrs. Lone shook her head. "I won't be part of this. I'll see you in jail first."

"Maybe. But I'll be out in two years, when I'm eighteen." She looked into Mrs. Lone's eyes, letting her feel the truth of it. "And I know where you live."

Mrs. Lone shook her head. "I can't live with this. I can't."

"You won't have to. After you call nine-one-one, call your brother. Rick. You're upset now over the loss of your husband. You don't want me in your house. You never did. You want Rick to take me in, just for the rest of this year and for my senior year, while you deal privately with your loss. Do that, and you'll never hear from me again. Don't do it, and the whole town will know your husband was nothing but a sick, disgusting child molester."

Mrs. Lone brushed away tears. "Don't you talk about him that way, you tramp. He had his flaws, his demons. But he was a great man."

"It's not me talking about him you have to worry about. It's the town. And when they learn what he really was, I think you'll be hearing more about his flaws than his greatness."

"How dare you, you—"

"But you can prevent that. Make the call. You think he had a heart attack. Get his belt back on him, unless you want people to ask why it was off. And then call Rick."

"My brother will never take you in."

"You better hope he does. Because if he doesn't, someone else will. Someone in Llewellyn. I'm a brave little refugee girl who's suffered such a terrible ordeal, remember? And if I stay in Llewellyn, you'll never be rid of me. Ever."

37—THEN

Paramedics came to the house and tried to revive Mr. Lone. They couldn't. They took him to the hospital, where he was pronounced dead.

Mrs. Lone told the right story. Chief Emmanuel asked Livia some questions, and she corroborated Mrs. Lone's version. She could tell the man had doubts. She could also tell he didn't want to indulge them. Because how could the chief of police, no less, have been so close to a man like Mr. Lone, and not known what his friend was up to? Better to avoid those issues entirely.

The next morning there were a lot of visitors. The Lones' sons. Senator Lone and his aide, Matthias Redcroft. People from Mr. Lone's businesses. And Rick, who had driven all the way from Portland.

Livia stayed in her room and could hear them all talking, though she couldn't make out the words. She was amazed at how good she felt. She knew things might not go well. There could still be an investigation. Maybe Mrs. Lone would change her mind and tell. Probably not, but maybe.

But if that happened, Livia would deal with it. She almost didn't care. Compared to the satisfaction, the . . . excitement of killing Mr.

Lone, what might happen next seemed almost irrelevant. She felt like something had changed in her. Like she had somehow become . . . more herself again. Or who she was meant to be.

She kept imagining it, over and over. The way he'd shouted at her. What he told her he was going to do to her. The momentary satisfaction on his face when he was between her naked legs, pressed against her, rubbing against her. And then how he realized he was wrong. That she was in control, not him. That she was the one who could do anything she wanted, no matter how he tried to stop her. And that what she wanted was to make him die. Thinking about it, remembering it, made her feel a strange . . . tingling she didn't recognize or understand. But she loved the way it made her feel. She loved thinking about it.

After a few hours, there was a knock on her door. Even if he hadn't been dead, Livia would have known it couldn't be Mr. Lone. He never knocked.

She got off the bed and opened the door. It was Rick. Just Rick.

"Hey," he said. He looked at her closely, his expression concerned. "How are you doing?"

"I'm okay." She tried not to be nervous, not to think about how much might hinge on what he said next.

"I'm sorry about Fred."

She wondered how sorry he really was. Maybe sorry for his sister. "It's okay."

"Dotty . . . this is a big shock for her. A lot to handle. I think it's going to take some time to put the pieces back together, you know?"

Livia nodded. "She told me."

He tilted his head slightly, as though confused or flustered. "She did? Oh. Okay."

They were both quiet for a moment. Then he said, "Dotty told me you were pretty upset. That you might benefit from . . . a change of pace."

"Yes."

Again, he looked a little flustered. Maybe he was expecting Livia to not know what was coming, to be more reluctant. He was trying to process what it meant that she seemed to know what was going on. And to welcome it.

"So . . . Dotty and I wondered whether it might be better for you to finish up high school in Portland. You know, away from all this . . . tragedy. I mean, you've already been through a lot. But we just want what's best for you. Would you want that, Livia? To live with me in Portland?"

"Yes. Please that."

He nodded slowly, as though putting together pieces he hadn't previously recognized were there. "It wouldn't be like this, you know. Just a small apartment. I mean, there's an extra room I use as an office now, I could clear that out, move my gear to the kitchen, and the office would be your bedroom. It's small, but comfortable. But it's nothing like my sister's house."

"It sounds nice."

"And I don't know much about . . . about raising a teenager. You know I've never had kids."

She smiled at his awkwardness and thought of the time he had given her coffee with the milk and turbinado sugar. "I think you know more than you realize."

He chuckled and rubbed the back of his neck. "Well, let's hope so, right?" He looked at her. "Are you really up for this, Livia?"

"If you are."

There was a pause. Then he held out his hand. She shook it.

"The funeral's tomorrow," he said. "Dotty wanted to get it over with."

That was good to hear. It meant Mrs. Lone was intent on getting the body in the ground before anyone outside Mr. Lone's cohorts thought to look at it too closely.

"The truth is," Rick went on, "I'm glad. This isn't a great week for me to take off from work. She's got all the boys here anyway, so she doesn't need me right now. I'll come back soon, when they're gone. She'll need the support then. But right now, she'll be okay. That means you and I will drive back first thing in the morning, day after tomorrow. Can you pack by then?"

Livia looked around her room. She almost told him she could leave right now. But she'd already revealed some of her eagerness, maybe even too much. So instead she just said, "I don't have much."

And that was true, up to a point. The real truth, though, was that the things she cared about most were things that couldn't be packed. Things that nothing could separate from her.

Or that she couldn't take where she was going, no matter how much she might want to.

38—THEN

It snowed the morning of the funeral. There were limousines to drive the family from the house to the church, and a police honor guard to escort them. Livia went with Rick, and as they pulled up, she saw there were mourners standing outside already, huddled under umbrellas against the falling snow, far too many to fit inside. The casket was closed—a good sign, Livia thought, as it indicated Mrs. Lone's commitment to ensuring no one could see whatever damage might have been visible on his neck—and surrounded by so many flowers, they must have been flown in from out of state. Senator Lone gave the eulogy, going on about the family's long history with and love of Llewellyn, and how they all owed it to themselves and the town to try to live by Fred Lone's example, and to continue his great work on behalf of prosperity and blah blah blah. If Livia hadn't been so glad he was dead, she might have thrown up.

The Lones owned a family mausoleum in Llewellyn's oldest cemetery, and that was where they buried him, alongside his parents and a sister who had died when he was young. Hundreds of people stood silently on the frozen grass, among the markers dusted in white, while the priest Livia had been forced to listen to so many times at Sunday services said some words about how Mr. Lone, a good and God-fearing man, was now with his Lord.

Livia hadn't seen Sean or Malcolm at the funeral, and assumed they hadn't been able to come inside because of the crowds. But they were at the cemetery. She'd never seen them dressed up before. She was surprised at how much older Sean looked in a suit and tie. And handsome.

When the priest was done speaking, they came over and told her how sorry they were, though Malcolm was looking at her in a way that made her feel he understood she wasn't exactly traumatized by her loss. Then he went off to express his condolences to Mrs. Lone, leaving Sean and Livia to themselves under the gently falling snow.

"I missed you at Katy's party," Sean said. "I wanted to call you, but I know you don't like getting calls at the Lones' house."

That was true. A few kids at school had cell phones, but not her. Mr. Lone had claimed they were frivolous. Probably he just didn't want her to have more access to the outside world than necessary.

"I thought you blew me off," Sean went on. "And then I heard about Mr. Lone. I'm really sorry."

Livia looked down, then back at him. "I would never blow you off."

"I know. I was being stupid. I'm sorry."

They were quiet for a moment. She was dreading what she had to tell him. She didn't know how.

Sean wiped some melting snowflakes from his cheeks. "So . . . will you be back in school soon?"

His expression was so open, so concerned. It hurt to look at him, and she glanced down again.

"No," she said. "I'm going to stay with Mrs. Lone's brother for a while. In Portland."

"What? Why?"

"Mrs. Lone . . . she needs some time to herself."

"But . . . when will you be back? What about school?"

"I'll finish school in Portland."

"B-but . . ."

He stopped. It was the first time she'd heard him stutter in longer than she could remember, and it made her want to cry to think she was the cause of it.

"You don't have to go to Portland," Sean said. "You could stay with my dad and me. For as long as you want. I could ask him. I know he'd say yes."

She shook her head. "I can't. I'm sorry."

"But why?"

"I just can't."

There was a long silence. Sean said, "Well, when do you leave?"

She'd never heard him sound so forlorn. She could feel her eyes wanting to fill up and willed herself not to cry.

"Tomorrow morning."

"But that's so soon!"

"I know."

"I . . ." He stopped. "Jeez, Livia. Who am I going to train with?"

She laughed softly. "Everyone wants to train with you. You're the best wrestler on the team."

"No, you are. And what about jiu-jitsu?"

His words were like a knife twisting inside her. She knew he didn't know it, that he couldn't understand, but still it hurt so much. "Sean, please . . . I'm sorry."

"I just don't understand," he said, and the sadness and helplessness in his voice had her on the verge of crying. She had to get away. Had to hide.

"At least meet me tonight," he said. "At the playground."

She couldn't speak. But she nodded.

"Ten o'clock?" he said. "Can you sneak out?"

She nodded again. With all the people in the Lone house, it wasn't as though anyone would notice. Or care, even if they did.

39—THEN

It was still snowing when Livia slipped out of the house and walked to the playground. She liked the snow. It was still so strange to her, and she hoped she would never get used to it or take it for granted. It was lovely, the way it covered everything and made the world look so fresh and clean.

Sean was waiting for her, wearing a wool hat and a down jacket like she was. He smiled as she walked over. "You want to sit on the swings?"

She didn't, actually. Tonight she wanted to be able to see him, not sit side by side. She smiled back and said, "Let's just stand for a while."

He nodded. "Okay."

She looked around, realizing this might be the last time she saw the playground. She would never miss the rest of Llewellyn. But the playground was special. A place she associated with Sean. With that night, a year earlier. There was even a moon again, like the year before, though this one was behind clouds that suffused everything in a soft glow. This would be a nice way to remember it, she thought. Blanketed in white, with the whole world hushed by the gentle, falling snow.

"Is everything okay at the house?" Sean asked.

"It's okay. There are a lot of people."

"My dad wrote you a letter," he said, reaching into his jacket and pulling out an envelope. "I don't know what it says. He said you could open it now, if you want. Or wait until later. It's up to you." He handed it to her.

She hesitated for a moment, then pulled off her gloves and opened the letter.

> *My dearest Livia,*
>
> *This is just a short note from a man who's never been prouder of anything than to be Sean's father and his and your teacher.*
>
> *I know Sean told you that you could stay with us if you need to, for as long as you like. That invitation is from both of us. It will always be there. It's never going away, not for anything. I told you, girl, you have people who care about you. So if there's anything you ever need—anything, ever—you call on us, and we'll be there.*
>
> *All that said, we understand you have your reasons, and we respect them whatever they are.*
>
> *Remember that your talent is your ticket. And never stop believing in yourself. Those two things, and nothing's ever going to stop you.*
>
> *I'm not going to say goodbye, because I feel certain our paths will cross again. Until then, thank you for the privilege of being your teacher, and I'm looking forward to seeing whatever you decide to make of yourself. I have a feeling you're just warming up now, and the best parts are all yet to come. I love you, girl.*
>
> *Malcolm*

By the time she was done reading, her tears were all over the paper. She handed it wordlessly to Sean. While he read it, she wiped away her tears and managed to stop crying.

"Wow," Sean said.

She sniffled, then laughed. "He always makes me cry."

He handed the note back to her. She blew the snow off, folded it, and put it back in the envelope, then put the envelope in her coat pocket. She'd known even before she finished reading that she would keep it with the photograph of her and Nason.

"Everything he said . . . you know I feel the same."

She nodded. "Thanks."

"I mean it."

"I know."

"Even if you did abandon me to Eric and his friends my first day of school."

She looked at him in shock, and he started laughing. "I'm kidding!" he said. "I'm just teasing."

She made a mock angry face. "You better watch it."

He smiled. "I know."

She really liked his smile. And his face, which had little flakes of snow melting on it. She was so used to seeing that face—his eyes, his smile—and now she wouldn't.

"My dad told me not to keep asking you," he said. "Because he said it's your business and it sounded like you'd made up your mind. But . . . are you sure you have to go? You really could stay with us."

She wished she could explain why she had to get away from Llewellyn, from everything about the Lones and their house and this town. And why it was so important that she go to Portland, where Nason had disappeared. She knew it would sound silly if she said it, but she felt like she would be able to look for Nason in Portland. Maybe she could find her, even though Rick hadn't. Not going to Portland when she had the chance would be to forget Nason. Or acknowledge she must be dead. And she would never do that. Never.

She had known it would be hard to see Sean, but not like this. She'd felt so good before. So satisfied. And that delicious . . . tingling feeling, when she imagined choking Mr. Lone. But now it was this goodbye that was real. She wanted to go back to her room and hide. But she also wanted to stay.

"Remember last year?" she said. "When you walked me here after the party?"

"Yeah. That was a good night."

The first part had been good, yes. Of course, he didn't know what Mr. Lone had done to her after. But that didn't matter anymore. It felt far away, detached. Mr. Lone was dead. He would never do anything to her again. He would never do anything to anyone.

"I remember so many things about that night," she said. "It was warm. There was a full moon. And the trees looked silver."

He smiled. "I remember you laughed a lot. I really liked that."

She looked at him, and felt her eyes get wet again. "I remember you touched my shoulder in such a nice way. And my hair. And my cheek. Do you remember that?"

He nodded quickly, as though afraid to speak.

She felt the tears spill over. "Would you touch me like that again?" she whispered.

He didn't say anything. He just looked at her, and what she saw in his eyes made something melt inside her. He took off his gloves and brushed away her tears. His fingers were warm and gentle. Then he touched her hair, and her neck, again so gently. And then her face again.

A tear ran down his cheek, mingling with the melted snowflakes. "Don't go," he said.

She stifled a small sob. "I have to."

"I don't want you to."

"I don't want to, either. But I have to."

"I don't understand."

"I'm sorry."

She brushed away his tears the way he had hers. She looked at his lovely face and smiled, even though she was still crying. And then he leaned in, so slowly, and kissed her.

His lips were so soft, and so warm, and they felt so good against hers. She kissed him back, softly, the way he was kissing her, thinking how good it was that he was finally kissing her, and how long she'd waited for this moment, maybe longer than she'd realized. After a while, she felt his mouth open a little, and she opened hers, too, and she felt his tongue against hers, and a little bolt of pleasure shot from somewhere deep inside her and spread through her whole body.

She wasn't sure how long they stood there like that. Long enough for him to hold her face in his hands, and for her to do the same to him. Long enough to feel hot inside her jacket, even though it was still snowing.

Eventually, the kiss broke, and they stood there for a moment, looking in each other's eyes. Sean's mouth was open. He seemed slightly dazed. She thought she had never seen an expression more honest. More naked. More vulnerable.

"I love you, Livia."

Her eyes welled up again. "I love you, too."

"Then why?"

She shook her head. "I'm sorry."

"I feel like I'm never going to see you again."

"You will."

"Maybe this summer?"

"Maybe." But she doubted it.

He smiled, but his eyes stayed sad. "Maybe we'll go to college together. Maybe we'll be on the same wrestling team."

Again, she doubted it, though she couldn't say why. "Maybe."

"I mean, we're only a little over a year away from graduating. That's not that long."

She could tell he was trying to comfort himself as much as reassure her. She didn't answer. Instead, she touched his lovely face again, then leaned in and kissed him some more. Part of her wished they could stay in the playground forever, just the two of them and the gently falling snow.

But in the morning, she had to go. And she knew everything would be different when she did.

40—THEN

Livia liked Portland. Rick's apartment was small but comfortable, just as he'd promised. And he never entered her room without knocking first and then waiting for her to invite him in. He never said anything about her locking the bathroom, either—in fact, he probably didn't even know whether she locked it, because when the bathroom door was closed, he stayed away until she was out.

The apartment was on the top floor of an old five-story brick building in the southwest of the city—a neighborhood called Goose Hollow. Rick's office, now Livia's bedroom, overlooked Interstate 405, and Livia had a little trouble at first adjusting to the sounds of highway traffic so close to her window. But in less than a week, she couldn't even hear the cars anymore unless she listened for them.

The high school was called Lincoln, and it was less than a ten-minute walk from the apartment. Compared to Llewellyn High, Lincoln was enormous—almost fifteen hundred students, grades nine through twelve. With so many students, Livia thought she would be harder to notice, and was glad. But word had gotten out about the wrestling phenomenon from Llewellyn. Some pretty girls asked her to sit at their table in the cafeteria—the popular ones, the queen bees. Livia knew the type, and wanted nothing to do with them. She had survived a nightmare trip across the ocean, then a childhood in a land whose language she didn't know and where her "savior" was in fact a filthy, disgusting rapist. And she had killed that rapist, killed him with her own hands using the skills she had painstakingly acquired, then engineered her own deliverance to a new life in Portland. Most of all, she had a sister she would die for. What would she have to say to a bunch of manicured socialites who cared for nothing but fashion and makeup and trying to impress popular boys?

So she sat at the table with the nerdy kids instead. They were nice. And smart. And more interesting. At least they knew what it was like to grow up without everything just being given to you and making you think you had done something to deserve it all.

But despite her efforts to steer clear of the popular crowd, various football players and other jocks kept inviting her to parties on weekends. She never went. None of them asked if she was "into chicks," at least, but they probably speculated. She didn't care. She didn't know what she was into. Sean, she supposed. The way her body had felt when they were kissing . . . she had never felt anything like that.

No, that wasn't quite right. She felt something similar when she remembered killing Mr. Lone . . . the same excitement, the same tingling, the same feeling that she needed something more, much more, even though she wasn't sure exactly what form that thing might take.

Sometimes, she imagined killing Mr. Lone just to bring on the tingling. And one night, while she was lying in bed, restless, her eyes closed, remembering, the tingling became so intense it was unbearable. Without thinking, she touched herself, and was shocked at how good it felt. She pressed harder. She was wet, and her fingers slipped easily inside. That felt so good it made her gasp. She imagined more—*his red face, his bulging eyes, his tongue sticking out.* She brought her other hand down and rubbed, panting now. *The bones of her forearms slicing into his neck, cutting off the blood, the oxygen.* Oh, that was so good, it felt so, so good. *The rattling sound from his throat while she looked into his dying eyes—*

Something seemed to explode inside her, a shockwave of pleasure and relief she could never have imagined. Her body shook and she clamped her jaw to keep from crying out.

It went on for a long time, cascading through her. When it finally abated, she lay there, sweating, gasping, stunned. That was it. That's what an orgasm was. That's what people were talking about when they talked about "coming." She was so revolted by what she knew of sex, she hadn't really believed orgasms were real. Or, if they were, she thought it would be impossible for her. But it wasn't impossible. She started laughing in delight, and put a hand over her mouth to muffle the sound. And then the laugh changed to tears. This was what Skull Face and his men and Mr. Lone had tried to take from her. And what they had taken, almost certainly, from Nason.

She waited for the tears to pass, then lay there for a while, her limbs heavy, her mood languorous, sleep slowly infiltrating her mind. She supposed it was strange that she had made herself come while remembering killing Mr. Lone. She knew other people wouldn't understand. But then, they wouldn't understand her, either. She didn't care. As long as no one else knew, as long as what she did and what she imagined were hers and hers alone, the rest didn't matter.

The safest things were secrets.

41—THEN

It was spring, and off-season, but the wrestling coach practically begged her to join the team for the following year, when she would be a senior. She told him she hadn't decided about sports—she was still feeling overwhelmed by all the changes. He told her he understood, but that it would be an honor to be her coach and please would she think about it.

She missed Malcolm, and Sean even more. But it was liberating, glorious, to be away from the Lone house and Llewellyn. To live in a place where she didn't have to dread someone coming into her bedroom. Someone forcing her to do disgusting things. A place where she was known as a champion, not as a victim. And where she didn't feel like a victim, either.

There was nowhere to do jiu-jitsu near Rick's apartment, but she found a place called Portland Judo in the northwest of the city that was easy enough to get to by bus. It was run by a man named Roy Kawamoto, a fifth-dan judoka from Hawaii. Rick took her there the first time she went, and would sometimes drop by to take her home, too, depending on his shift. She didn't mind, but she told him he didn't have to. He said it was good for people to know she had family. She thought about what had happened with Skull Face and Mr. Lone, when it was obvious she didn't have family, and she thought she understood what he meant.

Not that he needed to worry. She had developed a sense for the vibe predators put out, and Kawamoto-sensei didn't have it. He had even been a stepfather twenty years before to two brothers when their father had died—two brothers who had come all the way from Hawaii with him to become the top instructors at his new school. They all treated Livia with kindness and respect—and even awe, because her judo was so strong. The mat work was a lot like jiu-jitsu, of course, so she was hardly a beginner. But she had a knack for the standing techniques, too, and by the end of summer, they promoted her to black belt because she was defeating experienced black belts not just on the ground, but with throws, too. Her favorite move was the flying triangle, where she would go for the strangle even before her opponent had hit the mat. She learned her opponents weren't usually expecting that. They conceived of fighting on their feet and fighting on the ground as two separate arenas, and were therefore vulnerable during the transition, which to Livia was the most promising arena of all.

Rick let her read the file on her and Nason. It wasn't very thick. There were several ships from Thailand that had berthed in Portland around the time it was assumed Livia had been moved onto the barge destined for Llewellyn. By the time Livia was discovered, all the possible ships had departed. Worse, they were all flying under "flags of convenience," which meant they were owned by people in one country and registered in another, a practice that could make it difficult or even impossible to determine who the real owner was. In other words, a dead end.

The barge should have been a better lead. She was called the *Vesta*, and the captain and crew had been questioned. But they all claimed to have no knowledge of the container of smuggled people on board, nor of the three men who had kept the smuggled people captive. The captain and crew all had clean records. The captain had been charged some sort of fine, but that was it.

The survivor of the three men who had kept her on the barge would have been the best lead. He was the one Rick had told her about in Llewellyn, Timothy "Weed" Tyler. Weed had been belowdecks when the police raided the boat and hadn't been involved in the gunfight, which was why he had survived.

Weed had been sent to the federal prison in Victorville, California. Livia asked Rick if there were some way she could go to the prison and question him. She was afraid Rick might belittle her—a high school girl, wanting to interrogate an imprisoned white supremacist—but Rick treated her request with understanding and respect. Even so, he talked her out of it. If Weed had been willing to cooperate, Rick explained, he likely would have done so in exchange for a reduction of that twenty-year sentence. Now that he was in prison, no one had any leverage over him.

"Why do you think he wouldn't talk?" Livia asked one night as they sat for dinner at the small table in the kitchen. "Is it possible he really didn't know anything?"

Rick served her a miso-glazed salmon steak. "Well, not impossible, anyway. But remember that time in Llewellyn when I said you had good cop instincts?"

She nodded, eager for him to go on. He glanced at her salmon steak, a subtle reminder that he liked her to eat while the food was hot and at its tastiest. She took a forkful, chewed, and swallowed. "It's delicious," she said. And it was. But, as usual when her mind was on Nason and related matters, she didn't care about food. Or anything else.

He smiled. "Thanks. Anyway, yeah, I think Weed knew a lot. The reason being, I talked to the AUSA, and he told me that in response to his offer to reduce Weed's sentence in exchange for information, Weed wouldn't give him *anything*."

"What does that mean?"

Rick took a mouthful of salmon. "Damn," he said, chewing. "That is good." He swallowed, then said, "Well, here's how it works. When a prosecutor threatens a bad guy with a long prison sentence, the bad guy will try to bargain. Offer to testify against his cohorts, that kind of thing. In exchange for a reduced sentence. Defense attorneys and prosecutors dance these dance steps all the time. It's a routine. The ugly truth is, prosecutors are almost always looking for a plea deal. It saves them time and energy and they're all overloaded."

Livia was horrified. "But that's not fair."

"No. It's the system. And the system is never fair."

He twisted the cap off a beer and poured it into a glass. Livia had juice in hers. "Anyway. So when a guy looking at a twenty-year stretch refuses to offer up anything at all, you know he has information. But he's scared."

"But how do you know . . . I mean, you said it's possible, or not impossible, he didn't know anything?"

He glanced at her salmon again. She ate a big mouthful, along with some bok choy and cabbage.

He smiled appreciatively and drank some of his beer. "Right, but here's the thing. *All* bad guys know something. A street dealer who's rumored to have killed someone. The scuttlebutt on who really raped that girl in the projects. Where the Brown Pride Sureños are getting their guns. *Something.* And if they really don't know anything, which never happens anyway, they make something up. Because hey, why not, right? Facing twenty years in the can, what have you got to lose?"

"So then why didn't Weed offer anything? Or make something up?"

"There's only one reason someone dummies up the way Weed did. What do you think it is?"

Livia remembered to eat while she considered. After a moment, she said, "Fear."

"Bingo. Because when a defendant is scared, he doesn't want any-one to think he's talking about *anything.*"

"But scared of what?"

"Scared of getting killed. By anyone the bad guy might hurt testifying. So when you get someone who refuses to say even a word, that's what you're dealing with. Someone whose silence is a message to the people who could have him killed: 'I'm not talking, so please don't kill me.'"

"So what it does it mean that Weed was scared?"

Rick sipped his beer. "You tell me."

She considered again. "It means he knows who hired him and his brother. And the third guy. And that whoever hired them is . . . dangerous."

"Exactly. Now the thing is, Weed is part of a white supremacist gang, affiliated with a prison gang called the Aryan Brotherhood. That would give him automatic AB protection in prison."

"Aryan Brotherhood?"

"Yeah. The US prison population is dominated by three gangs—black, Latino, and white. It's a little more complex than that, but you get the idea. Anyway, the Aryan Brotherhood is the white gang. Numerically they're the smallest, but they're feared because they're so ruthless. So Weed was either afraid that if he testified, he'd get no protection from AB, or that AB would turn on him, or—"

"Or that even if the Aryan Brotherhood wanted to protect him, they wouldn't be able to."

Rick nodded, clearly pleased with the way she was thinking it through. "And what would that mean?"

"It would mean . . . whoever Weed is afraid of, they're stronger than the Aryan Brotherhood. Because they could kill him even if the Aryan Brotherhood tried to protect him."

"Exactly. So it's a reasonable inference that whoever hired Weed and his gang has a lot of juice. Unfortunately, that doesn't dramatically narrow the list of possibilities."

Livia hated it, but she had to admit that for the time being, Weed was . . . dormant. She would find another way to keep looking.

Rick did mention, though, that with time off for good behavior, Weed could be released before his twenty years were up. Livia decided she would keep track of that. And track Weed down when he got out of prison. Maybe at that point, he'd have a new reason to talk.

Or she could find him one.

42—THEN

She hadn't expected Rick to be any kind of parent figure—she knew he was single, with a busy job, and besides, after what she'd been through, just a safe place to stay while she finished high school would have been more than enough. But he seemed to enjoy the kinds of things parents do. He was a really good cook—he knew how to make lots of dishes, including his special salmon, and chicken tandoori, and bouillabaisse, Livia's favorite. He went to PTA meetings. He helped her research colleges. But she wasn't sure college made sense for her, and one night, at the dinner table, she told him of her doubts.

He paused with a spoonful of lentil soup halfway to his mouth. "I'm not pushing back," he said, "but do you mind if I ask why? Because college would create more options. And that's as important in life as it is on the mat, right?"

She hesitated, then said, "I think . . . I think I want to be a cop. Like you."

She was afraid he would belittle the idea, or otherwise try to talk her out of it. But instead, he looked down for a moment, then said, "The first thing I want to say, and it's the least important, is thank you."

"For what?"

"For saying you want to be a cop like me. And if you wind up going that route, you'll see one day how much that means."

She wasn't sure what he meant, but the way he'd said "if," acknowledging at least the possibility, made her smile.

He set down his spoon. "And for what it's worth, Livia, I think you'd make a great cop. One of the best."

Suddenly, she had to blink back tears. "Really?"

"Really. You're smart. And compassionate. You know how to sift through evidence, piecing together what makes sense, picking apart what doesn't."

He paused. "But that's not even the half of it. You know what would really make you such a great cop?"

She shook her head, afraid to speak.

"Your personality. You know, most people are like sheep. Nice, harmless creatures who want nothing more than to be left alone so they can graze. But then of course there are wolves. Who want nothing more than to eat the sheep."

He looked at his soup, then back to her. "But there's a third kind of person. The sheepdog. Sheepdogs have fangs like wolves. But their instinct isn't predation. It's protection. All they want, what they live for, is to protect the flock."

Livia blinked, but the tears got past her. Rick smiled. He knew she wouldn't want to be touched. But he handed her his napkin. And that was enough.

"Look," he said. "In the end, I just hope you find your thing, the thing you're passionate about, the thing you're best at, and do that. I don't want you to feel I'm invested in anything more than that. I don't want you to feel any . . . I don't know. Pressure from me."

She shook her head. "I don't."

He smiled. "Okay, good. Then I can say without worrying about any undue influence that when I look at you—all that strength, all that compassion—if you decide you want to spend your life protecting the flock, I think you'd be great at it."

She wiped her face with the napkin. She felt he had seen so clearly inside her. Like he had X-ray vision. Not for the first time, she wondered how much else he might know, or at least suspect.

Rick went back to his soup, giving her a moment. And when she felt a little more in control, she said, "Thank you, Rick."

He smiled again. "No, thank you, Livia. But don't rule out college, okay? Remember, it's about options. And it might even make you a better cop. All I'd ask is, keep it in mind."

She promised him she would.

Sean sent her letters, mostly news about Llewellyn High. She wrote back, telling him about her new life in Portland, but it was awkward. He explained he had an email account now, and asked if she could get one, too. She could have—unlike sick Mr. Lone, Rick let her use his computer whenever she liked—but she didn't want to make it too easy to be in touch. What she and Sean had in common, she didn't know how to express in writing. So they stuck with snail mail. His letters started to arrive less frequently, and she took longer to respond because being reminded of him made her sad. Eventually, the hiatus from his last letter grew so long that she sensed there might not be another. She told herself she could always write back, but the days passed and she didn't.

Rick had a motorcycle—a 1999 Kawasaki Ninja ZXR that Livia loved the second she saw it—and he taught her how to ride it. He was a member of a machine shop, where he brought the bike to do all the maintenance and repairs himself, and he taught her how to do all that, too. She liked using tools, and working with her hands. It seemed to reconnect her with who she was before all the terrible things happened, to a time when she had caught and butchered and cooked her own food, when she was more self-reliant and felt so much more free.

Rick wanted to teach her to drive a car, too, but he couldn't let her drive his, because it belonged to the Portland Police Bureau. She asked what car he had used when he drove to Portland—it wasn't his police car.

The question seemed to fluster him slightly. "Ah, when I need a car for something like that, I borrow one from a friend."

Livia had wondered before, and almost asked now. But Rick had always been scrupulous about respecting what she needed to keep private. It would be worse than rude, it would be a betrayal, not to do the same for him. So she said only, "I'm glad you have a friend like that."

He looked at her for a long moment, almost nervously. Then he said, "Yeah. I think . . . you'd like him. And he'd like you."

She shrugged as though it wasn't a big deal. "You could introduce us sometime. If you want. I'm sure I'd like your friends."

He smiled, looking both frightened and relieved. "Well, maybe he'd let me use his car to teach you to drive. I could ask him."

They developed an easy rhythm. Livia did the shopping, the cleaning, and the laundry, too. Rick told her it wasn't necessary, but she didn't listen. She didn't want to be a burden, something he took on because of a feeling of obligation, something he felt stuck with. She wanted to be valuable, and it made her feel good to know she was. She liked making the coffee, and had a cup every morning, with milk and turbinado sugar.

Sometimes she went to the port. She would stand and stare out at the water, the containers, the machinery, the ships. Then she would close her eyes and listen to the sounds—the thrum of huge engines, the cries of scavenger birds, the lapping of water on the docks—and try to imagine where Nason could have been taken, try to feel where she could be right that moment. She told herself if she concentrated hard enough, she would remember something, imagine something, conjure something that would help. But nothing ever came.

One day, on the way home from school, she came across a thick branch that had fallen from a tree. On impulse, she picked it up and carved it into a Buddha like the one she had made so long ago in the forest—legs crossed in the lotus pose, one hand down and the other out. She placed it by the window in her bedroom, next to the photograph of her and Nason. And every night, without fail, she looked out at the sky and whispered in Lahu, "I love you, little bird. I will never forget. I will never stop looking. And one day I will find you."

Rick told her that because he always had his service weapon either on him or within easy reach, it was important for her to learn how to handle firearms safely. "You don't just childproof your guns," was how he put it. "You also gun-proof your child."

Livia was thrilled. She wanted to learn about guns. About all weapons. To her, anything that wasn't a weapon was a weakness. And she was never going to be weak again.

They went over the four rules of safety: Always assume a gun is loaded until you've checked it yourself. Never let the muzzle cross something you wouldn't be willing to harm. Finger off the trigger until you're ready to fire. And know your backstop—what a bullet would hit if it were to miss or go through your target.

Safety was important, of course, but she told him she also wanted to learn how to shoot. So they went to the gun range, where he taught her the fundamentals: smooth draw, aggressive stance, firm grip, front sight on the target, press the trigger. She listened carefully and shot well, but afterward, in the parking lot, Rick told her the range was nothing like the street—that adrenaline, ambiguity, bystanders, someone shooting back . . . the street changed everything.

"Did you ever have to shoot someone?" she asked.

"I did, yeah."

"Have you killed anyone?"

He nodded. "Two people."

"Were they bad?"

"Very bad."

"What did they do?"

"You don't want to know."

"You can tell me."

He looked at her, then nodded again. "One of them was a drug dealer. He was shooting people in a house and we had to charge inside to stop him."

She felt her jaw clench. "The people in the house . . . he killed them?"

"All but a little girl named Lucy. He had beaten her unconscious and left her for dead. But she's fine now. She's in school and she's going to be a nurse." He smiled. "She called me not so long ago, on her eighteenth birthday. She said, 'You probably don't remember me, but you saved my life. I wouldn't be alive if it weren't for you.'"

"Did you remember her?"

He laughed. "Are you kidding? I told her, 'Remember? Lucy, I'll never forget you.'"

The story brought tears to Livia's eyes. She wished Rick had been there when the white van had pulled up. Or someone like him.

"Wow," she whispered.

He looked at her and shrugged like it wasn't a big deal, but she could tell the memory had moved him, too. "Yeah," he said. "Sometimes you get to really save someone. Makes all the bullshit worthwhile."

"What about the other one?"

"Gangbanger determined not to go back to prison. He shot two officers before they could get their guns out, and had my partner pinned down. I flanked him and shot him in the head."

"You saved your partner?"

"Well, that's what they said on the commendation, anyway."

She could tell he was being modest again. "I'm glad you killed them."

He frowned and said, "I'm not sure you should feel that way, Livia."

"But they would have hurt more people if you hadn't killed them. Killing them *saved* people."

He nodded slowly, as though reluctant to concede the point. "I guess . . . I just don't want you to be glad about killing. You're so young."

She felt the dragon stir, and suddenly she badly wanted him to understand. She looked at him. "I wish you could have killed the people who took Nason and me."

The way he was looking at her, she thought he understood the full meaning of that word, *took*. He nodded again, slowly, and said, "Point taken."

"Or I wish *I* could have." She didn't add that she wished she could kill them still. She didn't want to worry him any more than maybe she already had.

But she did wish it. And if she ever found a way, she would.

43—THEN

That summer, Livia took a knife course with an Oakland instructor visiting Kawamoto-sensei's dojo—Maija Soderholm, a blonde, dreadlocked, cigar-smoking, heavily tattooed edged-weapons expert Livia thought was the coolest woman she'd ever met. The woman could make a knife move like a fan, like liquid, like a creature with its own mind. Livia realized that as formidable as she was in judo and jiu-jitsu, against someone like Maija, armed with a blade, she would be in terrible trouble. So she resolved to become that kind of trouble herself. She stayed after class to train more, and Maija, impressed by her intensity, spent hours of extra time with her.

One night, Livia asked what it was about edged weapons. "I'm not really sure," Maija told her. "When I was a little girl, I picked up one of my father's knives, and it just . . . spoke to me. It felt right. And I never got over it. I found a Filipino sword master named Sonny Umpad, and started training with him. Sonny taught me that every weapon you put in your hand has a personality, and that a properly designed weapon will tell you its function just by its feel. When he told me that, I knew exactly what he meant."

Livia told her it was the same with her and jiu-jitsu. The first time she'd put on a gi and grappled on the mat . . . it all just made sense.

Rick, aware of her new fascination, bought her a knife Maija had designed: the Vaari. It was a gorgeous, handmade weapon with a curved eight-inch blade and a handle wrapped in waxed reindeer leather. Livia practiced with it incessantly, moving it in her hand the way Maija had taught her, with lots of dodges and feints.

In the fall of her senior year, Rick finally introduced Livia to his friend, a Portland sex crimes detective named Gavin. Gavin had a warm, open smile and didn't treat Livia with pity or like a kid, and Livia liked him immediately. No one needed to say aloud what Livia had long since known. She was glad Rick had someone special in his life, someone he trusted, someone he loved. She thought that must be wonderful, even though she sensed it was something she could never have for herself.

Livia asked Gavin a lot of questions about his work. She had thought she wanted to be a homicide detective, like Rick. But talking to Gavin made her feel like sex crimes would be her true calling. It would be a better way to protect girls like her and Nason. And to avenge the ones she couldn't protect.

Gavin knew about Nason, too. He was one of the cops Rick had told about her case. He hadn't been able to find anything, and he agreed that until Weed was out of prison, they had no good leads to follow. She could tell he didn't think Weed would be worth anything, either, but he was too kind to say so out loud. And even if he had, she would have refused to believe him.

After that first meeting, Gavin was in the apartment pretty regularly, sometimes spending the night. Livia felt bad knowing that, for a while, she had been one of the people Rick felt he had to hide his life from. But she was glad he didn't feel that way anymore. She knew how much he trusted her, letting her see something he kept secret even from his own sister. That kind of trust felt sacred to her. But it wasn't in her to trust someone the same way.

Rick used his Thai police contact to check with Livia's parents again. The contact reported back that they hadn't heard from either of their daughters. Livia hadn't been expecting anything, but still it hurt to hear that there was no news of Nason. She asked Rick if his contact could check again—maybe in a year or so. Just in case. He told her he would make sure of it.

From time to time, Livia thought about changing her name. She'd read online that she could when she turned eighteen. She wouldn't even need Mrs. Lone's permission then. But as time went on, the urge faded. She'd never minded the name Livia, even though Mr. Lone had chosen it for her. Initially, it had felt like a disguise, and that was good. She had liked being a girl named Labee who was pretending to be someone called Livia. But after a while, it had started to feel like she wasn't sure which she was, or who. And now . . . Livia just felt right. Like who she was, or who she had become.

As for the name Lone, it depended on context. Fred Lone was Fred Lone. Livia Lone was just her. She could always change the name someday, if she wanted to. But she began to think she probably wouldn't.

She kept training in judo. Kawamoto-sensei promoted her to second dan and asked if she would be interested in a job at the dojo—teaching a women's self-defense class. Livia was so surprised, honored, and overwhelmed at the notion that she could help teach other women to fight, that for a moment the old emotions welled up, and she had to pause before she could answer.

"Yes," she told him, her eyes glistening. "Please that."

So two nights a week, she taught women a blend of judo, wrestling, and jiu-jitsu, focusing on techniques and tactics geared to bigger, stronger opponents. She tried to make clear that technique was actually just a small part of it, that will and attitude were much more important. She knew in retrospect that, physically, she could have stopped Mr. Lone much earlier. So what had prevented her? Only her mind. Without the right mind, the body was useless. But conversely, when the mind was right, the body would find a way. So her philosophy was to teach technique to train the mind.

Her classes were small at first, and composed mostly of elementary and middle school girls. But word got around, and soon the classes included high school girls, too, and then the mothers who were bringing their girls to train. Livia went from two nights a week to three, and then added Saturdays, too. The Lincoln wrestling coach tried again to get her to join the team, but she demurred. Teaching girls to protect themselves was more important to her. Besides, she liked having a job. She wanted to make money so she wouldn't have to depend on anyone, not even Rick.

Kawamoto-sensei was thrilled by her popularity. In addition to her hourly pay, he started giving her a bonus based on the new members signing up for Livia's class. He told her most women's self-defense courses were taught by big, muscular men who might not understand what it meant to have to fight a heavier, stronger opponent, so having a class taught by a girl who weighed maybe 125 pounds was smart and special. That made sense to Livia. And even though the class was focused on women, she encouraged boys from the dojo to come, too, because in her mind, a woman learning to fight but not training against men wasn't preparing for the real world.

That fall, the dojo had a visitor: a teacher named Devin Asano from Kawamoto-sensei's previous school in Hawaii, who had won a silver medal at the 1988 Seoul Olympics. Livia had never seen judo as powerful, elegant, and focused as his, and trained with him whenever she could during the month he was staying with Kawamoto-sensei. Luckily, Asano-sensei seemed to enjoy training with her as much as she did with him, and told her he had rarely encountered someone with her talent.

Before he returned to Hawaii, Asano-sensei told Livia he had contacts at San Jose State University in California. SJSU was Asano-sensei's alma mater, and it had one of the best judo programs in America. They were going to call her.

Livia was reluctant because she wanted to start being a cop right away. And she didn't want to leave Portland, which felt like where she might find Nason, even though she knew the feeling made no real sense. But it turned out SJSU had a great criminology program—called "justice studies"—which intrigued her. She thought it would be useful to learn more about criminals. And of course the chance to train in judo with some of the best talent in the world was attractive. Rick and Gavin told her they thought SJSU would be a smart move—college would give her a wider range of opportunities no matter what career she ultimately decided on. So when the school offered her a scholarship, she accepted. She would go to SJSU. Train hardcore in judo. And learn everything about criminals.

And then she was going to be a cop. And somehow, find Nason.

44—NOW

Two weeks after her conversation with Masnick, Livia was riding the Ninja east on Highway 20. She would have preferred the Ducati, and the Jeep would have been more practical, but depending on how things went, she might need anonymity—not to mention the full leathers she was wearing.

The air grew colder as the elevation increased, the surroundings changing from fields to pine forests to craggy, snow-topped peaks brilliant under a clear blue sky. She'd never been out this way, and if the occasion had been different, she would have stopped repeatedly to appreciate the primal beauty of the lakes and rivers; the end-of-the-earth remoteness of the North Cascades Highway; the strangeness of tiny towns with names like Corkindale and Marblemount and Diablo, nestled in the mountains like diorama depictions of the Old West.

But she was here for something more important than sightseeing. Weed Tyler was finally out of prison. She'd been counting down the years, and then the months, the weeks, the days. And now she was just hours, maybe mere minutes, from what she'd wanted for so long.

Masnick had revealed Tyler's reward for the fall he'd taken: the Hammerhead meth distribution network into Canada. Tyler would be making regular runs from a cook operation in the hills surrounding the tiny Washington town of Hamilton all the way to Oroville, where the gang knew a guy who had a way of floating the product north on Osoyoos Lake, which straddled the border. The gang had given Tyler a dark gray Ford Super Duty as a coming-home present—suitable for the remote terrain, and one of the most popular vehicles in the region, so not one likely to be noticed or remembered. Tyler would be keeping clear of highways, staying well under the speed limit—and carrying several pounds of meth hidden in a custom compartment under the driver's seat.

"He'll be armed," Masnick had added. "And carrying that much meth, I don't think he'll go quietly. Just so you know."

Livia knew what Masnick was thinking: better for Weed to die in a gun battle than be sent back to prison. From Masnick's standpoint, "killed by arresting officers" would be cleaner. More permanent. On top of which, with the passage of time and appropriate discretion, Weed's death would pave the way for Masnick and Jardin to be open about their relationship, if not about when and how it had begun.

She used the modified Gossamer, duct-taped to the handlebars, to pace him from about a mile back. Carrying that much product, he'd be tail-conscious. She could have just attached a flasher to the bike and pulled him over, of course, but again, with that much product, she'd as likely get a gun battle as compliance. No, she wanted him off the road and out of his car when she finally approached him. Someplace she could talk to him in private, at last.

Just outside the remote town of Twisp, Livia saw from the Gossamer that Tyler was pulling over. It had been nearly three hours now, and she guessed he'd found a rest stop. This was it. Her heart started thudding in anticipation.

She drifted over to the gravel shoulder and used the Gossamer to confirm no other Hammerhead phones in the area. Unlikely Masnick would have set her up—the risk/reward ratio would have made no sense—but it paid to be cautious.

She continued on for another mile, and saw she'd been right. A rest stop along the Methow River. She eased off the highway, onto a gravel road, and into a little clearing carved out among the dense pine trees. She took in a couple of log cabins, not much more than outhouses. A maintenance shack. A lonely vending machine perched between signs for the women's facility and the men's. A picnic table. And a single vehicle in the parking lot: a gray Ford Super Duty, a light coating of road dust dulling the shiny new paint.

She parked about twenty feet away from the truck so Tyler wouldn't spook when he came out, took off the helmet and set it down on the seat, and squatted alongside the engine so she would see Tyler as he emerged and could watch him as he approached. Just a female motor-cycle enthusiast in full leathers, out for a ride on the glorious back roads along the Canadian border, examining her bike.

With luck, Tyler might even stroll right up and offer to help with any repairs she needed. Of course, if he did, there was a chance he'd spot the Glock she was holding alongside the cylinder head.

But not until it was too late to do anything about it.

45—THEN

Livia loved everything about San Jose State—the green campus in the middle of the busy city; the glorious weather; the classes on criminals and the justice system; the intense judo; most of all, being in a place where nobody knew her. She was just another freshman in a sea of more than thirty thousand students, in a city of more than a million. It was the most liberating feeling she'd ever known.

Her roommate was a blonde from Berkeley named Cindy. She was nice enough, but Livia didn't like having to share a space. She needed a haven, a place where she could lock the door and keep everyone out. Where she could set up the Buddha and the photograph, and whisper her nightly vows to Nason without feeling awkward or having to explain.

Cindy picked up on her private nature, and seemed to understand it wasn't personal. Probably she stereotyped Livia as a typical Asian kid, bookish and shy and obsessed with her studies. Livia was happy to play the role. It got people to leave her alone, and besides, she had to admit that on the surface, it wasn't exactly inaccurate. But beneath the surface . . . she wasn't sure what she was. Despite her newfound feeling of freedom, she still felt . . . apart from other people. She doubted any of the prosperous-looking students around her could even imagine the events of her past, let alone have survived them. That, and the secrets she kept locked deep inside, felt like a wall between her and the rest of the world.

At random moments, but especially when she was enjoying herself, she felt guilty. Maybe she shouldn't have gone to college. Maybe she should have become a cop right away, so she could try to find Nason. But she knew it didn't make sense to feel that way. Rick was a cop, and so was Gavin, and they hadn't been able to find Nason. She didn't see what she could do until Weed Tyler was out of prison. So there was nothing wrong with her going to college. But still, it hurt to remember her little bird, and she made sure to say her vows every night before she went to sleep, though when Cindy was in the room, she had to say them silently.

There was a boy on the judo team she liked—Colton, a junior, who had come to SJSU from Los Angeles specifically for the judo and who a lot of people thought had Olympic potential. He had light brown hair and green eyes, and a face full of freckles that reminded Livia of Sean. And he was a lightweight, close enough to Livia's size so that they practiced together a lot, though she also made sure to train with bigger, stronger opponents. She knew life was less fair than the tatami.

One afternoon after practice, Colton asked if she wanted to get a drink. She didn't trust alcohol because that time in Llewellyn it had made her feel out of control, albeit in a good way. But she said yes. They went to a bar near the school, and Livia had a beer. It made her feel buzzed, but not so much that she didn't like it. Afterward, Colton walked her back to her dorm and kissed her goodnight. Livia really enjoyed kissing someone again—the kissing, and the tingling it caused. She wanted to do more than kiss, but after everything that had been done to her, she was afraid to try.

The next few times they went out, they kissed more. And then, one night, after several beers instead of the usual one or two, he asked if she wanted to come back to his apartment. She was afraid, and furious at herself for feeling that way—furious enough that she would have gone with him even if she hadn't wanted to, because she was never going to be ruled by fear again.

But she did want to. She was afraid of what it would be like. But she wanted to try.

He put on some music—Rihanna's "Pon de Replay," a song Livia liked. Then they sat on his couch and kissed for a while, but it wasn't like the other times, when she had felt the tingling. She supposed that, even buzzed from all the beer, she was too nervous. Colton started touching her, running his hands along her hips and breasts, and it reminded her of what Mr. Lone used to do, which was awful. But she wasn't going to stop. It would have felt like a victory for Mr. Lone. So she let Colton undress her, and she undressed him, her fingers trembling as she did so. He eased her back on the couch and she tried to relax while he touched her, but it didn't feel good, she wasn't wet and tingling the way she was when she touched herself.

"I have a condom," he said, breathing heavily. "Is it okay? Do you want to?"

She didn't, but she knew she had to get past it. Had to at least try. So she nodded and whispered, "Yes."

He leaned away and pulled something from a drawer, then fumbled to get it on himself. She didn't watch. She was afraid seeing his penis would make her remember too many horrible things.

He pushed her legs open—gently enough, but she didn't like it, didn't like it at all. Too many memories were being stirred up, too many terrible feelings. The way Mr. Lone had pulled the towel off her. And made her stop covering herself. Those things. And then Colton moved on top of her, and his weight was on her, and his arms were under hers, and she felt him poking at her, trying to push it in. But she wasn't wet, and it hurt, and she just . . . she couldn't. She just couldn't.

"Stop," she said. "Colton, stop. I can't. I don't want to."

"Wait," he said, breathlessly. "We're almost there. Just a little more. Just a little more, Livia."

"Stop," she said again, louder this time, angry he wasn't listening. "I don't want to."

He put more weight on her and gripped her more tightly. He pushed harder, trying to get inside.

"No!" she shouted, suddenly enraged. "I said no!"

She hooked a leg under one of his and flipped him off the couch onto the floor. She kept the hook in and stayed with him as he crashed onto his back, landing in a straddle across his torso—the mount, the dominant jiu-jitsu position. She took hold of his throat with one hand and raised up the other to smash his nose into his face—a palm heel, one of the strikes Malcolm had taught her.

Colton was stronger than she was, but whatever he saw in her face must have frightened him. His eyes widened and he lay perfectly still for a moment, as though too shocked or afraid even to defend himself.

She looked down at him, suddenly acutely aware of the hot skin of his stomach pressed against her. She shifted slightly. That tingling. More than tingling. It was like an electric current. She realized she was wet.

Keeping one hand on his throat, she reached down with the other and took hold of his penis. It had softened, but the condom was still on it. And as soon as she touched it, it got hard again. Colton watched her, his mouth open, his eyes wide.

She rubbed his penis against herself. It felt good. It slipped in a little. It made her gasp.

She held it more tightly and spread her knees more, lowering herself onto him. It went in a little more. It hurt, but in a good way. She eased up, then pushed down again.

Colton tried to reach for her. Without thinking, she tightened the grip on his throat. "Don't move!" she said. He froze, then slowly lowered his arms back to the floor.

She kept easing her knees wider, and each time she did, it went in deeper. Finally, her hips were against his and there was no more deeper to go. It didn't hurt anymore. It felt good. Really good. Like when she touched herself, but different. More . . . all over, or something. She started moving, back and forth, up and down, riding him, finding the right spot, the right rhythm. She was panting now. She could come from this. She was *going* to come. He tried to move again, and she squeezed his throat hard. He stopped. She realized she was fucking him, fucking him the way she wanted to, and that he was afraid, and she moaned without meaning to and felt the explosion building, and she fucked him harder, moving exactly the way she wanted to, and then it happened, she was coming, coming so hard, and it was so much, it was so good and so different from the orgasms she gave herself.

When it was over, she slumped against him, panting, and eased the pressure on his throat.

"Oh, my God," he said. "What the hell was that?"

She smiled and thought, *The dragon, you idiot.* But she only said sweetly, "Did I do something wrong?"

46—THEN

In her sophomore year, Livia decided to make forensic science the focus of her justice studies major. She had enjoyed the survey forensics course the year before, and thought there would be nothing more useful to her as a cop than expertise in the science of catching criminals. Not that the other courses she took—gangs, victimology, criminal procedure, and others—weren't interesting. They were. But those were areas for which she felt she already had good instincts, or would quickly learn on the job. A forensics focus, on the other hand, with its related classes in chemistry, biochemistry, and microbiology, was different. She thought expertise in forensics would be like a superpower—enabling her to find clues criminals didn't even know they had left behind.

For a while, she toyed with the notion of becoming a prosecutor. One of her course books was *Sex Crimes*, by a former New York prosecutor named Alice Vachss. Unlike the prosecutors Rick had told her about, Vachss didn't want to offer plea bargains. Vachss was a warrior who fought to put rapists in prison *forever*. Livia read the book in a single day and night, crying at some of the horrors recounted, and relating to the woman's passion, her cold, determined hatred of the monsters who preyed on the weak. The office cowards Vachss had to work around and outmaneuver sounded horrible, but Livia could see doing what Vachss did. Putting together the case. Arguing in court. Sending rapists to prison to rot.

Around the same time she read *Sex Crimes*, an assistant US attorney named Daniel Velez came to the school to guest lecture on his experience fighting human trafficking. Not long after Livia's arrival in Llewellyn, Congress had passed a new law—the Trafficking Victims Protection Act—which turned what had previously been loosely understood as "human smuggling" into a new federal crime, with huge new resources devoted to combating it. The details Velez shared were horrifying, and Livia was moved by his passion for his work. He had prosecuted a Ukrainian gang that kidnapped women and sold them into sex slavery in the United States; agricultural interests that enslaved undocumented workers by threatening to murder their Central American families; a company that provided kitchen and cleaning laborers to dozens of restaurants, all of them beaten into working sixteen-hour days and paid next to nothing.

Although it wasn't the focus of his talk, Velez mentioned that many of the people his office had rescued had been sexually abused, and that even in labor-trafficking cases, this was common. Livia didn't need a lecture to know that. She knew what men did to women and children the men perceived had no power, no recourse. No ability to fight back.

After the talk, Livia approached him and asked where in America trafficking was worst. He told her it was everywhere.

"But how does it work?" she said. "I mean, you've rescued sex slaves, agricultural slaves, domestic-labor slaves . . . How do the people who want a certain kind of slave . . . I mean, how do they . . ."

Velez rubbed his goatee. She guessed he was about fifty, but there was something appealingly boyish about his face, and she wondered if the goatee was intended to make him seem older. "You're asking, is it like a help-wanted ad in a newspaper?"

"Yes, that. How do the buyers connect with the sellers to get the kind of slave the buyer wants?"

"Believe it or not, it's a market, in some ways like any other. It starts at the wholesale level, and moves down to retail. Say a Mexican coyote gets a truck across the border. There are a hundred people inside. The coyote's contacts will include smaller wholesalers—some looking for domestic labor, some agricultural, some nail salon, some sex workers—"

"And children."

"Yes, unfortunately, children, too."

She nodded, processing the information, trying not to let herself have feelings about it. "And then, what, these smaller wholesalers distribute to even smaller ones?"

"That's right. Until the buyer is, say, a restaurant that needs a single dishwasher. In many ways, it's a lot like any other market. Take produce, for example. There's a farm that grows all kinds of crops. The farmer takes the crops to market. There, wholesalers say, 'We'll take ten bushels of wheat, a hundred pounds of tomatoes, a thousand ears of corn . . .' based on what the wholesaler thinks he can sell. And then the wholesaler takes the produce to another market, where supermarkets and restaurants say, 'Oh, I'll take a hundred of those radishes, the same number of lettuces . . .' Eventually, you have individual shoppers buying these items one by one in a supermarket. Or as part of a meal in a restaurant."

Despite her efforts, she could feel her normally suppressed grief over Nason moving closer than usual to the surface. She pushed it back. She couldn't think about Nason now. She needed this information.

"You said . . . a hundred people. In a truck. You mean a shipping container truck?"

"Yes, exactly. In fact, in Texas in 2003, nineteen people died in a container attached to the truck that was carrying them from Mexico. So many of them were packed in, they couldn't breathe."

"But didn't the traffickers want to sell those people? They can't sell them if they're dead."

"It was over a hundred degrees that spring, and I doubt the coyotes thought they would lose so many. But remember, when you're trafficking people, there's a ratio. If you don't lose any, you're not bringing enough. Here's what I mean. Say you bring ten people in a shipping container and no one dies on the way. Okay, you get paid for ten. But if you bring a hundred, and ten die, you get paid for ninety. The expense of the container, bribes, logistics . . . it's all the same either way. So is the risk. So the financial incentive is to pack in a lot of people. It's no different from the slave ships that brought Africans to the American colonies. They had a ratio, too. The shippers didn't expect the entire cargo to make it. They preferred that all would suffer and a few would die. That's how they maximized profits."

Livia wondered why the shipments from Bangkok to Portland, and from Portland to Llewellyn, had been so small. At the time, it had been horribly uncomfortable, and such a small space with a dozen or so other people in it had felt cramped and claustrophobic. But from what Velez was saying, sharing a container with only a dozen or so other people was practically deluxe. Well, she supposed there was a range, with containers packed lightly, on one end, and deadly overpacking like the one in Texas, on the other. She imagined slowly suffocating in a packed, furnace-like, stinking metal box, with similarly terrified, suffering people jammed together on all sides. It sounded even worse than what had happened to her and Nason.

Or maybe not.

She thanked Velez—for the talk, for the additional information, and most of all for the work he did, because what he did was so important.

But as much as she appreciated people like Vachss and Velez and was tempted to follow their path, she realized that police work was her real calling. She wanted to carry a gun. And not just prosecute the monsters, but hunt them. Catch them. Snap handcuffs around their wrists and put them in prison forever.

Or else put them in the ground.

47—THEN

She was still seeing Colton. He had been intimidated by their first night together, but not so much that he didn't want to try again. Over time, Livia got used to other positions. But she found that nothing was better than turning the tables, taking control the way she had that first night. At a minimum, to come, she had to be on top. And as much as Colton wanted it, oral sex was out of the question. She didn't enjoy the vulnerability of having it done to her, and even the thought of doing it for Colton was a sickening flashback straight to the deck of the ship at night, the smell of curry and diesel fuel, the scratchy Astroturf under her knees . . . all of it.

On balance, though, she felt good about the relationship. She was secretly proud that she could have any kind of sex at all, after what had been done to her. And that she could actually enjoy it was practically a miracle. She thought she'd just see how it went and not think too much about it.

By spring semester, though, their romance had cooled. Part of it seemed like jealousy on Colton's part: he hadn't done well enough in events like the Grand Slams and the Pan Ams to qualify for the

Olympics, while Livia's wins in those events kept her in the running. But part of it was Livia's own growing dissatisfaction with the relationship. After the rush of that first night, the sex, even when physically adequate, just wasn't overall as fulfilling. Knowing what to expect in bed, having a routine, seemed to . . . well, if not ruin it for her, then at least diminish the experience.

She started dating other guys. But whatever it was she needed, she found it wasn't something she could satisfy just with other students, and she started going farther afield, taking new risks. She had bought a used Ninja, like Rick's, and she would ride it out to some of San Jose's seedier bars, the ones far from the SJSU campus, the kinds where students knew they weren't welcome. She was pretty, she knew that, and a lot of men fetishized Asian women. Inevitably, some tatted-up day laborer or construction worker would sidle up next to her at the bar and ask if he could buy her a drink. These were rough men, bigger than most of the students she knew. They worked with their hands, they weren't masters of the universe and weren't going to be, and they didn't like hearing no from a woman. Especially after they'd bought her a drink. And taken her to a motel, or back to an apartment, which in their minds entailed a certain quid pro quo. Many of them fought back when she flipped them off her and straddled them, giving in only when they realized they were still going to get laid, just not quite the way they'd expected. Mostly they seemed to treat it as a crazy new experience, like something they'd see in a porn movie, though maybe not one they would have thought to rent themselves. She'd give them a fake name and number afterward and never see them again.

One night, she let a guy who called himself Park buy her a drink, even though she wasn't sure about his vibe. On the one hand, he seemed normal enough. He was pretty solid-looking, but clean and well groomed, not tatted up or anything like that. She'd learned that past a certain point, most guys at least tried to be persuasive, and many let their attempts at "persuasion" get a little too aggressive. But that tended to be more of a heat-of-the-moment phenomenon. It wasn't a kink for them; it wasn't a conscious plan; they'd just gotten so tantaliz-ingly close to what they craved, they couldn't stand to have it taken away. She told herself this guy might be like that, and that would be fine. At any rate, he didn't have the predator feel she recognized. Still, there was something . . . missing about him, a kind of weird blankness in his eyes or affect she couldn't place. Whatever it was that was off, she decided to ignore it.

It was almost a very costly mistake.

The moment he'd locked the motel door behind them, he turned to Livia and as casually as if he were brushing back his hair shot an uppercut into her belly. She'd been unprepared for anything like that, and though she was in top judo shape, it still knocked the wind out of her. She doubled over and staggered back. Her legs hit the bed and she sat heavily on it, holding her stomach, realizing belatedly this was no run-of-the-mill, potentially date-rapey sort of guy. No, this guy was a freak, like the ones Alice Vachss fought to put in prison. Livia tried to scuttle away, and again, with no emotion at all, the guy hit her across the side of the head with a massive, openhanded shot. It blew her onto the bed on her side, but years of jiu-jitsu muscle memory kicked in and she twisted to her back. She went to kick him, but he was already inside her legs. He hit her again, his face as expressive as if he were doing a math problem or playing tic-tac-toe, rocking her head back, causing an explosion of white behind her eyes.

If he'd known what he was dealing with, he would have pressed his advantage then and continued to hit her until she was unconscious. But he miscalculated. He thought he'd hurt her enough, and cowed her enough, to get right to the main event. He shoved up the skirt she was wearing and tore away her panties, then unbuckled his belt and started opening his pants.

And suddenly, he was Skull Face, and Dirty Beard, and Square Head, and Mr. Lone. He was all of them, and the red haze descended, and the dragon awoke.

She scooted forward and bumped against his pelvis. It surprised him—he was ready for her to try to pull away, not to push closer. Before he could figure out what was happening or how to react, she jackknifed her body, slamming her legs into his back and driving his torso forward into her arms. She underhooked one arm and overhooked the other and scissored her legs behind his back, then hung on for a moment while he struggled to shake her loose, catching her breath, getting her bearings, waiting for her opportunity. He was strong and managed to slam her back, but she let him—it didn't matter, the mattress absorbed the impact.

He slammed her again, then a third time. "Fucking bitch," he said, and she could hear his breathing was already getting labored. "Let me go or I'll fuck you up for real."

He tried to reach down with his right arm, and she knew instinctively he was going for a weapon. She kept the overhook tight, tying up the arm, and waited.

He went to slam her yet again. She felt it coming—he obviously didn't know what else to do, and was flailing now. As soon as his body tensed, she opened her guard, hooked one of his knees, and flipped him on the bed, rolling on top of him into the mount. He had no training, and instinctively scrambled to his stomach to try to establish some sort of base. She let him, taking his back. Keeping her left leg across his stomach, she reached around his throat with her right hand, took the left side of his shirt collar, shot her right knee up into the space between his arm and the back of his neck, and leaned back while jamming the knee forward, forcing his throat forward into the shirt cloth cutting across it. A variation of *okuri eri jime*, a strangle she liked. A sound came from his throat, like broken glass grinding, and then the cloth cut in more deeply, silencing him. He groped back for her with his left arm, and she swam her own left inside it, keeping it away from her. His right arm was trapped under his body, and now all he could do to save himself was twitch and vibrate. Which was not going to be enough.

"You going to fuck me up now?" she panted, straining to crank the choke tighter. "You going to fuck me up?" His left arm waved weakly, as though requesting a timeout or a do-over, then went rigid, and then went limp, along with the rest of him.

She held him like that for a long time. She could have let him go. If she had, he probably would have wakened at some point after she had gone. But she didn't want him to waken. She knew she wasn't the first woman he'd done this to.

But she could damn well make sure she was the last.

48—THEN

Back at her dorm, she examined herself in the mirror. Her hands were shaking. Thank God she'd moved into a single for sophomore year; it would have been bad to have to explain her obvious distress to a roommate.

No scratches she could see. So presumably, no skin under his nails. And she'd thought to push him off the bed and roll up the bed cover, which she'd left in front of a homeless encampment on the way back to campus. The police wouldn't find it. Or, if they did, hopefully it would be contaminated with the DNA of the last thousand guests who had stayed at the hotel, and of the homeless who were using it now, too.

She'd been right about a knife—a folder, clipped inside his right jeans pocket. In plain sight, if she'd thought to look for it before he'd belted her. All right, a good lesson, thankfully learned at little cost. She hadn't touched it—better to let the police find it. It would make him look like more of a bad guy.

Still, there were a dozen things, a hundred, she knew from her forensics classes that she hadn't had the presence of mind to consider at the time. She hadn't planned things properly. She hadn't prepared. She'd always known that one of these encounters could get out of control, but she hadn't anticipated something happening so . . . suddenly. With someone who gave no warning, but just instantly flipped a switch to violence and rape. Not as a way of getting something else he wanted, but because violence and rape *were* what he wanted.

She breathed deeply, in and out, calming herself. Her left eye was beginning to swell, and she put ice on it. That would be explainable, at least. She must have taken a shot to the eye at practice without realizing at the time. It had swelled up afterward. It happened. And it would hardly be the first time she'd been marked by bruises and abrasions. Judo was a contact sport.

What if someone had seen her? She hadn't gone to the front desk with him, so she was safe that way, at least. But what if the police knew she'd met him at the bar, and asked witnesses for a description? And the marks on his neck—would they know someone had used a judo strangle? That could lead them to the SJSU team. They would see her eye, and ask where she was when the guy was killed. *Studying in my room*, she would tell them, but would that hold up?

She paced back and forth, naked. She'd tossed the panties in a sewer. Wouldn't want to have to explain how they'd gotten torn that way. She had marks on her left outer and right inner thigh. That made sense—the guy had been right-handed, and had ripped the panties off right to left. The elastic around the leg holes must have held for a moment and cut her before giving way. Again, explainable as a minor judo injury. Or at least, she hoped, not provable otherwise.

Worst case, she would explain what happened. Claim self-defense. Which is what it had been, of course. At least up to a point. She'd say she hadn't meant to kill him, but when she'd released the strangle—which she'd been forced to use to save her own life—she couldn't revive him. She panicked and fled. Not good, but maybe good enough. But even if she avoided prison, the thought of being some sort of campus tabloid fodder was horrifying. People would ask questions. Her past, at least parts of it, would be revealed. Maybe people would even wonder what had really happened to her revered adopted father, whether she was suffering from PTSD. And what would all of it mean for her career prospects as a cop?

She considered every angle she could think of. Maybe she should have taken his wallet, to make it look like a robbery? She hadn't thought of it at the time—she wanted to touch as little as possible, disturb the scene as little as possible, something she knew about from her classes. She wasn't sure now which would have been the better course, but she hadn't considered it when it mattered.

Eventually, her exhaustion and the post-adrenaline backlash began to overwhelm her. Overall, she thought there was a better-than-even chance the body wouldn't lead back to her. But she couldn't be sure. She should have been more careful.

Well, next time, she would be.

49—THEN

It was on the news the next night. Parker "Park" Crader, forty, of Campbell, California, was found dead in a motel room. Police believed a sex worker had lured him into the room, where a waiting accomplice ambushed and strangled him. Crader had a record: two charges of rape. Both times it had been a sex worker in a motel room, and both times he had pled down to misdemeanor assault. He'd been out of prison for less than a year. The working theory was that this was payback from a victim who was connected to, or could afford, some kind of muscle for hire. It didn't seem to occur to the police that a woman could have strangled Crader by herself.

The police spokesman said they were following up leads, but Livia had a feeling he was talking about the women who had accused Crader of rape before, and presumably those women would have alibis, or otherwise be impossible to place in the motel room at the time of Crader's death. Everyone knew SJPD was overworked—the city had a serious gang problem, among other things. She thought of Rick, of what he'd told her of his job, how he worked leads and prioritized cases. Unless something panned out right away, she couldn't see a homicide detective spending a lot of time trying to solve the killing of someone like Crader. Her assessment of better-than-even chances of not getting caught went to more like ten-to-one.

She still felt nervous about it, especially late at night, alone in bed. But when a week passed and nothing happened, she started to feel more confident. By the end of the semester, she barely even thought about it anymore.

Except, sometimes, to fantasize about it.

The rest of college passed without incident. From time to time, the craving for a dangerous encounter became overwhelming, and she would get on the Ninja and find the right kind of bar. After that first time, she made sure always to travel outside San Jose so as not to leave an easily traceable pattern. Salinas. Bakersfield. Visalia. Stockton. If anyone ever thought to try to map any of the resulting deaths, San Jose would be at the periphery. The locus would look like Fresno. Not a particularly likely scenario, considering the obvious degenerates she was leaving in her wake. But she'd learned to be careful.

She knew on some level that her hobby, as she liked half humorously to think of it, was fucked up. Certainly no one would ever be able to understand it, and realizing this only enhanced her sense that she was different from other people, separate from them, like something human on the surface but alien underneath. But she didn't care. She imagined a lifetime of psychotherapy, administered by a doctor who could have no notion of what it was like to be sold like a farm animal by your own parents. And victimized the way she had been afterward. And to be unable to protect your own sister from being victimized, too, despite bartering with the most desperate currency available to your thirteen-year-old self.

Yeah, maybe that.

Or maybe fuck that. Maybe she would just deal with it her own way. Keep her secrets buried down deep, the way she always had. And rid the world of a few monsters along the way. She didn't have to explain herself to anyone. Justify herself to anyone. What she did was her business, and no one else needed to know anything about any of it.

She traveled to the Beijing Olympic games as an alternate. She didn't compete, but to even travel with the team was a notable achievement. Everyone told her that London, four years hence, would be her event.

She knew they could be right. She was only twenty, and had probably a decade, maybe more, before she was past her physical peak. That was a lot of time to continue to become a more skilled competitor. She knew an Olympic medal was possible. Maybe even gold.

But she had never stopped wanting to be a cop. She still whispered her vows every night, and felt them deeply. They weren't just words, an empty mantra, a tradition bleached of meaning. Nason might need her. It was one thing to study criminology and get a college degree. That was all calculated to make her a better cop, and she believed it had been worth it. But four more years of full-time judo, just so she could maybe earn a medal? How would she ever explain that to Nason, or live with it herself?

And besides. As much satisfaction as she took in knowing that the men she had killed, starting with Mr. Lone, would never hurt anyone again, it wasn't enough. She didn't lie to herself: she craved the sexual rush killing a would-be rapist provided. But that wasn't the only point. Rick had been right: she was a sheepdog. She needed to protect people, people like Nason, and she felt damaged, diminished, incomplete when she wasn't doing so. There were predators in the world, lurking, waiting, wanting to hurt someone, ruin someone, and they would do it if they could. She hated them. She needed to fight them. Not just some of the time. All of the time.

And she had waited long enough.

50—THEN

Portland Police Bureau would have been a natural fit. Rick and Gavin were there, of course, and she liked the town enough. More important, Portland still felt like the closest connection she had to Nason, the actual place where she and her sister had been amputated from each other. But she also knew those feelings weren't logical. Rick and Gavin and others like them had done all they could in Portland, and had found no trace of Nason. What could she do there that they hadn't?

So she started thinking about Seattle. The best lead, she knew, was the imprisoned white supremacist, Weed Tyler, who had survived the police raid on the barge from Portland and whose gang, Hammerhead, was based in the area. Moreover, she had learned that the Seattle region, with its variety of ports, vast rural stretches, proximity to Asia, and location on the Canadian border, was a hotbed of trafficking, and particularly child trafficking. And the city was doing something about it, too—SPD had a newly formed Vice & High Risk Victims Unit, which investigated sex crimes involving children and all forms of child trafficking, with detectives cross-deputized with the FBI's Innocence Lost Task Force and the Department of Homeland Security's Investigations unit.

That meant federal dollars, federal databases, and federal resources, but with a local focus. Livia couldn't imagine a better combination.

So she applied for a position. There was a written test, a physical fitness test, and a battery of interviews. They all went well, and her interviewers made clear that if she passed the background check, the psychology tests, and the polygraph, she was a shoo-in.

She had a little trouble with the psychology test and the polygraph. She thought she was saying the right things, but apparently her hostility to rapists and child abusers leaked through her attempts at bland "serve and protect" professionalism. And they told her there was some evidence of deception regarding whether she had ever committed a serious crime. She was surprised about that, because she didn't consider anything she had ever done to be criminal. Not really. But she stuck with her answers, and in the end, the powers that be must have decided that a few psychological blips and some indicia of deception weren't much compared to a straight-A student with a degree in criminology who was a top judo competitor and a minority female on top of it. They offered her a position, and she immediately accepted.

That summer, she sold the Ninja, rented a truck, put her few possessions in back, drove to Seattle, rented a cheap walk-up in the International District, and entered the Basic Law Enforcement Academy. For the next six months, she studied the Constitution and the law of justified use of force, much of which she already knew from SJSU; various Washington State and Seattle ordinances; pursuit and precision driving; proper entry and clearing rooms; handcuffing suspects; use of firearms, the Taser, and pepper spray, and much more. As part of the training, everyone had to get pepper-sprayed and tased. Being tased was excruciating, but she didn't mind. She knew it was important for recruits to know the effects of weapons, and to know they were tough enough to keep fighting even when they were hurt. But it made her uncomfortable when everyone laughed at the tased recruits' contorted faces and howls of agony. She was stoical about her own pain. But it hurt her to see pain in others.

Unless, of course, they deserved it.

She missed the Ninja, and though the Pacific Northwest climate was nowhere near as good for riding as what she'd left in the Bay Area, she broke down and bought a new bike: a Ducati Streetfighter. And a battered, used Jeep Wrangler, for when the weather made the Streetfighter unsafe to ride.

She excelled in all her courses, and quickly developed a reputation as a star. Not everyone liked that. She knew there were rumors that her success was due to her looks, and maybe even sexual favors. None of it was true. Yes, she got a lot of attention from the male trainers, but she didn't seek or even want any of it. There were some good-looking SPD cops—a detective named Mike Devine in particular, who was one of the lecturers and who had a cowboy vibe she liked—but she wasn't stupid. She wasn't going to let anyone she worked with get inside, literally or figuratively. It was too likely to cause trouble.

Although the irony was, refusing all advances, refusing even to flirt, caused trouble anyway. The cops who came on to her and got shot down told their buddies she was probably a dyke. Because of course, a woman who didn't share a man's inflated opinion of himself could only be a lesbian. Meanwhile, there really were lesbians on the force, but she kept them at arm's length, too. Her sexuality, like her life, was a mystery, which of course only made the topic more alluring. In retrospect, she wondered if she would have been better off putting on a ring and pretending she had a husband before entering the academy. But the idea came to her too late to matter.

Her self-defense skills were another source of attention. There wasn't an instructor at the academy she couldn't crush on the mat. Everyone knew about the judo, of course, and reactions varied. Some of the guys had to test themselves against her, and were embarrassed by the results. Some were intimidated. A few, though, were respectful and appreciative, and had no problem asking her to share her knowledge. And a few of the women, too, rather than being jealous and treating her like a freak, asked if she would teach them. She was happy to, and made her first friends in the process.

A year after arriving in Seattle, she was a full-fledged patrol cop. Rick came to her graduation ceremony. Gavin couldn't make it, but Rick brought a gift from both of them: a SIG Sauer P238 subcompact with black pearl grips—"petite, beautiful, and not to be fucked with, just like you," Rick said. She was so overwhelmed at finally being a cop, and by the perfect gift, that she hugged him, and was surprised when she let him go to see he had teared up a little. He gave an embarrassed laugh and said, "You've just never been much of a hugger. But that was nice. Really nice. I'd even take another, if you don't mind."

She didn't mind. She was never going to be as physically affectionate as most people, and she didn't want to be. But she'd gotten used to off-the-mat contact. With someone like Rick, it didn't cause the kinds of associations it once did. She was proud of that.

They went out for dinner to celebrate, but first, Livia had to make a phone call. She hadn't forgotten Rick's story about the little girl Lucy, and she wanted to make a call like that to Tanya, the cop who had been so kind to her when she had been rescued in Llewellyn.

"You probably don't remember me," Livia said. "I'm called Livia now, but when you met me, my name was Labee. I'm the girl who got trafficked to Llewellyn. I was so scared and alone, and you were so nice to me. And I wanted to let you know"—she felt the tears coming, and paused for a moment while she willed them back—"I just graduated. Seattle PD. I'm a cop now, like you. I'm going to help people, like you helped me. And I should have called you sooner, but I . . . I think I just wasn't ready. And I'm sorry for that. And thank you."

There was a long pause, and then a familiar voice: "Livia. You think I wouldn't remember you? Even if I hadn't heard about all your wrestling exploits over the years. You were the skinniest, scaredest-looking thing

I'd ever seen. But you know what? I could tell how brave you were, too. And look at you now. I hope this won't sound condescending, honey, because I didn't have anything to do with it, but I am so proud of you."

Livia tried again to will the tears back, but this time couldn't. "Thanks, Tanya."

"Thank you, Livia. You just made my day. More than my day, really. If you're ever in Llewellyn or I'm ever in Seattle, we'll get a drink, okay? We sister cops have to stick together."

Livia told Tanya she definitely would, and they exchanged cell phone numbers. She didn't add that it would have to be in Seattle. She was never going to set foot in Llewellyn again.

Following the academy, there was an eight-month probationary period—half student, half cop. Her evaluations continued to be outstanding. On free weekends, she would head out of town—Olympia, Vancouver, Port Angeles—and look for the kind of sex she liked, where the man got aggressive and she wound up in control. A few times, she found it. And once, in Pullman, she wound up with a genuine freak, like Crader in San Jose. She put him to sleep with *hadaka jime*—"naked choke"—which didn't leave marks the way the cloth strangles did, and then smashed an ashtray into the back of his head to give the coroner a cause of death that didn't look like something done by a martial arts expert.

Of course she was more careful now than she had been in San Jose. She'd assembled a backup bike from salvaged parts, for one thing, something totally untraceable. And she exploited her ever-deepening knowledge of forensics and crime scene investigations. She prepared much more methodically, too. Still, it was bad enough that SPD knew about the judo. If word got around about the kind of sex she liked, people could easily start asking questions. So she kept turning down all the cops who asked her out.

Twice a week, she taught a women's self-defense class at a Seattle Krav Maga school, using the same approach she had at Kawamoto-sensei's dojo in Portland. And, just as had been the case in Portland, word got around, and her classes grew.

Sometimes after a workout, she found herself thinking of Sean. She wondered what he might be doing. She could have found out—you didn't need to be a cop to use Facebook or the like—but she never did. Her memories of him, and of Malcolm, were too tied up with Llewellyn. With Mr. Lone. With all that. But at the same time . . . it would have been good to see him.

At the end of her mandatory minimum of three years as a patrol cop, she did a year with the gang unit. And then she passed her detective's test and started working sex crimes, at last getting to find and catch rapists, as she'd always wanted. She developed a reputation for being good with her victims—respectful, methodical, and above all empathetic. Her clearance rate was excellent, and though there were a handful of excessive force complaints from suspects she arrested, the complaints were all dismissed as unfounded.

And every now and then, when she couldn't get a case to one of the prosecutors she trusted, and got stuck with one of the careerists Alice Vachss described so well in *Sex Crimes*, and a known predator got pled down and served too short a sentence because his victim was a prostitute or a drug user or otherwise not what the careerist coward thought would make a winning victim in front of the jury, Livia made sure justice was served another way.

Those extracurricular cases had been good preparation for Billy Barnett. And Barnett had brought her to Masnick, and Masnick to now, this very moment, squatting by the Ninja in the windy chill of a Highway 20 rest stop outside the tiny town of Twisp, waiting for Weed Tyler to emerge from a privy so she could make him tell her what for sixteen years her mind had been shrieking to know.

How to find Nason. Or at least . . . at least learn what had happened to her.

51—NOW

She recognized Tyler the instant the wooden door swung open. Of course, prison had aged him, even beyond the sixteen years since Livia had last seen him, on the barge from Portland. He'd been about twenty-five then, but now his face looked closer to fifty, the skin looser, a network of seams around the eyes. But the gait was the same, the expression, the businesslike don't-fuck-with-me attitude. The sleeves of his fleece were rolled up, and she saw the tats she remembered on his forearms, though on the barge she hadn't understood their significance. Lightning bolts and Iron Crosses—white supremacist symbols. Probably there was a lot worse under his shirt. On the barge, the other two had been beefy while Tyler was lean and sinewy, but the lean aspect was gone now, replaced by probably twenty pounds of new muscle. Well, not much to do in prison but work out.

Her heart started pounding as all the emotions of that horrible time came surging back, and she closed her eyes for a moment, concentrating on her breathing the way she once had before matches, walling off the nervousness, reassuring herself she had trained for this, she could do it, she was ready.

He had a gym bag slung over his shoulder—the meth, no doubt. He wasn't stupid enough to leave it in the truck, even for a quick bathroom break. She saw him log her, then check his perimeter as he approached, the same as she had checked hers, his head swiveling, confirming there was no one else here, this wasn't a hit or a heist. And once he realized it was just a petite, pretty Asian woman out for a ride, his shoulders relaxed. He smiled and rolled right up to her, just as she'd hoped.

"Little engine trouble there?" he said over the wind, when he was about ten feet away.

"Nothing I can't handle, thanks." She could see the bag was unzipped. A safe bet he had a weapon inside it. She was glad. If he thought he could access a weapon, it would relax him, increase his confidence. While at the same time, making no difference. She was already holding the Glock on the other side of the engine. He couldn't see it, but it would sure as hell be faster than anything he might try to pull from the bag, or from anywhere else, for that matter.

"You sure?" he said, coming closer. "I'm pretty good with engines. Nice Ninja, by the way. I'm strictly a Harley man myself, but hey, it takes all types to make a world."

She looked at him over the seat of the bike. "You really don't remember me, do you?"

He frowned. "Remember you?"

"Yeah, remember me. I mean, how many thirteen-year-old girls have you kidnapped and brought to Llewellyn from Portland by barge?"

He stared, squinting, and she could see the recognition. And the fear. Then his expression hardened. "What the hell's this about?"

"Then you do remember me."

He glanced around. "I don't know if I remember you or I don't."

"Then why are you looking over your shoulder?"

He hesitated for a moment, then said, "I don't know what you're talking about. So excuse me, but I've got places to be." He took a step in the direction of the truck.

"You mean meth to deliver?"

He stopped. She saw what he was thinking and raised the Glock over the Ninja so it was pointing at his chest.

"Don't. Seattle PD." She pulled her badge from the jacket pocket and held it up so he could see it.

He lost a lot of color and started breathing rapidly. She realized he might panic and do something stupid. That would be catastrophic. He'd be useless to her dead.

"Be cool, Weed," she said. "I'm not here to arrest you. I just want to talk."

"What is this?"

She glanced at the picnic table. "Why don't we sit over there? It'll be more comfortable. We have a lot to catch up on, right?"

He shook his head. "If you think I've got anything to say to you, you're crazy."

She returned the badge to her pocket and stood, the Glock still pointed at his chest. "You know I have probable cause to believe you've got meth in that bag. Along with a weapon a felon like you isn't legally permitted to carry. But I don't want what's in the bag. I want what's in your head."

He glanced at the pistol, then at her eyes, then held up his hands, palms forward. "All right, look. It was a long time ago. I told the AUSA back then, I didn't know anything. I didn't, and I don't."

"You don't seem to understand. Right now, I just want to talk. If you tell me what you know about how I wound up on that barge, I'll be grateful, and that'll be the end of it. If you want to dummy up, I'm going to arrest you and search that bag."

There was a pause. She could see the gears turning in his mind as he weighed the options, the risks.

"All right," he said. "You win."

She nodded toward the picnic table. "Over there."

He hesitated, then started walking. She grabbed the helmet with her free hand and followed him, keeping behind him and to his right.

If he went for a weapon, he'd have a hell of a time acquiring her from there before she dropped him. Though she hoped he would be more sensible than that.

When they reached the picnic table, she said, "Set down the bag on the far side of the bench. Then sit opposite. Your back to the parking lot." She wanted the tactical view for herself.

Again he hesitated.

"Weed," she said. "You just did sixteen years. You have a wife and daughter and a lot to live for. Do you really want to die today, in the parking lot of some highway shithouse? I'm not here for anything more than confidential information."

He looked at her and shook his head disgustedly. But he did as she directed.

She circled around to face him. "Now, palms on the table. Good. Keep them there, where I can see them." She straddled the bench, left leg under, right leg out, a flexible, mobile position. The benches were integrated with the table, and sitting the way he was, Weed didn't have a move. But that didn't mean she shouldn't seize every advantage, either.

She held the Glock under the table. If anyone showed up at the rest stop, she and Tyler would look like just a couple of people taking a break from the road and chatting under the pretty blue sky.

A gust blew a snack wrapper past them and shook the pine trees. She paused for a moment, almost afraid to ask, afraid that after so long, what she thought would offer the way to Nason would be revealed as a dead end.

Come on, Livia. Do it.

"All right," she said. "I want to know who hired you for that boat."

He sighed. "Like I just said. I told the AUSA I don't know anything. I didn't handle any of the arrangements. That was my brother, and the cops killed him."

She glanced over at the bag, then back to him. "Last chance. Then I search the bag."

There was a long silence. Then his shoulders slumped and he sighed. "It was a Thai group, all right?"

Her heart started pounding, but she kept her expression placid. "Which one?"

"Which one? I don't fucking know which one. The one we always dealt with."

"The one *you* dealt with. Not just your brother. You."

"Yeah. All right."

"What was your contact's name?"

"He called himself Kana."

"What did he look like?"

Tyler shrugged. "Tall for Asian. Big cheekbones. Kind of a bony face. Okay?"

Her heart beat harder. "That's the guy who handed us over to you? Kana?"

"Yeah."

"Did he look different compared to when you'd seen him previously?"

"Different? No. Well, I mean, his face was bandaged. Actually, one of his guys was cut up, too. They said a steel packing strap broke loose and whipped across their faces. Sounded like bullshit, but I didn't ask."

"Bandaged how? Where?"

"His eye. It was, you know, like an eye patch."

Skull Face. It had to be. He was telling the truth. So far. She took a few slow and steady breaths, working to ease her rampaging heartbeat. She so hoped she had cut Skull Face's eye out. Yes. Please that.

"Why you? What was the arrangement?"

"No arrangement. Just . . . look, I'm cooperating, okay? Like you said, I have a wife and daughter. They've been waiting a long time for me. I give you what you want here, and you let me walk, right?"

"I want the truth. All of it. You give me that, and you walk. But only for that."

He nodded. "We'd never done a shipment of people before, okay? And I didn't want to. It wasn't something I wanted to get mixed up in."

"Then why did you?"

"Why do you think? Kana offered a sweet deal."

"Sweet compared to what?"

"Compared to dope. Up until then, it had always been just marijuana. I mean, where do you think I got my gang name? The Thai dope was super high quality, much better than the domestic or Mexican. They tell me these days you can buy Thai and a lot better in any Washington State cannabis store, but back then, the profit margins were crazy. Like what you'd get for coke. That's what we moved for them. Just ganja. High-quality Thai ganja."

"So then Kana comes to you and says, 'Hey, I have some people to move.'"

"That's right. And that they'd pay us five thousand a head. Which was, shit, a lot of money."

"How many heads?"

"Kana said ten. Six adults. Four kids."

She kept her face frozen. "Tell me about the kids."

"Well, first he said ten people. But I said, look, I need to know what we're moving. How much food to bring. Blankets. I mean, fuck, we're practically putting together a week-long camping trip, how do we prepare? He said, okay, six adults, four kids. I said, what the fuck do I know about taking care of kids? He said, don't worry, the adults will look after the children, and anyway, two of them are sisters, they'll take care of each other."

She suppressed the urge to raise the Glock and shoot him in the face. "There were only three kids. What happened to the fourth?"

He cocked his head slightly as though in thought. "What, was the fourth one your sister? Is that what this is about?"

Her gun arm trembled and she fought to keep her voice level. "What. About. The other. Kid."

He raised his fingers from the table. "Okay, okay. He didn't explain. We met at Terminal Six in Portland, which was the plan, and all he said was, turns out nine people, not ten, he'd been mistaken."

She wanted to scream. She was so close to knowing. She could almost feel Nason. Feel her, but not touch her.

"Nothing else about the sister?"

"Nothing. I swear. I'm telling you what I know."

"Who arranged the barge?"

"Kana, I guess. It wasn't us. He just gave us the information. We got on the barge. The container with you and the other people was already loaded. Our job was just to get you to Llewellyn."

There was so much here she needed to examine. She pushed it away and forced herself to focus.

"Why didn't you give any of this to the AUSA? You could have saved yourself a lot of prison time."

He laughed. "Yeah, getting killed isn't exactly my idea of how to save myself prison time, but thanks."

"Why were you so afraid?"

"Are you kidding? Everyone knows how well the Thais are connected. They've got every kind of organized crime in Bangkok—Russian, Italian, Japanese, Mexican. They do business with everyone. And if you say one word about the business, your shortened prison sentence will end even shorter with a shank in your kidney. Hell, you think the Brotherhood would have protected my peckerwood ass from Black Gangster Nation and the Mexican Mafia if I'd come in with a snitch jacket? Are you crazy? Everyone would have known why I got the easy time. Especially when there were follow-up busts. I would have been a dead man."

She thought about his story. It tracked with what she knew. But what was he leaving out?

"You said you'd never moved people before this."

"That's right. Just ganja, that's it. Hey, you mind putting away the piece? I told you, I'm cooperating, all right?"

She ignored him. "So why did Kana want you to move people this time?"

"I asked the same. He said they had a buyer, simple as that."

That told her nothing. She clenched her jaw, walling off the emotions, willing herself to think.

"Kana," she said. "Did he deal with anyone else in the Northwest?"

"You think he would have told me if he did?"

"I didn't ask what he told you. I asked what's known. The way it's known his people are connected with the various international criminal organizations you just mentioned."

There was a pause, then he said, "No. I never heard of him dealing with anyone other than Hammerhead. I mean, why else would he have used us for you and those other people? If he knew other smugglers experienced with that kind of cargo, I'm guessing he would have used them instead, right?"

"Maybe," she said, thinking aloud. "Or maybe . . . you think a little Thai ganja offers profit margins? You should see what traffickers make moving people. Dope gets smoked and it's gone. But slaves? Slaves are an investment."

"Well, I don't know anything about that. I told you, I never moved people before, or obviously since. The one time I tried it, my brother and best friend got killed, and I got sentenced to twenty years in Victorville."

"My point is, maybe you peckerwoods were small-time to your guy Kana. Maybe he used you because his organization didn't care if you got rolled up."

"You think I haven't wondered about that? I had sixteen years to wonder it. But why would Kana set us up? Paid us fifty thousand to move that cargo, and the cargo never even gets to the buyer? Doesn't make any sense."

No, it didn't. But . . .

And suddenly she was hit by a cop epiphany. He saw it in her face and flinched.

"You ever think it was strange, Weed, that some of your cargo didn't make it?"

He swallowed. "What? I told you. Kana just told me they were one short. It had nothing to do with me."

"I'm not talking about the fourth child. I'm talking about the ones who were on the barge." She felt the dragon stirring and breathed in and out steadily, trying to calm it. "You know, the ones who died of food poisoning. Along with one of the adults."

His eyes shifted from side to side as he looked for the right lie. "I don't know what you're talking about."

"Except it wasn't food poisoning, was it, Weed? It was just plain old regular poisoning."

He shook his head. "That's crazy. You don't know what you're talking about."

"I'd never thought about it before. I didn't have the context. The way you and the other two fed us on the barge. Handing out the food individually. Watching us eat. Collecting the waste. Why were you so careful to monitor who ate what?"

"We weren't, we just, it was just—"

She pulled the Glock from under the table and pointed it at his face. "You better tell me what I already know. Or I will search that bag and send you back to Victorville for the rest of your fucking life."

He looked at the muzzle of the gun, his eyes wide, and then to her face. "Okay," he said, raising his hands, palms forward. "Okay. Kana gave us a vial and told us to put five drops in the other kids' food when we were a day away from Llewellyn. Only theirs. Not yours. He said it would just make them sick."

"Why?"

"I don't know. I didn't ask, and he wouldn't have told me anyway."

"What about the woman who died?"

"He said we had to do some adults, too. We did. But I'm telling you, we thought it would only make them sick."

Five drops. A fatal dose for a child, probably. Probably borderline for an adult.

"Why the other children? Why not me?"

"I don't fucking know. Think about it, why would Kana tell me something like that?"

No, she realized. That would have been too much to hope. Probably Tyler was telling the truth, at least about that much.

For the first time, she glanced down at the bench to her left, where he'd set the bag. It was unzipped, but she couldn't see inside it. She reached over and moved one of the flaps. Inside was a large, plastic-wrapped brick of what must have been meth.

On top of it, a Smith & Wesson .357 revolver.

"Don't," he said. "Don't look in the bag. Come on, this is bullshit, we had a deal. I told you everything. I did. I don't want to go back. Don't fucking send me back. Like you said, I've got a wife and daughter. Please."

"You're not going back," she said. "I'm leaving. You stay here after I'm gone." She pulled on the helmet.

His shoulders sagged with relief. He nodded and smiled. "Okay. Good. I gotta say, you scared me there for a minute."

She dropped the visor, pulled the revolver from the bag, and shot him in the heart.

He jerked back and his hands clapped over his chest. "*Oh!*" he groaned. "*Oh, guhhhh . . .*"

He tried to stand, then sat back heavily. He looked at her, his face contorted with pain and surprise. Then he slowly pitched forward, his hands still compressed against his chest. His face hit the picnic table. His body twitched once, and then he was still.

She looked at him for a moment, the dragon fiery inside her, then stood to go.

"They're not going to miss you," she said.

52—NOW

She tossed the revolver and the meth from a bridge into the Methow River just south of Winthrop. She'd been wearing her riding gloves the entire time and hadn't touched anything. And any gunshot residue on the helmet or the leathers wouldn't survive the long ride back to Seattle. Not that a little GSR on a cop's clothes was so difficult to explain regardless. Anyway, her connection with Tyler was ancient history. She doubted even Rick would suspect she had anything to do with it. And Masnick would take their conversation to his grave—because he knew he'd be in that grave a lot faster if he didn't. No, when the shooting victim was someone like Weed Tyler, the working theory was typically Drug Deal Gone Bad. Which, in its way, in this case wasn't so far from the truth.

She didn't want to go straight back to headquarters. Seeing Tyler, killing him, recounting the past, putting together some of the pieces . . . she had so much to think about. She needed air. She needed to move. To let her emotions wash through her so her mind could be clear.

Back at the loft, she changed out of the leathers, pulled on jeans and a fleece, and drove the Jeep to Alki Beach, where she walked north along the water. The air smelled clean, and the only sounds were the wind, the crunch of her boots on the gravel path, the waves lapping against the shore.

She stopped at the northern point and looked out at the Space Needle and the lights of downtown across Elliott Bay. The wind whipped her hair around, and she tied it back in a ponytail, then zipped up the fleece and just stood there, watching the silent passage of the Bainbridge Island ferry, the slow-moving lines of distant traffic, feeling cocooned by the wind. The city looked so peaceful from here, so clean. You'd never know the vile sewer underneath.

She had saved a baby girl raped so many times by her father the child's rectum was prolapsed. Rescued an elderly woman kept in a dungeon, chained in her own filth, her legs infested with maggots, imprisoned by the son who was cashing her Social Security checks. And caught the Montlake rapist, of course. The system had worked for that one. But every time she thought about the way he had used his victims' love for each other to control and further torment them, she couldn't help wishing the system had failed, so that she could have gotten justice for those women another way.

She had taken psych courses at SJSU, and knew that protecting others, avenging them, was sublimation. If she'd been raised Catholic, she might have understood the behavior as atonement instead. Either way, she couldn't save Nason, and would spend her life trying to make up for that failure by saving others in Nason's place.

She really did help people, she knew that, and when it happened, it was just . . . magic. And when helping wasn't possible . . . when a repeat rapist slipped through the system . . . sublimation took the form of her hobby. And it wasn't just sublimation. She also understood that her high-risk activities, even her decision to become a cop, were ways of proving to herself over and over that she wasn't a victim anymore, and never would be again.

It was interesting how much insight you could have into your own pathologies, and how little impact the insight would have on your underlying needs.

Or on your behavior.

At times, though, none of it mattered. At times, all the sublimation and atonement in the world weren't enough. And the only thing that might help would be to know what had happened to Nason. Just to know. Just to know. Nothing more than that. Just to *know*.

Facing Tyler, she realized, the culmination of a decade and a half of anxiety and desperate hope, had overwhelmed her defenses, and made all the horror and loss immediate again. And now, looking out at the city, she felt so . . . empty. Alone. So fucking bereft.

She shivered against the wind and watched the lights and let her grief have its way. After a while, she was able to think clearly again.

Four kids. Not three. And two of them sisters.

Why such a specific cargo? She thought back to her conversation with AUSA Velez, and how he had explained the way trafficking worked—wholesale down to retail. So had Skull Face sent them all off to market just hoping buyers would turn up?

No, that didn't make sense. Skull Face was using a gang with no experience moving people, only with drugs. Why would he do that, unless he had a designated buyer somewhere in the vicinity? A buyer who wanted, who had ordered, something specific, forcing Skull Face to turn to Weed Tyler and his gang despite their lack of relevant experience?

Or maybe . . . it was *because* of their lack of experience?

She made a mental note to log in to the FBI's crime database, to see if she could cross-reference the name Kana. It was a long shot, but worth a try.

So someone had, what, bought them all? Ordered them, the way you would order a pizza?

She imagined it. *Get me a Guatemalan housemaid. Get me a Chinese busboy. Get me a little Thai girl to rape.*

No. Not just a little girl. Two sisters.

Where had that thought come from? Maybe from the way the Montlake rapist had used his victims' love for each other to manipulate and control them. The way Skull Face had done the same to Livia with Nason.

The way Mr. Lone had done.

Was that why she had found herself thinking about the Montlake case? Was her unconscious trying to tell her something?

She shook her head. It didn't make sense. How could Mr. Lone have arranged it? All the way from Thailand? It was a coincidence. A sick, evil man sees a powerless little girl, and takes advantage of his good luck. A crime of opportunity, not of planning.

His brother. Ezra Lone. The senator.

It was still too far-fetched. She didn't believe it. But . . .

Assume both brothers are that sick. And assume they have the connections to pull off something like what you're imagining.

Okay, but there were still too many pieces that didn't fit. Like the fact that there had been other girls in the container from Thailand. Why had Skull Face and his men left the rest of them alone? Why had they been interested only in Livia and Nason, the sisters? If Livia and Nason were some kind of special shipment, wouldn't Skull Face and the others have abused someone else?

She remembered the way Skull Face had looked at her, when despite her own fierce hunger she had given her food to Nason.

Could that have been it? Was that the sick kink he couldn't resist? The opportunity to control a little girl by manipulating the girl's love for her own sister?

And then the opportunity to rip away even that small victory, by violating the sister anyway?

But Nason hadn't even made it to Llewellyn. Skull Face and his men had sold her somewhere else. Or . . .

. . . killed her. Because no one would want to buy merchandise as damaged as that.

She pushed her fist to her mouth and bit down on the knuckles. She hated thinking it, but of all the possibilities, that the men had killed Nason seemed by far the most likely. The only thing that made the thought even remotely bearable was that it didn't feel true. Her mind could say what it liked, but in her heart, she had never stopped believing her little bird was alive, out there somewhere, and that one day she would find her, envelop her in her arms and never, ever let anything bad happen to her again.

She waited again for the emotions to pass and her mind to clear.

All right. Maybe the Lones had wanted sisters because sisters would be easier to use against each other, easier to control, something like that. Maybe some kind of sick turn-on. The same sort of thing Skull Face had found so irresistible. The same sort of dynamic involved in the Montlake rapes. But then . . . Nason would have been on the barge from Portland with Livia. And Skull Face and his men never would have damaged her the way they had.

Unless they hadn't meant to damage her. Not the way they did. Only to use her, like they had used you. And then you cut them, and Skull Face forgot he was handling merchandise ordered by a customer, merchandise he was supposed to deliver more or less intact. He lost control. He needed to hurt the helpless victim who had just cut out his eye. Hurt her in the worst way imaginable. Through her sister.

She choked back a sob. Many times before, she had suspected it was her fault the men had hurt Nason so badly. But it had never felt so true.

She remembered how afterward, Skull Face's men had restrained him from going after her. He'd wanted more revenge, but cooler heads—dollars-and-cents heads—had prevailed. She tried to find holes in the theory, but couldn't. It was simple. Skull Face was supposed to deliver two intact sisters. But he'd lost control and hurt one so badly that he could only deliver the other.

She'd been just a little girl when it happened. She'd only been trying to protect Nason. She knew it wasn't her fault.

But it was her fault. It was. If only she hadn't attacked the men . . .

She closed her eyes and gritted her teeth. She pushed aside the guilt and forced herself to focus. *Focus.*

If the Lones had wanted sisters, why bring other children on the barge from Portland, just to poison them? And why poison some of the adults, too?

Because Mr. Lone couldn't adopt four kids. He had wanted something he could control. Four would have been too many. But they didn't want it to look as though they were singling out the children. An adult, or adults, needed to die, too, or at least get sick. So it would look random. Accidental.

It was as though a window she had been trying for so long to see through, a window on what had really happened, was suddenly clearing, at least partly. It was what she had hoped for. But it was also almost too much. She staggered over to a bench and sat.

The Lones wanted sisters. But Fred Lone couldn't go out and just adopt a pair—it might have caused speculation, suspicion, even in a town as devoted as Llewellyn to not seeing what he really was. So they arranged for a shipment somehow. A shipment that was supposed to be a mix of adults and kids, but with the sisters the only kids surviving the journey. The ones no one would know what to do with. Except Fred Lone, the great benefactor. He would adopt them.

She could feel her mind still trying to resist it. For so long, she'd believed she and Nason had been the victims of circumstance. But a conspiracy?

And they needed a bust, of course. That's why someone phoned in an anonymous tip to Chief Emmanuel. But there was no tip. Mr. Lone told Emmanuel exactly what to do. Save the victims. Execute the traffickers. Tie up loose ends.

But Tyler . . . he survived.

Remember, there were federal agents, too. Emmanuel had to do the whole thing by the book to avoid scrutiny. He, or he and his men, tried to kill all three, but somehow they couldn't get to Tyler. Maybe the feds got to him first. Whatever the reason, they went to plan B: not a word, Weed, or your ass gets shanked in prison.

Besides, Tyler didn't know that much, anyway. But they would take as few chances as possible.

She tried to imagine it from their perspective. How it would look when it was done.

It's the perfect appearance: routine human trafficking. Heroic local police and federal action. Adoring coverage in the press. A group of adults, all subject to repatriation. And two poor little refugee sisters no one knows what to do with.

No one except Mr. Lone.

But Livia had told them her parents were dead. They couldn't have predicted that. What if she had told them what had really happened?

Lone would have just argued that they couldn't send the poor children back. Their parents would only sell them again.

She put her hands to her head and moaned aloud. How could she have missed it all, for so long? Was it because she didn't want to see?

No. It wasn't that. It was information she had lacked, not insight. Before Tyler, she had no reason to believe she and Nason were anything other than routinely trafficked children, just two among thousands, hundreds of thousands. Why would it have occurred to her that the two of them might have been specifically requested by a degenerate—a degenerate whose brother had the political connections to order a customized set of child sex slaves?

The political connections. She needed to look into that. Who would a senator have to know to order two sisters all the way from Thailand? He'd need the contacts. A conduit. A circuit breaker, for deniability. How would Ezra Lone have set up all that?

She thought of his "legislative aide," Matthias Redcroft. That would be one piece—probably the go-between, the bagman. But how would the senator know where to place the order? He trusted someone, and they trusted him. Enough to do this kind of business. And what did he pay? Was it cash? Political influence? Something else? Whatever it was, it was valuable enough so that whoever had paid Tyler and his gang to move Livia and the others to Llewellyn didn't mind losing fifty thousand dollars in the process. And the cargo, too, obviously.

She remembered her initial impressions of Llewellyn. How she had always sensed something rotten about the town, something she could almost smell. She'd read a book in high school called *Watership Down*. It was about rabbits—well, rabbits as people. And there was one group of rabbits that lived on a farm, accepting the farmer's food, grateful that he shot foxes and stoats, their natural enemies . . . and accepting that he laid snares, so that anytime he wanted to make a stew from one of his nice, fat rabbits, he could.

She realized that's what Llewellyn felt like. The people had known. But they found a way to not know. Because they wanted what Mr. Lone and his brother provided. The ammunition factory. The mill. All the people they employed, through Mr. Lone's businesses and Senator Lone's votes. Against all that, why would they care if the Lones decided to snare a little refugee girl . . . and eat her?

The theory felt right. In fact, her own discomfort, her resistance to believing it, suggested it was sound. Still, there was one thing missing, one imaginative leap she knew needed to be bridged. She wasn't trying to make a case that would stand up in court. But she needed all the pieces to fit. The whole thing had to be solid enough for her to take the next step. Whatever that might be.

She'd always assumed Fred Lone was simply a freak. Maybe there was an explanation—he'd been molested by a priest or a teacher or a coach, and infected by evil. She'd certainly seen enough of that. Or maybe he'd just been born twisted. She'd encountered plenty of that, as well. Evil with no explanation, no origin.

But two brothers, and both of them monsters? That wasn't a coincidence. Something had happened to them both, when they were boys. If she could find out what that thing was, maybe she would be one step closer to finding Nason.

She thought about Fred Lone's funeral. The family crypt, with the sister who had died when Lone was young. Livia had never thought to ask about that before. She'd never cared.

Well, she did now.

53—NOW

She walked back to the parking lot. She was getting cold, and anyway it was too windy for a phone call.

She turned up the heat in the Jeep and pulled out onto Admiral Way, heading toward the West Seattle Bridge and Georgetown. The streets were quiet, the windows dark in the buildings she passed.

She called the number Tanya had given her when they'd talked after Livia had graduated from the academy. *Answer*, she thought. She didn't want to wait for this information. She'd waited so long already.

The phone rang only once, then Tanya's voice: "Livia Lone, as I live and breathe."

Livia smiled, relieved. "Tanya. You must be on call."

"You guessed it. Not that you'd be waking me anyway. I'm a night owl. How are you, sister?"

"I'm good. I'm sorry to bother you this late, but I have a strange question, if you don't mind."

"I never mind, and I told you, for me it's not late. Tell me what I can do to help."

"Thanks. You've lived in Llewellyn for a long time, right?"

"Born and raised. Went to Llewellyn High School, just like you."

"Well, even born and raised, this would have been a little before your time, but . . . what can you tell me about Fred Lone's family? I mean, when he was a boy. I know about his older brother Ezra, the senator. But there was a sister, too, right? Who died when they were young?"

There was a pause, probably while Tanya considered asking what this was about. Then she said, "Actually, there were two sisters. One was the oldest child. She committed suicide. That's the one buried in that fancy mausoleum. And the youngest child was also a girl. She left Llewellyn after high school, and the word is she's never been back."

Livia felt her cop instincts prickle. There was something there. She just didn't know what yet.

"Suicide? Why?"

"No one knew why. Not really. Supposedly there was a history of mental illness. There were several attempts before she finally succeeded. Threw herself out her bedroom window onto a fence. Picket fence."

Livia frowned. What had Eric and his bully friends used to taunt her with, when she was new in the school? *Hey Lahu, when are you going to jump out a window onto a fence and kill yourself?* She had never known what they were talking about. But it must have been that. Some kind of town lore.

"How old was she?"

There was a pause, then Tanya said, "Seventeen, I think. It was the summer before her senior year."

Livia imagined how desperate a teenage girl would have to be to hurl herself onto a row of wooden stakes.

Though it was more remembering than imagining.

"What was her name?"

"Ophelia, believe it or not."

Livia thought of *Hamlet*, which she had read in one of her high school English lit classes. "Unlucky name."

"I'd say so."

"So you weren't even born when all this happened."

"That's right, I came along ten years later. But you know the Lones. They've always been a big deal in this town, going back to Fred Lone's grandfather, who started the paper mill. In a town like Llewellyn, news is like throwing a rock in a lake—the bigger the rock, the bigger the ripples, and the farther they go. Ophelia Lone killing herself the way she did . . . shit, kids were still talking about it when I was in high school, and that was almost twenty years later. 'They took the fence away, but that's the spot where she landed, and the fence posts went through one of her eyes, her mouth, her heart, her private parts' . . . depending on how gruesome the teller wanted to be. You never heard any of this when you were in school? I guess the talk finally died out."

"No, there was still talk. I just didn't know what it meant."

"I'm not surprised. It's like a ghost story, you know? People want to keep telling it around the campfire."

"How old were the brothers and the other sister when it happened?"

"They were each only a grade apart. So figure Ezra was sixteen. And Fred . . . he was a tad younger, so fourteen. And Rebecca, who they called Becky, she was thirteen."

"Sounds like Lone Senior was a man with a mission."

"Yeah, he wasn't giving the missus long breaks, that's for sure."

"You said Becky moved away."

"That's right. Caused a minor scandal by going to Berkeley rather than Yale."

"Why a scandal?"

"The family was a big Yale legacy, going all the way back to the grandfather, and then the father, and Ezra and Fred were both Yalies. I think there's even a Lone building somewhere on campus—that's how much money the family donates. Plus you know how conservative the

Lones are—church every Sunday, a flag out in front of the house. And back then, Berkeley was a hotbed of hippie radicalism. So a Lone going to Berkeley . . . hell, it was like changing religions, or something. Becky was the black sheep of the family."

"You have any idea where she wound up?"

"After Berkeley? No, I don't. But like I said, I never heard of her coming back to Llewellyn. I don't think she was even here for her brother's funeral."

"No. She wasn't."

"Well, even for a black sheep, that's a little odd, now that we're talking about it."

Maybe, Livia thought. *Or maybe it makes perfect sense.*

There was a pause, then Tanya said, "I'll tell you what, Livia. I won't ask what this is about. But if you ever want to tell me, I won't tell you not to."

She couldn't tell Tanya. Or anyone. Not without telling all of it. Which she was never going to do.

"It's probably nothing," Livia said. "But if I'm wrong about that, I'll . . . try to find a way to let you know."

Tanya chuckled. "Fair enough. Either way, I'd still enjoy that drink sometime."

"So would I. This is the second time you've been really good to me. I hope I'll be able to repay you at some point."

Tanya laughed. "You don't owe me anything. Just seeing what you've made of your life makes me smile. I will let you buy the drinks, though, okay?"

Now it was Livia's turn to laugh. "It's a deal. And thanks, Tanya."

She clicked off.

Mental illness. Is that what they called it, when the father, or the brothers, or both, were raping a teenage girl and destroying her dignity, her self-image, her peace of mind, ripping apart everything about her until she reached the point where a row of stakes twenty feet down looked like a blessing?

She swung the Jeep around and drove to headquarters. She had a feeling Rebecca Lone had changed her name, and maybe a few other identifying details, too. She was trying to hide—hide from the past, hide from her guilt, hide from her shame.

Or maybe even something worse than all that.

It didn't matter. Livia was going to find her.

54—NOW

She spent most of the night at her desk at headquarters. The coffee was burnt, so she made a fresh pot, then poured herself a large mugful, cutting it with milk and a scoop of the turbinado sugar she kept in a desk drawer.

Senator Lone was the easy part. All she needed was his website and Wikipedia. It was so obvious, now that she had some of the pieces.

He'd been active against human trafficking since his time as a freshman senator. Wrangled himself a position on the Senate Foreign Relations Committee, where he worked to raise consciousness on the issue. Multiple trips to Thailand, to pressure the Thai government to do more against the scourge of trafficking. And every time he was out there, Livia knew, he would have fucked every impoverished child he could get his disgusting hands on.

His website trumpeted his work, claiming his efforts had led to the protection and rescue of thousands of children and unprecedented cooperation from governments that had formerly turned a blind eye to trafficking—countries like Thailand, where Lone had fostered joint law enforcement efforts that had led to the near destruction of Thai organized crime groups involved in trafficking.

Unsurprisingly, she found nothing about a Thai gangster going by the name Kana. But there were dozens of old news articles on Thai criminal groups generally. It seemed that once there had been three large ones, all of which were known to move human cargo through Southern California and, to a lesser extent, San Francisco and Oakland.

But no known instances of people-smuggling through Portland.

So maybe they used Hammerhead because they knew there was going to be a bust. Not despite Hammerhead's lack of experience moving people, but because of it, as she'd wondered when talking to Tyler. If a bust was indeed the plan, they wouldn't have wanted to bring heat on their profitable California routes. If they had to sacrifice something, it would be a relatively small-time narcotics operation in the Northwest, and the expendable peckerwoods they used as distributors there.

She thought of her conversation with AUSA Velez again, and how he had told her containers were usually jammed full of trafficked people because packing the container was just sound economics and risk management. Well, of course that's why there were so few of them on the barge. They knew the shipment was going to be intercepted. It was *supposed* to be intercepted. The less wasted cargo, the better. And likewise the shipment from Bangkok. It was a decoy operation. They probably didn't have local buyers. Those other children, the Hmong boy Kai . . . Skull Face and the rest probably had to ship them individually to wherever they had buyers, at additional cost and risk.

Or simply dispose of them. But Livia couldn't allow herself to accept that. It was too close to Nason.

So whatever they were getting in exchange for this one shipment, it was worth more than the fifty thousand they'd paid Tyler and his gang. Worth more than the sacrificed cargo. It was worth risking an entire Pacific Northwest Thai ganja operation.

She kept reading. It seemed two of the three Thai gangs had been crushed with multiple arrests and prosecutions. The third had been seriously weakened.

All around the time she and Nason were trafficked to America.

All around the time Ezra Lone was on a crusade to get the Thai government to crack down on trafficking groups.

She put her elbows on her desk and rested her forehead against her knuckles. Could that have been it? Some kind of quid pro quo?

She imagined Senator Lone pitching it to some of his corrupt government contacts, or even directly to one of the criminal groups. Or maybe to both. *There's a storm coming,* he would have told them. *I can't head it off. But I can give you an umbrella. Joint law enforcement to destroy your rivals. Adoring press coverage about your unprecedented cooperation. I report to the Senate that Thailand has made tremendous progress in the battle against trafficking, with more investigations, prosecutions, and convictions than ever before. The Senate recommends to the State Department that Thailand be upgraded from Tier 3 trafficking status, the worst, to Tier 2, or maybe even Tier 1, with all the trade benefits the improvement entails. We clear the field for you. And bring in a boatload of US trade. You'll make more money, have more power, than you ever dreamed. And all I want in return is that you provide me children to fuck when I visit on my periodic fact-finding missions.*

And two custom-ordered sisters, who you'll obtain and ship to America per my instructions.

Probably she was wrong about some of the particulars. But she was pretty sure she had the general contours. The sisters part especially. It explained why her parents had given out the photo of her and Nason—so the Lones could select exactly the type of girls they wanted.

She remembered a concept from one of her college psych courses: the "breastplate of righteousness." It was a biblical phrase referring to the armor of God, the goodness required in the battle against evil. But in psychology, it meant a protective shield of super-propriety, like when a closeted man railed in public about the evils of homosexuality—attending church regularly, proclaiming the importance of "family values," and overall cloaking himself in political conservatism. Sometimes it was a defense mechanism. More often, it was a deliberate attempt to avoid or deflect suspicion, like that anti-gay senator who had been caught soliciting anonymous gay sex in a Minnesota airport restroom, or like any of the countless fire-and-brimstone ministers and politicians who had been similarly caught out in their hypocrisies.

Why her and Nason, though? Did the Lones want hill tribe girls? A certain age? Sisters? Some combination?

Just sisters, she sensed, thinking again about how Skull Face had used Nason against Livia, how the Montlake rapist had used those two women against each other.

But she needed to be sure.

She finished her coffee, then ran a search on Matthias Redcroft. Zero hits on social media. One hit for tax records—he was indeed employed by the senator. And one hit for military service—twelve years in the army, the last six with Special Forces. What the hell was a former SF guy, with the social media profile of a ghost, doing as a "legislative aide"?

She lifted her head and rubbed her eyes. She could see the opportunity. And most of the means. And the motive was obvious, in the very abuse she herself had suffered. What was missing was the pathology that had created the motive. She could sense it, but not yet see it.

If they'd wanted sisters, if that had been important to them . . . then maybe there was a chance. The smallest chance, but still a chance. That Nason was alive somewhere. That Livia could find her.

But no matter what, there was another chance, too. The chance that she could just know. Yes. Please that. Just to *know*. Before she died herself, just to know what had happened to her little bird.

She took a deep breath and blew it out.

And started searching for Becky Lone.

55—NOW

None of the available police and federal databases had anything on a Rebecca or Becky Lone. A social media search was similarly fruitless. Not surprising—it had all happened decades earlier. And if Livia's intuition was right, Becky would have kept a low profile anyway.

But her intuition suggested a few other things, as well. Someone fleeing an abusive past and desperate to build something safe and secure. A new family. A new life. And someone who wanted those things not far in the future, but soon. Maybe as soon as graduating from college, or soon after. Maybe Becky had met a boy, the right kind of boy—sane, stable, reliable. She'd married him, and taken his name. Probably a California boy, since about eighty percent of Berkeley undergraduates were from California. And Livia knew from having lived in the Bay Area herself that people from there tended to stay. That gave her a lot to cross-reference with alumni organizations, property records, car registrations, voter registrations, and vital records databases. Of course, she could have been wrong about any of the particulars, in which case she would have to expand the search. But her gut rarely failed her, and she sensed she was using the right parameters.

As the day's first light began to creep through the windows, though, she was starting to doubt herself. It had all felt so right. But she wasn't finding anything. Becky Lone had just . . . disappeared.

And then, as she was on the verge of deciding she'd been wrong and was going to have to figure out a completely different approach, Livia found her.

She was called Rebecca MacKinnon now, married to William MacKinnon. Same class at Berkeley. MacKinnon had been a partner, now some kind of emeritus, at a big Bay Area law firm. They lived in San Francisco—Vallejo Street in Pacific Heights, a high-end neighborhood. Three children. Two small grandchildren. One of the children had a Facebook page with a photo of a birthday party—the baby, the parents, the grandparents. Livia saw the wide-set eyes of the grandmother and knew she was looking at Becky Lone. She looked up the woman's mobile phone number and confirmed its current location. Pacific Heights. She was home. Probably still sleeping.

Her heart pounding, Livia started writing an email to Lieutenant Strangeland. She wasn't going to make it to roll call this morning. It seemed she needed a personal day.

56—NOW

Livia arrived by taxi a block from the MacKinnons' house at a little past noon after a nonstop from Seattle. She didn't like Lyft and Uber. Whenever possible, she preferred not to leave a trail.

It was a postcard day in San Francisco—cool, clear, breezy, hard blue skies. She could smell star jasmine in the air, and it reminded her of college. She liked this city, and in fact had considered joining SFPD after graduating. But Seattle was her best route to Nason, and that had trumped everything.

She walked up Vallejo and stood for a moment in front of the house, the sun warm on her face. It was a relatively modest place for the neighborhood—on the small side, with a brown wood façade, and a shingle roof rather than the tile of some of the enormous dwellings nearby. Unlike the Lone mansion in Llewellyn, it felt real—designed to be lived in, not to make a statement. Still, the back faced north, and would command spectacular views of the Golden Gate Bridge and the bay. This was no starter home.

She went through the gate, stepped under the archway, and rang the bell. She looked up and saw a security camera. Well, so much for not leaving a trail. Not that it mattered. She was only here to talk.

A moment later, the door opened. The woman in the Facebook photo—no question, Becky Lone, a.k.a. Rebecca MacKinnon. An attractive woman, mid-sixties, fit-looking, prosperous, well preserved. She had short gray hair and a minimum of makeup, and was dressed in a smart navy pantsuit. A lady who lunched, Livia thought. And maybe lunch was in fact where she was heading.

Beside MacKinnon was a large German shepherd. The animal neither barked nor growled. It simply remained still and watched Livia. It was obviously well trained, and intimidating in its calm watchfulness. Livia had the sense that if it hadn't been for the dog, MacKinnon wouldn't have opened the door, even though it was only a petite Asian woman in the security camera feed.

"Can I help you?" MacKinnon said.

"Yes, ma'am," Livia said, holding out her badge. "My name is Livia Lone. I'm a sex crimes detective with Seattle PD."

At the mention of Livia's name, MacKinnon's pupils dilated and her face paled. The dog remained silent, but seemed to tense slightly. Livia realized it would take no more than a word from MacKinnon and the animal would launch itself. She didn't think it would come to that, but she ran a mental play of stepping offline and bringing out the Vaari from the side pocket of her cargo pants. She could deploy the blade faster than she could the Glock. Traveling as a cop had its advantages, among them being you didn't have to disarm to get on a plane.

"I'm not here in any kind of official capacity," Livia said, "but I'd be grateful if you could help me understand a few things."

"I don't . . . really know what I could help you with," MacKinnon said, taking what looked like an unconscious step backward, her hand gripping the door.

"Becky," Livia said evenly, "I think you do."

At that, the dog growled.

The woman pursed her lips and slowly shook her head. Her knuckles whitening on the door, she said, "I don't want to talk to you."

"No. I'm sure you don't. I'm sure you don't want to talk to anyone. But your refusal to talk? Your refusal to say anything? It's why your brother Fred was able to do to me the same things that happened to you. So I think you owe me that talk. I think you owe me at least that much."

She wasn't positive she was right. But MacKinnon's behavior so far had strengthened her suspicions, and emboldened her to bluff. If she was right, it would be a powerful gambit—when a suspect became convinced the detective already knew much of what the suspect might say, the suspect became significantly more inclined to confess. Because what was the harm, anyway?

For a long moment, Livia thought the woman was going to close the door in her face. Or maybe sic the dog on her. Then her body seemed to sag. She nodded and opened the door.

Livia stepped inside, the dog's head swiveling to follow her as she passed. She had been right about the view. The windows in back were massive, and she could see everything—the bay, sparkling in the sun; the bridge spanning it; the green hills of Marin on the far side. She noticed MacKinnon's bare feet, and that there were shoes lined up by the door. She took off her own. The tile was warm. It must have been heated.

MacKinnon closed the door. "Why don't we sit in the kitchen," she said. "Can I offer you something?"

Her tone was so chilly and begrudging, it reminded Livia of Mrs. Lone's courtesies. Though the kitchen was encouraging. The living room was for putting people off. The kitchen was always where business got done.

"I don't want anything from you," Livia said. "Just the truth about your brothers."

MacKinnon stared at her, then dropped her eyes. "I don't know what you mean by that."

"Becky. A minute ago you heard my name and it looked like your breakfast was going to come up. You knew. You learned your brother Fred had taken in a little Thai refugee girl. You knew why." Her voice started to rise. "You knew what he was going to do to me. *You knew what that was like.*"

The dog growled again. MacKinnon did nothing to calm it. Livia looked in its eyes. *You want to try me?* she thought. *Come on, then. Let's see who's faster. And who has sharper claws.*

MacKinnon glanced at the dog. "Easy, girl," she said. "Easy."

Livia wasn't sure which of them she was talking to. She didn't care. After all she had endured at the hands of MacKinnon's brother, the notion that the woman would feign ignorance was enraging. "So don't tell me you don't know what I mean," she went on. "You know *exactly* what I mean. I want to know what happened to you. And to your sister, Ophelia."

By the time she was done speaking, MacKinnon had lost so much color that Livia thought the woman might pass out. She seemed to wobble for a moment, then righted herself. "Won't you please sit," she said, gesturing to the kitchen. "I'll make some tea. And we'll . . . we'll talk."

Livia sat at a wooden table next to another enormous window overlooking the bay, making sure the handle of the Vaari protruded just slightly from her pocket so she could reach it instantly if she needed to. MacKinnon filled a kettle and put it on the restaurant-style stove. Livia glanced around, taking in the fine cabinets, the high-end appliances. It looked like law had been good to William MacKinnon. Or maybe his wife had built a career, too. Although somehow, Livia doubted it. She felt she was looking at someone who had built a home instead.

Or rather, rebuilt one.

"Green tea?" MacKinnon asked. "I drink jasmine myself, but we have several."

"Jasmine's fine. Thank you."

"Honey?"

Livia wanted to shout, *Enough with the stupid formalities, tell me what I want to know!*

But she'd interrogated enough suspects, and cajoled enough reluctant witnesses, to understand the value of respect. And patience. This woman was about to discuss matters she had prayed for close to half a century would never catch up to her. She was collecting herself, bracing herself, and it would be foolish not to allow her time to do it.

"Honey would be lovely. Thank you."

MacKinnon led the dog to another room and closed the door, and Livia had the strangest sense the woman didn't want it to hear what she might say. Whatever the reason, she was glad it was gone for the time being.

Then the water had to be poured, the tea had to steep, the honey had to be stirred in. And Livia had to take a sip, and acknowledge that it was delicious, thank you. And then she waited again, letting the silence do its job.

MacKinnon took a sip of tea, then set the cup back on the saucer. Livia waited. It was so quiet she could hear the hum of the refrigerator.

MacKinnon put her hands on the table and looked at them. "My father was a monster," she said quietly.

Livia didn't speak, or even move. She did nothing except wait.

"He . . ." There was a pause. MacKinnon was still looking down, and Livia couldn't see her face. But she sensed the woman was crying.

"He . . ." She exhaled sharply, then looked at Livia, her eyes glistening. "Please don't make me talk about this. Please."

The woman's expression was so dignified, and her pain so poignant, that Livia might have felt compassion for her. And maybe she did feel something. But she pushed it away. This woman was the key to Nason. And that's all that mattered.

"I had a sister," Livia said evenly. "Her name was Nason. Sixteen years ago, she went missing. I've been searching for her ever since. What you know could help me find her. So please. Go on."

MacKinnon took a deep breath and let it out. She adjusted herself in the chair. "My father. He believed . . . daughters belong to their fathers. Do you understand?"

Sometimes, euphemisms and other vague references could help a reluctant victim give a statement. This time, Livia sensed brutal truth would be the better tool. "Your father believed fathers should be able to fuck their daughters."

MacKinnon winced. "He believed a daughter's body was her father's right. Until she was married, when her body would belong to her husband. And he believed . . . that brothers, also . . ."

"He believed brothers should be able to fuck their sisters."

MacKinnon sobbed. "Please don't make me talk about this," she whispered.

"Your father. Your brothers. They were abusing Ophelia, weren't they?"

MacKinnon got up and tore off a length of paper towels from a rack on the counter. She wiped her eyes, blew her nose, wadded up the towel, and threw it into a garbage container under the sink. Then she grabbed another length and came back to the table.

"My father started abusing Ophelia when she was thirteen."

She paused for a moment, as though collecting herself.

"Your mother?" Livia said, already knowing the answer from having worked too many cases of fathers raping their daughters and stepdaughters.

MacKinnon shook her head. "She was terrified of my father. And she blamed Ophelia for what was happening."

She paused again, then said, "When Ezra turned thirteen, my father made Ophelia service him, too. And when Fred turned thirteen, it was the same. All three of them." Her voice cracked. "Using her. Whenever they wanted. However they liked. Her *father*. And her *brothers*."

She wiped her eyes. "Then, when I turned thirteen, it was my turn to be put to use. And . . ."

Her voice cracked again, and she broke down for a moment, her face downcast, her shoulders shaking. Then she took several deep breaths and wiped her eyes again. "And Ophelia . . . she wouldn't let them."

"Your sister tried to protect you," Livia said, and for a moment, she wasn't sure who she was referring to, herself or Ophelia. Both, maybe. Despite all the years of professional reserve, she felt her own eyes well up.

MacKinnon nodded. "She fought them," she whispered.

Livia could imagine her little bird so clearly. The blood between her legs. Her thumb in her mouth. Her vacant eyes. Her unresponsive body as Livia held her and cried.

"But they did it anyway," Livia said.

MacKinnon looked at her, her face twisted. "They made her watch," she said, and her voice cracked again.

Livia made no attempt to hide her own tears. "I'm sorry, Becky."

"And then they made me watch. My father said, 'You see, boys? This is what we do to disobedient girls.'"

Livia remembered Fred Lone's fixation on her own "disobedience." She forced away her disgust.

MacKinnon wiped her eyes again. "So. Now you know about my family."

There was a long pause while they both collected themselves. Then Livia said, "I think your brothers, at considerable risk and expense, arranged for my sister and me to be shipped to Llewellyn from our village in Thailand. Could what you've been telling me be why they wanted sisters? I was thirteen. Nason was eleven. Could your brothers have wanted to . . . I don't know, recreate what they were doing to you and Ophelia when you were a similar age?"

MacKinnon looked like she might be sick. "Oh, my God," she said. "I'm sorry."

It made sense. It fit. And as horrible as it was, there was satisfaction in piecing it all together.

She thought of how she had felt after what Skull Face and his men had done to Nason. How she had wanted to die. How the only thing that had made her keep eating, made her keep herself alive, was that Nason might need her. Looking back, she was amazed she hadn't succumbed to her longing for oblivion. For Ophelia Lone, it seemed, the sirens of oblivion had sung louder.

"Is that when Ophelia jumped from the window?" she said.

MacKinnon looked at her, her face slowly contorting. "That's a lie," she hissed.

Livia blinked. "What?"

"They told everyone she jumped. But she never would have. *Never.*"

Livia stared at her for a moment, feeling like she'd been hit by a throw she hadn't seen coming and slammed into the tatami. She had been remembering her own despair, her own longing for death, and had projected it onto another tormented teenage girl. And the projection had blinded her to another, even more horrifying possibility.

She would never have made a mistake like that as a cop. But this, she realized . . . this was too close to her. It was interfering with her judgment.

She shook her head, as though doing so might clear it. "You think your father—"

"I think it was Ezra. But"—her voice cracked again—"she was the only one who loved me. She would never have left me alone to them. Not for anything."

"Why do you think it was Ezra?"

"Because he was the most horrible. For my father and Fred, it was mostly about power. And sex, of course. But Ezra . . . he liked to hurt us. And . . . he told Ophelia he was going to do something to me. Something he liked to do to her. And she told him if he did that, she would tell. She would go to the police. He could do what he liked to her, but not to me. And you know what he told me after she died?"

Livia was afraid she did know. But she said nothing.

"He told me, 'That's what will happen to you if you ever say anything.' And then he did the thing to me anyway. I begged him. I was screaming. I told him he was killing me. And he just laughed and did it harder. After that, I don't even remember. I think I blacked out."

A moment went by. Then MacKinnon said, "I knew better than to scream, but I couldn't help it. Whatever made me scream became his favorite thing. So I learned not to. Just to be passive, and wait for it to be over. But really, that only made it worse. It frustrated him, and made him look for new ways to make me scream."

Livia looked at her. "Why didn't you ever tell anyone?"

MacKinnon returned her look. "Why didn't you?"

Livia scrubbed the back of her hand across her wet cheeks. "Because no one would have believed me. I was just a little refugee girl. And your brother was the most revered man in Llewellyn."

"Well then, you already know why."

"But all these years . . . don't you understand? Your brothers . . . they had my sister and me taken all the way from Thailand. And who knows how many other children they've raped, traumatized, destroyed, that we'll never even know about? You could have stopped that. Maybe not when you were a child, but any time after."

"Don't you dare judge me. Look at you. What have you ever done to stop it?"

"I *did* stop it."

She said it before she could think not to.

There was a long pause. MacKinnon looked at her, understanding slowly dawning in her eyes. Livia thought she was going to ask, and prepared a denial.

But the woman only nodded grimly. "Good," she said, and her tone was as cold as the frozen grass over Fred Lone's grave. Then she added in a whisper, "I hope you made him suffer."

Livia said nothing.

MacKinnon blinked, then straightened. She took a sip of tea, then returned the cup to the saucer. "For what it's worth, if I could go back, I would have said something. But in college, I was just overwhelmed to finally be free of them all. I didn't want to do anything that could jeopardize that. And then I met Bill, my future husband. He didn't know about any of it. And I didn't *want* him to know. Didn't want any connection between what they had done to me and the life I was trying to build. And then we had children, and I couldn't bear to put them through all that. And Ezra . . . he always told me he would kill me if I ever told. And I believed him. I still believe him. You know what he did when our first child, David, was born?"

Livia looked at her and again said nothing.

"He sent me a baby outfit and a card, congratulating me on the birth of his nephew. And telling me David reminded him of Ophelia. No one else would know what that meant. But I did."

They were both quiet for a moment. Then MacKinnon said, "Do you see? I hadn't been in touch with Ezra since leaving Llewellyn. I never told any of them I was getting married. Or taking my husband's name. Or moving to San Francisco. Or my home address. I did everything I could to keep all that hidden. Ezra was telling me none of my efforts mattered. He was watching. He could get to me. And he could get to my children."

She took another sip of tea. "So. I am sorry. Truly sorry. For what you and your sister have gone through. And if there's a way I can . . . redress that, I hope I'll have that chance. But in the meantime, I hope you'll at least understand. I've had my reasons."

Livia nodded. "I do understand."

MacKinnon looked at her, her face carefully set. "Thank you."

There was a long pause. Then Livia said, "But if you're serious about redress, I have an idea about how."

57—NOW

When Livia was done laying it out, MacKinnon was almost there. But she wasn't quite persuaded.

"Why do you need him to come out here?" she said. "Couldn't you just march into his office and flash your badge the way you did me? And leave me out of it entirely?"

"I don't think your brother would tell me what I need to know in his office. He'd be in a familiar, comfortable environment, surrounded by all the trappings of his power. I want to confront him someplace unfamiliar. Where he doesn't know the terrain. Where he'll be off balance."

A long moment went by while MacKinnon considered this. Finally, she said, "All right. We'll look up his office number. And I'll . . . I'll call him. But let me do it from your phone. I don't want him to know my number."

Livia shook her head. She understood the woman knew better, and at this point was just protesting as a way of proving to herself that she was in control of at least some of what was suddenly happening to her, no matter how trivial.

"That won't work. It would be too easy for him to check my number, and figure out something's wrong with your story. Besides, if he's sent you baby gifts, he already knows your number. Or could easily get it."

There was a pause while MacKinnon considered this. Then she said, "I just need a minute."

"Of course," Livia said. This woman was about to face a monster from her childhood. A minute would be the least she'd need.

MacKinnon stepped away. Livia heard a door open, then close. She had a feeling the woman needed to be with the dog. It didn't surprise her. One of the victim support services she worked with had a rescue dog, a shepherd-mastiff mix named Argus, and Livia had never seen an abused child emerge from a scarred shell the way some of the support kids did when they spent time with that devoted animal. Livia thought it had something to do with recognizing the existence of a creature at once powerful and yet incapable of hurting you—incapable of doing anything other than loving and protecting you. She sensed that kind of bond between MacKinnon and the shepherd.

And indeed, when she returned a few minutes later, the dog was with her. It sat alongside her at the table while she did an Internet search on her phone.

"Okay," MacKinnon said, nodding. "Okay. Okay." She took a deep breath and blew it out, summoning her courage like someone about to leap from a cliff into dark waters.

She input the number. There was a pause, then she said, "Yes, hello. My name is Rebecca MacKinnon, formerly Becky Lone. Senator Lone's sister. It's urgent that I speak with him."

Livia was impressed by the confidence in her tone. The woman had found her composure, at least for the moment.

There was a pause, then, "I don't have his mobile phone number. We haven't been in touch in quite some time. But it's urgent that I speak with him now."

Another pause, then, "Yes, please give him this number. If you're thinking this is some sort of prank, it isn't. When you tell him it's Becky and that it's urgent, I assure you he'll want to call me immediately. If you wait to deliver the message, you'll be making a mistake."

She clicked off.

Livia looked at her. "You okay?"

MacKinnon nodded but said nothing. Then she started to shake. She reached for the dog. It whimpered and licked her hand.

"I'm sorry," Livia said. "I can imagine what this is stirring up."

MacKinnon smiled grimly. "Well. I think you can more than imagine."

"That's true."

MacKinnon stared out the window at the sparkling bay. "It never goes away, does it?"

Livia wished there were an answer to that. But there wasn't.

A moment ticked by. MacKinnon said, "I don't know if he'll get back to me right away."

"He will. If that receptionist is smart enough to get him the message promptly."

"I hope so. Can you wait for a bit?"

Livia glanced at her watch. It had been close to an hour. Plenty of time still to get back to the airport, and there were dozens of non-stops to Seattle. She nodded and said, "Yes. Let's see if he has a smart receptionist."

MacKinnon left her phone on the table and made them another pot of tea. She looked tense, and to take the woman's mind off her dread of confronting her brother, Livia said, "What's the honey you're using? It's really good."

In fact, it was good, though Livia didn't expect anything would soon displace her affection for coffee with milk and turbinado sugar.

"Sonoma County Wildflower," MacKinnon said. "I get it at the farmers' market. Glad you like it. I'm afraid I'm a bit of an addict."

"Well, I could see where that would be a danger. Wish they sold it in Seattle."

MacKinnon returned to the table and they sat wordlessly for a moment, sipping the tea. Livia asked about the dog, her kids, life in San Francisco. Safe subjects. Comforting ones. She wasn't sure if it was helping, but it was better than silence.

MacKinnon's phone buzzed and the woman jumped. "Speakerphone," Livia reminded her, leaning forward.

MacKinnon nodded and looked at the phone. And kept looking at it. It buzzed again.

"Becky," Livia said.

MacKinnon looked at her, her eyes wide, then at the phone again. Her mouth twitched and her expression wavered between fear and determination.

The phone buzzed again.

"Becky," Livia said. "You can do this."

MacKinnon nodded. She closed her eyes, and then opened them. And Livia could see the determination had won.

MacKinnon pressed the speaker button. "Hello."

"Becky, it's Ezra. Is everything all right?"

Hearing his voice conjured his face, and that of his brother, and again Livia had to suppress a wave of disgust. Apparently MacKinnon was having a similar reaction. She closed her eyes and swallowed, then said, "A reporter came to my house today. Asking me questions. About Father. About when we were children."

"Hold on a minute, hold on. What reporter?"

"I don't know. She wouldn't even give me her name, or organization. But she said she had information, about when—"

"Hold on, hold on. How do you even know she was a reporter?"

Livia nodded grimly. She had predicted Lone would be afraid to talk about anything specific over the phone. That he would be afraid to discuss this in any way other than in person. So far, she'd been right.

"Well, who else could she be?" MacKinnon said.

"I don't know. Some crazy person. Someone unstable who thinks she can make things up to blackmail us. Who knows? Now, did she say anything specific? Just yes or no, Becky. You don't have to tell me details."

MacKinnon glanced at Livia. "Yes. Extremely specific."

Perfect.

"I need to talk to you, Ezra. I need to know what's going on. If this is going to affect my family."

"Nothing's going to affect your family, Becky. Everything's going to be fine. Now, I can't talk right now. I'm in Bangkok and it's the middle of the night—"

Bangkok? Livia thought.

"—and I have meetings starting early tomorrow and then throughout the afternoon. And the next day. It took a lot to set up these meetings with the Thai government people, and I can't get free for a bit. I just can't. But I can stop in San Francisco on the way back. Why don't I come by? I can stay with you—"

"Absolutely not. You will not stay in this house."

Perfect, Livia thought again. It was exactly the way they'd role-played it. *You have to sound reluctant*, Livia had coached her. *Not like you're trying to draw him in—like you're trying to keep him out. Otherwise he could sense a trap. So make him work for it. Make him feel* he's *trying to persuade* you.

"All right, fine. I'll stay in a hotel. We can meet in the lobby. Or anywhere else you like. But I think we should talk about this in person. Not over the phone."

MacKinnon glanced at Livia. Livia nodded.

"When?" MacKinnon said.

"Three days. I'll get my itinerary revised and text you my flight and hotel information as soon as I have it."

"If that woman comes back to my house . . ."

"Listen. Whoever she is, if she contacts you again, try to get a name. Or at least a phone number. Whatever information you can. Then you get that information to me, and I'll find out what we're dealing with. And I'll handle it. In the meantime, you tell her nothing."

Livia glanced at MacKinnon and made the okay sign with her thumb and forefinger.

"I don't like this," MacKinnon said, again playing it grudgingly.

"Neither do I, Becky. It's probably just some crank who wants to hurt us. I'll be out there in a few days and we'll figure it all out. And . . . it'll be good to see you. It's been too long."

MacKinnon clicked off.

Livia glanced at the phone to confirm the connection had been broken, then looked at MacKinnon. "You were great, Becky."

MacKinnon nodded, then started shaking again.

"I know," Livia said. "I know. But you were great. Completely convincing."

MacKinnon leaned over and nuzzled the dog's head. "We're okay, girl," she said. "We're okay. We're okay."

A moment passed while she collected herself. Then she straightened and said, "Can you be away for three days?"

"No," Livia said. "But I can get back easily enough."

But what she was thinking was, *Bangkok.*

There was one more thing she needed. Instinct had told her she should wait to bring it up, wait until MacKinnon had first taken some concrete action, like calling her brother. Then what came next would seem a smaller leap. But still . . . it would be a leap.

"The problem is," Livia said, "I don't think he's going to tell me what I need to know unless I have some leverage."

MacKinnon's eyes narrowed. "What do you mean?"

"I've dealt with a lot of suspects. Hundreds. And there are various ways you can get someone to cooperate, if you have a knack for these things. If you had a good mentor, like I did. But with someone like your brother . . . I can't just ask. I need something to threaten him with."

MacKinnon shook her head, apparently sensing where this was going, and not liking it at all. "You said you would tell him you tricked me. Pretended to be a reporter. That he would never know I helped you."

"Yes, I did. And I could do it that way. But what's really going to get his attention is you and me working together. Two of his victims, with no connection between them other than his crimes, corroborating each other's stories."

"No. Absolutely not. You told me. You promised."

"And I'll keep that promise. But Becky, if we do this right, it will never come out. The threat will be enough."

"And what about his threat to me? And my family? And if you're going to tell me next that you'll protect us, please, just spare me. I wouldn't believe you now anyway."

There was a long pause. The request had been just the opening, and Livia hadn't expected it to be decisive. Now she had to close.

"Becky. Ophelia did everything she could to protect you. She *died* trying to protect you." She paused, then went on. "You can keep faith now with what Ophelia did. With who she was. You can protect someone, too. *My* sister. Nason. Please."

MacKinnon shook her head. "No. I told you, no."

But Livia knew what it felt like when a suspect's defenses were wavering. It felt like what she was seeing now in MacKinnon's face, and hearing in her tone.

"She protected you," Livia said. "And you can never pay that back. But wouldn't she want you to pay it forward? By protecting someone else?"

"I *am* protecting someone else. My family."

"Ezra is your brother. He's not the bogeyman. And you're not that little girl anymore. You're strong. You're a survivor. Don't let him control you with fear. Stand up to him, Becky. The way Ophelia did."

As it had before, MacKinnon's expression wavered between fear and determination. Then it dissolved and she started crying again. "He *killed* her."

"Yes. And you had no choice but to let him get away with it. But now you *do* have a choice. You have a weapon. Me. Use it."

That was it. There was nothing more to say. There was nothing to do but wait.

A minute went by. Then another.

Finally, MacKinnon said, "If your sister is alive, and Ezra tells you where she is, you'll be able to help her."

"Yes."

"And if she's . . . not alive . . ."

"Then I'll deal with that."

MacKinnon nodded. "But you don't want a scandal any more than I do."

"That's right."

"You want to threaten him with exposure. And if the threat works, then you don't actually need to expose him. It's something like . . . you're pointing a gun at him. And if he complies, you don't actually need to fire."

"Yes. That's exactly what it's like."

"But then we'll have protected your sister. Or at least found out what happened to her. But we won't have done anything to protect the other girls my brother has victimized. The victims yet to come."

For the second time that afternoon, Livia felt she'd been hit by a judo throw she hadn't seen coming.

"So," MacKinnon continued. "What are we going to do to protect them?"

Livia said nothing.

"I'll help you," MacKinnon said. "You can tell my brother we're working together. Tell him we'll both testify, go to the media, whatever. And if he thinks you're exaggerating, or bluffing, or making the whole thing up, and he calls me, I swear to you I will back up everything you say."

Livia said nothing.

"But in exchange for that, you can't leave him to hurt anyone else the way he and Fred hurt us. You can't."

Despite herself, Livia was impressed. She had created so many boxes for suspects in the interrogation room. It was disconcerting to experience one from the suspect's perspective.

Not that it mattered. She had already known she wasn't going to just walk away after bracing Lone. If she'd been forced to choose between finding out about Nason and letting Lone live, there was no question she would have chosen the former. But she didn't expect to have to make that choice. She would squeeze everything possible out of him. And as soon as she was convinced he had nothing more to offer, she would leave him, the way she had left his sick brother. The way she had left Weed Tyler.

But she hadn't exactly planned on discussing any of this with MacKinnon, either. She realized again her moves were off. She wasn't as in control as she usually was, she wasn't as aware of what was happening at the periphery of the game. The Lone girls' tragedy . . . it was just too close to hers and Nason's.

All that said, she wasn't worried the woman would be any kind of risk. MacKinnon was too motivated to keep her secrets. Protect her family. Continue to live the life she had painstakingly created for herself. Beyond which, of course, she *wanted* her brother dead. It was about the last thing she would object to, or go to the police about.

"It isn't fair," MacKinnon said. "They victimize us in secret, and then the only way we're allowed to fight back is to be raped again in public? By scandalmongers, by the tabloid press, by gawkers rubbernecking at every disgusting detail of what they did to us against our will?"

Livia sighed. The woman had great instincts. But she hadn't yet learned not to sell past the close.

MacKinnon held out her hand. "Do we have an understanding?"

Livia hesitated. Then reached out.

They shook.

MacKinnon held on to her hand. "And this is just a request. It's not a quid pro quo. Not a demand. No more than a favor, really. But . . ."

She leaned closer and gripped Livia's hand harder.

"You make him suffer," she whispered. "For us. For Ophelia. For Nason. You make him fucking suffer."

Livia nodded and withdrew her hand. It wasn't something she could promise, she knew.

But she wasn't going to rule it out, either.

58—NOW

Less than thirty-six hours later, Livia was in Bangkok.

She'd flown back to Seattle from San Francisco, emailed the people at the Krav Maga academy to tell them she wouldn't be able to teach for the next few days, and called Donna to tell her the same—a few days for a personal matter. She'd never before asked for personal time, and was less concerned that the request would cause an administrative problem than that it might attract suspicion. She didn't care. She didn't care about anything other than Nason.

She didn't bring a gun. She didn't have time to figure out what regulations would govern US law enforcement trying to bring firearms into Thailand, and even if it had been possible, she didn't want the attention. Nor did she bring the Vaari, which was big and intimidating, and therefore might raise eyebrows if someone searched her bag at customs. She decided instead on a Boker Plus Subcompact—about four inches extended, two folded. Small enough to clip to a bra. Sharp enough to cut to the bone. And the kind of thing a careful female tourist might be expected to carry on holiday. She considered what she might be up against, and decided to bring a pen-sized pepper spray, too. Not police issue, but one of the quality civilian versions. And one last item—a six-inch, injection-molded nylon Kubotan impact weapon, about the size of a large marker pen. Unlikely any of it would be found in a checked bag. If it were, she'd deal with it. On balance, the risk felt worth taking. She made reservations online, packed a bag, grabbed her passport, and caught a post-midnight flight through Taipei, landing at Suvarnabhumi Airport a little before noon local time.

Passing through the airport was strange. Seeing so many Thais, hearing the language, smelling the food. Even as a child, she'd never felt Thai—she had always been hill tribe, Lahu. And now she was American. Even the rudimentary Thai she'd learned as a child was mostly gone. So why was being here making her feel so . . . what, mournful? Nostalgic? She wasn't sure. Whatever it was, she hadn't been prepared for it.

She caught a cab to her hotel—the Anantara Riverside Resort. She'd found it online, and it seemed like the kind of place a "tourist" like her might choose. Moderately priced; lots of pools and bars and restaurants; close to the Grand Palace and other attractions. And big enough to offer a comfortable degree of anonymity. She'd taken a course with Narcotics, where one of the instructors, a CIA veteran, explained that you had to live your cover. Not just because the cover might get probed, and so needed to have as much depth and breadth as reasonably possible, but because the more you lived your cover, the more you would feel it, and the more you felt it, the more you would look it. "If you want to fool, you have to feel," was how he put it. And while there was only so much she could do on such short notice to prepare and inhabit a cover, having the right hotel reservation when she arrived was a no-brainer.

The cab ride took over an hour. It wasn't far, but the roads were colossally jammed—honking cars, gear-grinding trucks, buzzing tuk-tuks, motor scooters with engines that sounded like chainsaws and with two, three, sometimes even four people perched on them. Even on a full-sized motorcycle in America, you never saw more than a single passenger, and witnessing how much these people could do with so little made Livia feel a pang of remembrance for her childhood in the forest.

As they drove, she glanced back and forth through the left and right windows, taking in as much as she could. Had the city always been so dense, so teeming? She had never been here, and had only caught glimpses as they passed through during that nightmare trip in the white van. But no, there couldn't have been this kind of noise back then, and construction, and energy. There was so much money now. She could see it at work in the high-rises sprouting everywhere like freakish mushrooms, the glitzy façades of shopping malls, the smartly dressed women carrying fancy bags. But there was so much poverty, too—beggars, children who looked like they lived on the street, people practically in rags. What had William Gibson said? *The future is already here—it's just not very evenly distributed.* That's what money felt like in Bangkok. It existed. But only for a few.

She was surprised at how many people asked if she was Thai—the customs officer at the airport, the cab driver, the hotel receptionist. She didn't think she looked Thai. Not even Lahu. She didn't feel it, not anymore. But there must have been some vestige. She wasn't sure what that meant. Or how she felt about it.

The room was pleasant and functional. Not that it mattered. All she needed was a bed. She'd been too keyed up to sleep on the plane, and had spent most of the trip reading a couple guidebooks she'd bought at the airport, trying to learn as much as possible about the city, gaming out approaches, gambits, when/then scenarios. She needed to know the layout, the clothes, the customs. She needed to be able to move without disturbing what she moved through. In America, that had become easy. In this new place, it was going to be a challenge.

She bolted the door, showered, dried off, and lay down. Her mind was still racing, but she'd been awake for over forty-eight hours and her mind quickly lost to her body. Her sleep was black and empty at first, but then there was an awful dream where she had found Nason but there was something wrong with her—she was dead, but somehow Livia had brought her back to life, and Nason was saying, "Why, Labee? Why?"

She woke with a groan and sat up, looking groggily at the bedside clock. She'd been asleep for almost four hours. It was already evening.

She rubbed her eyes and tried to shake off the dream. She'd had many like it when she was a teenager, but the last one had been a long time ago.

She'd left the air-conditioning on too strong a setting, and the room was cold. She shivered. What was she doing here? How could she get away with this? A United States senator? What was she thinking?

She realized that something about being in Thailand, about facing the past, was making her feel like that long-ago little girl. She'd thought the girl was gone, that to the extent the girl lived on at all, it was only as a shadow, a distant memory.

But no, she'd been wrong. That little girl was still here.

And she was scared.

Come on, Livia. We can do this.

Because she wasn't that little girl anymore. That little girl had grown into a champion wrestler and judoka. A self-defense teacher. A cop. A killer. A *dragon*. And it wasn't the girl who was going to face Ezra Lone. It was what the girl had become.

No. That was the wrong way to put it.

Ezra Lone was going to face *her*.

59—NOW

She showered again to clear her head, then got into character. A lot of makeup. Oversized, horn-rimmed eyeglasses. A short black skirt. A cream-colored blouse with a black bra underneath. Flats, because while heels would have been a little more in keeping, there were some tactical concessions she just couldn't make. And a brown Coach handbag with no labels. The Boker was clipped to her bra in front of her left armpit, easily accessible from under the blouse with a right-hand draw. Just in case.

She took the elevator to the lobby and headed out to the street. She was surprised at how oppressive she found the evening heat and humidity. She'd really gotten used to the glorious weather in San Jose, and then to the chill and the damp of Seattle. She wasn't acclimated to the tropics anymore. And yet, at the same time, it felt so familiar, like fragments of a dream she'd forgotten upon waking.

She took the modified Gossamer out of her purse and used it to locate Lone's cell phone. Having been trained on the device, she knew it would work anywhere in the world, but still she was irrationally afraid that being abroad would somehow screw up its functioning.

There were other possibilities, of course, involving calling for Senator Lone at various high-end hotels, or having Becky Lone contact his office on a pretext . . . that sort of thing. But the Gossamer was the surest, lowest-profile, most accurate way of pinpointing his exact location, right down to the room.

As it turned out, there was nothing to worry about: it took the Gossamer only a few seconds to zero in on his phone. It was at 96 Narathiwat Ratchanakarin Road, about two miles away—probably twenty minutes by tuk-tuk in Bangkok traffic. She wanted to look up the address to see exactly what she was dealing with, but couldn't use her own phone, which she'd powered off before leaving Seattle. She didn't want anyone to be able to track her the way she was tracking Lone. Not that anyone would, but regular use of Gossamers was enough to make anyone paranoid. And even beyond creating a record of her movements, she didn't want to leave a record of anything she looked up on the Internet. A layered defense, as always.

She walked until she found a store selling prepaid mobile phones. The saleswoman set the whole thing up for her, selecting English as the language, installing the SIM card, and charging the unit while Livia waited. When it was ready, Livia headed out again. She input the address into the browser and got two hits. It seemed Lone was dining either at Vogue Lounge on the sixth floor of the CUBE building, or at L'Atelier de Joël Robuchon on the fifth floor. Livia looked up both and couldn't decide which it would be. Both stylish, and the kind of high-end establishments where she expected local government officials might entertain a visiting dignitary. She thought about reconnoitering, but decided against it. Probably Lone would be in a private dining room where she wouldn't be able to confirm his presence. But if he wasn't, he might see her. She doubted he would recognize her after so many years, out of context, in disguise, and against a background of countless other Asian faces, but it would be bad if he did. It would ruin the surprise she had planned for later.

So she weaved along the Chao Phraya River while the last light faded from the cloud-studded sky, checking the Gossamer periodically to see whether Lone had moved. She passed endless sidewalk food stalls, their plastic tables crowded with families eating, laughing, conversing animatedly in a language that sounded weirdly familiar but that Livia could no longer comprehend, like a melody she recognized, the lyrics of which she no longer knew. There were tiny corner shrines and a massive, multi-tiered wat; luxury hotels and corrugated shacks; men in dark business suits and saffron-clad monks. Even in the midst of the city, she could hear the buzz of insects in the trees. It brought her back to the forest, and she found herself thinking of her parents. Were they even still alive? The last time Rick's police contact had checked had been years before. After so much time and so many reports of no news, the exercise had become pro forma. If Livia went to them, would they even recognize her?

She decided she didn't care. The only thing she might want from them was that they understand the horror into which they had delivered their own daughters. But why would it matter to them, anyway? They'd say they didn't know, they didn't realize, they had been desperate, it wasn't their fault.

No, she wanted nothing from them. If she ever saw them, her mother she would ignore. Her father, she would spit on. Beyond that, whether they were alive or dead or happy or sad or comfortable or in pain meant nothing to her. And likewise her brother. All he had ever done was receive from their parents everything that should also have been for Nason and Livia.

She passed an outdoor market and browsed the stalls—handbags and Thai silks and stuffed animals and lingerie and every kind of tourist trinket. She paused in front of one of the pavilions, and selected a platinum blonde wig, affixing it carefully, checking it from all angles in a mirror, and paying cash before moving on again.

At just past ten o'clock, Lone's cell phone started moving. Livia felt a little kick of excitement in her chest. She watched its progress until it stopped—Thanon Khao. A short street in . . . Dusit, the east bank of the Chao Phraya. She checked the address on her phone, and found a nursing school, a fire station . . . and the Hotel Orient. Her heart kicked harder.

She read some online reviews. Hotel Orient . . . one of Bangkok's oldest and, following a multimillion-dollar update several years earlier, most fashionable. She zoomed in using a map and satellite view, and saw the building was a long rectangle facing the Chao Phraya. At each end of the rectangle was a protrusion—suites, she guessed, with windows in three directions. The property was popular with dignitaries, it seemed, because Dusit was the government district. Famed for its guest list, assumed to be comprised of various international celebrities and power brokers; its discretion; its triple-glazed windows and soundproofing. She wondered about that last feature, and whether it was part of the attraction for Lone.

One way or another, she was going to find out.

60—NOW

She waited until close to midnight. His phone hadn't moved for more than an hour, and it was a safe bet he was in for the night now. Maybe his "aide" Redcroft was close by, but beyond that, she didn't expect him to have bodyguards. He never had in Llewellyn. And he was a senator, not the president or secretary of state. Besides, she thought he would value his privacy while he was in Bangkok. Three days, for government meetings? Maybe. But she thought he was here for something else. Something that might be difficult to explain to a bunch of Secret Service agents, or anyone else watching him closely.

She had a tuk-tuk drop her off a few blocks from the hotel, then walked. The moment she turned onto the street, the sounds of the city faded, and within a short distance the urban tumult had become no more than a steady hum in the background. This was a residential neighborhood, dignified and quiet. To her left were genteel apartment buildings; to her right, a long wall with tall bamboo behind it, protecting and concealing the hotel.

Halfway down the street, she came to the entrance—an ornate metal gate, open, with a small wooden building along the stone road behind it. Two uniformed guards were inside behind a glass window; another stood in front, holding a flashlight and a mirror attached to a telescoping pole. She caught a glimpse of a security camera affixed to the underside of the eaves, and was glad she was disguised, and keeping her head down. The guard outside nodded to her pleasantly enough, and she walked past, the soles of her shoes crunching softly on the gravel path, glad she hadn't been asked for ID. Probably their job was to search the trunks and undersides of cars for explosives. Pedestrians, it seemed, were okay. But it was unnerving to encounter guards at the perimeter of the hotel at all. It made her aware of how much she didn't know, how much she was winging this.

But she had to. She might never get a better chance.

The hotel's façade was dramatic and imposing: four stories of white stone, surrounded by palm trees swaying in the evening breeze; tall, rectangular, black lattice windows; square turrets on the top floor. There were a few concessions to Thai architectural tradition—the sinuous lines on the corners of the roof, for example—but for the most part, the structure was starkly contemporary, the ambiance that of an elegant fortress. Livia didn't like it. Or maybe her feeling was just a reflection of what she was here for.

She walked inside. The lobby was equally imposing: a long rectangle lined with planters, and open to the guest floors and a latticed glass roof above. During the day, it would probably be flooded with light and feel airy and open, but just then, it struck Livia as a luxuriously decorated prison cellblock.

She wandered around for a while, getting acclimated, developing a feel for the layout of the place, taking in the vibe. A lot of foreigners—*farang*, a word she still remembered. All well dressed and prosperous-looking, some on the chic side, others more conservative. Hushed acoustics and soft music muting the sounds of conversation. An impeccable bar, with accents both classic and contemporary. Overall, an atmosphere of privilege, power, and discretion, old money mingling synergistically with new. *You're on the inside now*, the place seemed to whisper. *Where everyone else wants to be.*

She noticed a security man by the elevators, checking to ensure guests who passed him had room keys. Damn, she hadn't thought of that. She could have just paid for a room, assuming one was available, but didn't want a record of having been here, let alone having stayed. But she thought she knew a better way regardless.

She went to the lounge, sat at the bar, and ordered a white wine. It didn't take long for one of the *farang*—an all-American guy with designer sideburns, a dark linen sport jacket, and a white shirt open at the collar—to sit next to her. She smiled. How many times had she done this very thing, trolling for the kind of sex she liked, or better yet for a rapist?

"Buy you a drink?" he said, offering her a smile of his own.

"Oh," she said. "You're nice. What's your name?"

He held out his hand, the sleeve pulling back to reveal a duly fabulous watch. "Mike. And you?"

Americans. They were so confident. She took his hand and said, "Hi, Mike. I'm Betty." She smiled and held on to his hand a beat longer than might be expected.

He glanced at her wineglass, which was still about half full. "So, how about that drink, Betty?"

She leaned against his shoulder. "The thing is, Mike, I've had three already, and . . ." She stopped, laughing.

He laughed, too. "And?"

She was still pressed against his shoulder. "And . . . oh, man, I'm already pretty wasted." She laughed again.

"Well, that's okay. I'm pretty wasted, too."

"Are you really?"

"Yeah. Closed a big deal tonight. The client took everyone out to celebrate."

Men, she thought. *Always such little peacocks.*

"Well, hey," she said. "Congratulations."

"Thanks. Thought I'd have one more by myself before turning in, just to savor the moment, you know? But I'm glad I ran into you."

She looked at him appreciatively. It wasn't hard; he wasn't a bad-looking guy. "So, are you staying here?"

He nodded. "I am indeed. Suite with a nice minibar. You?"

"No, I'm at the Sukothai. With my boyfriend and another couple. But he's being a jerk, and . . . I don't know. I heard they had a nice bar here."

"I'm sorry he's being a jerk. But, you know, if you want to just chill here for a while, my suite is your suite."

She gave him a long, lascivious smile. "You're bad."

He smiled back. "Only if you want me to be."

She glanced around. "But . . . I don't think I should be seen going up with you. I mean, I wouldn't want anyone to get the wrong idea or anything like that."

"No, no, I totally get it. Why don't I head up now, and you just follow me in a few minutes?"

She gave him the smile again. "That sounds nice."

"Yeah. So, Room 217, okay?"

"Got it, 217."

He glanced at her wineglass. "Can I at least buy you that one?"

"No, no, it's paid for." She stretched, giving him a look at her body. "But if you like, you can offer me something from the minibar."

He stole a not terribly discreet glance at the scenery. "That's a deal."

He stood. It would have been better if he'd thought of it himself, but it didn't look like he was going to, so she said, "Oh, I don't need a key for the elevator or anything, do I?"

"Oh, right. Good point." He reached into the breast pocket of his jacket, fished out a chip-card key, and handed it to her. "I'll go to the front desk, show them ID, and tell them I left mine in the room. They'll give me another. So I'll see you in a few minutes, okay? Room 217."

Confident, she thought. *And way too trusting.*

She smiled. "See you soon."

She waited ten minutes, then headed out. She flashed her room key to the security guy and took the elevator to the third floor. When the doors opened, she glanced left and right. The corridors in both directions were empty. Okay.

She stepped out of the elevator and turned right. Soft, blue-hued lighting. Recessed doors. The carpet soft and deep. As quiet as a recording studio. She checked the Gossamer. Lone's phone was less than two hundred feet ahead. She followed the signal until she came to the end of the corridor. There were rooms to either side, and one right in front of her—the protrusion she had seen on the map, with the windows on three sides. But the phone was still fifty feet away. Too far for it to be one of the rooms on this floor.

She looked at the carpet, then the ceiling. Was he below, or above?

Above, she decided. He'd want to be on the fourth floor, the highest, above it all, looking down at people. If she was wrong, she'd just go down to the second floor.

But she didn't think she was wrong. Lone was in the suite directly above her.

She returned the Gossamer to her purse, blew out a long breath, and headed back down the corridor.

61—NOW

Livia came out of the elevators and made an immediate right. The fourth floor was a repeat of the third—the lighting, the thick carpeting, the hush. With one difference—the man in the dark suit seated outside the suite at the end of the corridor.

Livia recognized him instantly—the blond crew cut had some gray in it now, but the protruding ears were the same, and so was the solid build. Matthias Redcroft. World's most versatile "legislative aide."

She'd already worked out how she would handle this eventuality, and didn't hesitate or otherwise show any sign of concern. She just walked slowly in his direction, checking room numbers left and right as though searching for one in particular. She wasn't worried Redcroft would recognize her. They'd only spoken once, and the last time he had seen her, she had been a skinny teenager. She was a different person now, and disguised on top of it.

Still, as she got closer, her heart began to pound. Redcroft looked up from his chair, watching closely. She kept one hand on the strap of her handbag and the other loose at her side, sauntering along like a high-end call girl dispatched to service some rich guest of the hotel.

When she reached the suite, she stopped and looked at Redcroft.

He raised his eyebrows. "Can I help you?"

"Are you the one who called?" she said, releasing a trace of Lahu into her accent.

"I'm sorry?"

She pointed to the number alongside the door to the suite. "Room 428."

"I don't think anybody called you from that room."

"This is where I was told to go."

"Told by whom?"

"My boss."

"Who's your boss?"

"The service."

"Look, I don't know what service you're talking about, but it sounds like there's been a mistake. Why don't you check with your boss and get it straightened out?"

"I can't reach him now. Anyway, his information is always good."

"Yeah? How'd you get past the guy checking keys in front of the elevators?"

"They know who I am. Now, could you please excuse me? It took over an hour to get here and I'm already late."

He looked her up and down. "What do you charge?"

Shit, was he going to try to just pay her fee to get rid of her? She shook her head. "Too much for you, I think."

"Ha. Try me."

She thought of a ridiculous number. "I charge fifty thousand baht," she said. That was close to fifteen hundred dollars. Doubtful he'd cough up that much just to get rid of a Thai hooker.

He leaned back in the chair and looked her up and down again. "You know what?" he said. "It's about time for my break anyway." He inclined his head toward the room to the left of the suite. "Tell you what, that's my room right there. Why don't we make me your appointment. We'll fix the mistake that way, okay? And everyone goes home happy."

She thought quickly. She'd been hoping she could persuade him to knock and get Lone to open the door. But adjacent rooms, one of them a suite—probably there was an interior connecting door. She could make that work, too. And if she was wrong, she'd just keep improvising.

"You seem like a nice guy," she said, making sure not to play it too eager. "But I have a client. How about you in two hours?"

"I am a nice guy. And two hours from now won't work. So I'll tell you what. Because you're already here, I'll give you an extra ten thousand for blowing off your other client. Okay?"

She frowned. "My boss . . . he won't be happy."

"Well, he's the one who sent you to the wrong place to begin with, right?"

She gave him an uncertain smile. "I guess so."

"All right," he said, coming easily to his feet. He pulled a room key from his jacket pocket, walked over to his door, opened it, then held it for her. "Please."

She had hoped he would go first. That would have allowed her to slip the pepper spray from her purse while his back was turned. Beyond which, after that near miss in San Jose, she didn't like turning her back on a man when she walked into a room. But it would look strange if she objected. Anyway, the main thing was, she would be able to get out the pepper spray easily enough while he was behind her.

She walked in. The lights were already on. A long, wood-paneled, marble-floored corridor, the room itself visible at the end of it. The purse strap was over her shoulder, the bag itself below her elbow, and she slipped her hand unobtrusively inside and curled her fingers around the canister, her thumb on the trigger.

She kept moving. She heard the door close behind her, the bolt closing into place with a dull mechanical clack. She heard his footsteps, about ten feet behind her. She'd walk into the room, stop, and let him move in just a little closer. Then she'd turn and spray him. Follow up with the Kubotan until he was down and disabled. Finish him. See if he had a key to the senator's suite. If he didn't, kick down the adjoining door. If there was no adjoining door, go back into character and return to the main door of the suite.

She took in an immaculate king-sized bed. Pewter carpeting, mahogany furnishings. She heard his footfalls moving up the corridor behind her. She breathed in deeply. Let it out. Braced to spin—

"I don't know what's in your hand, Livia, but unless it's faster than the pistol I'm pointing at your spine, I'd recommend you put it back in your purse."

She froze. *Livia?*

"That's right, I know who you are. Just let it drop, Livia. Back in the purse. Slowly."

She glanced back. Saw the gun. He raised it—a good, two-handed grip.

"Turn the fuck around," he said, his voice louder now. "Face forward."

She did.

"Now, last chance to drop whatever that is in the purse. And I won't have to shoot you in the back, okay?"

She dropped the pepper spray into the bag and slowly raised her hands, the fingers splayed. How the hell had he recognized her? Could they have known she was coming? Could Becky Lone have . . . no. It made no sense. Even if the woman had believed Livia might go to Bangkok, she never would have warned her brother. Whatever this was, it wasn't that.

"Good, keep those hands up. Now walk. Don't turn around. You know, you're pretty good. You probably could have fooled almost anyone, but unfortunately for you, I never forget a face. Never. It's one of the reasons the senator pays me the big bucks."

She moved farther into the room. All right, it sounded like just bad luck that he'd recognized her. Not good, but not as dire as if this were an ambush. He was improvising now as much as she was.

"Even so," he went on, "I gotta say, you almost had me. Out of context, the makeup, the glasses, the wig . . . took me a minute to place you."

She saw the adjoining door. Whatever happened, it was going to happen in here, or in the suite. They wouldn't be going back to the corridor.

"I mean, shit, you look like a real, high-class Thai hooker. Hell, I'd fuck you. Maybe I even will."

She said nothing. Her only move was to wait for an opening.

Or make one.

"Well, we'll check with the senator first. He might have some ideas. He usually does. You want to know something weird? I think he's actually going to be glad to see you. It's been a long time. What have you been up to?"

He didn't know, then. About the judo, about her being a cop. They hadn't kept tabs since she'd left Llewellyn. They'd look at her as just a slightly older version of that scared, helpless little girl.

That was her play. Maybe her only play. To foster that impression. Make them underestimate her. An instructor had once told her that when you recognize someone is dangerous, it automatically makes him less dangerous.

But the opposite was also true.

"So, Livia, this is what you're going to do. First, I want you to slowly lower that bag to the floor. And just by the way? If you think I'd be afraid to shoot you because of the noise, you'd be wrong. The Orient has the thickest walls in Bangkok. You could set off a fucking suitcase nuke in one of these rooms, and no one would even be disturbed in his slumber. On top of which, for security, the senator always takes both adjacent rooms and the one below. We clear on that?"

She did as he said. She still had the Boker, but she didn't think he would be stupid enough not to search her. His tactics so far had been sound.

She heard him pick up the bag. "What do we have in here? Oh, pepper spray. Well, that would have hurt. And I guess you were going to hit me with this Kuboton after that? What, did you take some kind of self-defense class? What is this? What are you trying to do?"

She said nothing.

"And what's this? Some sort of cell phone tracker?"

The modified Gossamer. Again she said nothing.

"How'd you get hold of something like this?"

"I bought it."

"Where?"

"Here. In Bangkok."

"How'd you get the senator's cell phone number?"

"Private detective."

"That's a pretty good private detective. What's his name?"

He had the interrogation instincts of a cop. Time to change the dynamic. "I'm not saying anything else," she said. "Not until you tell me what happened to my sister."

"Is that was this is about? After all these years, that?"

"Where is she?"

"That's up to the senator. Maybe if you're good, really good, he'll tell you."

"Why don't you tell me?"

"Well, now, that kind of decision is above my pay grade. We'll talk to him, though. I told you, I have a feeling he's going to be happy to see you. But first, I want you to put your palms against the wall next to that interior door. At about, oh, say, tit level. Then I want you to step back and spread your legs until your elbows and knees are straight and your weight is on those palms. You with me? I'm going to pat you down. Make sure whatever you brought with you was limited to your purse."

She recognized the commands. She'd patted down countless suspects from the same position precisely because it made sudden aggressive action so difficult. She'd been hoping he would take her so lightly that he'd be sloppy, but no, so far he was being careful.

She did as he said.

"More, Livia. Feet farther apart. And farther from the wall."

Again, she complied. On the other side of the door, she heard . . . was that a scream? Something high and plaintive, like a child in pain. It was so muffled she wasn't sure.

She heard Redcroft move up close. Felt his hand along her back—his left, she thought. Not that it mattered which. She sensed his gun hand was well retracted, and regardless, a disarm from this position was damn near impossible.

He ran his hand up her left side, then her right. He stepped in close, between her legs, his crotch against her ass.

"You don't have anything in there, do you, Livia?" He rubbed himself against her. "I don't have to search you in there, do I?"

Positioning himself between her legs was his first deviation from sound tactics. He was underestimating her. Not enough to create the opportunity she needed. But it was encouraging. She reminded herself to project fear. Helplessness.

He reached around and felt her breasts. "Oooh, these are nice. Grew a little since the last time we saw each other, didn't they? And oh, what do we have here?"

He'd touched the Boker, as she'd known he would. She felt the muzzle of the gun press hard into her kidney. Again, a deviation from sound tactics—the closer he was, the better her chances at a disarm—but not quite the opportunity she needed. Still, if he kept this up, an opening would present itself. She just had to be patient.

He reached under her blouse and pulled free the Boker. "Jesus, Livia, you're a regular fucking Rambo, you know that? So, what was the plan, tie the senator up, get him to talk, something like that, hmmm?"

She heard the Boker hit the carpet with a quiet thud somewhere behind them. Then he reached around again and squeezed her breasts. "Was that it? Was that the plan? Come on, you can tell me. Come on."

His voice had gone husky and he was getting hard where he was pressed against her. She felt rage begin to smolder inside her. The dragon, stirring awake.

No. Not now. Not now.

"You like that, Livia? My cock against you like that? You like it?"

"Where's my sister?" she said, and was pleased that her tone was fearful, almost childlike.

"Oh, your sister again. All right, we really should get you to the senator. Damn, and here we were just starting to have fun, right?"

He felt her belly, then ran his hand up and down her legs, finishing by rubbing her ass, and then her crotch. Then he yanked off the wig and tossed it aside.

"That's good," he said. "I think the senator will like you better like this. And let's lose those glasses, too." He pulled them off and dropped them.

He stepped back. "Okay, Livia, why don't you open that door for me. Just unbolt it and pull it open. Give it a good tug, it's heavy and fits pretty snugly in the frame."

She did as he said. He was right, the door was heavy—at least two inches of what looked like solid mahogany. There was another like it on the other side, presumably bolted from inside the suite. She'd been wrong about kicking this in. It would have taken a battering ram.

She heard that plaintive sound again. Still faint, but through the single door it was unmistakable. A child's wail. What was happening in there? She felt the rage rising again and fought to push it back.

"Yeah, I was afraid of this, we're interrupting the great man at play. Well, that's another reason he pays me the big bucks—command decisions. I'm pretty sure he'll be happy to switch up once he sees it's you.

So just go ahead and knock on the door. Hard, with your knuckles, so they'll hear you."

They'll. Lone, and who else? The child she thought she heard screaming?

She knocked. A moment later, she heard a muffled voice on the other side. "What is it?"

The voice sounded weirdly familiar. And was that a Thai accent?

"It's me. Open up, Chanchai, the senator will want to see this."

"Can it wait?"

"Trust me. He won't want to wait."

Livia heard the bolt draw back. The door opened.

It was Skull Face.

62—NOW

She stared at him, suddenly seething. For an instant, all her years of training deserted her, and all she could imagine was launching herself at him, knocking him down, ripping his face apart with her teeth and her nails.

No. Scared. You are scared.

Skull Face looked almost exactly as she remembered him. The hair, the face, everything. Like Redcroft, he was wearing a suit, though on the boat he had always been either bare-chested or in a dirty tee shirt. Beyond that, the only thing different was a black eye patch. She wanted to tear it off his head and jam her thumb all the way into whatever was behind it.

Scared. You are scared.

Skull Face was looking at her intently. In confusion, at first. And then with slowly dawning recognition. He looked to Redcroft, then back to Livia, then to Redcroft again.

"This is . . . this is that girl."

"Yeah, it's her. The one who took your eye, right? Well, she's always been a fighter, I guess. You should have seen what I took off her just now. Mace, a Kubotan, sweet little folding knife . . . Hey, man, you're welcome. She probably would have taken that other eye."

Skull Face smiled. His hand shot out and he grabbed her by the back of the hair. She had to force herself not to take him down and break his neck.

Scared. You are scared.

He twisted her head back. She didn't fight him. He said something in Thai.

"Where's my sister?" she said, grimacing.

He looked at her. "What?" he said in English. "You forget your Thai?"

"What did you do with her?"

He smiled and pulled her closer. That curry smell . . . it was exactly the same. It made her feel she was back in the box again. On the boat. On her knees. A nightmare from her childhood bursting into the present.

"Everything," he whispered.

And suddenly the dragon was gone. She was just Labee, in the clutches of the man who had hurt her. Who had hurt Nason. It had never stopped. It was never going to stop.

Skull Face pulled her by the hair across the room, Redcroft behind them, his gun still out. She caught a glimpse of a couch and chairs, an enormous flat-panel monitor, a dining room set. Then they were at an interior door, presumably to the suite's bedroom. Skull Face rapped sharply on the door.

A voice came from the other side. "What on earth is it?"

Senator Lone. Even if she hadn't already known it was him, even after so many years, even muffled by the door . . . she would have recognized that voice. So much like his brother's.

"Come out," Skull Face said. "You need to see this."

A moment went by. Then the door opened. It was Lone, tying the belt of the hotel robe he was wearing. Unlike the other two, he looked older, his hair thinner, his cheeks sunken.

Livia heard quiet sobs coming from inside the room. She strained to look. And saw a naked girl, on the bed, handcuffed to the back of the latticed metal bedframe. She looked like not even a teenager.

No, she thought. *No. Please. No.*

Lone looked at Livia, then to Skull Face, then to Redcroft, then back to Livia. "Is this who I think it is?"

Redcroft nodded, the gun still pointed at Livia. "She wants to know where her sister is. Came all this way to ask you."

"Just tell me," Livia said. "Just tell me where she is." And she meant it. If she could know that, she wouldn't care anymore. About fighting. About anything.

Lone clapped a hand over his mouth and stared at her as though he couldn't believe what he was seeing. Then he pointed at Skull Face. "Call your people. Have them come and take the girl. This is so much more interesting."

Skull Face pulled a mobile phone from a jacket pocket, held it to his ear, and said a few words in Thai. Then he replaced the phone and pulled a pistol from a cross-draw nylon shoulder holster. He pointed it at Livia. The holster . . . it was the way she'd expect a cop to carry. Not a criminal. And the gun was a SIG Sauer P320. The full version. Again, not something your average bad guy would favor—the size made it too hard to conceal.

She glanced at Redcroft's gun. A Glock, and smaller than Skull Face's. She wondered how he'd gotten it into Thailand. The diplomatic pouch maybe. Or maybe Skull Face had supplied it.

Redcroft slipped his gun into a holster at the back of his waistband. That's where he carried—and why she hadn't seen any telltale bulge when he'd first stood to open his room door. He went into the bedroom and unlocked the handcuffs, then pulled the sobbing girl off the bed. She looked maybe eleven.

Nason's age. When they'd taken her.

The girl was bleeding from between her legs. It was too much. It brought Nason too close. Livia clenched her jaw and tried to stop herself. But she couldn't. She began to cry.

Redcroft tossed the handcuffs on the bed and helped the girl into her clothes. The girl was shaking all over. It looked like it was all she could do just to stay on her feet.

Redcroft led the girl out of the bedroom. She looked at Livia as they passed as though beseeching her to do something. And all Livia could do was cry harder. She shook her head and whispered, *I'm sorry*, over and over again. She watched Redcroft lead the trembling girl through the living room and into Redcroft's room. A moment later, there was a knock on Redcroft's door. When he came back, the girl was gone.

Livia was still crying. But deep down, under all the pain, and grief, and horror . . . something stirred. Only a little. Just a tiny movement, something no one else would notice. As though the dragon was letting her know it understood now, it had to be quiet. It had to wait. But that it was still there. That it was ready to do what it had always done. So ready.

All she had to do was let it.

63—NOW

Redcroft said, "All right, she's gone. I should go back out and keep watch."

Lone smiled. "I don't think that's necessary. Nobody's coming. Well, somebody already did, but she's here now. I think you can stay."

Redcroft looked at Livia. "You see? This is part of why I like working for the senator. He knows how to treat his employees."

Lone gestured to the living room. "Why don't we go in here? It'll be more comfortable."

Skull Face gestured with his gun. Livia moved into the living room, the men behind her.

Redcroft settled into one of the overstuffed chairs. Skull Face gestured with his gun to the couch across from the chairs. Livia sat on it. Lone took the chair next to Redcroft. Skull Face remained standing next to the couch, keeping his gun on Livia.

Livia blinked away the tears and looked at Lone. "Tell me what happened to my sister. Please, just tell me that."

Lone glanced at Redcroft, then at Skull Face. "Well, what do you think. Should we tell her? It seems unkind not to."

Skull Face smiled at that. But Redcroft's amused expression faded, replaced by something closer to . . . concern. Livia didn't know what it meant, but she didn't like it.

"Well, Livia," Lone said, "what happened was this. Your sister Nason was supposed to join you on that boat to Llewellyn. My brother was going to foster you both. But you did a stupid thing. You made Chanchai very angry."

Chanchai. His name was Chanchai. Not Kana, as Tyler knew him. But to her, he would always be Skull Face.

"And . . . Chanchai went a little too far. But he knows that. He apologized for it. Told me everything. That's part of why we're friends. Because we trust each other. Isn't that right, Chanchai?"

Skull Face nodded. He was smiling, clearly enjoying watching Lone torment her.

"Now, Chanchai asked Fred and me how we wanted to handle things, given your sister's . . . condition. That is to say, we couldn't very well have my brother take in a little refugee girl who was that traumatized. At a minimum, she needed special care. I have to tell you, initially I was not happy at the news. Nason was supposed to be mine. Plus, how was Fred going to manage you without a sister for you to worry about protecting?"

He rubbed his brow and looked down for a moment. "Ah, it's making me miss him. Anyway, Fred said, 'We'll make do. As long as I just tell her I'm trying to find her sister, and eventually that I know where her sister is, it'll be almost as good.' And he was right, wasn't he? He always was the clever one. It's why he stayed in business while I pursued politics. Although, in the end, I suppose we both did all right."

None of it was surprising. It all fit what she had already pieced together on her own. But it was still agonizing to hear. It was as though his words were ripping away scars and probing the wounded tissue underneath.

"Fred actually thought we should get rid of your sister, given her state. But honestly? I thought that would be a waste. I thought she sounded interesting. So I told Chanchai to find a way to bring her to me. I wanted to meet this zombified little girl. Maybe I could help her."

Livia could feel the dragon, its ears flattening, its eyes glowing, its breath getting hot.

Not yet. Not yet.

"And Chanchai, good man that he is, knew it was the least he could do following the momentary lapse of professionalism that had caused the problem in the first place. So he brought Nason to me. And I entrusted her to the care of Matthias."

"I think you've told her enough," Redcroft said.

"No," Livia said. "Please. What happened to Nason? Please."

Lone smiled and glanced at Skull Face. "Chanchai, she really does want to know, doesn't she?"

Skull Face nodded and looked at her, his expression burning with hate. "Yes. She wants that. Yes."

"Well, is there anything she could do that would persuade you to fill her in on the rest of the story?"

Skull Face smiled. "Yes. I think so."

He stared at Livia. "You were so fun on boat. So fun. Maybe you be fun again, we tell about your sister."

Livia shook her head. The dragon was struggling now, straining.

Skull Face raised the gun and pointed it at Livia's face. "No? Two choice. You be fun now. Or I fucking kill you."

Lone gave her a sad smile. "Why don't you make him happy, Livia? You know what happens when he gets angry. And really, I think he missed you. The way he talked about you . . . you were special to him. I want to see what was so special. I want to watch. And then, if you make him happy, I'll finish telling you about Nason."

The dragon was practically screaming inside her now. She'd never felt it so huge before. So undeniable.

Skull Face pointed the gun at the carpet, then aimed it at Livia again. "Knees," he said. "Like on boat. You so fun on knees."

Livia got to her feet. She was trembling. Skull Face saw it and nodded with satisfaction. He thought it was fear. In fact, it was effort. She was doing all she could to hold back the dragon. She didn't think she could contain it much longer.

She stepped closer to him. This would be her best chance yet, maybe her only chance, for a disarm. Just a little closer.

But Skull Face retracted the gun, holding it closer to his body. He knew her too well, and she'd hurt him too badly. He wasn't going to take a chance.

Skull Face pointed to the carpet with his free hand, his gun hand keeping the pistol trained on her. She didn't have a move. Not yet. She was going to have to do this.

She got on her knees. She could see how hard he was. He moved closer and pressed the muzzle of the gun against her temple.

"Pants," he said. "You open."

In her peripheral vision, she could see both Lone and Redcroft lean forward in their chairs. Probably out of anticipation and interest. But with Redcroft, the posture would create quicker access to the waistband holster at the small of his back.

It didn't matter. She couldn't fight the dragon any longer even if she wanted to.

And she didn't want to.

She opened Skull Face's pants. He pressed the gun harder. The muzzle bit into her skin.

He moved aside his underwear, exposing himself.

"Mouth," he said. "Mouth. Like you did on boat. Like your sister did."

Livia took him into her mouth. Deeply. As deeply as she could, the way she knew he liked.

He moaned. The dragon saw its chance. It spread its giant wings and filled its lungs with fire.

Skull Face grabbed the back of her head and thrust deeper, wanting to make her gag, to make her choke, the way he always had on the boat. It was all right. She wanted him to. She let him push as deeply as she could stand.

And then, in a single blur of movement, she shot her palm up into his gun hand. Jerked her head down.

And clamped her jaws together.

Skull Face shrieked. The gun went off inches from her ear. She barely heard it. She grabbed the barrel and torqued it toward the ceiling and bit harder, screaming, roaring through the clod of blood and tissue in her mouth. Skull Face shrieked again and shook, unable to pull away, frozen by shock and pain. Livia pushed the gun hard to the left and tore her head viciously to the right. The gun came loose. So did the rest of him.

She fell to her back, bringing the gun into her right hand on the way. Redcroft was already moving offline, his hand going for his gun, but she'd anticipated the move and tracked him easily, firm grip, front sight on the target, just the way Rick had taught her.

She pressed the trigger. The first round caught him in the side. He twitched and continued to fumble for his weapon. She shot him again in the side. Tracked up. Shot him in the neck. He fell to his knees. She lowered her sights. And blew his jaw off. A geyser of blood erupted from where his lower face had been. His hands went spastically to the wound as though he could somehow arrest the damage, and he looked at her for a moment, his eyes wide, as though imploring her to explain how this possibly could have happened. Then he pitched forward onto the carpet.

Livia stood, keeping the gun on Redcroft. She spat the bloody chunk of meat from her mouth onto the carpet. Lone watched wordlessly, frozen in his chair, his face a mask of shock and horror.

Skull Face was on his back, shrieking, writhing, his hands clasped uselessly over his crotch, blood flowing through his fingers and saturating his pants.

Livia pointed the gun at Lone and said, "Stay." Then she walked to where Redcroft lay and put one more round in the back of his head. She pulled the gun from behind his pants and threw it to the far corner of the room.

She knelt next to Skull Face and patted him down, keeping the gun on Lone. Skull Face continued to shriek and writhe. He was clean. He'd only had the SIG, and now the SIG was hers.

She stood and walked closer to Lone. "The bedroom," she said. "Move."

"I'll tell you about your sister," he said, panting. "I'll tell you everything."

She spat out another bolus of gore and wiped the back of her wrist across her bloody mouth. She smiled at him.

"I know you will," she said. "I know."

64—NOW

She handcuffed Lone to the bed, the same way he had handcuffed the girl, making sure he could see into the living room. Then she went back for Skull Face.

He was still shrieking. She set down the gun and scooped the bloody remains of his cock off the carpet. She could taste his blood, smell it everywhere. She dipped her head and looked at him for a moment, letting him see her, letting him know what was coming.

He cried out and rolled to his stomach, his hands still covering his amputated crotch, then started twitching away from her like an earthworm.

She moved in, grabbed him by an ear with her free hand, and dragged him onto his back. He shrieked, "*Mai! Mai!*"

That much Thai she remembered. It meant "No! No!"

She gripped his hair in her left hand. Put her left foot behind his head and planted her right knee in his throat.

He kept his mouth shut and tried to twist away. She pressed harder with her knee. He struggled for another moment. She pressed harder.

His mouth popped open. She shoved his severed cock into it, clamping her palm down over his mouth and nose to hold it there.

"*Mmmmmmphhh!*" he screamed, the sound muffled by her hand and what was under it. "*Mmmmmmphhh!*"

She was crying now. "You so fun!" she shouted, staring into his bulging eyes. "You so fun!"

She gripped his hair and bore down with her hand and knee while he choked and twitched and struggled. He grabbed her wrist and tried uselessly to pry her hand away. Then he began to vomit. She pressed harder. His body convulsed. She stared into his agonized eyes until they went vacant, until his twitching body lay still.

She stood, her breathing ragged, heaving, and took a moment to collect herself. She looked at Lone. He was bleating in terror, rattling the handcuffs against the bedframe, desperately trying to break loose.

Nason, she thought. *Nason*.

The dragon seemed to settle and fold its wings. But its breath was still hot, its eyes still glowing.

It was telling her it would wait again.

But not for very long.

65—NOW

Livia walked into the bedroom. Lone strained harder at the handcuffs, moaning in terror. She stopped at the foot of the bed and looked at him.

"Don't hurt me," he said, panting. "Please. I'll tell you about your sister. Tell you everything. Please."

Livia pulled a chair from against the wall and positioned it so it faced the bed. She sat and looked at him. "All right. Tell me."

"You won't hurt me? You won't kill me?"

"You and your brother. Fred. You wanted children to rape again, didn't you? But not just any children. You already had that, on your 'fact-finding' trips to Thailand. No, you wanted sisters. Sisters who loved each other, who would do anything to protect each other. Like Ophelia and Becky. Like the good old days."

He looked at her in horror.

"Yes," she said. "I'm not a reporter, like Becky told you. I'm a cop. That's what I became, after surviving your sick brother. Becky told me everything. And I know a lot on top of that. So what you tell me now better fit with what I already know. If it doesn't—"

"It will. Just promise. You have to promise you won't hurt me. Or kill me."

"If you tell me the truth."

"Swear. Swear on your sister."

"All right. I swear on Nason. If you tell me the truth."

A moment went by with nothing but the sound of his frantic breathing. Then he said, "I told you. Chanchai brought her to Washington. Well, to Maryland. Matthias hired discreet people to care for her. And, sometimes, he would bring her to me."

He looked at her fearfully.

"It's all right," she said. "I swore. But only in exchange for the truth. Whatever it is."

He nodded. "It wasn't good. The state she was in . . . she wouldn't come out of it."

"It wasn't good . . . you mean, she wouldn't scream when you hurt her."

Beads of sweat broke out along his brow. "Please," he said. "Look at me. I'm an old man. And I'm sorry."

"All I want is the truth. All of it. I swore on Nason, remember?"

He swallowed. "She wasn't . . . she just wasn't there. And there was nothing anyone could do. So Matthias . . . he . . ."

There was a pause. Then he said, "Matthias killed her. I'm sorry."

She heard the words. But she couldn't feel them yet.

"What did he do with her after he killed her?"

"He left her in Little Bennett Regional Park."

"Was she found?"

"Yes. He wasn't trying to hide her. It didn't matter. There was no one who could identify her."

Well, not no one, Livia thought, feeling strangely detached. *There were the "discreet" people who had been "caring" for her. But why would they have ever known? Or given a damn, even if they did?*

"When? When was she found?"

"This would have been . . . the fall after you arrived in Llewellyn. October."

She'd always suspected Fred Lone was lying about having to protect Nason. Though apparently he had known where she was. Or rather, where she had wound up.

It didn't matter. The state of Washington had protocols for the disposal of unclaimed bodies. She expected Maryland would be no different. It wasn't what she had hoped for. But now that she was hearing it out loud, she realized she had always known, on some level, that it must be true.

Her little bird was gone. And she had been gone for a long time.

"Please," he said. "I told you the truth. You swore."

Livia nodded. "Yes. I did."

She walked back to Redcroft's room.

"Where are you going?" Lone called out. "What's going on?"

She saw the Boker where Redcroft had thrown it. She picked it up and returned to the bed.

"All right," she said. "Now there are a few things I guess I should tell you."

He looked at her wordlessly, his eyes wide with fear.

"First, your brother didn't have a heart attack. I killed him. Strangled him with my own hands, and looked into his desperate eyes while the life ebbed out of him. It's funny, the things he used to do to me are some of my worst memories. But killing him? Making him die? That's one of the best."

The fear on his face was now tinged with horror.

"Second, I know how well the hotel is soundproofed. So well that no one would have heard those gunshots. Besides, your man Redcroft told me about your arrangements. The empty rooms adjacent and below. He said it was about security, but come on. We're being honest with each other. We both know it was so no one could hear a child screaming in agony. And if no one could hear a child scream, why would anyone be able to hear you scream?"

He began to pant again. "Why are you saying that? You promised. You swore on Nason!"

"Third, do you really think a promise about my sister, who you tortured and raped and murdered, could control me the way threats about her controlled me when I thought she was alive?"

"Please!" he said, almost sobbing now. A dark patch began to spread on the sheets as his bladder let go. "Please, please, please, please, please!"

"Shhh," she said. "Shhh. There's a final thing. I want you to hear it."

He looked at her, panting again, his eyes terrified.

"Becky wanted me to do something for her. As a favor." She opened the Boker. "And you know what? I think I will. And not just for her. For Ophelia, too. And for Nason."

Ezra Lone began to scream. It was a long time before he stopped.

66—NOW

One month later, Livia was back in Thailand. She flew from Seattle to Bangkok again, but this time immediately transferred to a connecting flight to Chiang Rai. Where the hill tribes lived. Where she had lived, when she had been a little girl. Before she became someone else.

She had cleaned up the scene at the Hotel Orient that night as well as she could, but really all she had been able to do was wipe her prints from the surfaces she remembered touching. Whether she got away with it, she knew, hinged on how much effort the authorities would expend on an investigation into the murder of a US senator. Ordinarily, such a thing, particularly overseas, involved significant manpower, NSA surveillance databases, and the FBI's forensics lab, which was probably the finest in the world. She had done what she could to cover her tracks beforehand—using the Tor Browser for her searches on Ezra Lone, for example. But she'd also made liberal use of various law enforcement databases, and those records would remain, if anyone thought to check them. And there was Tanya, who might wonder at the coincidental timing of Ezra Lone's passing. And Becky Lone, who was also a potential vulnerability. Overall, given the speed with which she'd put the whole thing together and the level of improvisation required, she doubted she could survive full-scale federal scrutiny.

So it would all come down to what the authorities decided should be the official story. If they wanted the truth, they would investigate. If they wanted to hide the truth, because the truth was too embarrassing to various powers-that-be or otherwise undesirable, an investigation might be just pro forma. Or there might be none at all.

It was in the news the very day she arrived back in Seattle: Ezra Lone, the senior senator from Idaho, had died on official business in Bangkok—part of his lifelong efforts to combat the evils of human trafficking. A heart attack. It seemed heart disease ran in the family: tragically, some twelve years earlier, the senator's younger brother, Fred, had suffered a similar fate. The president offered his condolences to the entire Lone family, describing Lone's death as "a loss not only to the world's greatest deliberative body, but indeed to the entire nation Senator Lone dedicated his life to serving."

One day later, there was another story: a fire at the Bangkok morgue where Senator Lone's remains had been moved to await transfer to the US authorities. The senator's body had been burned beyond recognition, though his remains had been identified via dental records and were now on their way back to the United States, where they would be interred at the family mausoleum in Llewellyn.

Livia had searched for other news, and came across an article in the *Bangkok Post* lamenting the untimely death of one Chanchai Vivavapit, chief of the investigative branch of the Thai National Police. A heart attack. His body would be cremated in accordance with his family's wishes. Livia suspected those wishes might have been the product of a generous financial inducement.

So Skull Face had been with the National Police. She'd sensed as much in the hotel that night. She could only imagine the number of children he had trafficked during a lifetime in the trade, all the while moving up in the ranks of law enforcement. And obviously, he hadn't been acting alone. His organization would still be up and running, pimping children like the one Lone had raped at the hotel that night.

She came across another article in the *Bangkok Post* not long after. Apparently, one morgue worker claimed Senator Lone's body had been badly mutilated—"like wild game caught and prepped for the cook pot," was the worker's lurid description. But a day later, the worker retracted his account, claiming to have been talking about a television program he had once heard about, and describing Senator Lone's body as having been perfectly intact before the unfortunate fire. The story was bizarre, and other media outlets seemed uninterested in pursuing it.

Tanya never called. That was good. No doubt she would have heard about Lone—they were burying him in Llewellyn, after all. So maybe she simply had made no connection between his death and Livia's questions. Though more likely, she just wasn't inclined to ask. It was odd. Livia didn't have many friends, but somehow this woman she barely knew had managed to become one of them.

She'd been back for a week when a package arrived for her at police headquarters. There was no return address, though it was postmarked San Francisco. Five pints of Sonoma County Wildflower honey. And a note that said only, *Maybe it does end after all.* Livia nodded grimly when she read the note and thought, *Maybe.*

Everything else took a little time. There were favors she needed to ask, and chits to call in, but eventually the necessary paperwork had been processed, and the Maryland authorities exhumed the Jane Doe who had been discovered by hikers in Little Bennett Regional Park in the autumn shortly after Livia had first arrived in Llewellyn. The body was that of a young Asian girl. The coroner had determined she had died from blunt force trauma to the head after being repeatedly sexually assaulted, and the authorities had buried the girl in the state's own potter's field. DNA tests confirmed the body was that of Livia's sister. Livia flew to Maryland, had the remains cremated, and brought them back to Seattle. And from there, to Chiang Rai.

She rented a dirt bike, like the ones she'd seen trekkers riding so many years before, and rode it up into the hills, the urn containing Nason's ashes secure in a pack against her back. Gradually the road grew steeper, the air became cooler, and her ears repeatedly popped over the whine of the engine. It was strange to be back. Everything seemed smaller now. In part because she herself was bigger, of course, and because her frame of reference was so much broader. But in part because the world had gotten smaller, too. There were telephone and electric lines now where once there had been only trees. Paved roads where there had been only dirt. Storefronts on what had been empty fields.

Other things were different, too. Some of the distant hills were startlingly, almost unnaturally green—terraced with exotic teas now, she had heard, a cash crop the hill tribes had embraced in preference to the subsistence agriculture of Livia's childhood. But much was still the same. The red dirt that had once caked her bare feet. The smells of the earth and the plants and the trees. The gentle blue of the sky. The villages she passed were still marked by rickety wooden shrines, intended to ward off evil spirits. She hoped they were more effective now than when she had been small. But she doubted it.

She rode on, higher, deeper into the forest, until the trail beneath her stopped and she could go no farther. She took off her helmet, wiped the sweat from her forehead, and looked around. She smiled. Nason would have liked this spot. There was an opening in the forest here, framed by trees to the left and right, looking out over a valley surrounded by lush hills and a line of green mountains beyond. A haven overlooking a beautiful, emerald world, a place where they had known hardship but still had been happy, and innocent, and safe, before anything truly bad had ever happened to them.

She opened the kickstand and dismounted. Then she set down the helmet, took off the pack, and unfolded the portable shovel inside it. She began to dig a hole at the base of a small durian tree. She liked the idea that as it grew, the tree would absorb Nason's ashes. From the tree's branches, Nason would have an even better view of the forest paradise that had been her home during her brief time there. And it seemed right that she would become part of the tree that produced the fruit she loved so much.

For a while, as she shoveled out clods of the red earth, Livia's mind drifted. She forgot what had brought her here. She was just back in the forest. Digging a hole. It might have been a dream.

And maybe it was a dream, because the forest felt different now. How, she wasn't sure. Something seemed . . . missing. Or maybe it was just her memory playing tricks on her.

When the hole was deep enough, she stopped and mopped her face with her sleeve. It was good to use her hands like this again. To be in the forest, sweaty and dirty from hard work.

She retrieved the urn from the pack, knelt, and carefully emptied Nason's ashes into the hole. Then she went to the pack again and brought over the wooden Buddha she had carved as a girl in Portland. She placed it atop the ashes. "To help you sleep," she whispered.

She stood and filled in the dirt. When she was done, she knelt again.

She put her hand on the spot, as though she might feel Nason's presence there. As though her touch might comfort her sister, the way it always had before.

"Goodbye, little bird," she said, and started to cry.

Suddenly, around her, the forest came to life with the calls of hundreds of birds. She looked up, startled. That's what had been missing. The sounds. The birds Nason had once imitated with such uncanny accuracy.

She knew they must have gone silent at the sound of the bike's engine. And of her digging afterward. It was no more than that.

And yet. And yet. And yet.

She looked around at the trees and smiled through her tears.

"I love you, little bird," she said in Lahu. "I found you. I won't look anymore." Her voice caught for a moment. Then she said, "But I will never forget."

She stayed and listened to the birds for a long time. When the sun began to get low in the sky, she started back.

She didn't know where she would go from here. Well, Seattle, of course. She had several cases, victims who needed her help.

But beyond that?

She thought about Malcolm. She had never really thanked him for everything he had done for her. And not just the jiu-jitsu. Everything.

Of course, if she contacted Malcolm, she would have to ask about Sean. And who knew where that might lead. But for some reason, the thought of it leading somewhere didn't make her feel bad.

She thought about the Homeland Security task force Donna had mentioned. She thought if this task force involved Thailand, there was a good chance she might join it. Dirty Beard and Square Head, and the other man in the van, and the man who had whipped Kai—they were all probably somewhere in Bangkok. Probably cops, like Skull Face. She wanted to find them. Settle those last debts.

But even more than that, she wanted to find that little girl—Lone's last victim. The one who had looked at her so beseechingly. She badly wanted to help that girl. Needed to.

And she would. She would help her. And others like her. She would. One way. Or another.

NOTES

CHAPTER 1

Why does Billy Barnett assume he can get away with raping a woman he met and chatted with in a bar?

https://the-cauldron.com/my-astoundingly-typical-rape-406b427bcac2

If you're curious about Livia's deployment of a jiu-jitsu triangle choke (in judo called *sankaku-jime*), Bas Rutten has a nice demonstration of the fundamentals here:

https://www.youtube.com/watch?v=TwMIBqOKHoc

And the page-by-page description starting on page 124 of *Brazilian Jiu-Jitsu: Theory and Technique*, by Renzo and Royler Gracie, John Danaher, and Kid Peligro, is also great.

http://www.amazon.com/Brazilian-Jiu-Jitsu-Theory-Technique/dp/1931229082/ref=asap_bc?ie=UTF8

CHAPTER 4

I had a lot to learn about container shipping before I could write the sequence where Livia was trafficked. This documentary was invaluable and fascinating.

https://www.youtube.com/watch?v=rG_4py-t4Zw

CHAPTER 5

"This Life in Ruins"—love this photo collection of derelict Georgetown.

http://thislifeinruins.blogspot.com/2010/06/rainer-brewing-georgetown-seattle.html

These videos of huge objects being run through metal shredders are weirdly addicting. Or maybe the weirdness is just me. But still.

https://www.youtube.com/watch?v=b7ex3ejXnEo

CHAPTER 10

Though Seattle PD was kind enough to give me a tour of their head-quarters, I've taken a few novelistic liberties with my description of the layout of the building and the processes involved with checkout of equipment, creating something that's more a composite of various police departments than something specific to SPD itself.

The Montlake rape/murder is based on an actual case. I am in awe of the bravery of Jennifer Hopper, the survivor, and of her murdered partner, Teresa Butz. And of the dedication of SPD Homicide Detective Dana Duffy.

http://www.thestranger.com/seattle/the-bravest-woman-in-seattle/Content?oid=8640991

http://www.thestranger.com/seattle/i-would-like-you-to-know-my-nam/Content?oid=9434642

CHAPTER 13

Here's what happens to a cell phone (or, presumably, a Gossamer) in a fight with a hydraulic press.
https://www.youtube.com/watch?v=eCgVgaEYFAM

CHAPTER 26

The flying arm bar is courtesy of Dave Camarillo's excellent book *Guerrilla Jiu-Jitsu: Revolutionizing Brazilian Jiu-Jitsu*, a must for any serious grappler.
http://www.amazon.com/Guerrilla-Jiu-Jitsu-Revolutionizing-Brazilian/dp/0977731588/ref=sr_1_2?s=books&ie=UTF8&qid=1374452406&sr=1-2:
Obviously, Sean is a great grappler, and things turned out well on the schoolyard with those bullies. But like any tool, grappling in self-defense ought to be used judiciously. Here are some excellent thoughts from Marc MacYoung, putting grappling in a larger context
http://conflictresearchgroupintl.com/on-grappling-marc-macyoung/
http://nnsd.com

CHAPTER 36

Here's a good video primer on the cross-collar choke Livia uses with lethal effect. I've done it, and had it done to me, many times, and it's as effective on the mat as it is for Livia. If you want to argue that Livia probably wouldn't be able to look her attacker in the eyes while she did this choke, in general I'd agree. But I'm glad she managed it anyway.
https://www.youtube.com/watch?v=NqGIs_UEv6o

CHAPTER 41

Livia's flying triangle specifically, and her philosophy of combining judo and jiu-jitsu more generally, suggest she must have trained with Dave Camarillo.

http://www.davecamarillo.com/jiujitsu/

CHAPTER 42

Rick's recollection of the woman who thanked him years later for saving her life when she was a little girl is based on something that happened to SPD Homicide Detective Dana Duffy, who I was honored to interview while writing this book. Made this hard-boiled thriller writer cry.

CHAPTER 46

In 2003, nineteen smuggled people died from heat and asphyxia in a locked truck packed with approximately one hundred people.

https://en.wikipedia.org/wiki/Coyotaje#Media_portrayals_ and_controversy

CHAPTER 47

Here's a good photograph of the kind of choke Livia uses to end the encounter with the guy who picked her up in that San Jose bar.

http://www.grapplearts.com/some-recent-pics-see-me-get-choked/

CHAPTER 55

This will give you an idea about how much information cops can access about citizens.

https://www.eff.org/deeplinks/2016/03/eff-pressure-results-increased-disclosure-abuse-californias-law-enforcement

It's possible Livia's access to and use of SPD cell phone tracking devices is beyond what the average detective could get away with. It's also possible her use of such a device in Bangkok wouldn't be technically feasible. It's hard to know the answer to the first because Harris Corporation insists on draconian confidentiality agreements with the law enforcement agencies that purchase its cell phone monitoring products. As to the second, if it's not feasible today, it will be tomorrow.

https://theintercept.com/2016/03/31/maryland-appellate-court-rebukes-police-for-concealing-use-of-stingrays/

http://arstechnica.com/tech-policy/2013/09/meet-the-machines-that-steal-your-phones-data/1/

CHAPTER 61

The concept of something becoming less dangerous just by your recognizing it's dangerous—and the opposite—is courtesy of Marc MacYoung. http://www.nononsenseselfdefense.com

SOURCES

Robert Christensen's *Out of the Darkness and into the Blue: Surprising Secrets, Tactics, and Training Concepts: A Memoir from One of Kalamazoo's Top Cops*
 https://www.amazon.com/Out-Darkness-into-Blue-Surprising/dp/1495301052
 Miles Corwin's *The Killing Season: A Summer inside an LAPD Homicide Division*
 https://www.amazon.com/Killing-Season-Miles-Corwin/dp/0345483006
 Patrick Radden Keefe's *The Snakehead: An Epic Tale of the Chinatown Underworld and the American Dream*
 https://www.amazon.com/Snakehead-Chinatown-Underworld-American-Dream/dp/0307279278?
 Lee Lofland's *Police Procedure & Investigation: A Guide for Writers*
 https://www.amazon.com/Police-Procedure-Investigation-Writers-Howdunit/dp/1582974551
 Moisés Naím's *Illicit: How Smugglers, Traffickers, and Copycats Are Hijacking the Global Economy*

http://www.amazon.com/Illicit-Smugglers-Traffickers-Counterfeiters-Hijacking-ebook/dp/B000MAH5NS/

Steve Osborne's *The Job: True Tales from the Life of a New York City Cop* (and for God's sake, if you like audiobooks, listen to Osborne read this one in that tailor-made New York accent!).

https://www.amazon.com/Job-True-Tales-Life-York/dp/1101872144

Adam Plantinga's *400 Things Cops Know: Street-Smart Lessons from a Veteran Patrolman*

https://www.amazon.com/400-Things-Cops-Know-Street-Smart/dp/1610352173

David Simon's *Homicide: A Year on the Killing Streets*

https://www.amazon.com/Homicide-Killing-Streets-David-Simon/dp/0805080759

Maija Soderholm's *The Liar the Cheat and the Thief: Deception and the Art of Sword Play*

https://www.amazon.com/Liar-Cheat-Thief-Deception-Sword/dp/1505407672/ref=sr_1_1

Randy Sutton's *True Blue: Police Stories by Those Who Have Lived Them*

http://www.amazon.com/True-Blue-Police-Stories-Those/dp/1250051258/ref=pd_bxgy_14_img_2

Alice Vachss's *Sex Crimes: Ten Years on the Front Lines Prosecuting Rapists and Confronting Their Collaborators*

https://www.amazon.com/Sex-Crimes-Prosecuting-Confronting-Collaborators-ebook/dp/B01FTBDKJM

ACKNOWLEDGMENTS

Police work is less familiar terrain for me than espionage, and I did a fair amount of research while preparing to write this book. I'm deeply grateful to the following officers of the Seattle Police Department, not just for their time and generosity, but for the work they do, the risks they take, and the costs they bear on behalf of the public:

Clay Agate; Megan Bruneau; Dana Duffy; Mike Freese (more on Mike below); Diana Freese; Michael Devine; Alvin "Big Daddy" Little; Suzanne M. Moore; Donna Strangeland; and Lauren Truscott.

I have to share an anecdote here. On a late-night ride-along, Mike Freese asked if I might want to see Seattle's "Jungle"—the sprawling area under Interstate 5 and various other overpasses, occupied by homeless, transients, and other trackless people. I told him I did. We stopped, got out, and went through a hole in the fence. Mike was careful to shine his flashlight at the ground, and as I came through the hole after him, he raised his finger to his lips and pointed at a sleeping bag under a tarp. "Shhh," he whispered. "People are sleeping."

As I prepped for this book, I asked a lot of cops what they thought was the top quality in a good officer. The most frequent response was, "Compassion." That moment in the Jungle was a demonstration of it.

A few other cops I want to thank for their time and generosity:

Loren Christensen, former army MP and Portland cop, who knows a thing or two about martial arts and self-defense, as well.

http://www.lorenchristensen.com/martial-arts.html

Montie Guthrie, former Texas cop and federal air marshal, who for years has given me great feedback on everything about firearms and more despite being traumatized by the love scenes.

Randy Sutton, former Las Vegas PD officer, who made the call that got things rolling for me with SPD, and who possesses a wealth of knowledge about police work. Plus his books are great and damn you, Randy, your stories always make me cry.

http://thepoweroflegacy.com

John Vanek, former San Jose PD officer. I highly recommend John's book, *The Essential Abolitionist: What You Need to Know about Human Trafficking & Modern Slavery*. It's just what the title says, and along with John was an invaluable resource for writing this novel.

http://www.amazon.com/Essential-Abolitionist-Trafficking-Modern-Slavery/dp/0997118008/ref=sr_1_1

http://www.johnvanek.com

Thanks also to Gloria Fichou, former DHS Homeland Security Investigations; Andrew Huang, Assistant US Attorney; Mary Petrie, former San Francisco PD; and Daniel Velez, Assistant US Attorney, for terrific background on law enforcement work against human trafficking.

Thanks to Prasong Taja, for being the best Chiang Rai guide a writer could ever ask for.

Thanks to Xeni Jardin, for her insights into the psychological consequences of childhood abuse.

https://twitter.com/xeni

Thanks to Emma Eisler for her amazing insights into, and patient explanations regarding, the inner world of teenage girls.

Thanks to Maya Levin, for telling me a true story about Sean Uenoyama, and thereby inspiring the character named after him.

Thanks to Tony Bartholomew of SF Moto, who took time out of a busy morning to patiently and enthusiastically answer all my questions about motorcycles and riding.

http://sfmoto.com

Thanks to Justin Bell and the other staff at TechShop for answering my somewhat unusual questions about metal shredders, oxyacetylene torches, and hydraulic presses, and for showing me the equipment in action.

http://www.techshop.ws/ts_menlo_park.html

No one knows more about the evils of child abuse than novelist and protector of children Andrew Vachss, and the hours he generously spent talking to me about Livia's origins and character were a master class in close listening, informed insights, and terrific ideas. He corrected what I was getting wrong, made me more conscious of what I was getting right, and shared two great concepts that Livia wound up borrowing: that behavior is the truth; and what isn't a weapon is a weakness.

http://www.vachss.com

Livia's firearms skills are courtesy of Massad Ayoob, who I've been privileged to train with.

http://massadayoobgroup.com

More about Maija Soderholm and the Vaari knife here. The Vaari wasn't around when Livia was in high school, but hopefully I can be forgiven for transporting it back in time a bit.

http://www.somico-knives.com/about-us.html

Sometimes I wind up listening to a certain album a lot while working on a book. This time around it was Ray LaMontagne's *Ouroboros*.

Thanks to Rex Bonomelli for another knockout cover.

http://www.rexbonomelli.com

Thanks to Naomi Andrews, Daniel Born, Wim Demeere, Grace Doyle, Alan Eisler, Emma Eisler, Judith Eisler, Montie Guthrie, Mike Killman, Lori Kupfer, Dan Levin, Maya Levin, Genevieve Nine, Laura Rennert, Ken Rosenberg, Johanna Rosenbohm, Jennifer Soloway, and Alice Vachss, for helpful feedback on the manuscript.

Most of all, thanks as always to my wife Laura Rennert, who's also my literary agent and a great editor and collaborator. Even more than the characters in previous books, Livia Lone was a joint effort. Thank you, babe, for everything.

ABOUT THE AUTHOR

Photo © 2007 Naomi Brookner

Barry Eisler spent three years in a covert position with the CIA's Directorate of Operations, then worked as a technology lawyer and startup executive in Silicon Valley and Japan, earning his black belt at the Kodokan Judo Institute along the way. Eisler's award-winning thrillers have been included in numerous "Best of" lists, have been translated into nearly twenty languages, and include the #1 bestseller *The Detachment*. Eisler lives in the San Francisco Bay Area and, when he's not writing novels, blogs about torture, civil liberties, and the rule of law. Learn more at www.barryeisler.com.